PRINT EDITION

Bewitching Hannah © 2017 by Mirror World Publishing and Leigh Goff
Edited by: Justine Dowsett
Cover Art by: Jan Doseděl

Published by Mirror World Publishing in September 2017

Mirror World Publishing
Windsor, Ontario
www.mirrorworldpublishing.com
info@mirrorworldpublishing.com

ISBN: 978-1-987976-31-1

To Brian, Carson, & Chase

Bewitching Hannah

by
Leigh Goff

M|W mirror world publishing

"Most gods throw dice, but Fate plays chess, and you don't find out til too late that he's been playing with two queens all along." –Terry Pratchett, Author

1.

I didn't know if fate could be altered, but I hoped for the possibility. The reason was simple—sometime ago, my bewitched ancestors co-mingled and permanently effed up my life. Thanks to them, the inherited magic I'd have sacrificed my virginity to live without was stirring again, most likely triggered by the stress of leaving Green Briar. It whispered to me from its lair like a beast luring a curious creature to her doom. *Not now*, I thought. I was twelve hours away from starting fresh at Truxton High and desperate for an ordinary junior year, not to mention a deliriously ordinary life.

Chillax, Hannah.

What was that damn mantra? Right. Acknowledge, focus, and breathe deeply. I inhaled enough air to make myself dizzy. Crap. This was *not* working.

The magic hummed to life, quiet at first, then loud like a banshee unleashing in my head. On the outside, I tried not to make the weird face. Instead, I focused my gaze on the dashboard and clenched my jaw, waiting for the magic's slow crawl back to its dark cave.

Aunt Jocelyn, or Aunt J as I liked to call her, tapped her thumbs against the steering wheel to a crappy disco song on the radio. "Everything okay, darling? You look like you have cramps."

Ten minutes from her home in Annapolis and I was already wishing I was back at Green Briar, mostly because of the cramps comment, but the bad music wasn't helping. I swiped a blonde tendril away from my eyes and shot her a look. "Gross. Not cramps. Head hurts."

She pursed her lips in the way that always filled me with dread. "Your head hurts? Or are you trying to suppress the family legacy?"

A hard lump formed in my throat as she unleashed her suspicion. "You know I don't want to talk about it." Tears welled in my eyes. I couldn't talk about if I wanted to. A year and a half ago that legacy of magic drove my mom so crazy she killed herself. A few months later, my frustrated dad followed her lead. If only I'd done something to stop them. If only.

"Days after your dad's funeral, when you begged me to send you to Green Briar, I guessed it wasn't just grief and anxiety that was overwhelming you, but I let you go because it was what you wanted. However, it's been a year now, and all I'm asking for is the truth."

I hated when her guesses were spot on. "I wanted help—to deal with *it*." A single tear betrayed me, trailing down my cheek.

"How could ordinary therapists help you stifle your extraordinary magic?"

I ignored her attempt at a compliment and wiped my face dry. "I needed to learn how to suppress the emotions that bring it to life." She'd witnessed the damage it had caused.

"Where's the fiery spirit you once had?"

My gloom phased to anger and my eyes flashed fire. "It's dead along with my parents."

8

"That's enough." She lowered the radio volume. "It's not dead. You're suppressing it, but you can't suppress what you are. Only in accepting your true self can you live a happy life."

On the verge of my fresh start, my aunt had the nerve to sound like a philosopher. Didn't she understand that all I wanted was to not be a Fitzgerald for once? "I'm not worried about my spirit, or being happy. I just want to be ordinary and I don't want to talk about it anymore."

"Ordinary? As if you could be."

I bit down hard on my tongue, crossed my hands in my lap, and focused on the piece of jewelry I cherished. Beneath the passing streetlights, the enchanting gold ring shimmered in a rhythm that was almost hypnotic.

"I always loved seeing that ring on my own dad's finger. He always told me the Irish heirloom held tight to a secret."

I nodded, not taking my eyes off the Fitzgerald crest. "That's what Dad always said to me. He promised one day I'd prove worthy enough to unlock its mystery, but I don't feel very worthy. And don't say it's because I'm suppressing what I am."

She said nothing.

"I just don't feel much of anything."

"You'll feel better once you take something for that headache. I have magnesium citrate powder at home. Your dad used to take it."

I shot her a half-dazed glance. "Magnesia what?"

A subtle smirk appeared on her face, hinting at a secret. "Don't worry about it." She stopped at a light before entering the city limits of Annapolis.

"We're almost there." She probably forgot I wasn't a little kid who couldn't remember where she lived, although now it was where I lived, too.

"I know." I glanced out the window at the historic marker noting the Witch's Grave—a gnarled tree leaning over the Spa Creek bank where centuries before three witches had been executed and buried beneath its shade. A shiver shook through me. What else could come of being a witch? Nothing good—I knew that much already.

"And everything will be *chrysanthemum*."

"I'd nearly forgotten about your shop talk," I said with a half-smile.

"That's what happens when you work with flowers all day."

"Chrysanthemum means wonderful, right?"

A breeze swept through her cracked window, tousling runaway strands of chestnut brown hair across her prominent cheekbones.

"Yes, everything will be wonderful," she said with certainty in her voice, but I wasn't so absa-freaking-lutely sure.

Lightning flashed, followed by a rumble of thunder, jolting me alert. A tempest churned over the Chesapeake Bay and was rolling toward town. I stared at the clouds, ready to calculate how much time we had before the rain hit. Another bright flash of white-hot lightning forked across the purplish-black sky. One, two…twenty.

Boom.

The storm was at least four miles away. I pressed a hand over my chest, feeling the thumping slow.

I glanced at Aunt J, who was no longer bopping her head to the bad music. Instead, she blinked over and over, and rubbed her eyes with one hand.

"If you're tired, I can drive." Who needed a license when I'd already mastered a moped along with the Green Briar golf carts?

Her slender fingers searched for me as if I were a ghost she could only hear. She grasped my arm tightly.

"Hannah?" Panic drenched her voice.

My eyes widened. "What's wrong?"

"I can't see. I mean, I see something, but it's not the road. What's wrong with me?"

I peered out the windshield. A distant telephone pole grew bigger as her foot stuck to the accelerator.

A frightening swell of adrenaline flooded my veins, sending my heart into a frenzy. "Stop!" I yelled, but she was frozen with fright. I grabbed the steering wheel and threw my leg over to jam on the brake pedal.

It was too late. Absolute silence fell over us in the grim second before we plowed into the pole. My lower body slammed into the dashboard while the seatbelt squeezed hard against my ribs. Metal groaned. White bubbles deployed. Glass shattered with a scream. Or maybe the scream was mine. The car groaned to a halt with a hiss and clank.

Stillness settled over us. My head was reeling as I checked myself for injuries. Bursts of pain sparked from my chest and leg.

"Hannah?" Aunt J's quivering voice reached out.

I pried my eyes open. She had escaped her seatbelt. Her lips and hands were trembling, but I saw no blood or broken skin. Inwardly, I sighed with relief.

"Are you okay?" she asked.

I sucked in a shallow breath. "Me? Fine," I managed, not wanting to stress her out, but I struggled to breathe and my left leg was wedged under the intruding dashboard.

She reached over, wiping her hands across my cheeks and forehead, dusting away crumbs of glass. She touched her trembling fingers to the seatbelt release and pressed on it, over and over. "Come on, dammit. Let go."

I pushed her hand away, restraining a whimper. "It's okay. Go get help."

She nodded and with a hard push, shoved her door open. "I'll be right back."

A heavy silence fell over the car's interior until a hiss sounded from the engine. Within seconds, the smell of burning oil seeped in through the vents.

One toxic breath went deeper than I meant it to. "Ow!" I coughed and writhed beneath the unyielding seatbelt like a five-year-old having a tantrum. Panic swept over me as I struggled for freedom.

Stress vibrated deep in my gut. Self-soothe, self-soothe, I reminded myself. The air grew thicker with burning oil and a starburst of pain wracked my body. I was going to die. Unless...

No. How could I even think it? There had to be another way because what if I couldn't send it back? What if it took me to the same terrible place it had taken them?

I peered out the windows, searching. There was no one. I turned my focus on the glove box. Maybe Aunt J kept a knife in there or a pair of floral scissors. I pushed the button hard, again and again. Jammed. My heart raced.

A burst of smoke puffed into the car's interior. I coughed and closed my eyes. The pressure on my leg intensified and the sickening fumes filled me with dread. Eff it. I balled my hands into fists.

I recalled the spell I'd overheard my dad utter once. I recited it in my head before casting, making sure I had it right. "By the power of fire, I do summon and churn, and call thee forth to blaze and burn."

I stopped breathing, trying to sense any changes. I felt no different. And then it filled my core like a warm sphere of energy. Quickly, the power expanded into a blazing inferno. My back arched, pressing me harder into the seatbelt as my internal fire surged. Every cell jolted awake. My heart pounded out of control as I imagined channeling the smoldering energy. Suddenly, my hands tingled with intense power. I swallowed hard and aimed my fingers at the strap. The fiery threads trickled out in a wiggly pattern until I steadied my hand. The seatbelt burned orange, then cooled to black before separating.

I sat there wide-eyed for one full second, partly in disbelief and partly in revulsion. I leaned back, drained, feeling the heat recede up my arm and back into my core where it simmered down. I squeezed my eyes shut and waited to feel ordinary again.

A thunderous boom roared. The car shuddered, sucking me out of my daze. Flames licked up from the engine and through the broken windshield. Suffocating billows of black smoke glugged in from the vents, urging me to get the hell out of there.

With shaky hands, I jerked the loose belt through the latch and grasped the door handle. I jiggled and jiggled, while shoving my shoulder into it over and over, with no success. I leaned toward the driver's side to escape, but a jolt of pain shot up from my trapped leg. Crap. I rammed my shoulder into the passenger side door again as hard as I could. My weakened muscles quivered. I slapped the vents flat and bashed my hands against the partially open window.

Another flash of lightning streaked across the sky, illuminating a tall, shadowy figure in the distance. Was it a hallucination? Was I already going crazy from tapping into the magic? I stared hard.

The figure approached quickly—like mercury racing toward the car. I drew back, stunned, while he fought with the door. He seemed real enough.

"Who are you?" I asked through the window's narrow opening.

Darkness obscured most of the boy's features. However, the glow from the fire radiated on the skin of his neck where the tendons strained as he wrestled with the jammed metal. The faint light also illuminated his eyes. The color was several shades lighter than arctic ice, lending them an otherworldly quality.

Thunder rumbled louder. "Someone who shouldn't be here," he replied. The tenor of his voice caused my heart to pause on a whisper of breath before speeding up again.

"W-what does that mean?" I stammered, pressing a hand to the window.

His gaze settled on my ring as if he were taking in the details of the Fitzgerald crest. Then he froze, his chest and shoulder muscles bunching beneath his black jacket.

My lungs filled with another gulp of rancid air. I coughed and gagged, fanning the smoke away. I glanced over my shoulder, remembering the family picture that was tucked away in my duffel bag. I wasn't leaving it behind.

My gaze drifted back to the boy. He was no longer frozen. Instead, his hands slipped from the car door and gripped around the sides of his head. Then he doubled over as if he were in agony.

My stomach dropped. "Oh, no. What's wrong? Tell me. Please."

He straightened slightly, offered me an unforgivable look, and took off running into the darkness.

My hands slapped against the hot glass. Was he leaving me, too? I couldn't handle another person leaving me when I needed them. Inwardly, I freaked out. Tears trailed down my cheeks. "Don't go. You can't go. Come back!"

I moaned from the intense pressure on my leg. This was not happening. I was so not going to stay trapped in a fiery sedan while the remnants of a stupid disco song played in my head.

I sniffled the tears back and stared at my plastic captor. With a huff, I worked on the dashboard, trying to free my leg. After several intense palm heels, my hands went numb. Drained of energy, yet desperate, my eyes searched for another way; a possibility. Then I saw something by my feet—a spraypaint can, probably dislodged from under the seat during the crash. I reached for it and brought it closer to my eyes—water-based floral spray in midnight blue. My aunt's flower language came to me without effort; I'd never been so *agrimony* in my life.

The smoke grew thicker. I held my breath and wrapped both hands around the can, aimed, and thrust the hard cylinder against the glass, over and over. A small crack appeared and filled me with hope. Operating on pure adrenaline, I threw my shoulders into the action and slammed the can as hard as I could against the barrier.

Smash.

The safety glass crumbled. I used the can to clear a bigger opening and then I gripped onto the window frame and pulled. My arm muscles shook. A shock of pain shivered through my leg. I screamed, but kept heaving my body upward. With one last grunt-filled effort, my leg released.

I dropped onto the street in a fume-filled stupor, hacking and gasping for air. I groaned from the hard landing, but I didn't care about the pain. All I could think about was how that bonehead had left me. Who leaves a girl trapped in a burning car? *A shadow of a boy*, I thought. Then I remembered my bag. Crap. The rough cement pressed into the tender skin of my palms and the blood pulsed through my tingly left leg as I struggled to stand.

I wrestled with the back door, which wasn't as damaged. After several heaves it opened just enough to remove the duffel. I hobbled across the street with my hard fought prize and plunked onto the curb.

Alone and in the dark, I peered around at the empty side street.

"Hannah!" Aunt J shouted.

"Over here."

She rushed to me, cupping my face in her hands. "Holy salt, sulfur, and mercury."

I glanced at her with surprise. "That's what Dad used to say when he messed up one of his chemistry experiments."

"Chemistry?" she remarked, turning her head toward the burning wreck. Stress washed over her features, causing every tiny facial muscle to crease. "The parking garage attendant called nine-one-one. I'm so glad you got out." She tilted her head. "How *did* you get out?"

I bit my lip, not wanting to worry her with what happened. "The seat belt finally released."

"Well, that's a relief."

Who cared about the seat belt when that wretched shadow of a boy had left me pissed off and with a zillion questions in my curious brain?

Sirens screamed, growing louder as they raced toward the blazing car. Within seconds, the area filled with firefighters, working to extinguish the flames. I looked at Aunt J. "What went wrong with your eyesight?"

"I don't know." She stared at the wreck; her eyes glazed over with shock. "And now..."

I squeezed her hand. "And now, we'll be fine." I assured her even as I silently cursed the instincts that told me that was a big, fat lie.

he storm winds off the creek stirred the Tree of Life wind chime hanging from Aunt J's front porch, setting the copper leaves tinkling like raindrops. After a shortcut and a four block hike, we stepped inside. When Aunt J shut the door, the storm unleashed itself on the house with a roar.

"It's going to be a long night," she said, wiping her brow while I took in the familiarity of my surroundings. As always, her homemade bee balm flower essence perfumed the house and the first floor rooms, painted in a rainbow of soft pastels, soothed my frayed nerves. I peered around wide-eyed, making sure everything was as it used to be when I'd visit. It was an easy way to distract myself from the tears welling up behind my eyes.

"You'll be sleeping in the rose room at the top of the stairs, two doors down on your right." Aunt J was my dad's older sister, but more whimsical in her ways than he ever was. She was in her late thirties, obsessed with the nineteen-seventies and flowers, and had never had children of her own. When she volunteered to be my guardian, she assured me her shop made enough money for the two of us to live comfortably, and I loved her for the ordinary-enough she was offering, even if she wanted me to be far from ordinary.

"Thanks, Aunt J. Thanks for everything."

Her cheeks tugged up. "I wish you *moonflower*, darling." She easily read the confusion on my face as I struggled to recall the meaning of that one. "It means 'dreams of love'."

A boom of thunder vibrated through the house, shaking the floor beneath us.

"That's a beast of a storm out there. A little too ominous for my taste, especially on your first night back." She sounded rattled. "If you need the magnesium citrate powder for your headache, it's behind the bathroom mirror. Take one teaspoon with water."

I was more worried about swallowing that chemistry experiment than I was about the storm. "Thanks." I hugged her goodnight and trudged up the winding wooden staircase and into the hall bathroom.

I tossed off my pink T-shirt and kicked out of my dirty jeans before stepping into the shower. Steaming hot water rinsed away the chargrilled smell and relaxed my strained muscles. I dried off and staggered zombie-like into my bedroom, relieved my duffel bag was safe next to my bed. I removed my parents' picture and set it on the night table. I stared at our similar faces, remembering. My shoulders heaved up and down with each sob, matching the tempo of the rainstorm lashing against the windows. I tried to stifle the sound as best I could so Aunt J wouldn't worry. She'd been so strong for me, and I needed to show her that I could be strong now, too. I wiped away the tears. Tomorrow would be better. A new beginning.

With a few sniffles, I carefully slipped under the pink flower quilt draped over the full-sized bed. After the bizarre trip from Green Briar I'd barely survived and the horrible encounter with the Shadow I'd never forget for as long as I lived, sleep beckoned like a comforting embrace calling me into unconscious oblivion.

The eerie mist surrounding me gave way to a flash of brightness. Climbing flames licked off the masts of a tall merchant ship that was like something out of the bedtime stories my mom used to tell me. The blaze illuminated the night sky and everything around it, including the unfamiliar, yet beautiful, gold and white gown I was wearing. I leaned over a man holding tight to a tricorn hat. A layer of smoke fragrant with tea drifted between us and prevented me from seeing his face, but somehow he was familiar. So familiar, yet I couldn't recall his name.

"Elizabeth, we've broken their rules," he whispered with a hushed groan. His voice was gruff and concerned, and his eyes misty.

"Dude, I'm so not Elizabeth." My sight had to be failing me, so I relied on my other senses.

"Aren't you?" He tugged me closer so my face hovered just an inch from his lips. His warm breath brushed across my cheek. I inhaled his musky scent and reached for his hand. Stomach-tightening tension sent my heart racing.

"Do you know what I am now?" His voice phased to another's. Now he sounded like the Shadow.

Curiosity outweighed my anger. "Tell me."

The cool evening air chilled to a wintry temperature and the smoky wind whistled its warning. The hair on my arms stood on end as I waited for his reply.

"Cursed," he whispered.

Everything went black. A blinding light exploded in front of me, whisking me from the fiery past to a hazy present. The brightness faded. A girl's silhouette creeped in along the edges of my dream. Curious, I tried to make out her face, but a dense fog obscured her features.

Wake up, Hannah.

She pointed at me, drew a hand to her face, and blew a glistening powder into the sky. Screams rose from a sea of faceless people below her and a sense of urgency descended like a black vortex, sucking the life out of me.

No!

I shot up in bed and wiped my damp forehead with pruned fingertips. My eyes flitted back and forth until my panting slowed. I wasn't at Green Briar anymore, but after the creepy dream I wondered if maybe I should've stayed there. In the near distance, chimes tinkled like a glass chandelier being played by a storm. I waited for the memories of the strange dream to subside before I tossed the quilt to the side.

Outside, the storm had softened to a steady drizzle. I peeked into the hallway and listened, but the chimes weren't coming from outside the house. The music called to me from beyond the white door at the end of the hallway. I tiptoed toward the mysterious portal I never dared enter as a child, afraid of ghosts. However, I was no longer a little girl and the only ghosts I feared were those that haunted my grieving head and heart.

With a twist of the knob, I pushed in and pressed the door to the frame as quietly as I could. I sneaked up the steps toward the light, breathing in the strong cedar scent. On the far end of the attic I noticed another tree wind chime hanging near the half-open hexagonal window.

I scanned the cache of treasures, noticing Aunt J's old, red leather recliner and a desk with an antique sewing machine. Two different-sized steamer trunks hidden away long ago added to the normal atmosphere of an ordinary attic. With my family, everything always appeared normal on the surface, just like me. However, underneath the façade, dark secrets lurked, threatening to destroy any chance of ordinary. Annapolis, with its secret population of witches, wasn't much different in that way. I kneeled in front of the smaller trunk, my imagination running wild, wondering what was concealed beneath the pretty lid. I grasped the tiny padlock and tugged, but the lock held tight. I twisted and tugged again, but the iron did not yield.

"Humph." I ran my hand across the textured leather. "My dad would say I'm not worthy yet to know your secrets, but when I am, I can't wait for you to share them with me." Next to the trunk, my aunt had retired a stack of books. I eagerly searched through the titles and recognized my surname on one of them,

The Fitzgerald Dynasty. Why not? I was feeling sentimental like a child wanting to traipse through the pages of a familiar, although dark, Grimm's fairy tale. With a yawn, I plopped in the red recliner. A swirl of dust spun in front of me like a twister. I fanned it away and brushed a finger over the word *Dynasty,* leaving a trail in the thick layer of pale dust.

Dynasty of madness, death, and bad magic.

I glanced at the family tree that included the Irish Wizard Earl, Gerald Fitzgerald. I'd been told stories of the Fitzgerald enemies whose descendants liked to dabble in dark magic and how all of their heirs had sailed to Maryland, set up a coven, and became discreetly known as the Chesapeake Witches.

A groan hitched in my throat. There was no escaping my family history, especially now that the magic felt stronger than ever. I feared the Green Briar treatments wouldn't be enough to suppress the emotions that triggered the problem, and I wondered if therapy could have saved my parents. I recalled my mom's despair, brought on by her haunted visions, and my dad's extreme frustration from his failed experiments. All that was left was me, the potentially combustible product of an elemental witch of air and a wizard of fire.

With as much mental oomph as I could muster, I shoved the thought out of my head and flipped through the yellowed pages until the fingers of sleep lured me under again.

When I startled awake, the sun spilled through the small window. I leaped out of the recliner, showered, and applied mascara and lip gloss. I grabbed the first outfit my hands brushed across in my duffel bag, gray leggings and a T-shirt. Aunt J had already left to open her shop, so I heated up a scoop of crab dip and plopped it on top of a soft pretzel. I sunk my mouth into the warm, salty snack. Ahh, delish. It had been a year since I'd noshed on one of her crab pretzels.

I locked the front door behind me and cursed the nervousness bouncing around in my chest, concerned it might become a possible trigger. I twisted my ring round and round on my finger. If the whispering began, I'd have to quiet it down, because failing on my first day was not an option.

Truxton High was larger in size and number than the small Episcopalian school where I'd spent my elementary and freshman years, and profoundly louder than Green Briar where the tutors for my sophomore year had always spoken in librarian voices. As I made my way to the main office, pungent clouds of Axe Body Spray overwhelmed my nose and the squeaking of new Chuck Taylor's on the tiled floors hit my ears like a squeegee on glass.

I retrieved my schedule and locker number from the overwhelmed secretary and while I searched the bustling halls, I found my attention drifting to every tall boy, searching for some resemblance to the detestable Shadow. I wanted to unleash on him. Ask him what he meant when he said he shouldn't have been there, and how in the world he could have possibly left me like that. I shuddered from the memory.

"You look new." A girl's sweet, clear voice came from behind as I popped my locker open. Surprised, I spun around. She was exotic-looking, with lightly tanned skin, wide, emerald green eyes, and white corn silk hair.

"I'm Summer Roca. Looks like we'll be locker mates this year."

Her T-shirt said, *Baristas make it hot and creamy*. She looked around, seeming suddenly confused. "Do you smell crab?"

I cupped a hand to my mouth, exhaled, and sniffed. She must've had a good nose because I couldn't smell any trace of breakfast.

"Probably my bad." From my pocket, I retrieved a small blue tin and popped an Altoid in my mouth. "By the way, I'm Hannah." My gaze floated a few lockers down to a slender, model-like girl. She glimpsed her reflection in her locker mirror then tossed her head back and forth so the long, dark brown tresses swept over her shoulders. On each side of her stood an equally model-like friend.

Summer nodded toward the girl in the center. "You know *her*?"

I shook my head. "Never seen her before."

"That's Emme Blackstone. She's the head of the Queen Js, and FYI, she's not big on new people."

I returned my focus to shoving notebooks and pens into my locker. "She can't be that bad. No one's that bad."

She spun the lock on the locker beside mine and yanked it open. "You are new. Here's some free advice. Find someone other than a Queen J to like."

I winced from the potent peppermint burning my tongue. "What's a Queen J?"

"Has something to do with them all being related to a royal whose descendants settled in Annapolis ages ago. Some people rely on their ancestry to feel important."

"Not me," I volunteered. We peered back at them. They wore expensive clothes and shoes, and whispered as other students shuffled by. If I had a clique I'd never call them the Fitz Gs. I laughed inwardly at how ridiculous that sounded when a shocking thump sent me spinning. I pressed a hand to the top of my head.

"What the hell?" Summer shouted down the hall.

I stared at a football spinning by my feet.

"Sorry." A boy's voice broke through the first-day-of-school buzz as he waded through the throng of students. He wore an orange polo shirt and had a pleasant face topped by a brush of short, spiky brown hair. "There it is." He picked up the pigskin and tucked it under his arm before looking me up and down. "Transfer?"

The beauty of never having attended Truxton High before was that it afforded me the sweet luxury of anonymity. "Yeah. Name's Hannah Fitzgerald."

His eyes brightened. "Can I call you Fitz?"

Without thinking, I tossed him a Kristen Stewart peeved face. "Not if you want to breed." But I couldn't hold the hostile expression for more than a second. A soft laugh bubbled up. "I'm a junior. You?"

"I'm Chase. Sophomore. Hey, good luck here." His voice wavered with pessimism.

I drew back. "Will I need luck?"

A troubled frown marred his brow. "My older brother thinks so."

"Why's that?" I searched the hallway for an older version of Chase.

His gaze sank to his feet. "Let's just say he isn't at Truxton High anymore."

His bleak tone left me curious. Who was I kidding? I was curious as soon as he mentioned an older brother. "What happened?"

From the gloss coating his eyes, I instantly regretted asking. He cleared his throat. "When you're different, this can be a tough school."

Different was the last thing I wanted to be, even if I was, but I guessed that was how it went at any high school.

His attention drifted to my locker mate. His cheeks flushed a strawberry red. "Hey, Summer. You staying after for history club?"

She stared at her feet as a slight blush colored her complexion. "Not today. Have to work at the Bean."

"Cool. I mean, that's not cool, but maybe I'll catch you at the next one." His voice cracked. "The next meeting, I mean."

"Sure."

I watched him disappear down the hall and turned to Summer. "What did he mean about his brother being different?" I grabbed a notebook and pen and slammed my locker shut.

"Oh, that." She pulled an eek face. "My brother heard his brother contracted a rare illness last year and their dad took him out of school. Maybe he's quarantined or something."

"Quarantined?" It all sounded so eighteenth century. She shrugged. "So what's the Bean?"

A tan, dark-haired boy snuck up behind Summer, grabbed her by her ribcage, and tickled her into a wriggling fit. "I see you met my sister, the Pale One." His voice was deep and vibrant.

"That's his stupid nickname for me," she said in between fits of laughter.

He beamed his attention on me. "The Inca Coffee Bean is our parents' shop." That explained the hot and creamy T-shirt. "Who are you?" he asked.

"Hannah Fitzgerald."

Summer squirmed, but managed to elbow him in his stomach until he backed off. "This is my idiot brother, Mateo. We're twins, and I know, we look nothing alike."

I studied their faces, searching for any sign of twinsy. He was a contrast to her with his bronze skin and espresso-colored hair.

"You both have green eyes." Mateo's seemed to sparkle at my notice of them.

"Mine are greener," she said as if it was a competition. "I need to duck into the bathroom before class. Hey, maybe we'll be in some of the same ones. Do you know where you're headed?"

I flipped open the schedule from the secretary, but before I could see the classes Aunt J had registered me for, Mateo plucked it from my hand. "I got this." He scanned the paper, then set his eyes on me. His gaze lingered for a moment longer than necessary. "Follow me."

I appreciated the friendliness, while trying to ignore his flirty side.

Summer waved goodbye and the enthusiastic boy handed the schedule back, his fingers brushing against mine ever so slightly.

"So, sucks being new, huh?" He shifted his backpack to the shoulder farther from me and we started walking.

"Actually, I kind of like it. It's a fresh start."

"You're sixteen, right?"

I nodded.

"So why do you need a fresh start?" His tone thrummed with naiveté.

He looked totally normal and so he couldn't possibly imagine in a gazillion years why I needed a new beginning. "You ask a lot of questions."

He raised a single eyebrow with confidence. "It's one of my many charms. Besides, if I wasn't interested, I wouldn't ask."

I pressed a hand over my chest and tried to breathe through the grief that was like a searing hot knife jabbing into my heart. "Can't really say," I choked out.

"That's okay. So are you related to Jocelyn Fitzgerald?"

I nodded as I recovered. "She's my aunt."

"Cool shop she's got. It's not far from the Bean. Are you like her?" The question hung in the air for an uncomfortable second.

I looked up at him, trying to read his face for clues. My instincts told me there was something more to him that I hadn't noticed at first, but I couldn't figure out what it was. "I'm not into the seventies, if that's what you mean."

His throaty, ambiguous laugh floated between us. "Here we are." He stopped abruptly and stared straight ahead. I followed his gaze into Room 101.

"Thanks. Maybe I'll see you around."

He winked. "Count on it."

A spontaneous chuckle escaped my lips before I strolled into the white-walled, fluorescent-lit classroom. The generic desks all faced the front and along a side wall hung a world map with dozens of red flag pins. When I looked closer I realized the flags marked locations of famous settings in literature like Yorkshire from *Wuthering Heights* and Colmar, France from *Beauty and the Beast*, a childhood favorite.

My gaze wandered, accidentally locking on the three Queen Js who held court in the front row. A bout of nervousness swelled in my chest.

Breathe. Focus.

The Emme girl offered a cool smile that conveyed her status as an alpha. I smiled back. She crooked her index finger, gesturing for me to come closer, so I did. "Welcome. You must be Hannah Fitzgerald."

Breathe. Better.

"How did…"

She seamlessly interrupted. "My mother knows your aunt and everyone else in town," she smirked, "well everyone that matters."

My aunt and I made the Queen Js Who's Who list? Huh.

She tossed her hair over one shoulder and released an indifferent sigh. "I'm Emme." She flipped her slender wrist to her left. "This is Navan." The green-eyed girl had the palest complexion paired with shiny red hair that draped down her back. She sported a cool all-seeing-eye tattoo on the underside of her wrist and copper rings that decorated her fingers. Then Emme flipped her wrist to her right. "This is Arora." Arora possessed honey brown skin and deep-set brown eyes. She wore silver gauges in both ears and had black streaks running through her curly blonde Afro.

I offered a wave with my free hand. "Nice to meet you all."

Emme bit her plump red lip and stared at me. "Are you sure you're in the right class? This is *AP* Lit." She stressed the AP part with enough snark for me to choke on. So much for being on the Who's Who list.

I examined the outfit I'd thrown on in a hurry—leggings and a shirt with white flowers on it. No food stains and it didn't scream idiot to me. A sarcastic retort swirled on my tongue, begging to be unleashed, but instead I forced a smile.

"Well, I haven't officially taken an advanced literature course before, but in my free time I'm kind of into the Russians." My English tutor at Green Briar thought the Russian classics were amazeballs, and eventually, I joined Team Russian Lit, too.

She scowled. "Is that code for something weird you do?"

My pulse picked up and the magic whispered from the dark, cool void I'd returned it to. I inhaled a quiet breath. I'd better hurry this along. I stepped closer. "The Russians, you know." I glanced at her sidekicks' blank faces. "Tolstoy, Dostoyevsky, Nabokov."

"Nabo who?" Emme said.

"Vladimir Nabokov, the genius who wrote about chess in *The Defense*. But I'm sure you knew that. Since you're in here, right?"

Her forced smile didn't dare lift her cheeks. She nodded. "Mm hmm."

"Cool."

Navan and Arora sat wide-eyed as I stepped back, resisting the urge to do a Tiger Woods fist pump.

"Hannah!" Summer waved at me from the classroom door. Distracted, I stumbled like a drunk over Emme's foot that she jutted into my path. I mashed my lips together, ignored their snickers, and directed my focus forward, trying to breathe through the surfacing magic.

I plunked into the first empty desk I saw and pointed Summer to take the one next to me. The whisper intensified.

"What are you doing?" Summer asked.

Look normal, look normal, for your one chance at ordinary, look normal.

I applied my best toothpaste commercial smile. "What do you mean?"

She leaned closer and dropped her voice to a hush. "Are you messing with Emme?"

"I was merely shoveling back the crap she chucked at me." A muffled groan stuck in my throat. Effing eff. I grabbed the desk's edge, waiting for the inner banshee to hit maximum volume.

"Bad things happen to anyone who crosses her. I should've warned you, but I didn't think you'd try to mess with her on your first day. *Ay Dios!*"

I tilted my head and shot her a doubtful look. "So, you're superstitious?" I winced.

"I'm Latina. I was superstitious when I was an egg." She paused. "Are you okay? You look like you have cramps."

"I wish," I mumbled under my breath. "I mean, no. Just a migraine. I'll be fine." The magic began to quiet. "I just need to close my eyes for a minute." Having not slept so well last night, I shut my eyes and before I realized it, I drifted asleep.

A sharp burst of white light flashed in my head. As it dimmed, an unfamiliar boy took shape. He tripped over his shoelaces and fell to the floor. In the background, I made out white cinderblock walls that matched the walls in the school. I watched with confusion, breathing hard until the dream faded away.

I startled awake. What the hell was that? My instincts shifted into alert mode. Summer shot a tiny paper ball onto my desk. "Were you asleep, dude?"

"I guess I was."

I straightened and glanced around, catching Emme staring at me. She immediately whispered to Arora who glanced back with a look of incredulity.

Whatever. I stretched my arms out and yawned. "Didn't sleep well last night."

Summer shook her head. "Well, wake up. Miss Pam is getting ready to hand out textbooks."

After two more classes, I was wide-awake and out from under the Queen Js' scrutinizing eyes. Plus, it was lunchtime. I followed behind Summer past a cafeteria wall of windows with my orange lunch tray in hand. From the corner of my eye, I spotted the Queen Js outside. A Burberry blanket was spread beneath them as they lunched under the wispy green branches of a willow tree. But as I stared, the three of them suddenly stopped talking. In a subtle synchronized motion, they lifted their heads and stared back. What was their deal?

I whipped my head forward and continued toward Summer's table, but something sent my hair standing on end. A classmate raced past me, nearly knocking me over. I glanced down at his untied shoes, and the scene unfolded like instant replay. His feet caught up in the laces, which sent him tottering—exactly as the boy in my catnap dream had. Was I losing my mind? With my eyes locked on the boy, I dropped my tray on a table and lunged for his arm to steady him, but it was too late. He tumbled forward, his face smacking into his plate of gooey macaroni and cheese. All I could do was help him up and hand him a fistful of napkins with shaky hands. "Had to be déjà vu. That's all. I'm not going crazy," I tried to convince myself.

"What are you talking about?" he said.

"Nothing. Sorry about this."

The boy eyed me strangely. "Accidents happen. Not like you could've stopped it."

"Right." However, my instincts told me he wasn't right. A spinning sensation came over me. I feared I was experiencing a touch of something; the something awful that drove my mom over the edge and it was because I'd used my magic. Freaked out and in a tizzy, I snatched my tray from the table, wondering if the dreams from the night before were future glimpses, too, and if so, what the hell did they mean? Was I going to meet a weird girl who blew stuff in the air that made people scream and I wouldn't be able to stop her?

The sense of being eyeballed stifled my internal questions and sent a chill across my skin. My eyes flitted beyond the windows again. This time the Queen Js were standing, arms crossed over their chests and mean girl gazes locked on target. *Me.*

After school, I raced straight to Aunt J's shop to help with deliveries. Before I walked in, I glanced up at the sign that stood out from the others along the street. She'd changed the Os in the Flower Power sign to rainbow-colored peace symbols. It was so her.

Inside, recycled blue and green bottles and jars lined the wood shelves of her Bohemian flower essence boutique. A boxy glass refrigerator, humming against the sunshine yellow walls, displayed dozens of beautiful, fresh-picked flowers waiting to be arranged or processed into perfumes, oils, and essences.

She smiled as she let her slender fingers dance about the wood slab, chopping and dicing. The shop was her life since she had no partner and not much of a social life. She told me once she'd fallen in love, but the woman she gave her heart to married an abusive, old man and the sad betrayal had left her in pieces, unwilling to risk another go at it.

"How was your first day?" she asked.

"Um, it was okay." I smiled, relieved it was over, but regretful it wasn't as ordinary as I'd hoped. In my head, I kept replaying my strange interactions with the Queen Js. Did they suspect what I was? I wasn't sure, but I'd have to up my game at playing normal.

"Good. Now, I need you to deliver that." She gestured toward a pretty, white gift bag on the main counter.

"Sure. Rusty's in the back, right?" The moped wore a coat of red flaky dust, but was a ton of fun to ride.

"You can walk. It's not that far."

"Where to?" I grabbed a broom from the back and swept up bits of snipped greenery and fallen petals. She reached in the pocket of her bell-bottom pants and handed me the name and business address.

"Mallory Grey Blackstone, Historic Annapolis offices at Brice House on Forty-Two East Street," I said, reading the information out loud. "Her daughter's Emme, right?"

"You met her?"

"At school today."

"Her mother heads the historic foundation, among other things."

I guessed that was how she knew so much about everyone that mattered, although I still didn't know how we ended up on her VIP list. "Wait. Her middle name is Grey?"

"Yes, it's her maiden name. Why?" Her tone implied unnecessary suspicion.

"Doesn't her family have something to do with the urban legend of the Arundell Curse Mom told me about when I was little?"

She hesitated. "It's historic lore more than urban legend."

My eyes widened. "So you know it?"

A spark of knowledge glimmered in her brown eyes. "Yes, I know it. The night of October nineteenth, seventeen seventy-four, the *Peggy Stewart* ship, laden with British tea, was docked in Annapolis Harbor and set ablaze. During the tea party, a local patriot was injured. His love—a beautiful Fitzgerald witch, who happened to be your seventh great aunt—attended him. The head of the coven foresaw the offense and quickly discovered the young witch and her forbidden mate. She had broken a serious coven rule, so the Grey witch cast the Arundell Curse upon the forbidden ordinary. The curse ensured that if the two stayed together their progeny would forever bear the horrendous scars of her transgression. The irony is that the Grey witch didn't realize that by imparting the spell with such blackness in her heart she also cursed her own descendants." She paused and a sinking feeling came over me.

"What do you mean?"

"Nothing. What I've told you is enough for now," she said.

I shuddered. "I still have strange dreams about that story."

She tilted her head. "You do?" There was a hint of concern in her voice.

Just last night, I thought. "Yeah. I never understood why Mom liked that one so much."

"Maybe it's because stories like that impart valuable lessons." She frowned in grim silence. "Speaking of the *Peggy Stewart*, did you know the Two Hundred and Fiftieth Anniversary of the Annapolis Tea Party is in a few weeks?"

"Was the event really that big of a deal?"

"You're the one dreaming about it. You tell me." She handed me the order and nudged me out into the cool September evening.

"Forty-Two East Street," I said to myself.

The all brick, Georgian mansion with matching additions that flanked the central part of the historic house had a reputation for being the most haunted residence in town.

I dropped off the delivery to a sharp looking secretary and wandered around town for a while. St. Anne's chimes echoed through the evening air, sounding more ominous than they usually did. The church, with its huge stained glass Tiffany windows and soaring steeple, had been around since my ancestors first set foot on Annapolis soil, and I imagined the bells tolled out over many remarkable events where a Fitzgerald witch was present, including the tea party. Yup, no escaping my family history. Not even on a walk through town.

As I counted the chimes, I realized how late it was. I hurried up Main Street heading home, but soon found myself standing in front of Calvert Manor, staring at the old house from the sidewalk. The Calverts were the most revered non-witch family in their day, and as far as I knew, the all brick structure still housed their descendants. The brick walls looked slightly dilapidated beneath an abundant cover of ivy, but it was a hauntingly beautiful sight.

Above, twilight disappeared like a flickering flame extinguished by the clouds rolling in over the Chesapeake. Instead of heading back to the shop, my relentless curiosity urged me forward. I climbed the short set of brick steps and pushed open the rusted gate.

Their landscapers must've quit because within the garden walls, the property appeared decimated. Weeds grew higher than my knees and ivy covered not only the house, but climbed the trunks of the ancient chestnut trees that stood guard over the property. What had been the most lavish historic estate in town was now a shadow of its former self.

The rain-scented air trembled with thunder. I brushed away blowing strands of hair from my eyes before turning back. I grasped the gate hard, almost falling backward when it refused to release.

Can't anything be easy?

I touched my fingers to my forehead, feeling slightly stressed. My chest tightened, and worse, the magic hummed to life.

"Not now," I said to myself while I tried to conjure pleasant thoughts and wait it out.

"Dammit. Why is this getting worse?" Stressed out, I recalled the self-soothing mantra again. I focused on my phone screensaver, a pic of tree-filled view from Green Briar, and I wondered how much time I had left before the magic drove me out of my mind and right over the proverbial edge.

The wind whistled like a screeching witch and froze the crampy look I could feel on my face. I fluttered my eyes closed. "I refuse to succumb to this. I am going to be ordinary, ordinary, ordinary." I wished I were Dorothy tapping my heels together to get where I wanted to be. However, I wasn't Dorothy. I was Hannah Fitzgerald with an effed up problem even the great Green Briar therapists couldn't hypnotize out of me.

I grasped the gate and tugged again, but the old iron hinges resisted. With my feet dug in, I leveraged myself against it and with a *thunk* it popped open, tossing me onto the hard earth. Perfect.

I wiped the grass off my backside as the gate creaked shut, the screech like a drill on metal. With a leap, I escaped. The latch caught with a clack. I dashed down the stairs, peering back one last time at the gloomy state of the house.

Above it, lightning reached across the sky, resembling a luminous skeletal hand. I jumped and spun around, ready to bolt, but instead crashed into a slight figure. I shook my head, only seeing long, dark hair blowing in the wind.

Thunder cracked like cannon fire. The girl's bony fingers clutched at my forearm, twisting me to a frightened standstill. My eyes flashed wide. Anger set in as I realized who she was. "Emme? What are you doing? Let go."

Her black-cloaked figure blended into the night. "Hannah Fitzgerald, what a surprise to see you here," she said with such ice in her voice I assumed it was not a good surprise.

I glanced around. We were alone and all I had to keep me company was the chill snaking up my back. Perfect.

"Are those white flowers on your shirt? How pure and innocent of you," she said with an overdose of snark.

I planted my free hand on my hip. "Love your cloak. Out stalking small children for a nighttime sacrifice?"

A glint of sinister gleamed in her eyes. "Not children."

"You don't scare me. Now, let go of my arm." My tone was edged with impatience.

She ignored my request with an evil grin. "I need help with something, and I thought you were the perfect person for the job."

I wondered what her game was. "I don't even know you, and I'm certainly not helping you with anything."

She knitted her eyebrows. "You'll know me in time. Besides, we're sisters, you and me," she said in her vocal-fried purr.

Clearly, she'd inherited the Grey temperament. "What are you talking about?"

"My girls want to know if you're Queen J material."

Bleh. "What did you tell them?"

"I told them you were, but proof is needed." She inhaled deeply as if she was preparing herself for something strenuous.

My head throbbed. "I'm not interested in being a part of your clique, and I'm definitely not up for proving anything tonight."

She tapped her foot on the sidewalk. "Nonsense. Everyone wants to be a Queen J, but sometimes they need a push."

"Like off a ledge?" I growled, perfectly annoyed. "Besides, you can't force me to do anything."

The corners of her mouth curled into an impish grin as if she were saying, *Can't I?*

Another bolt of lightning crackled above and the wind picked up with a moan. Tiny beads of sweat lined my brow while I fought to pry her grip loose, but she held firmly. "You're seriously freaking me out."

She ignored my angst and sharpened her focus. Then she lifted her free hand to her lips, a motion that reminded me of the dream I had. Was it possible she was the girl shrouded in fog?

She blew a breath, sending a fine glistening mist in my direction. I whipped my head out of the vapor's path, but a second later I struggled to focus and numbness settled over me like a wet wool blanket.

"Did you give me drugs? What the hell?" I mumbled while I pushed against the clouds spreading across my brain like a blooming ink stain. I clenched my jaw tight as I braced myself for whatever was coming.

A ripping sensation tore into the middle of me as the menacing mist whirled in deepening hues of gray. Then the smoky haze whisked me to another place.

I roamed through a gloomy field of fog until I stumbled in the tall, wet grass, falling on my face. When I looked up, my gaze locked on a white marble headstone. I read the inscription—my name and today's date.

"*No!*" I screamed. The fog thickened and the ground softened to a cake batter consistency, sucking me into it. I scraped and clawed, panicked. Mud seeped into my mouth. I choked and gagged.

The fury within me rose up like a fire licking at my soul and the whisper of my magic drew me out of the nightmare. If magic drove me to take my own life, I'd consider that a tragic family legacy. However, to die in a muck-filled nightmare thanks to a witch like Emme—no freaking way.

I squeezed my hands into fists, preparing to do what I swore I'd never do again.

"From the power of fire, I do summon and churn, and call thee forth to blaze and burn." The whisper phased into a screech and searing hot energy surged into every cell in my body. I threw my head back and channeled the fiery heat from my core. Delicate ribbons of fire released from my hands.

Emme's scream of pain sifted through the remaining mist and the pressure on my arm released.

A searing white flash of lightning lit the sky over us. I fluttered my eyelids and saw her stumble backward, her eyes wide.

"No! You can't be the other one," she uttered under her breath, making no sense.

Rain sprinkled on my face, rousing me further. I pushed up from the street with my trembling arm. My vision cleared as I stared at my hands then my gaze darted to Emme.

Her eyes looked wild. She'd seen it.

Flush.

Yup. There went my hope of ordinary swirling right down the white porcelain high school toilet.

I gazed at her arm, hoping the burn I'd inflicted wasn't too bad, when a deep human growl sounded in the near distance behind Emme. She must've heard it, too, because she spun in that direction.

Beneath a white halo of streetlight stood the Shadow, in a black jacket, face-to-face with Emme. My mouth dropped open and my temper heated. Emme screamed again and backed away, but he matched her pace with intention until she fell backward, landing on the street. Her eyes filled with fear as she searched for a way around the threat the mysterious stranger posed. He wasn't hurting her, but he wasn't letting her out of his sight either.

Slowly, she regained her stance, keeping her hands in front of her as if she could ward him off.

He lurched. She jolted into a sprint, running until she disappeared into the rainy night.

The rain subsided as I sat there, my energy drained and my muscles shaking, and all I could think was that he had some nerve to be anywhere near me after what he did the last time.

Darkness cloaked his face, but once again I saw his pale eyes glistening. His gaze locked on mine. In the air I caught a faint whisper of his scent, amber mixed with sun-dappled woods.

I wobbled to my feet, barely managing to steady myself as the dizzy feeling from Emme's trip through Nightmare Alley dissipated from my head and rage rushed in. I tilted my chin up and jabbed him with the meanest look I could manage. "You're the jerk who left me to die in the burning car, aren't you?"

He was tall and exuded a youthful vibe that told me he was my age or not much older, but more than that he was angry. I sensed it wasn't because of me; he seemed pissed off about something else. *Welcome to my world*, I thought. I stepped closer and smacked my hands against his shoulders, expecting him to move backwards, but he didn't budge. Instead, something else happened. Sparks from touching him shivered through me. My eyes widened. The rush was intense, matching my rage which had reached a boiling point. "Why did you leave me? Why does everyone leave me?" I screamed.

He shook his head.

"Tell me!"

"I—I had to," he stammered.

I shoved my hands into him again. This time he stepped back. I matched his move. "I almost died. What were you thinking? Who leaves a girl trapped in a burning car? What kind of monster does that?"

"A monster that didn't want to—"

The Shadow crouched over like he had at the accident. It was as if his entire body was suddenly wracked with pain. He pressed his balled up fists to the sides of his head and inhaled hard gasps of breath.

My instincts should have been on high alert, but they weren't. I extended a cautious hand toward him. "What's wrong with you?"

"Get away from me. Get away from this property and never come back," he commanded, his tone abrupt and brutal.

His unexpected rudeness rankled me further. I stomped a foot on the ground. "You don't get to tell me what to do. No. You get to tell me why you left me there."

A low-chested moan vibrated out of him. "I did it to save your life."

My face went flat. "No. Don't say that. I've heard it before and I refuse to believe that's even a possible consequence of leaving someone in trouble. I refuse to believe it. Do you hear me?"

He threw his head back and grunted, and then turned on his heels to escape.

I was right. He was in pain. Part of me longed to follow him and demand answers. But I didn't. He disappeared into the darkness once again, and I returned to the light of Aunt J's shop.

I tucked my damp hair behind my ears and paced back and forth in the main part of the boutique, trying to make sense of what happened, what I did to Emme, and the wretched stranger's reappearance. What was wrong with him?

"Hannah?" Aunt J stepped out from the back, her hair splayed messily all around her face.

"Huh?"

"Where have you been?"

"Oh, I was, um, I delivered the thingy to Mrs. Blackstone and went for a walk."

She eyed my face. "You're wet from the rain. Is everything all right?"

No, it most definitely wasn't all right. What would Emme tell everyone at school? I scrunched my lips into a squiggly grimace as I debated what to confess. There was no point in lying since she could read me like a picture book, but I could get away with editing.

"I'm...I'm not sure." I slumped against the counter with my hands covering my face, replaying the whole bizarro thing in my head. There was no going back. Emme would do her best to make sure of it. "I got a taste of Emme Blackstone's psychotic personality."

Aunt J's face expressed dread, but not surprise. "Oh no. What did she do?"

"She Nightmare-on-Elm-Street-ed me."

"What are you talking about?"

"I'm talking about how she sucked me into a bad dream with a weird mist. It felt like there was no escape." My pulse picked up as I recalled the real feeling of soft earth squeezing through my fingers and into my mouth.

She clasped her chin between her thumb and index finger, seeming pensive. "That's odd."

"To say the least."

"No, I mean the night of the car accident, my vision went foggy like I was dreaming awake. All I saw were haunting images coming at me like in a bad dream."

I considered the possibility. "You think Emme had something to do with the accident?"

"Impossible. We were driving in a car."

If the Shadow was there that night, Emme could have been out there, too, like when we stopped at one of the traffic lights.

Aunt J frowned. "Hannah, there's something I need to tell you."

The metallic cluster of keys jingled as she closed the shop. "Come with me."

It was the last thing I wanted to do with so much stuff on my mind. Troubling stuff. No one outside of Aunt J would believe me if I told them what Emme did. I had no proof. However, if our classmates asked Emme about the burn marks on her arm that exactly matched my hands, now that would require explaining. How could I possibly explain what I did without everyone thinking I was the freak? Ugh. What had I done? And then there was the Shadow. What was his deal?

"I'm tired and hungry. Can't whatever it is wait?" My head ached and my stomach grumbled.

"Unfortunately, this is not a request. I'm telling you to come with me." She paused. "What if we stop at McGarvey's for a crab pretzel?"

I did a double take. "Bribery?"

"Well, you sound hangry."

Another stomach grumble convinced me to deal with the Emme witch-sitch later. "I do need to carb-load," I conceded.

"Good. Let's go."

We hurried along the old cobblestone streets near the docks. Waves from the Chesapeake Bay splashed against the retaining walls and the briny fragrance of steamed blue crabs from O'Brien's filled the air. A flock of seagulls squawked above us as we entered McGarvey's. After enduring an agonizing three-minute wait, I noshed on the hot, salty deliciousness that was a local tradition as we walked. I inhaled a breath between bites attempting to match her stride. "Are you going to tell me where we're going?"

"It's past time to introduce you to everyone."

I swallowed the last bite and brushed the crumbs from my hands. "Everyone who?"

"Everyone in the coven."

I drew a shaky gasp as a swell of nausea rose up in my full stomach. I should've known she would do this. Here I was trying to suppress the thing she celebrated with a coven of the same mind, the very thing that had robbed me of loving parents.

"I'm a firm believer in having roots in our hometown, especially when our family has been connected to it for centuries. So I took the liberty of filling out your membership papers."

I cursed under my breath. She could tear those papers right up. "Don't I get any say in it?"

"Of course you do, but it's a privilege to be a part of the Colonial Chesapeake Daughters."

"Sounds like a nightmare." I crossed my arms over my chest.

Sadness overcame her expression and filled me with guilt. "It's time to put the past away and move forward."

I sighed, feeling pathetic and ungrateful. I pressed a hand to my rumbling stomach. I wanted to escape my history, not dive into it, but now, seeing my aunt's sullen expression, I really didn't want to make her unhappy. "Fine." I agreed. However, I had no intention of embracing their pro-witch outlook—like, ever.

I glanced around and realized where we were. St. John's College, located in the State House's shadow, was steeped in colonial history. Red brick paths cut through the green grassy campus and ancient oaks hovered over the porticoed buildings. "Why does the coven meet at a college campus?"

She twirled her hair into a messy chignon and stuck a green floral pick in it to hold it in place. "Mallory Blackstone, our elected leader, is a St. John's alum, and she convinced the board members that the historic college, which was founded by four signers of the Declaration of Independence, was the ideal meeting place for the Colonial Chesapeake Daughters, a local civic club with equally old roots."

Since Emme's mom was the leader, then of course Emme would be there too. It was what she meant by us being sisters. Well, I didn't know many sisters who didn't hate each other, so she was right in that sense. Awesome.

Aunt J paused, ignoring my dread. "Hannah, your parents didn't properly educate you about your family." She grabbed my hand and tapped my gold ring like my dad used to. Then she shook her head, seeming frustrated. "They didn't tell you what was special about our bloodline."

I arched my eyebrows. "Special and bloodline are two words that don't go together when you're talking about our family."

"Did either of them tell you about Queen Jane Grey?"

"The queen's descendants, like the Fitzgeralds, became the Chesapeake Witches." So that's why her fashionable descendants named their clique the Queen Js. "Whatever."

She huffed at my brisk dismissal. "Did they tell you about the *Chesapeake Histories*?"

"What?" My curiosity awoke from its slumber.

She glanced at my ring. "That heirloom is more than a piece of family jewelry. The ring marks you as a descendant of the powerful Fitzgerald bloodline."

Powerful in a deadly way, I thought. I sighed with frustration. "So everyone in the family has told me, but go back to that *Chesapeake Histories* thing."

"Patience, Hannah. The *Chesapeake Histories* was renamed when our ancestors settled in this area. It contains stories of our coven's past and prophecies of its future. Mallory Blackstone

43

oversees the ancient book at every Colonial Chesapeake Daughters meeting."

"What does that have to do with me?"

Aunt J dropped her voice to a hush. "Did your parents ever mention something called the Witch's Breath?"

"No." All my parents wanted to do was leave their heritage behind them. In the end, it was their heritage that drove them to leave everything else behind, including me. I shook my head, letting my anguish run its course.

"The Witch's Breath is a pair of elixirs, mystical substances capable of causing great change."

"Sounds like a mythical Holy Grail." I didn't mean to sound snarky.

"I'm serious," she stressed. "With Mallory Blackstone's seven-year term coming to an end and the prophecy beginning, the balance of good and dark has become…unbalanced."

"Whoa—what prophecy?"

"Within the *Chesapeake Histories* is a prophecy that foretells of one witch from the thirty-third generation, your generation, rising above the rest. At the time she acquires the Witch's Breath, a rare elixir—she will be the most powerful witch in our coven's history. She will either be strong and take the coven to new heights, or she will be indulgent to her own fears and desires and destroy the coven along with all the ordinaries that get in her way."

I stared at my aunt with incredulity. "Are you being serious?"

Her lips thinned with impatience. "Deadly serious."

I pressed a hand to my forehead. "What about the election process?"

"The next one will be the only one that is suspended."

"Naturally. Go on."

She sighed. "There were quite a few Chesapeake witches born in your generation. One of them even shares your birthday."

That coincidence stunk like a bad egg. "Which one?"

"Emme. Anyway, from among this group two will be extraordinary."

Bad egg was right. "You said only one rises above the others."

"According to the *Chesapeake Histories*, that's correct."

A chill raced down my spine. "What happens to the other one?" Was she doomed to die before experiencing a life-altering first kiss?

"You see, the other one dies before her seventeenth birthday. Her death will mark the beginning of our next chapter, my dear."

"The other one." The hair on my arms stood up as I recalled Emme's response after scalding her arm. I inhaled a deep breath. "I haven't wanted to talk about our family magic, but there is something I can do like Dad, whether I like it or not."

Aunt J listened intently while I explained the fire summoning. "I knew you'd carry on the Fitzgerald legacy, and it doesn't mean anything bad is going to happen to you, Hannah. Now, what about your mom's gift?"

"I'm not clairvoyant, but I do have strange dreams, like déjà vu, sometimes." A chill shimmied through me, but I didn't want her to see it.

"You seem concerned," she said, reading my face anyway. "Does anything terrible happen to you in these dreams?"

The evening air had cooled, yet I was sweating. "No. Should it?" I'd witnessed what the magic did to my parents. Did I really need to see what it was going to do to me?

"I don't know." She offered a tender smile. "Follow me." Her brisk stride outpaced mine once again. I hurried to catch up. She pointed to the glass hurricanes in the front windows of an old college building. "The blinds are drawn, and the black candles are burning blue flames. Before your dad stopped attending the meetings, he created those blue flames with a special copper chloride solution."

"Sounds like something Dad would do, but why?"

"It's a signal that it's safe for us to gather."

I peered over my shoulders, scanning the grounds for danger.

She answered without me asking. "In the past, ordinaries posed a threat to our kind because they feared our powers. Today, Mallory Blackstone believes the ordinaries have disillusioned themselves to think we don't exist and that's a powerful place for us to be."

I had a feeling Mrs. Blackstone's motto was, 'Evil grows in the dark.'

"It's why she ruled that we must wear street clothes to meetings instead of the traditional black cloaks. However, the effort to blend in and keep our magic hidden is stirring up a deep resentment toward the ordinaries and causing unrest within our ranks."

"Do you resent the ordinaries?"

"Of course not. I think if presented with the truth they would be tolerant, but I'm not the one making the rules."

"No, you're just following them."

She huffed. "I'm not in a position to break them. Besides, there's no harm in blending. The beautiful thing about being a Chesapeake witch is that we're not famous like our Salem and Wethersfield sisters. In a world where *not* being a witch is essential to thriving—even in present time—our anonymity is *delphinium*, a blessing."

I glimpsed my family ring. "You totally embrace your witchiness, so why was it such a burden for my parents? Why did they have such horrible luck with it?"

Her focus drifted as a solemn expression washed over her face, sending off alarms in my head.

"Spit it out."

Her gaze flashed to mine. "Your parents believed you were one of the two witches in the prophecy."

I gasped. "Do you mean the one that's really extraordinary or the one that dies?"

She released a grim sigh. "We can't be sure of anything."

My pulse picked up. If my mom and dad thought I was the one who would survive, then why did they do what they did? The only explanation was the worst one.

She lifted her chin in the air. "The future is subjective and we need to be positive."

I wiped the perspiration from my brow. "How can I be positive when my parents couldn't be?"

"They wanted to be, but they were distraught about what was coming."

"You mean death, like mine?"

"I didn't say that. What I'm saying is that your dad turned his back on his gift and tried to use alchemy and chemistry to alter fate."

"I think it's safe to say that didn't work out so well."

"You don't know that. You don't know that he didn't set a change in motion."

Emotion swelled in my chest as childhood memories flashed back of his experiments gone awry. The magic called to me in a whisper. I recited the mantra. "Acknowledge, focus, and calm the hell down with a deep breath." Maybe they were trying to save my life. Maybe it was my fault they were dead. My fault. Hyperventilating commenced.

She grabbed my hand and shook it. "Stop it, Hannah. I know you're trying to suppress your magic, but what you don't know is that it might save your life one day and that day may come sooner than you expect."

"What difference does it make if I'm fated to die anyway?" My voice escalated in pitch.

"Not even the best clairvoyant knows what the future holds." She released me and knocked three times, paused, then knocked another three. The white double doors sprawled open and a pleasant face filled the wedge of light.

"Is this our newest member?" the kindly-looking woman asked, focusing her attention on me.

My stomach churned. I tried to calm my breathing. A polite smile formed on my guardian's face as she greeted her auburn-haired acquaintance and turned to me. "Hannah, this is Mrs. Meier. She's a Jewitch."

"What's that?" I said, barely paying attention.

"A Jewish witch. Her particular type of magic comes from her Canaanite roots and her talented ancestors date back much further than our own. She and her daughter are members through her late husband who was a Chesapeake wizard."

Mrs. Meier scanned the tree-filled campus behind us then welcomed me with a smile. "I had a feeling you'd come tonight. Welcome to the Colonial Chesapeake Daughters."

"Thanks, I think."

Aunt J tossed me a sideways glance soaked with disappointment. I stepped past her into the enormous hall that resembled a Puritan meetinghouse right out of seventeenth century Salem. Dangling chandeliers illuminated the main space. Antique wood chairs added to the centuries-old ambiance along with the plaster ceiling moldings, gold-framed oil portraits, and wide plank wood floors. About thirty witches of various ages flitted about and socialized, seeming pleased to be there.

Aunt J came up behind me and gently spun me around. "I can see it in those big gray eyes of yours." She frowned. "It was not your fault."

"You don't know that."

She cupped my cheek with her warm hand. "I'm confident that I do."

"Where are the guys?" I asked desperate to change the topic.

"The Colonial Chesapeake Sons meet on a different evening than we do."

"Perfect." Disappointment underscored my tone.

She pointed to a group of girls in the corner. "Take a few minutes to introduce yourself and be quick. Our leader is very *red columbine* about getting the meeting started."

"Anxious?" I recalled her using that flower term when I explained why I wanted to go to Green Briar as in, *I think you're more than red columbine, but you won't tell me.*

"Very good."

I glimpsed Mrs. Blackstone's raven-colored bob that was so intensely black it was almost blue. Aunt J nodded toward the woman. "Her husband is a wizard-slash-plastic surgeon, although from what I've seen and heard he's not very good at either." She flitted a knowing look at me. "Your parents on the other hand were very talented, but..." She narrowed her gaze at me. "The idea, 'To whom much is given, much is required', means we are responsible for the power we have. Your dad turned his back on his power because fear undermined his confidence. Fear ruined both of them. You must have confidence in yourself and what you can do to undermine your fears," she said, the warning implied.

Anxiety rose up. I shifted my focus to a clock stuck to the wall and paced my breathing.

She pointed. "Emme's over there."

I locked eyes on the dark-haired witch who had ditched her black cloak for the meeting. She met my gaze with cool indifference as if she didn't just try to kill me an hour ago. And then, gasp, she gestured for me to join her and her mean girl clique. What if she pulled her little trick in front of everyone? What if I had to show mine? At least Aunt J would think I was confident if I did. I wafted handfuls of air to my nose, trying to keep the crab pretzel down.

Chill the hell out, Hannah.

I shored up my attitude and approached them. The three girls wore matching Chanel T-shirts in different colors. Emme stared at her red-haired friend.

"Navan, what are you doing?"

Emme snapped her fingers together, gracefully producing a cerulean mist that hovered six inches above her palm. *Probably toxic like its maker*, I thought. Best not to inhale any more calming breaths.

Navan startled and dropped her tennis ball-sized crystal, which shattered into thick shards, scattering paper-thin copper flakes across the wood floor. I jumped. She screamed before gathering the sharp pieces in a panic.

"This was my great grandmother's. Dammit, Emme."

"Get over it," Emme said. Then she crisscrossed her hands in the air and waggled her fingers. She stared intently and pursed her blood red lips. "Give to me, oh clouds on top, from the air, drops and drops." Her voice was breathy. She cupped her empty hands and raised them above her head.

I leaned into Navan. "What's supposed to happen?"

"Shh."

When she lowered her arms, a small puddle of water filled her palms. She tossed it up. The liquid crackled mid air and froze into an eerie mist. She winked at me. I was desperately losing hope that she'd keep my secret. "You're new here so I'll fill you in. Water is my element and I work it like a tasty treat."

The witch had ovaries, great big ones. She turned to Arora. "Show Hannah what you can do, since Navan is struggling this evening with her fortune-telling." Arrogance underscored her words.

Navan grunted. "I hate it when you call it that. It's clairvoyance and it's seriously difficult, Emme. One day I'll show you what—"

Emme shot her an I'm-the-alpha glare and Navan snapped her lips shut.

Arora searched the wall of windows, landing her sights on a fuzzy black fly. With cat-like speed she pinched it by one of its wings, and then clasped it between her hands; her silver bangles jingling like tiny chimes of death. "*Je t'ordonne de te soumettre à ma volonté et de mourir à l'instant,*" she whispered in her exotic Caribbean accent.

"I've had two years of high school French, and I have no idea what you just said."

Her eyes hardened to chocolate diamonds, yet she managed a smile. "I'm happy to translate," she said. "By my command and desire, your pesky little death I require." A cold shiver shook through me as she opened her hands, revealing the lifeless fly lying on its back.

Whoa. I cringed and looked away, wondering if her spells were limited to bugs.

She scoffed at my disapproval. "My mother is a Voodoo priestess and I'm an aether witch—as if the black lowlights in my blonde Afro left you any doubt."

I rolled my eyes while Emme beamed a shimmery ray of alpha approval on her friend. She flipped her bouncy waves over one shoulder and turned her sharp focus on me. "Why don't you show the girls what you can do, Hannah?"

I shrugged, completely disinterested in their game. "Can't do anything." I held on tight to one last shred of hope she'd keep her mouth laser sealed.

"You're here for a reason, and you've seen what we can do. It's only fair you show them." She tilted her head and added a smile that only evil can produce.

"Yes, show us," Arora pleaded.

I inhaled a deep breath while their eyes burned into me. "I said I can't do anything." I dropped my voice to a hush. "Emme, whatever happened earlier between you and me was a mistake. It was nothing."

"Maybe it's nothing because everyone in the coven knows how magically inept the Fitzgeralds are. The Wizard Earl was a laughing stock among our kind," Navan quipped.

I bristled under her summation of my family.

Emme subtly concealed the bright red handprints on her arm before listlessly arching her eyebrows. "So if you're better than the rest of your bloodline, prove it."

Their faces were eager. "I never said I wanted to be a part of your clique."

"So your talent must not be that good, huh?" Arora said.

Navan crooked her lip.

"I'm sure you all are much more gifted."

A scoff caught in Emme's throat. "You make it sound like it's a competition when it couldn't possibly be." Everything about the way she looked at me signaled a deep, dark desire to end my existence.

I could feel my jaw muscles tighten. Why did I agree to come with Aunt J? Oh right, crab pretzel bribe. I cursed my carb addiction then shot her a warning look. She set her jaw telling me she wasn't going to back down so I blurted it out. "Wasn't it just an hour ago when you said I was the 'other one'?"

Navan's eyes widened as she leaned in with interest. "Wait. Are we talking about the prophecy?"

Arora drew back with attitude. "As if a Fitzgerald could be one of the two. We're wasting our time."

I leveled my gaze on her.

She turned to Emme. "Where's she going to sit because only royal queens, not drama queens, get to sit with us for the meetings, right?" The way she said it made it sound more like a suggestion, which was über-fine with me.

Emme relaxed her tensed expression and the cool smile reappeared. "She's more than welcome to—once she passes our test." Her gaze floated beyond me. "Uh oh, it looks like you're wanted elsewhere."

Aunt J patted the seat next to her. I welcomed the relief that washed over me. "See ya."

Emme sashayed to her chair in the front row while Mrs. Blackstone checked her appearance in a compact mirror. She popped a pill from an iridescent bottle and swallowed it dry.

I plunked in the seat next to Aunt J in the last row. "Why are we sitting in the back?"

"This is where witches like me and Mrs. Meier, and those two young ladies, Renner and Ava, assign ourselves."

"You mean, according to bloodlines and talent?" I asked simmering with annoyance after Navan and Arora's remarks.

She patted my leg, seeming to understand. "Don't worry about them. They'll come around."

I hoped they didn't. Like ever. I twirled a strand of hair tight around my index finger. "What do the other witches here do?"

"The younger ones are very gifted. The girls you were talking to can do amazing things with dark magic incantations, clairvoyance, and water spells."

I elbowed her. "We know who casts the dirty water spells, huh?"

"Emme's been raised to be a little competitive."

Two tall, young women dressed like Vogue magazine models in high heels clacked to the front of the room and grabbed a handful of something from the podium. "That's Marabella and her mirror image twin, Bellamara. They both excel at creating protection stones and act as the coven's honorable commissionaires."

They approached each door in the room and hung a leather pouch over the knobs.

"What's in the bags?"

"Altered hematite. The stones cause the metal to seize up, barring intruders until the pouch is removed." Our attention was drawn to Mrs. Blackstone who summoned a girl to the front.

"What's going on?"

Aunt J leaned over, her voice dropped to a grim whisper. "That's sixteen-year-old Eve, Mrs. Meier's daughter."

The leader cleared her throat and snapped her fingers, creating a brilliant blue cloud that floated above the tip of her glistening thumb. With a puff of breath, she blew it away like birthday candle smoke.

Like daughter, like mother, I thought. "How did she do that, and is it toxic?"

"Emme taught her how to use her nimbus mist. She keeps a vial in her pocket along with a bottle of anti-aging capsules her husband concocted. And no, the mist is not toxic."

Shocking, I thought.

"Sisters, we are starting tonight's meeting off on a disappointing note." An implied *tsk tsk* edged her tone.

52

"Miss Meier will be leaving for rehabilitation at Camp Sea Haven on Smith Island tomorrow morning. Her crime," she paused dramatically, "is breaking a serious rule. She forgot that dating a forbidden crossbreed is strictly prohibited and is equally as punishable as dating an ordinary, revealing our knowledge to an ordinary, or using witchcraft that does not benefit the Colonial Chesapeake Daughters."

She closed her eyes and pressed a hand to her narrow waist as if the thought of being near a forbidden was totally repulsive. "We know nothing about these outcasts, their bloodlines, their talents, or their insanity, and history has taught us that crossbreeds can't be trusted." She slammed her open palm against a large, thick book resting on the podium that I could only assume was the *Chesapeake Histories*. Aunt J shot me a look that confirmed my suspicion. "If they do not come to us through a formal letter from their coven then they shall be considered forbidden and dangerous." She puckered her lips and turned to the accused. "Your boyfriend wasn't just any forbidden, was he?"

Dressed in a black skirt, tight sweater, and a salacious grin, Eve appeared completely without remorse. She eyed Mrs. Blackstone with a flash of spellbinding hate.

Mrs. Meier gave her the universal mom look that relayed a warning to not say or do anything she'd regret. It was then the girl clenched her hands together. Her knuckles whitened from the pressure as if she were afraid something terrible might happen if she kept them loose.

"He was definitely not just any forbidden, Mrs. Blackstone," the raven-haired girl said with a whisper of lust in her voice.

I didn't know anything about her, but I wished she were staying.

Mrs. Blackstone's eyes bulged. "Enough of your insolence. Tell your sisters his name."

Her long, wavy hair cascaded around her shoulders like a black waterfall and the chandelier lights glinted off the gold Star of David dangling from her necklace. She stared hard at our leader, her eyes sparkling as she thought of him. "Tommy Bladen."

Mrs. Blackstone pounced on the uttering of his surname. "The forbidden is a dangerous product derived from the mixing of one of our royal bloodlines with an ordinary family and not just any ordinary; one directly descended from William Bladen." She threw a hand in the air. "William Bladen, the Annapolis judge in seventeen fifteen who participated in the odious prosecution of our witch sister, Virtue Violl. He wanted her to die for doing what came naturally to her."

I leaned my head closer to Aunt J's. "Oh, but falling in love with a crossbreed, an act that came naturally to Eve, is a crime?"

"Shh. Remember the story about the Arundell Curse?"

The Queen Js in the front row snickered at Eve. Mrs. Blackstone pointed a bony finger at the girl.

"You are a weak sister. Return to us stronger and re-committed."

I nudged Aunt J. "I thought Smith Island was known for its ten-layer cakes, not witch rehab centers."

"Camp Sea Haven is like Green Briar, but for witches. There, our rules and goals will be reinforced to help her rejoin her sisters."

Her acceptance of the unpleasant consequences seemed completely bizarro as I imagined mystical shock therapy and incandescent injections to make Eve's mind more receptive to being a proper Jewitch. "This is wrong."

Renner and Ava stared at me, their matching brown eyes wide with dismay.

"Shh," Aunt J eked out through gritted teeth. "Not here. Not now."

"She can't do this."

"She presides over the coven which, because of your bloodline, is now your coven, whether you like it or not. Mallory Blackstone enforces the rules, rules meant to keep us *clematis vitalba*."

"Safe?" I dropped my volume to an angry hush. "I don't feel safe, and I doubt Eve does either."

"That crossbreed rule has been honored for hundreds of years and has kept us safe from the ordinaries and safe from our darker sisters."

My chest tightened. Did I walk through a time portal when I crossed the building's threshold? "Who cares if the Jewitch dated a crossbreed? It's a new millennia. Time to chillax the old rules."

Her tender eyes pleaded with me to shut up and not ruffle Mrs. Blackstone, who possessed the cunning look of a woman who knew how to make someone suffer, but what she was doing to this girl seemed extreme.

Eve marched to the front double doors and waited for Marabella to remove the Hematite pouch. Her mother sat three chairs down from us and pressed a hand to her wet face trying to suppress the sobs as we all watched.

I hated the watching. I stared at the podium wanting to be anywhere but here. A moment later the door shut and Mrs. Blackstone snapped her fingers creating another bright blue cloud above her thumb and blowing it away. "On to the next agenda item. It is that special time again," she said as if nothing had happened, and that was when the seriousness of the coven and its rules hit me.

"Every year the head committee for the International Witchcraft Club requests an undercover recruiter to choose one witch or wizard from our young ranks to join them in London for a summer internship. We do not know who the recruiter is. She could be one of our own or a visitor. We will be hosting a talent exhibition to allow our young sisters and brothers the opportunity to demonstrate their best skills. Take note, the recruiter, whoever she may be, will be present at this event, and the winner will be chosen later this fall. To all of our weaker young witches here this evening, I recommend practice, practice, practice."

Emme and Arora snickered, seeming unconcerned with perfecting their talents. Mrs. Blackstone tossed them a grin before continuing. "Only the best witch will be selected for this prestigious honor." Her eyes filled with pride and flitted to Emme, who raised her hand in a wave to her mother.

On her fingers, I noticed one of her gold rings resembled mine. I pressed the clasp on mine and unlatched the engraved bezel, revealing the mother-of-pearl cabochon beneath with its mesmerizing pearly swirls.

Mrs. Blackstone cleared her throat and spoke again. "That's all, my sisters. Please go forward and remember the great words of our ancestors. 'We are the daughters of the witches they couldn't burn'."

he next day I lunched with Summer and Chase. He struggled to finish his cafeteria spaghetti while he sat next to her, wide-eyed and attentive. I struggled to finish mine, too, but it had nothing to do with Summer. I swirled the noodles round and round on my plastic fork.

She tapped the table with the flats of her hands. "Where are you?"

I dropped my sauce-stained utensil. "I'm here. I've just had a weird few days. You know, being new and all." I wished that was all it was, but no.

"That's how the first week of school always is, especially if you're new. Speaking of weird, Mateo wanted me to ask you to meet him later this evening at the Bean. Said he has a favor to ask."

"Sure."

"If he's being weird, just tell him to stop."

"He's not weird at all." I patted my lips with a paper napkin. "Need to meet with guidance before next period. See you then."

"See you," she and Chase said in unison.

Their combined cuteness caused me to pause for a moment as they tipped their heads toward each other. "Aww."

"What?" Chase asked, seemingly unaware.

I grinned. "Nothing. Bye." I hurried to meet with Ms. Russell. I tapped on her door.

The slender, blonde woman greeted me and gestured to take a seat. Her shoulder-length blonde hair was styled neatly around her face and her expensive navy blue suit seemed fancy compared to my simple pink knit dress.

On one wall, a framed print grabbed my attention as the word *chaos* changed like magic to *order* in four lines.

On the opposite wall was a beautiful painting of pink roses basking in a golden dawn. "You needed to see me?"

"Miss Fitzgerald, take a seat," she requested, reclining back in the tall chair behind her desk. She nudged her reading glasses up her nose and opened my file. "What are your goals for the future?"

I sat on the edge of the green pleather chair. "Go to college and figure it out then."

She clasped her hands together and rested them on her desktop. "And what conclusion do you think you will come to?"

I twisted my lips to the side, clueless. Taking a hint from her impatient eyes, I knew I needed to toss out something good. "Maybe run my aunt's shop one day."

She picked up my file with a look of inexplicable expectation. "You don't have higher aspirations than that?"

I sank back in the chair, disappointed with her abrupt dismissal of my spontaneously awesome idea. "What's wrong with running a small business?"

She set the file down and pursed her lips. "I saw you a few minutes ago dining with Chase Calvert in the cafeteria."

Why hadn't Chase mentioned he was a Calvert? The family had a prestigious background, unlike mine, and their coat of arms made up the state flag. It was definitely brag-worthy, yet he hadn't said peep about it. "I'm sure he was there for Summer Roca's company, not mine."

"I want to tell you that the boy comes from an undesirable situation. You would be better off not associating with him."

"What about Summer?"

"She's not one of my students."

Harsh, but why was Ms. Russell focusing the convo on Chase Calvert? "If he's a danger, shouldn't we all be warned?"

"I didn't say he was a danger."

My brow creased with confusion. "I don't understand. He's descended from Maryland's first family, likes football, and seems to be a nice boy. Doesn't sound undesirable to me." Was this guidance counseling or just meddling? "Is there some kind of problem with him that will affect my G.P.A.?"

"All I'm saying is that I sense you have great potential, and the test scores from your freshman and sophomore years are stellar."

"What does that have to do with Chase?"

She clasped her hands together again and tensed the muscles in her jaw. "I'm saying to stay away."

Her condescending tone annoyed the hell out of me, however my curiosity remained firmly in place. "Look, if you can't tell me what the problem is, then you can't tell me to stay away from him. Besides, if his situation were that undesirable—" I paused to finger wrap air quotes around the word "—the school wouldn't allow him to be here, right?"

"His brother no longer attends. You should question that."

I drew back, stunned. So his mysterious brother was the problem, but why? What happened that had people on edge? "Is that all?"

She tapped her French manicured nails on the desk, looking miffed. "That's all. For now."

At the end of the day I bent down by my locker, shoving stuff into my backpack, when a small white envelope with a black border drifted down onto my pile of books.

I clutched the mysterious note to my chest and peeked over my shoulders. The hallway was nearly empty, except for three oblivious mathletes tapping like speed demons on their calculators. I slipped a thumb under the seal and slid the stiff white notecard out.

> *If you want a chance to beat Emme in the dangerous game she's playing, come to the gardens at Calvert Manor, eight o'clock tonight. Don't be late.*
> *~W*

I traced over the cursive W with my finger before concealing the envelope in my pocket. Who knew anything about what had happened between Emme and I except for the Shadow? And he definitely didn't seem to want to get to know anyone. I was one thousand percent sure there were zombies less interested in getting to know anyone. I slammed my locker shut and slung my backpack over my shoulder, my head buzzing with W names. There was Warner from kindergarten who was probably still a weenie. Then there was Wren who used to live down the street from Aunt J. Wren was cute and good at basketball, but he had moved away ages ago.

I cut across town and past the State House until I reached Flower Power. The shop bell announced my arrival. I stepped inside and inhaled the sweet scent of early summer flowers being processed.

"Ah, just in time. What do you think of this fragrance?" Aunt J stepped out from the back room wearing pink bell-bottoms and a flowery top. She pointed to a crystal atomizer on the counter. Her rich brunette hair falling out of the hapless knot barely held in place with a pick marked the busy day she had.

I glanced at the bottle while W's note burned hot in my pocket. My hand brushed across the subtle outline of it. I was aching to reread it a million times over, but instead I smiled and spritzed the atomizer—enchantress roses. They were my favorite. "This is beautiful, but it must've taken hundreds to produce this much perfume, and their blooming season is almost over."

She angled her head and smiled. "Flowers are never out of season for me, and it took five hundred to be precise. You're worth it."

She did possess magic when it came to coaxing flowers to bloom, even five hundred roses. I arched my eyebrows up. "For me? Seriously?"

She nodded. "You don't want..."

I clutched the bottle to my chest. "No, I do want. I love it, but it's too much." I looked beyond her at the open backroom door that revealed her antique perfume-making equipment. I'd been around her shop my whole life so it always seemed normal to me, but after being away for a year, the stuff now resembled rickety, medieval torture devices. "You really should get new equipment."

She peered over her shoulder with a sentimental glimmer in her eye. "If it works, why would I change it?" She tapped her chin in a pensive manner. "Although, there was one malfunction a few months back."

"No surprise there."

"It was strange really. I mixed up a plant compound hoping to create a new classification on the fragrance wheel, but the pentathlum broke down, ruining the mix. The altered formula splattered onto my solid gold bangle and made it as pliable as rubber."

"Pliable metal? That sounds a like a valuable accident."

"Humph. I poured the crazy mix on a few items at home, including a pair of decorative, gold-plated shoes I picked up at a flea market for the sake of whimsy."

My aunt was nothing if not whimsical.

"It was fun, however, the fragrance didn't turn out so well. It smelled—industrial. Since then, I've been careful to maintain the equipment. After all—the fractionating and aludel flasks, ashpits, and the pentathlum, it's all been handed down to me through the family, and it's irreplaceable."

I eyed her with concern.

"Stop worrying about the shop, darling." She reached for the knob and closed the back door.

I sniffed the rose perfume. "Beautiful. Did you add gloxinia?"

"You can smell it?"

I cocked an eyebrow. "All those summers of your flower instruction paid off."

She beamed a smile. "You're a smart girl. I hope you continue to be a smart girl."

I flashed her a surprised look. "What does that mean?"

She clenched her hands together in an uptight way. "With all the family tragedy you've suffered and learning about the coven and its rules, I fear it's been too much for you."

"I'm dealing with it. All of it." What else could I say?

"Good. It's finally slowed down around here, so I'm going to lock up and extract oil from these begonias for a homeopathic essence."

My gaze trailed over the waxy pink petals. "That's ironic."

She looked at me with a puzzled expression. "What is?"

"Begonias mean beware."

Her face glowed with pride. "That's my darling girl. Now, why don't you go home and I'll meet you there in twenty?"

"Um," I twirled my hair tight around my finger, "would you mind if I went to see a new friend this evening?"

"What new friend?"

"Mateo." I did plan to meet Mateo, but there was one stop to make beforehand. "His parents own the coffee shop where he works. He has a twin sister, and they're both really nice."

"Oh yes, the South American ordinaries. Very *white zinnia*. I know his mother from the Chamber of Commerce events."

I rolled my eyes. "They are very nice, but do you have to call them ordinaries?"

It sounded über-unflattering, especially since my instincts told me they were more than ordinary.

"They're not witches or wizards, so what should I call them?"

"That sounds snobbish and he only had nice things to say about you."

"Ordinary isn't a derogatory term, darling. It's a fact." She pursed her lips. "How much homework do you have?"

A chuckle started in my throat and eased out as a smile. She was trying to say what a parent should say, but the mom-hat didn't quite fit like her daisy hairband did. "Finished it in study hall."

"Go ahead, but don't stay out too late. I have a surprise for you when you return this evening."

When I was little she had told me about the flowers that were the happiest of flowers and how the buttery cookies she baked with them imparted love and longevity. My mouth watered from the memory. "Sunflower crisps?"

She winked. "Something better than that."

"Lavender honey macarons from Sweet Hearts Patisserie?" They were the most amazing little delights; a melt-in-your mouth combination of whipped egg whites, honey, and French lavender extract.

"Even better than that."

She had ignited my curiosity, which wasn't hard to do, and I hadn't had a good surprise since my dad gave me the family ring. "What is it? Please, tell. I won't be able to stand it!"

"Darling, one of the best gifts we can give ourselves is the chance to be surprised," she said with a twinkle of mischief in her eyes.

Scurrying down back streets and skulking through unlit alleys to be sure I wasn't seen, I hurried to Calvert Manor. I peered over my shoulder before facing the imposing seven-foot-tall brick wall, the only obstacle between my curiosity and the mysterious W.

A spike of nerves sent my hands trembling. What harm was there in meeting someone who wanted to help me? That was a good thing, right? But why Calvert Manor of all places?

I stared at my feet, contemplating. Maybe some surprises weren't good. *Maybe I should leave.* After all, Mateo was waiting at the Bean. I weighed the risks as I looked at the time on my phone. Nearly eight. *Don't be late*, the anonymous W had written. I pressed a knuckle to my lip. I could walk away, or hang out with a potential psycho stalker in a secluded, walled-in garden. I stared at the bricks. Where I stood was safe and ordinary, but the unknown on the other side might be everything else.

Standing on tippy toes, I reached for a sturdy vine of English ivy and heaved myself high enough up the wall to survey the vast, terraced gardens. Disappointment left a pout on my face as I realized that beyond an abandoned family chapel behind the house, the garden was empty.

I slapped my hands on top of the bricks and hoisted myself higher. I peered around at the towering chestnut trees and the golden weeds, but saw no one. Was this a game? In that moment of disappointment, my right foot slipped and my hands dragged down the gritty surface. "Ow!"

I shook off the scrapes and scrambled up again, throwing a leg over so I was awkwardly straddling the wall in my pink dress and tights. No biggie.

Then I saw a flicker. Candlelight danced in a side window of the two-story, semi-hexagonal, brick chapel that looked like it had been abandoned a century before. My eyes flashed wide and without thinking, I threw my other leg over and pushed off. My body crashed to the hardened earth, rattling my bones. Ignoring the unpleasant jolt, I bounced up and raced toward the light.

I staggered to a standstill and cupped a hand to my mouth. "W?" I whispered into the breeze. My heart thumped fast as my imagination reached its peak.

I tiptoed along the cracked brick path where moss chewed away at the gray mortar. I inched closer to the narrow double doors, my curiosity dying to be indulged.

I reached for the handle, expecting it to be locked. With a click, it released. The scent of candle smoke and incense wafted past me as I peered into the glowing sanctuary with cautious eyes.

The imposing entrance segued into the main part of the old family chapel. Shadows flickered across the white walls as candlelight streamed down from an ornate iron chandelier cradling clear-colored hurricanes. Angelic sculptures hung between the arched windows and beneath the cloud-painted ceiling that Michelangelo himself would have envied, four wooden pews graced each side of the aisle.

I tiptoed farther in and spotted another black-lined white envelope on the altar. I was definitely in the right place.

My fingers trembled as I traced the letters that formed my name. This was way beyond ordinary, but why and—more importantly—who?

"W?"

A hint of the Shadow's amber and woods scent mixed with the faint candle smoke of the chapel. "No. Way." I spun around ready to stomp right out of there.

In that moment, a heavy gaze fell on me and the air felt charged with electricity. I searched right and left, seeing no one. "W? Whoever you are, show yourself."

"This will be the hardest thing you've ever done." His potent voice reverberated off the walls and seemed to come from everywhere, including the inside of my head.

I locked my wandering gaze on the loft above the entrance where I spotted his silhouette. "Was leaving me in a burning wreck the hardest thing *you* ever had to do? Was it?" I raised my volume. "Who are you? Why did you leave me for dead?"

His intake of breath was audible. "I would never. I mean. I didn't want to do that. I don't."

"Oh, lucky me." I stuck my hands on my hips and tapped an impatient foot on the floor. "If you don't want to finish me off, then you lured me here to do what, exactly?"

"To help you. I want to help you."

"Ha!" The sarcastic laugh burst out before I could stop it. "You've done a bang up job inspiring my confidence and trust in that department."

He simmered in silence for a moment. "What do I have to do to inspire you to follow my directions?"

Following someone else's directions was definitely not my strength. I grimaced, but curiosity got the better of me. "What do you want?"

"You read the note."

His desire to remain in the shadows was increasingly irritating. "I consider myself a very smart girl, so when a guy who left me in a burning car tells me he wants to help me take on a different deadly problem, I have to wonder if he's not setting me up to fend for myself again. What's your motive?"

I dropped my eyes to the envelope, turning it to and fro.

"Emme Blackstone is a mutual enemy and means us both harm." A tinge of anger laced his tone.

The anger, I understood. After all, we were talking about Emme, but there was also a hint of sadness that intrigued me further. "Why do you think Emme means *you* harm?"

"It's inevitable—because of what I am."

What was he besides completely contemptible?

"It's in her blood and I believe it's in her destiny to wreak havoc, especially against someone who can challenge her in talent like you can."

I dropped my hands to my sides, still clasping the enveloping. "Whoa. Like me? You don't know me. You don't know anything about me. How could you? I've been gone for the last year."

A chortle caught in his throat. "What's a year when you come from a bloodline with hundreds of years of history? A history that's written down and available to certain people with the right—pedigree."

Confused, I creased my brow as I continued to stare at his silhouette. "Have you been cyber-stalking me on *Ancestry.com* or something?"

"Hardly." There was disdain in his voice as if he considered cyber-stalking to be worse than leaving a girl to die.

"Look, whatever you think you know about my family, I'm not like them. I'm not talented, and I don't want to challenge Emme. I just want to live a normal life. Normal." My voice escalated. "Do you hear me all the way up there?"

He huffed. "Normal? You don't get to pretend to be normal when you're not. It doesn't work like that. Not in Annapolis. Someone always knows. Someone always unravels your secrets."

I thought of the Witch's Grave. I pictured the women's slender figures dangling from sturdy, gnarled branches. Their tragic endings proved what I already knew. Magic only brought suffering and death. "You make it sound like I don't have a choice. I'm telling you I do, and I won't be a part of this." I stomped my foot hard on the floor.

He shifted from the shadows into a dim ray of light, seething. "You read the note and you know Emme won't stop. You need my help."

I glared, trying desperately to make out the details of his face. "I don't need anything from you."

"You don't have to like it, but that doesn't change the fact that you are a part of this. You know you are or you wouldn't have come here. However, if that's how you feel then you should leave." The cold in his voice crystallized.

My pulse escalated. "Yup. That's how I feel. And I'm only leaving because that's what I want to do, not because you suggested it. Bye." I marched to the door and wrapped my hand around the knob. I yanked it open. From the moment I'd first laid eyes on him, he'd been nothing but trouble. Horrible, awful trouble. However, as much as I hated to think it, he knew about me and the other witches in town. He was full of answers—answers I needed. I shut the door and turned back around. "How do you know all this about Emme and me?"

"I'm well informed."

He was frustrating is what he was. I marched back to where I had stood before and directed my voice toward the loft. "I'm not saying you're right, because you're definitely not. I don't want anything to do with any of this. However, hypothetically, let's say Emme and I are fated to be rivals. If that was even a remote possibility, what do you expect will happen?"

"What you've witnessed is only the beginning of the nightmare, unless we give you a fighting chance to take her on."

He sounded Biblical as I recalled my eerie dream of the girl blowing powder into the wind and the people's screams filling the air. "You think I can take Emme the Nightmare on because of—you and me working together?" I gulped loudly, not meaning to, but he was right about Emme being a nightmare.

"Are you afraid to try?" The question eased out as a whisper so faint I wasn't sure if he had said it out loud, or if I said it to myself in my head.

Frustration shook me to my core. "I'm not afraid of you. Or Emme, or her entourage." However, the prophecy was a problem. I didn't want to be the one who died, and I didn't want anything to happen to the coven or to the ordinaries.

A heavy silence shrouded the chapel while my gaze flitted to a painted statue of Saint Dymphna. I had learned about her at my

Episcopalian school. She was the patron saint of victims and her physical resemblance to me left me uneasy.

"What's your name?" I demanded firmly, my voice echoing off the plaster walls until it was quiet again.

"Like I said. Someone always unravels your secrets. In time, you'll unravel mine."

A challenge? Maybe he did know me. "So W is all I'm going to get from you. For now. Awesome."

He disappeared into the darkness of the loft, so without another word, I marched back toward the double doors. I reached for the handle and forced myself to leave. Outside, I glanced up at the second-story window above the doors, hoping to catch a better glimpse of him. Nothing. Disappointed, my eyes flitted to the brick walls surrounding me in the Calvert gardens.

I fanned the envelope in front of my face. I wanted to rip it to pieces or stomp on it and run away. Instead, I gave in and slipped my thumb under the seal to rip it open. I strained to read his writing in the moonlight.

> *Drop the seed and dare to be yourself. This means you may need to look inside to find a way outside. If you succeed, then return to the chapel Saturday at eight o'clock.*
> *~W*

A dare and a riddle all in one note. He was obnoxious, but clever, which left me more inquisitive than ever. Inside the envelope, one tiny black seed stared back at me. I glanced up at the chapel window and cupped a hand to the side of my mouth. "I'm doing this because I want to do it." I slipped the note in my pocket and dumped the seed onto the ground.

Little black leaves and stems burst from the earth. The midnight-colored sprout phased into a black rose vine with knuckled branches and gnarly onyx roots, both of which grew thicker by the moment. The vine rose up with great speed, spiraling around me and flourishing upward. "W-what the hell is this?"

With a crackle, the thorns grew spikier. The branches creaked as they reached taller. Black ends reached for other ends, touching, entwining, and growing thicker all around me. I was trapped within a six-foot-tall barrier of impenetrable razor-sharp blossoms and serrated plant talons that were closing in fast.

Why did I open the envelope? Why did I listen to that psycho? He was trouble, nothing but trouble. I reached through a gap, but a vicious branch snapped at my hand and a thorn tore across my skin. "Ouch!" I recoiled my arm. Anger escalated as a drop of scarlet blood trickled out. The branches inched closer.

Lines of sweat ran down the sides of my face as panic worked its way through my body. I recalled the riddle. *You may need to look inside to find a way outside.* What the hell did that mean? Oh my God, I was totally going to die. I sucked in my chest as the plant infringed on what was left of my personal space. I scanned the ground around my feet for a sharp rock or something—anything—that could free me.

Another branch snapped at my arm like a hungry alligator. The magic hummed. "Crap!" Time was running out as I realized what the riddle meant. The only thing left to do was look inside. I clenched my fists at my sides. "From the power of fire, I do summon and churn, and call thee forth to blaze and burn."

The magic exploded. The energy within me expanded into a fiery blaze. My back arched as the fire surged. I channeled the magic to my finger and aimed a smoldering ribbon of fire at the vine. The obsidian-colored plant glowed neon orange. I snapped my eyes shut again and with a push, the energy burned hotter and the fire rushed out.

Flames licked and crackled as they hungrily devoured the branches embellished with death blooms. The heat waves lapped at my face. I swept my hands through the smoke, stunned by the power rolling out of me.

The branches shifted and writhed, sending billows of black smoke into the air. The black rose bush sizzled and popped as it collapsed down on itself, while the heat in my hand receded up my arm and into my chest. I feared suffering my parents' fates if I continued to summon the magic, but what if I was destined to die anyway thanks to the prophecy?

A few intense minutes later, the bush spread out like a worn hoop skirt of a ball gown. I dragged myself over the smoldering heap and collapsed on the ground, hacking a smoke-filled lung up. My whole body shivered with exhaustion before I recouped enough energy to stand.

Whoever W was, he wasn't an ordinary. I knew that much from the color of his eyes alone, but if he was a member of the Colonial Chesapeake Sons, he wouldn't need to hide his identity from me. So how was it possible for an outsider to have access to a seed like this?

I cast an enraged glare up to the chapel windows, catching sight of his silhouette. I seethed. It didn't make any sense. How could my instincts be so off when he was clearly more threatening to me than Emme?

I swung the chapel doors open with ferocity. "Come down here, you bastard!" My shaky voice bounced off the walls and I cursed his infuriating silence under my breath. "Why would I worry about Emme when you've claimed first dibs on taking my life?" I stomped my feet. "You are a coward. Do you hear me?"

Exhausted, I backed away and headed for the front gate. I broke into a slow run up the terraced backyard. I dashed past the front door just as it creaked open.

My arms flailed out to the sides to keep me from falling on my face. Chase stepped outside, shutting the door firmly behind him. "Hannah? What are you doing here?"

Trying to stay alive for now, duh.

I panted, trying to catch my breath. "You startled me." After the last run-in with Emme in front of the manor house, I wrongly figured I was maxed out on trouble there. "I, um, took a shortcut around town and got lost." I didn't know what else to say. "How about you?"

"Uh, I kind of live here." He looked at me like I was the psycho, and then his gaze drifted down my arm to the bloody scratch on my hand. He closed his eyes, seeming upset.

Did he know about the candles burning in the old Calvert chapel or the murderous W living there? Was W a Calvert? The quarantined brother?

"Right. You're a Calvert. I should've realized you might live here." I laughed nervously and hid my hand behind my back. "Sorry. I'm being weird." I was being weird, but after battling the black vine of death, no thanks to W, I kind of had a good reason.

He didn't seem to mind though. "Let me help you with the gate. It's old and it sticks." He walked me to the front and fiddled with the rusty latch until it released. "Good night. See you at school."

"Good night, Chase." I stepped down the stairs and stumbled onto the sidewalk. I rolled my eyes at myself, but hesitated. As I turned around to ask him about W, I bumped into Emme. This time she was with her mother. I immediately wondered if her mom's presence would keep me safe from the nightmaring trick or if Mrs. Blackstone would join her daughter in the effort.

They both held tight to shopping bags from Forever Sixteen. They looked at me and then at Chase, an ordinary standing guard by the gate. I swore I saw a sneer tug at his serene expression, making me think he seemed rather brave for being an ordinary standing before the dark-hearted pair.

Mrs. Blackstone tried to crease her Botoxed forehead, but it only crinkled on the edges. "Were you with *him*?" She made it sound like he had cooties.

"Me, with Chase? No."

No, ma'am, no ordinary cooties on me. I snickered inwardly.

Emme offered a coy grin to our schoolmate, like a cat offering false assurance to its next meal. He stood firm in his stance and held a wary gaze on both of them. Did they all know each other?

I wanted to interrupt the hate-fest, but figured it was more important to get the hell out of there. "It's late. See you all around."

I staggered backward, shocked at the ease of my escape, and rounded the corner. I pressed myself up against the brick wall and leaned over, too tired to stand upright another minute. Blonde hair draped around my face. I grasped a wavy lock and took a subtle sniff. Ugh, it reeked of black rose vine smoke.

My phone buzzed, jolting my heart into my throat. I definitely needed to chill. I read Mateo's message.

Don't come 2 the Bean. Have 2 leave now 2 study. Did Summer mention the favor I wanted 2 ask?

Yeah. I texted back.

This Saturday, Quiet Waters Woods—will b an adventure. Need you there.

An adventure in the woods?

Yeah, that's the only hint ur getting.

I slipped my phone in my pocket next to W's note and dashed home, almost forgetting Aunt J had a surprise waiting for me.

When I arrived, she was asleep. Disappointed, I changed into pajamas and curled up on the quilt, staring at my parents' picture and thinking of the spine-chilling bedtime stories they used to tell me. Were they warnings just for me, or for the coven and everyone in town?

I nestled my face in the pillow and slipped my hands underneath, my fingers brushing against a cold metal object. I snatched it and flipped on the light. In my palm rested a key with a note attached.

> *For Hannah,*
> *You've earned it.*
> *Love, Aunt Jocelyn.*

My mouth dropped open as I played with the key. Could it be? She must have heard me the other night. Tiptoeing over the creaky spots in the floor, I rushed to the attic and kneeled in front of the elusive small trunk. I inserted the key into the little padlock. Was I worthy this time? With a twist, the lock unlatched, sending a thrill through me as I heaved the lid open.

On top of the strange contents rested a book with a note attached to the front.

> *To Hannah, I failed to find a solution to change*
> *what is coming, but maybe you will.*
> *Love Always, Dad.*

My eyes misted over at the unexpected sight of his message. I clutched the book to my chest and rocked back and forth on the floor, sobbing, until a breeze blowing through the hexagonal window set the chimes in motion and cooled my warm, wet cheeks.

I leafed through the hundreds of handwritten notes about his experiments. There were drawings and science terms I'd never seen before. Then I saw the title of the last experiment, *Alchemical Transformation.* I shook my head, remembering Aunt

J telling me how he had turned to alchemy. It seemed as if, rather than transmuting lead into gold, he had tried to change a dark fate into something bright and hopeful.

I studied his words, searching for a way to change the figurative lead problem into a golden outcome.

When my eyelids grew heavy, I set the book down and glanced back into the trunk. It was loaded with glass flasks, burners, and four glass jars filled with various compounds. I removed the antique sewing contraption from the desk and arranged the glass jars in a row.

Secrets—Dad's, W's, the family's. I collapsed in the red leather recliner and dropped my head into my hands.

The next morning, I woke with a pounding headache. I showered and dressed in a khaki skort and a pink shirt with a swirly logo on it. When I arrived in AP American History, Summer flagged me over with a panicked look on her face.

I dropped my book on the desk next to hers and slid into the chair. "You look as pale as mist. What's wrong?"

"History report due in two weeks and Mrs. Rivelli is taking us to the school library for, gasp, resources. Seriously, there are a million more resources on the internet. Why is she limiting us?" she complained as we lined up single file.

I pointed to a colonial poster with a broken up snake. "Join or die, Summer."

"That's not funny."

"It is funny and you're such a nerd. The library is so much better than sitting in this classroom reading tacked up quotes from the Constitution."

"Me, a nerd? You're the one who likes the smell of old books. And don't deny it. I saw you in English lit yesterday pressing a Wikipedia to your nose."

"I won't deny it, but you mean an encyclopedia." I liked old books, ones that had been sitting on a shelf for a while, untouched. They possessed the most pleasant scent—a mix of printer's ink, vintage leather, and musty parchment.

"Me, I prefer my iPad. I can rule the world with any handheld digital device."

"Yeah, but they don't smell good."

"They don't smell at all, which is how I prefer my reading material."

There was a collective grumble as we strolled under a covered walkway toward the two-story brick annex. My attention flitted to the sound of a trickling creek concealed by a row of swaying hemlocks on the right edge of the school property.

"This way, ladies and gentlemen," Mrs. Rivelli said, leading the way. The library's wood doors creaked as we entered.

Summer watched me inhale the book-scented air. "Kill me now."

Mrs. Rivelli clapped her hands. "Today, we're going back in time."

Summer elbowed me in the ribs and dropped her voice to a soft whisper. "Yeah. All the way to the Cretaceous Period."

Our teacher continued. "To a building that was the city library. From eighteen thirty-six to nineteen thirty-five, Arundell Library housed the city's library collection before the school was built, but there is another piece of history that our special guest, Miss Grayson from Historic Annapolis, is going to teach us. She is adding our library to the October Ghost Tour, which begins next month. After the lecture, everyone can break into groups of two and search for resource materials."

My eyes drifted to the pretty twenty-something girl with auburn hair that I had first met at Mrs. Blackstone's office when she took the Flower Power delivery. She had also attended the coven meeting I was at. Around her neck dangled a brilliant gold coin pendant engraved with a Celtic witch's knot. She aimed her sharp chin at Emme, who seemed overly pleased with her arrival.

The witch led us into a spacious reading pit where tall, deep-set windows invited light into the open area and nineteenth-century floors covered with rough gray carpet creaked under our feet. With the tables full, Summer and I snagged seats on the steps next to our classmates.

"Oh, look at this. What an interesting throwback. It's the original card catalog library patrons used." She pointed to a long wood cabinet with a thousand tiny drawers.

Arora raised her hand, her fingernails painted black. "What's a card catalog?"

Our ghost guide aimed her gleaming, bleached smile in her direction. "It was an organizational tool. This archaic contraption once housed index cards that contained printed information of every book in the library."

Arora raised her hand again. "Did you say index cards, as in paper?"

"Yes. Paper, as in the old days," Mrs. Rivelli interjected with a smirk.

She pointed to our left. "On this wall here, we have an oil painting of the original house Lord Arundell shared with his wife right here on this property at the time of the Revolutionary War."

I stared at the painting of the imposing colonial couple and they seemed to stare back.

"What happened to them?" Navan asked.

"Interesting question. After Lord Arundell died, the house burned to ashes. Legend says that his grieving wife was accused of summoning the fire using witchcraft."

I swallowed the lump in my throat.

Miss Grayson continued. "Months later, Lady Arundell was found hanging from the tree overlooking Witch's Grave. Today, her spirit continues to keep a watchful eye on the happenings here, and since she was known to be a collector of rare books, we've heard she's a *mostly* contented spirit residing in the archives room—in spite of being put to death without a trial." She bit down on her lip, hard. A tiny drop of scarlet blood oozed out before she swiped it away with the back of her hand.

I elbowed Summer. "Did you see that?"

"See what?" she said. I glanced around, realizing no one else seemed to have noticed.

A boy named George standing behind us smoothed his greasy hair and lifted his chin. "So, even with a broken neck, she isn't mad enough to haunt the place properly?"

Miss Grayson sneered ever so slightly. "I said mostly contented. Spectral experts have told us that Lady Arundell's ghost guards the collection of rare books her descendants bequeathed to the city library for safekeeping. She won't let anyone remove them without a fight," she continued, more as if she were talking to herself, "or a proper offering."

George's eyes popped. "How does she fight?"

She winked. "Every witch has her own method."

Another classmate's hand went in the air. "Can we see those books?"

"I'm afraid you can't. Your librarian, Mrs. Dockerty, told me she doesn't even like to go in there. When she does, a chill stabs her through, and on occasion the lights flicker. It can be quite frightening, which is why we've added this location to the October Ghost Tours. You'll have to come back then and see."

Emme shot her hand in the air. "You should add Calvert Manor to the tour." She turned her evil eye on me. "I heard they have a stalker on the grounds. Maybe it's a ghost." She winked, setting my jaw with anger.

Miss Grayson smiled and continued. "Please let me know if you have any encounters—of the spectral kind, and when you're done finding resources for your history paper, you are being treated to a paperback copy of *Annapolis Ghost Tales* courtesy of the historic foundation. Thank you."

Summer nudged my arm. "Talk of ghosts gives me the creeps."

Trying not to get wrapped up in Emme's game, I ignored her and searched the main floor. "I'd love to get a glimpse of those rare books."

"She said they're off limits."

"I heard her." I doubted it was a coincidence that Miss Grayson, who was part of the coven and worked side-by-side with Mrs. Blackstone at the foundation, was sent to give a ghost tour spiel only. My eyes flitted back to the group, but Emme had disappeared. "I'll be right back."

Summer nodded and stared at the time on her phone as if she were willing the seconds to move faster.

I sped toward a dark hallway and spied Emme's back disappearing behind a door marked 'Archives'. I counted to five and took a step.

A cold hand touched my shoulder. I spun around. "What the h—," I stammered.

Mrs. Rivelli eyed me. "You seem very curious, Miss Fitzgerald, but we've been instructed to not go near the archives room. Please find research books for your project."

The kid in me wanted to rat Emme out and earn her a detention, but I couldn't confirm my suspicions if I did. "Sorry, Mrs. Rivelli." I smiled and walked away, waiting for George Wardwell to distract her with one of his gazillion questions, which he did about one minute later.

I dashed down the dark hallway. Emme's voice drifted through the door. I leaned in close.

"I don't care if the ghost doesn't want the damn coin. I'm leaving with a book." She paused and Miss Grayson's voice rose up.

"Not just any book. Your mother said everything you need to know is in the ghost's most valuable book," she continued, sounding out of breath. "It's not hard to figure out from these rows of dilapidated hardbacks that it has to be this gold one with all the Latin writing. Leave the coin, take the book, and guard it with your life."

My feet remained glued as my curiosity surged.

Approaching footsteps drove me into the nearest bathroom where darkness absorbed me like liquid mercury. I pressed firm against the wall, listening.

A rumbling and crash sounded from the other side. The wall vibrated against my fingers like a mini-earthquake and the air suddenly cooled. An arctic chill swept over the prickled skin on my arms as a soft, white glow cast its illuminated reflection onto the mirror.

I had never seen anything like it in all my life. I reached out, unsure what it was. When I skimmed my hand through the light, a tiny electrical shock traveled the length of my arm. "Whoa!"

A moan emanated from the radiant ball. The light undulated into a willowy female shape wearing a flowing white gown. She opened her mouth in silent agony like the eerie scream painting I had studied in Ms. Peña's art history class two years ago. I wasn't afraid, but I didn't dare touch her again. Instead, I drew back as far as I could and waited.

Breathe, Hannah.

The lights flickered on by themselves and along the white wall, words formed. *The unworthy girl will regret her thievery*, she etched in charred black, as if her ethereal finger was exuding fire as she wrote.

What did it say about me that I could relate? "Wait. Who are you?" I'd already guessed.

Again the writing appeared, letter by letter, in the same ashy print that quickly faded. *Lady Arundell*, she wrote. An icy trail ran across my hand where I wore my gold family crest.

"Did you really die at Witch's Grave?"

Hung for being a witch like you.

"Who said I was a witch?"

You are a witch, but if you are a worthy one, you will bring me the truth.

"What truth?"

The lights flared, then dimmed to black without another word from her. My shoulders relaxed as I bent over to catch my breath, but all I could think was if a ghost knew I wasn't an ordinary I must really suck at pretending. I peeked back into the hall, certain a crowd was gathering from the disturbance, but there was no one and the door to the archives was ajar.

I sneaked a peek inside. My eyes popped while my mouth dangled open. "What the—?" I stepped in amid the destruction.

Two grand, overfilled bookcases were toppled and scattered books covered every inch of the floor along with dozens of white archival gloves. On the walls, framed pictures hung at odd angles and desk drawers dangled from their alcoves.

Slam!

I spun around and grasped the doorknob. I twisted and turned, yanked and pulled, but it wouldn't budge. My heart hammered. The magic whispered. "Not now." I slapped my hands against the door. "Help. Someone let me out!" I grabbed onto the knob again.

"Who's in there?"

I recognized Mrs. Rivelli's voice.

"Um, it's me. Hannah. I'm locked in." I jiggled the knob again.

"Ouch," she said. "Why is the knob so hot? What's going on in there?"

I released the door handle and stared at my hands. My magic must have trickled out. I threw my head back in frustration. "Try it now."

With a click, the door opened wide and so did my teacher's eyes. "Hannah Fitzgerald. What on earth did you do in here?"

I flung my hands out to my sides like the innocent victim I was. "Me? This wasn't me."

Shock phased to anger and colored her face red. "I don't see anyone else."

Mrs. Dockerty rushed up behind her. "Why is someone in...? Oh my goodness."

"Don't worry, Mrs. Dockerty. If you can get the janitors to stand the bookcases upright, Miss Fitzgerald will spend all of her study halls cleaning up this mess until it's perfect."

Appall shaded my attitude. "I don't mind helping to organize this, but it wasn't me. It-it was Lady Arundell."

A scoff caught in her throat. "The ghost? Really, Miss Fitzgerald? Do you want detention?"

"No, ma'am, but how could I possibly knock those heavy bookcases over? I'm not that strong."

She stuck her hands on her hips. "All evidence points to you since you're the only person in this room. Maybe you leveraged your weight against them. I don't know."

"But, but..." I sputtered. If she didn't believe it was Lady Arundell, she wouldn't believe Emme had anything to do with it, either. "Fine. I'll come back during study hall." Maybe suffering the punishment would prove my worthiness to the ghost.

I seethed under my breath as I bolted back to the reading pit. I joined Summer at her table.

"What's wrong with you?" she asked.

"Nothing. Why?"

"You look all—sweaty."

I wiped my brow dry with the back of my hand. "I'm fine. Wanted to find some good books for my paper before we left."

She glimpsed my empty hands with her sharp emerald eyes. "I see you found as many as I did. Good job."

Her sarcasm lifted my mood. "Did you see anything strange?"

"Besides Mrs. Rivelli's inappropriate fondling of the card catalog?"

"Huh?" I spotted Miss Grayson, minus her shiny gold pendant, chatting with Emme and the other Queen Js near the checkout desk. With one hand, Emme flipped her dark hair over her shoulder and with her other, she held the small, white, plastic gift bag in a death grip.

Summer pressed her head to the table. "I already know everything there is to know about my research topic. What I need is a good mythology book." She peeked up at me. "Did you hear me?"

"Uh huh. Mythology." I tore my attention from Emme and crinkled my brow. "I thought you were counting the microseconds until we escaped."

She smiled. "My mom's half Incan and half Greek so my heritage leaves me with a soft spot for powerful gods."

I returned my gaze to the Queen Js. "How about powerful beasts?"

"What do you recommend?"

"The original *Beauty and the Beast*. It's not so much a myth as it is a classic tale, but you can download it on your iPad."

A commotion grabbed our attention and Summer mimicked a sportscaster's voice. "Emme fighting with Arora, over, could it be…a free ghost book and tour coupon?"

What Summer couldn't see was Emme blowing a sparkly mist from her fingertip at Arora, and Arora ducking so the stuff landed on George's black T-shirt. The mist luminesced like glow-in-the-dark dandruff.

I kicked Summer's foot to distract her. "Hey, I need to use the bathroom. Can you grab me one of those free ghost books? I forgot where she said they were."

"Sure." She strolled past Miss Grayson as the Queen Js sashayed toward me all wearing the same coy smiles and Prada scarves in different colors. I stared hard at the bag in Emme's hand, straining to make out a title, but Emme switched it to her other hand, putting it out of sight.

Arora sidled up next to me and reached a honey brown hand toward me. "When are you going to take the test, Hannah?"

"I told you I'm not interested." I really needed to form my own clique.

Navan rested her copper-ringed fingers on my shoulder, which I shrugged off.

"You know what? I'm not feeling well," I moaned like a killer whale. "Bad crab pretzel for breakfast, I guess." I pressed my hand to my stomach and gagged. "Uh oh, it's coming up."

The Queen Js screamed. I yanked Emme closer and stole a better look at her bag. The thin plastic revealed a gaudy gold book cover, but no title. She wrestled free of my hold. I jerked straight up and smiled. "Not crab pretzel." I sniffed the air. "Just a bad reaction to the collective smell of your cheap perfumes."

Arora huffed and threw her hands on her hips. "Our perfumes are imported from France."

I snickered. "So is the smelliest cheese in the world."

Arora and Navan strutted away, while Emme remained. She leaned toward my ear. "You want me as an enemy?"

"After the nightmare you put me through, I assumed you were my enemy."

Her lower jaw jutted out. "If you're going to be one of us, Hannah, you have to be a big girl witch and toughen up."

I glanced at my pink shirt and black ballerina flats, and then stared her dead in the eyes. "I may not look tough, but looks are deceiving, aren't they?" I nodded to her forearm where my scalding handprints still glowed a faint pink.

She offered a smug half-grin. "That's the attitude I want to see from a potential Queen J."

I recalled W's warning about her, but if I let her think I was open to joining her stupid clique, maybe she'd tell me why she was risking a suspension to steal a ghost's book. "I'd consider being friends, but no more testing."

She purred. "Perhaps we can postpone the testing."

I shrugged. "Great."

"Great," she repeated. She lifted her hand and touched my hair.

I shoved her hand away. "What are you doing?"

"You had a piece of lint in your hair. That's all." She turned on her shiny, Italian leather, kitten heel to join the others.

Summer rushed up to me and dangled the gift bag in my face. "Hey, what's that stuff in your hair?"

"Huh?" I patted my hair and found a sticky mess where Emme had touched. My shoulders sagged. "Hopefully, just hair gel." I plucked several tissues from a box on the checkout desk and wiped away the goo.

Summer dabbed sugar cookie Chap Stick to her lips. "Queen Js and ghosts suck. Let's go."

When I glanced back at the dark hall, a thunderous tremble triggered a mutual gasp from the class. I whipped around and watched Emme cross over the threshold. As she strolled toward the covered walkway, the whole building swayed. More books fell off the shelves. Overhead lights flickered.

"Earthquake!" George yelled.

The Chesapeake area wasn't known for earthquakes, but it was known for ill-tempered witches and there were at least five inside the library at the moment.

At the end of school, I was slightly worn out from cleaning up Emme's book disaster during study hall; however, I was on a mission. I rushed to my locker because of its nearness to Emme's.

"What's up, Hannahbell Lecter?" Mateo shouted down the hall toward me. An inside draft tousled his chunky coffee-colored hair. He threw his big hand high in the air, wanting me to jump like a circus Chihuahua to give him five.

Short girl problems. I chuckled. "What's with the cannibal nickname?" I weaved back and forth to keep an eye out for my nemesis.

"I give all my best buds nicknames. It's kind of a privilege. You're welcome." He sounded serious.

"It's horrible, thank you. Now, drop the Lecter part?"

"No way." He shrugged, shoving the long-sleeves of his green polo shirt up his forearm.

"Fine, Mattyboy, why are you here?" A crowd of dispersing students mobbed the hallway.

"Waiting for Summer to drive me home after history club ends."

I hoped she and Chase were making progress in the boyfriend-girlfriend department. I should've asked when we were in the library.

"Why does she have a car and you don't?" I stood on tippy toes to see beyond him.

"Grrr. Another story for another day." He jumped up with one arm extended, shooting air hoops. "What are you doing right now?"

"Looking for a change of scenery," I joked.

"Ohh—sounds dangerous." His sarcasm was as thick as cold butter on bread.

I playfully flexed my bicep. "I seem to be attracted to danger." That was the problem with my curious nature. It took me to places I shouldn't venture, but this time I was willing to risk another trip to Emme's Nightmare Alley to satisfy it.

He pointed to a bedazzled poster plastered on one of the main doors. "Have you ever been to the Annapolis Tea Party re-enactment? The city roped the Bean into being a sponsor."

"I haven't, but I heard this year is kind of a big deal, what with the two hundred and fiftieth anniversary and all. So you and Summer will be there?"

"Summer snagged two tickets to the ball after, leaving my mom and me to work the coffee table at the re-enactment. You should come and hang out with me," he said, kicking a pebble to the side.

I fake-gagged, remembering the last historic event I attended. Eighth grade field trip to Williamsburg, and just as the Patrick Henry look-alike recited his famous speech Shaun McFarley slapped his wet lips on mine. It was like a slimy eel invading my mouth. *Bleh.* There was no way anyone would consider that a real first kiss because it absa-freaking-lutely wasn't.

"I'm not really into historic events." I shifted back and forth.

He paused, watching me bob left and right. "Why are you so distracted?"

I stopped and let my gaze drift upward. "I'm—waiting for someone."

He squinted, seeming disappointed. "I knew you were acting weird. Well, weirder than usual." He paused, his eyes begging to know more. "Who's the lucky guy?"

I gulped a big breath. "Emme Blackstone."

His eyes widened. "You roll that way? 'Cause I didn't get that vibe from you."

I shook my head. "You're an idiot. I'm not gay. She has something I want."

He turned around and scanned the crowd of students, his six-foot height an advantage I didn't have. "There's Queen E now with Arora." He pointed subtly. "Go on, girl. I'll sit here and wait for Summer and try not to laugh when the mean girl shuts you down."

I set a hand on my hip. "How do you know I'm not a mean girl?"

He snickered. "You're not. I can sense these things."

"Humph, but you couldn't sense I was a hetero?" I stuffed my backpack into my locker and then strained to listen to them talking, but the busy hall was filled with the loud buzz of chattering.

I sneaked closer. Without a plan, I waited and listened.

Navan appeared and flitted into the conversation. "I've finally decided what I'm doing for the talent exhibition. How about you, Emme?"

"Of course I have and don't even bother to beg because I've claimed Arora as my assistant." Self-absorbed as usual, the trio was completely unaware I was right behind them, separated only by a steady stream of classmates passing through.

Arora clapped her hands. "Who cares about the exhibition when the Governor's Masked Ball following the stupid tea party thingy is happening? I already bought my colonial dress and a vintage Prada evening clutch. I mean it's not vintage Revolutionary era, duh, but it matches my gown. It's so haute. Wait until you see it. You're going to calcinate."

I nearly choked hearing Arora use the chemistry term I recognized from my dad's notes because it had nothing to do with a reaction to fashion.

I peeked over my shoulder. Emme's back faced me while Arora's hands flew about, accentuating her vapid conversation.

Talk about the book, I thought.

Seconds later, Emme reached into her locker and retrieved a piece of paper. My eyes widened.

"Navan, grab your Latin to English dictionary."

"What for?"

"I tore this page from an ancient book and I want it translated. Looks like Latin to me."

Navan glimpsed it. "Yeah, it does."

"Are you any good at it?" Emme snapped.

"Uh, I've only survived three years of Latin with Mr. Brian."

Arora scoffed. "Shut up, Navan. You only signed up for that class because he's the hottest teacher in school."

She giggled. "I signed up for it because I foresaw him flirting with me, but that never happened."

"Foresaw? It's called wishful thinking," Emme said with a droll smile. "Besides, he's happily married."

Navan frowned. "Anyway, we didn't learn any of those words in class. What's it supposed to be about?"

Emme sighed with impatience. "Someone told me the info I needed was on this page, so translate and tell me what it means."

Navan grabbed a book from her locker and paged through it while I listened intently. A cluster of lacrosse players gathered in between us, shoving and knocking each other around until they bumped me into the bulletin board.

"Ow."

"Sorry about that," a tall boy said.

"Shh." I centered myself behind him, hiding, and realized intel-gathering sucked. Maybe W was right. I hated to think that was possible after his nearly tragic black vine prank, but my instincts told me we needed to work together and everyday the feeling was growing stronger—like if we didn't, all kinds of apocalyptic bad was going to rain down, and not just on me. I peered around the player.

Navan looked at Emme and smiled with satisfaction. "None of those words are listed in here."

"What the hell am I supposed to do?" Emme shook the page in the air.

"Why do you sound so crazy?" Navan questioned.

"I'm not crazy. I have big plans and I need this info."

"Big plans for what?" Arora asked.

"I want to be more than the head of the Queen Js. I want to be the prophesied one."

"You already know it's you," Navan added with a sly grin I couldn't quite decipher.

Emme paced. "I don't know anything. Not for sure."

I was dying to get a glimpse of the page, or better yet, snap a picture. I reached into my pocket, but my phone shocked me. What the hell? I shook off the tingling sensation and turned off the flash. I slipped my hand alongside a different player and aimed the phone in their general direction. I clicked the button over and over, hoping to get one good shot.

"You could hit up the language lab. Mr. Brian keeps a massive Latin to English dictionary on the shelf. It might be worth a shot."

"Come with me—in case I need your help. Arora, we'll see you later."

Navan bounced on her toes, seeming thrilled to be chosen for the task. I scrolled through the photos I snapped. Damn it. The pics were all blocked by Emme's big hair. I peered around the boys as the two witches disappeared down the hall and the other headed for the quad. At this time of day, there would be no one else in the lab so I couldn't follow them in there. Then an idea hit me. I raced toward the main office where a school map was plastered to the wall. I trailed my finger across the layout until I found it.

"Yes, perfect. Tricky, but perfect." I shoved out the main doors and dashed around the school building to the back classrooms that overlooked a wooded area. Every classroom had a wall of windows.

A robust crabapple tree with lots of long sturdy branches grew right outside the language lab. I grabbed hold of the gnarled bark and climbed, latching onto a contorted branch that ran above the top row of windows, one of which was open.

I felt like a five-year-old as I released my grip and dangled upside down so my head was near the open one. My curiosity was going to be the death of me. I only hoped it wasn't today, with Emme ten feet away.

The late afternoon sunlight illuminated the interior. I pressed my forehead against the glass. Emme and Navan hurried into the classroom, locking the door behind them. Navan pulled the huge dictionary from a shelf. After several minutes, she gestured to Emme to come closer.

Damn it. I scrambled over to another tree's branch that gave me a better view.

Emme held the torn page while Navan skimmed through the book.

I reached for my phone again, and this time her hair wouldn't get in the way of my zoom lens. My fingers fumbled for the device. Then I felt it—the magic hummed to life. I blamed it on the sheer terror of hanging upside down in a tree. "Not now." I clenched my teeth and focused on a leaf, trying to calm down, but it was too late.

A steady pulse of energy rose up. No, no, no. There was no explosion, but a micro-thin stream of fire seeped out through my fingers. I imagined drawing it back inside, but it didn't work. My hands got hotter. With a screaming pop, my phone exploded. The fried battery caused a flash and a sizzle, followed by a thin trail of black smoke that stunk like burning rubbing alcohol.

I muttered curses as I dropped the melting device to the ground. That had never ever happened before. Was I losing it? The smoking phone was real, not a hallucination, and so was the slight energy drain, which meant one thing—the magic was growing stronger. I wasn't sure that was a good thing, and even more dread settled in as I wondered if they'd discovered me. I cast a wary gaze into the classroom.

Emme seemed oblivious, and for once I was thrilled with her self-absorption. She looked at Navan blank-faced. "Crap." She stared at the book. "So mirror means the opposite in effect?"

I released a silent gasp and tried to focus on what they were saying, which was difficult with the rush of blood roaring in my ears.

"The two elixirs are opposite how?" She waved her hands in front of her. "Keep translating."

Two elixirs? I repeated in my head. I cast my attention back to the girls.

"Or do I have to do it myself?" Emme's icy gaze locked on Navan.

Her follower grabbed a pencil from the teacher's cup and wrote the translation right on the page.

Emme threw a hand on her narrow hip and tapped her foot on the floor, seeming eager to figure out the meaning. So did Navan, who jotted words down wearing that same mysterious grin. Finished, she read it over to herself before handing the page back to Emme.

"This is unbelievable. I've got to find it for my dad. Actually, I don't have to do anything. I know just the person who can be motivated to do the work for me." A hint of excitement sparked in her voice. "Tell no one what you translated," she warned before standing to give her friend an air-kiss.

I shuddered at their fakeness at the same moment Emme turned to stare out the windows. My leg muscles ached with nervousness. Then she set the translated page down on the windowsill and paced the classroom. The info I wanted was right there just a few feet away and she wasn't looking.

I eyed the branch below and to the right of the windows. I'd be out of view and closer to my goal. I counted to three and reached for the branch. I shifted with a fair amount of grace and grabbed onto the branch below. Then my leg twitched, throwing me off balance. With a jerky motion, I smacked my hands against the trunk to steady myself.

I froze, wide-eyed. Still high above the ground and near the open window, I peeked in. Navan had her back to me and Emme was out of view. Was she racing outside to catch me? I imagined her blowing her wretched nightmare mist in my face, and if I survived the nightmare, I imagined Mrs. Blackstone driving me to Camp Sea Haven—minus any delicious stops for a ten-layer cake.

My wild eyes flitted back and forth. My breathing stalled. Should I jump and run for it? I counted to ten then peered around. No one was coming. I wiped my breath fog from the glass and peeked in one last time.

Emme traipsed back into view, not seeming alarmed.

"I can't believe I'm this close to what my family has been looking for all these years. That this is a clue to the key," she said.

A crunch in the woods behind me caught me off guard. I swiveled my head, losing my grip. My body wobbled. The branch slipped out from under me. My stomach dropped.

I fell through the air, but instead of hard earth absorbing my momentum while imparting a concussion, a pair of warm, strong arms wrapped around me and scooped me up.

I slapped a hand over my mouth to stifle the scream. My heart sputtered. I inhaled his scent, the fragrance intertwining with mine as he held me for a second longer than necessary. Trying to stand, yet feeling unsteady, I grasped his strong hand without thinking, but in that moment the horror of the black vine flashed in my mind. I narrowed my furious focus on his face that was turned to the right. "Here to finish me off?"

W stood there, all pompous. Classic black Ray Bans and the hood of his jacket partially concealed his face that was angled to the right.

He nodded toward the smoking phone in the grass. "Does your warranty cover accidental fires?" he said with a heavy dose of sarcasm.

I gritted my teeth and lowered my voice. "Ha. You're super funny. Is that part of your serial killer act? Pretend to help me, lure me in with a riddle or tell a snarky joke, and then boom, watch me die?"

He peered into the lab. The Queen Js kept their backs to the windows. Then he tugged on my arm and gestured toward the woods.

"Yeah, I'd like to live through today, so I'm not going anywhere with you, like ever. Besides, I need something and they've got it."

He tugged again. "If Emme catches you out here, you'll never get whatever it is she has."

I recalled the last thing Emme said about a clue to a key, but what key? I crossed my arms against my chest, unwilling to budge.

"You know I'm right, but go ahead. Be stubborn and prove it to both of us."

I could feel steam shooting from my ears. "You are so wrong in so many ways. Let's review, shall we?" As I was about to list his failings, he jerked me back by my shoulders out of the witches' sights.

"What the hell?"

My gaze followed his finger as he pointed to the classroom. Emme and Navan turned and stood at attention, scanning the area outside the windows.

I bit down on my tongue. "Gah! Fine, but I swear, if you pull any tricks on me, I'll take you down."

"I don't doubt it. Now, come on." He moved swiftly, leading me through a thick cluster of trees until we were deep in the woods. We slowed to a stop.

Then I remembered I was still pissed about the vine trick he had pulled on me. Was there anything about him that didn't piss me off? Well, there was that clever thing. I yanked my hand back and brushed the hair from my eyes to see him better.

His black hood hid most of the short, straight, dark brown hair that peeked out around the edges. He was tall, probably six-foot-two. He kept his face turned away from me—until he didn't.

I drew a loud breath as I flinched. A long, jagged scar, red and puckered, marred his ivory complexion from just beneath the sunglasses. It looked like a knife wound surrounded by a severe burn, and the damage ran the length of his cheek.

With a growl, he faced me and offered a full glimpse of the disfigurement. "I'd flinch, too."

"I—I didn't mean to. It's just that I'm…" I averted my eyes.

"You wanted to look, so look. Look at me! Or are you too disappointed?"

I threw my shoulders back and lifted my gaze until it settled on his sunglasses. "Well, yes. I am disappointed," I said without fear or hesitation.

He sneered. "Because of my horrid face?" He turned his head to the right again to lessen my view.

With one finger, I reached for his chin and straightened him out. "Don't do that." I stared at the black lenses that created the wall he wanted between us. "You did surprise me." I paused for a breath. "However, my disappointment has nothing to do with your scar. I'm disappointed because I'm out here to get information and thanks to you butting in, I've missed out on it."

He shoved out his lower jaw and growled. "Is that why you're hanging out behind the school?"

"Why are *you* hanging out behind the school?" I demanded right back in an equally ticked off voice, straining to see the boy behind the black reflective lenses. Again, my instincts weren't screaming any warnings, however the magic was starting to whisper.

"I saw you and figured you were going to need help."

His presence had my heart racing. I shoved him away, but as my hands touched his chest, another spark surprised me. Blood rushed to my cheeks in a flash and a storm of unfamiliar pleasure swirled in my stomach. What the hell was wrong with me?

"H-how condescending of you," I stuttered as I mentally pulled myself together. "In case you forgot, I escaped the burning car by myself, got Emme to back off, and destroyed that killer plant you literally stuck me with."

He closed the distance. "You sound surprised that you did all that."

The whisper grew louder. "Seriously, what are you doing here?"

He took another step toward me. "You have a lion's heart, but your curiosity, lack of confidence, and pigheadedness are going to be a problem."

I closed my eyes trying to squelch the magic, but dealing with him was making it difficult. "My curiosity? You were spying, too, and I'm not pigheaded."

"You are, but don't worry. So am I."

His deep voice hummed in my head.

My eyelids fluttered open. We were nearly face to face with only an inch of electrically charged air between us. "Are you tr-trouble?" I couldn't see his eyes, but he stared straight into me, and my heart sputtered.

"Absolutely. That's why you need me."

My eyes nearly popped out of my head. Was he serious? "Ha. I so don't need you."

"Don't you?" he said with a snarl. "I saved you from that fall and our mutual enemy."

I narrowed my eyes. "You mentioned before that she was our mutual enemy, yet I don't see her going after you."

He rubbed his chin seeming pensive for a moment. "She will. Once she figures out I'm helping you, and she will figure it out, she'll stop at nothing to get rid of me."

"Wait a minute. Who said you're helping me? I never agreed to that. I haven't gotten past the car accident slash killer plant trauma, yet."

"I told you why I had to leave you and the rose vine was a test, which you passed."

"Lucky me," I said with smugness.

"I doubt you'll be so lucky if that witch confronts you again. You need to back up your courage with something equally as powerful."

"How do you know what...?" His ability to see the situation comforted and annoyed me at the same time. "You—you shouldn't have followed me."

"You should be grateful!" he hissed.

"Grateful? I went to a lot of trouble to find out what Emme was up to and you, you..." Thinking about the lost opportunity on the other side of the language lab window irritated the salt, sulfur, and mercury out of me. My cheeks heated as I silently counted to ten.

He continued, "If Emme caught you spying, I'm certain you'd have your second confrontation, and then you'd never see whatever it was you were after."

I dropped my head with disappointment, hoping he wasn't right, but there was the slightest, tiniest, most miniscule chance he was.

He lifted my chin with his finger. "I expect you Saturday evening at eight."

My pulse picked up. I pushed his hand away. "Not until I know who you are first, and how you got your hands on that deadly seed."

His potent silence was almost intimidating, but not quite. "You want to know? Really?"

I nodded.

"You know enough for now. Trust that." His tone was filled with unrelenting determination to leave me as curious as ever.

"At least tell me how you know what Emme and I are."

His mouth turned down at the corners as if there were some internal debate weighing heavily on him. "The question you want to ask is how could I know?"

He was annoyingly clever. "Because you're a wizard?" My instincts seemed to sense it, yet still no alarms. All I felt was an undeniably powerful connection between us. I studied him for a moment. He exuded confidence. It rolled off him in waves, but that scar; it seemed to leave him vulnerable. I could relate to that, except my wounds were on the inside.

A slight grin tugged on his left cheek, confirming my suspicion of what he was, but how? I was new to my aunt's coven; however, I remembered the rules. Any visiting witches or wizards were required to notify them.

"I trust you can make your way home without falling into danger again?"

"As long you don't follow me, I should be fine," I teased, but I wasn't fine. My desire to be ordinary had been flushed down the proverbial toilet, and I feared for the prophecy's conclusion that was bound to play out. I threw my hands in the air.

"Who cares about danger anyway when none of this even matters because I can't change how it's going to end?"

He grimaced. "What are you talking about?"

My frustration flowed. "I want a fighting chance to change my fate."

"You mean the *Chesapeake Histories*?"

My body went rigid at mention of the coven book. I searched his expression for an answer. "How do you know about that?"

He ignored my question. "You don't think you can change it?" he asked, derision vibrating in his tone.

The scoff caught in my throat. "My parents couldn't change theirs."

"Your parents aren't you."

"What are you saying?" My voice was edged with fire.

"I know Emme thinks she's more than she is, but she isn't, and you don't think you're much at all when—when you really are."

Frustrated, I dropped my face into my hands. "My parents were gifted and that didn't help them."

"But what you do with fire—it's powerful."

He had more knowledge about me than he should.

I glanced up at him. "You shouldn't have tested me like that with the vine."

His gaze seemed locked on my ring. "You're a gifted witch. It wasn't a far leap to assume you could handle it."

"You don't get it. It's not a gift."

"Having the element of fire literally at your fingertips is an extraordinary gift," he said.

I huffed. The tears welled up as I thought of my parents. The magic stirred faster and louder. "You don't know me. You don't know my life. I'm telling you the magic ended up being a curse to my parents and it could be that way for me, too."

"A curse?" He huffed. "You wouldn't know what a curse was if it knocked you off your broomstick." He spun away.

My whole head ached. Without thinking I snapped. "Said the wizard to the witch." As the word *wizard* tumbled off my tongue, I glanced at his scar again and wondered if it was a sign of something more.

"You're right. I'm a hypocrite, but fate hasn't exactly dealt me a fair hand." He stared into the distance. "However, for the first time in a long time, I believe there's a chance I can change mine. I need to know my life can be different."

The response summoned an expression of pure vulnerability, and I had to seize the moment. "What happened to you?" Desperation dug in—I needed to know him the way he seemed to know me. My gaze washed over his rosy lips that pursed with an invitation. A yearning took hold within me, and I couldn't shake it. I reached for his sunglasses.

With a cold, abrupt motion, he jerked back. "What are you doing?" His tone was harsh.

I recoiled. When I looked up at him again, his mouth formed a rigid line.

"What's happened to me is none of your business," he snarled. "I shouldn't be here. This was a mistake."

The repetition of his words stung. I glared. "You shouldn't be here. In fact, why don't you leave? Leave me alone forever."

The muscles in his neck stiffened as if he were fighting against an inner demon. He bit his lower lip. "If I don't leave now, I—," he paused, "I promise you this. I won't be there next time you fall and good luck dealing with Emme by yourself."

Anger singed my throat. My narrowed eyes flitted to his sunglasses, hoping he saw everything I was feeling at the moment. My insides quaked. "Perfect! If I die, it will be just what you wanted!" I doubted that was true, but I said it anyway.

He mashed his perfect lips together. "Ungrateful." He huffed as he stomped away.

"I heard that!" I hoped danger jumped out at me from every bush just to spite him. Every muscle in my body shuddered and the steady pulse of energy rose up again. "Grr," I growled and stared at the fiery threads undulating from my fingertips. I couldn't freaking afford to not have it under control. Not now.

8.

Days passed without a word between W and I. Thoughts of our argument consumed every minute I was awake and rocked my dreams at night. I didn't regret unleashing a bit of tempest on him, especially since he'd asked for it, but I shouldn't have tried to remove his sunglasses. I, more than anyone, understood what it was like to want to hide an unwanted trait. Not that he deserved my empathy, because he didn't, but I was certain the breach of trust voided the invitation to meet him later tonight. Of course it did. My feet dragged underneath me as disappointment weighed heavy like a dozen soft pretzels in my gut.

Aunt J waited by the front door for me. "Here's your replacement phone. I picked it up at the mall yesterday. Good thing there was a warranty on it, huh?" She retrieved the new phone from her fringed purse and handed it to me.

"Yeah. Good thing." I checked the settings to make sure everything had transferred to the new phone.

"Are you ready?"

"As I'll ever be."

We hopped in the van for a short drive to Quiet Waters Woods. "Have fun today," she said as I jumped out.

Gentle slopes of land were abundant with trees that stretched as far as I could see. Leaves dripping shades of crimson and amber drifted down like embers and the scent of spicy smoke filled the air. In the distance, I detected the subtle sound of waves washing up on the beach.

I spotted Mateo on the edge of a natural trail that cut through the woods. He was crouched down and lacing up a pair of hiking boots, and I suddenly realized the black leggings I had paired with my long white T-shirt and flat shoes were not going to suffice for the outdoorsy surprise he had planned.

"Yo! Hannah!"

Beyond him, another boy loped toward us. His build was similar to Mateo's, but his complexion was the color of burnt mahogany compared to my friend's warm bronze.

"Hannahbell Lecter!"

I smiled big, knowing he'd never drop the Lecter part. "Mattyboy!"

"Hey, girl, meet my cuz."

The boy was dressed in gray cargo shorts and a white T-shirt and his espresso-colored eyes matched the color of his wild, wispy waves of hair. "I'm Blaze."

Mateo snickered. "That's my nickname for him."

I crinkled my face. "Why Blaze?"

Blaze grimaced. "I'm kind of hot-tempered."

Mateo's eyes snapped wide. "Like your mom's food—*muy caliente*."

Blaze knocked into him. "Shut up, man!"

"So, what's the big secret?"

"I'm sure you already sensed that I am more than Latino," Mateo said with certainty while Blaze rolled his eyes.

"I did?" I did, but there was no need to inflate his already puffed up ego.

"Stop kidding, Hannah. What I'm trying to say is that I'm Incan. Blaze is Incan, too, and we're here to prepare for our rite of passage, if you know what I mean?"

He waited for me to catch up as if this was something I did every Saturday with my large posse of Incan friends.

I stared at him blank-faced. "What in the world are you talking about?"

He exhaled a long breath. "The Incan Empire may no longer exist, but its warrior descendants do." He pounded on his chest like Tarzan. "There is an Incan ceremony called Huarachicoy with requirements Blaze and I must fulfill."

"These requirements don't involve nudity or anything gross, do they?"

He waggled his hands at me. "No way. It's man stuff."

"Oh, like nudity and gross things aren't man stuff?"

He ignored my sarcasm. "When it's over, you'll have to call me Mattyman."

"Ha! Only if you drop the Lecter in my nickname."

"Not happening."

I shook my head at his stubbornness. "What part do I play because I didn't exactly dress for an Incan man experience?"

"I told you it was going to be an adventure. Blaze and I have to find our animal spirits." Excitement brimmed in his voice.

I, however, wasn't impressed. I crossed my arms over my chest. "That's the man stuff?"

"Yeah, and having a girl around brings good luck. And since you're like your aunt, and you work at a flower shop, it makes you more connected to nature."

Why did boys always say that kind of stuff? "I'm not a four-leaf clover, and you don't even know my aunt that well."

"I know enough," he said hinting that maybe he did.

I cocked my head, curious. "What do you know?"

"Summer is a well of useless knowledge, which you probably figured out already, but sometimes I actually pay attention to her."

I kicked at the leaves around my feet. "And what did she tell you?"

"That your kind has an old bloodline like we do and that it's touched by magic—like ours is."

"M-magic?" I stuttered. Paranoia washed over me. I wasn't sure if we should talk about it. Ever since the coven meeting where I'd watched Eve get the boot, I'd been concerned about breaking the unbreakable rules, mostly for Aunt J's sake. I lowered my voice. "All I can say is that I'm intrigued, Mattyboy, so I'll make you a deal. I'm only helping if I get to find my animal spirit, too."

His lips twisted to the side as he considered my demand. "Hmm. How do I say this? You don't have an animal spirit."

I straightened my lips into a serious line. "Because I'm a girl?"

He shook his head. "No. Actually, Summer already found hers, which is so unfair. What I mean is, for your kind, I believe it's called a familiar."

I'd forgotten all about it, but birds were always associated with the Fitzgeralds. My dad had a black crow named Gerry that had disappeared after he died. "That's totally swag!"

"You ready to begin?"

I nodded with anticipation. He raised his thick, dark eyebrows up and down.

"We open our minds, walk through the woods, and become one with nature."

I pointed a finger at him and chuckled. "You realize you sound like a Zen yoga instructor." Or the quirky eco-therapist at Green Briar that held group sessions in the bonsai garden.

He playfully shoved me backwards. "Miss Impatient, we wait for a sign."

I stared with incredulity. "Wait? That's your brilliant man plan?"

"Yeah, that's my man plan." He slapped his hands together as if to signal the start of our search.

Blaze seemed completely at ease with what might potentially be an all-day hunt. "Wouldn't it be easier to take a Facebook quiz, like *What's Your Animal Spirit*?"

He crinkled his face with disgust. "This is how it's been done in my tribe for thousands of years. That's right, I said *thousands*, so this is how we'll do it." He closed his eyes and puckered his mouth. "A Facebook quiz. Gah!"

Conceding, I tucked my hair behind my ears and the three of us hiked into the woods. Well, they hiked. I skipped and leaped over sharp rocks and sprawling poison ivy. A wild howl in the distance brought us all to a stop. When we caught sight of each other's stupefied expressions we busted into laughter, making me certain none of us knew what we were doing.

"What if you purposely look for an animal with sharp teeth or intense talons?" I wanted specifics on how it worked.

Mateo shrugged. "Doesn't happen like that. The animal finds you. And not on a Facebook quiz, so keep your phone in your pocket, Hannahbell."

I smirked. "What if a gerbil crawls over your foot?"

Annoyed, he slapped his eyes shut. "Then your animal spirit is a gerbil, but at least you discovered it the Incan way. That has meaning."

I threw my hands behind me, trying not to touch the gnat flitting near my face, just in case. A manly chortle burst out of Blaze before he hiked ahead of us.

Mateo stuffed his hands in his pockets and kicked at the pebbles in his path. "So what have you been doing at Calvert Manor?"

I shot him a curious look. "Gossip in Annapolis gets around faster than a digital download." Inwardly, I blamed Emme and her big mouth.

"Yeah, especially when the new girl starts hanging at the recluses' property."

"Recluses, huh? You make them sound like circus freaks."

He stopped hiking and grabbed my arm. His concerned gaze met mine. "Not freaks. Just—sickly."

I sighed with exasperation. "What do you mean sickly?"

"My uncle knew the Calvert uncle back when they both attended Truxton High. My uncle said in a matter of days something came over his Calvert classmate and what he saw would turn any Incan warrior pale. He said it was like a Dr. Jekyll and Mr. Hyde kind of sickness that possessed his body and killed the boy inside." He said it with a stone cold seriousness that left me quiet. "Then last year, Chase Calvert's brother left school because of some weird illness and no one has seen him since."

Angst filled my body. W had to be Chase's brother. "Aren't you worried about Chase Calvert being too sickly for Summer?"

"Summer can take care of herself."

"You seem to believe I'm a witch, Mateo, so I guess I can too. Right?"

He twitched his mouth. "I'm just letting you know."

I tried to swallow, but my mouth went dry. Was he right about the Calverts being cursed? I wondered if that was why Ms. Russell was concerned. I let a carefree scoff escape. "That's the dumbest thing I ever heard."

He huffed. "Then why are your eyes so big?"

Blaze, seeming uncomfortable with our argument, shouted back to us. "Hey, I'm gonna hike over by the water. Holler if you two see anything."

Annoyed, I tugged at my shirt. "I don't want to talk about the Calverts anymore. Why don't you explain this rite of passage thing instead? There's a ceremony?" Twigs crunched under our feet.

"Once we discover our animal spirit, there is an endurance test followed by the Huarachicoy." He aimed his moss green eyes at me. "Kind of cool, huh?" He seemed to be searching for acceptance.

I nodded. "It is cool." The Colonial Chesapeake Daughters had their talent exhibition, which was coming up soon, but it didn't sound nearly as cool.

A commotion stirred in the distance. "Come here. Quick!" Blaze shouted, excitement bursting from his voice.

We raced toward the beach.

"Awesome!" He kneeled down on the sand.

I stared hard, trying to figure out what he found. "Is that a hermit crab?"

Blaze shot me a what-the-hell look. "Do you see a hermit crab?"

I stuck my hand on my hip. "Have you ever seen one of those things fight? Hermit crabs are fierce."

"Pfft. Not as fierce as what I found."

Mateo kneeled next to him and touched the ground, examining the evidence that had Blaze animated. His eyes glimmered with pride. "Wolf tracks."

"Definitely wolf." Mateo stretched his long arm out to where the waves hadn't wiped the sand clean. "They continue over there." The two would-be warriors conspired together.

Mateo's rounded shoulder muscles flexed as he shifted. I forced my gaze onto the discovery. It didn't seem very extraordinary. "How do you know it wasn't a random dog? There are lots of retrievers in Annapolis."

Blaze's face radiated crimson, giving me a glimpse of his fiery side. "Wolves have extra-large feet with two large protruding front toes. Not smaller and rounded feet like dogs. See there?" He pointed to the details. "Wolf. One hundred-percent. I nailed down my animal spirit. Come at me, bro." The two boys jumped up and fist-bumped each other. "How about you, Mateo? Any luck?"

A shadow of disappointment fell over his face. "Nothing." He dropped his head and kicked the dirt.

"Chin up. We just started. I'm gonna follow the tracks and see if I find it." He jumped in the air again, kicking his feet together like a South American leprechaun. "This is the best day—ever!" He rubbed his hands together with excitement, oblivious to his cousin's huge disappointment.

The breeze blowing off the water sent a chill through my thin shirt. I touched Mateo between his broad shoulder blades. "Come on. You'll find yours."

He faced Blaze. "We'll catch up with you later."

As soon as there was distance between Blaze and us, Mateo groaned. "I wanted the wolf. What the heck am I going to find out here, now?"

"Why can't you find a wolf, too?"

He shook his head and frowned. "The chances of Blaze and me having the same animal spirit are slim."

"What's Summer's?"

He glanced at me sideways and the frown disappeared. "I suppose it's not surprising what hers is. After all, she looks so different from the rest of us. It's sort of fitting."

"What is it?"

He laughed. "I'll let her share that secret with you."

I pouted. "I hate secrets!"

"I can tell. You're easy to read." He rubbed his hands together with satisfaction. "But this secret is good. Just wait." He kicked a small rock out of the way and stared at the ground. "I only wish, I mean, this whole rite of passage means a lot to me, and I don't want to be the only guy at the ceremony with a ratty squirrel as my animal spirit. I'll be humiliated."

I patted his back. "You are so not a squirrel. Do you even like nuts?" I joked, trying to lighten his mood. "Anyway, I sense you're definitely a hunter of some kind." I wasn't kidding. The feeling was tangible.

He lifted his head and his smile reappeared. "Yeah?"

"Definitely." We wound our way around the trees purposely getting lost in the woods as if going off course would bring us luck. As we traveled deeper into the wilderness, I fell behind, searching for a familiar while naming the native blooms I recognized from my childhood flower lessons.

I inhaled the perfumed fragrance from a handful of pine tree pollen pods, and then spotted a vine ordinaries loved; hops, a flowering plant used to make beer, and medicinally known to be an amazing sedative. I touched its broad green leaves and squishy green cones, and brought one up to my nose. The cone imparted its strong, grassy scent.

I brushed my hand across an oak tree's knotty trunk, but felt something unusual beneath my fingertips. I lifted my hand and stared. My eyes darted around at the other trees, discovering another initial and then another. E, A, and N, each paired with a pentagram. I could only guess who had carved those in the middle of the woods. I spun around and no longer saw Mateo.

I cupped my hands to my mouth and shouted. "Mattyboy?" He didn't reply, but he was so loud, he'd be easy to find again. I searched around, unsure of which direction I had started from, but a shaking beneath me stopped me dead in my tracks. I threw my hands out to steady myself, but the ground dipped. I struggled to stay balanced as the earth caved in, taking me with it.

Leaves and rocks plummeted after me as I dropped into a hole as deep as I was tall. Unsteady, I pressed my hands to the earthy walls. I caught my breath and tried to think, but something cold touched my foot.

"Aaah!" I flinched. What was that? I reached down and grasped onto the freezing cold object. It was a doll-sized ice sculpture of a girl. I narrowed my focus on her face and sighed.

The freaking Voodoo ice doll resembled me, except her face was distended in agony. Nice touch, Arora.

"More of an adventure than I guessed it would be," I said to myself. I wrapped a warm hand around the doll's head and melted the face so it didn't look like me anymore. Unfazed by their little prank, I dropped it, brushed the crud from my face, and pushed my back against the ditch, keeping my legs parallel to the ground below me. Slowly, I walked myself up toward the sunlight.

Clutching the outer rim of the pit, which was covered in a layer of dewy leaves, I hoisted myself over the slippery edge. I stared all around, trying to gauge my location, but a bird of prey in the distance, diving up and down with war-like precision, distracted me. I stared at the beautiful white animal in flight, but what was it diving for? I watched, fascinated.

"Hannahbell Lecter?" Mateo shouted.

"Over here."

In seconds, he closed the distance with his long stride. He shook his closed fist in the air, excited.

"What is it? Show me," I asked, silently relieved to see him again.

In his palm, a shiny porcelain figurine glistened, a charm, probably fallen from a child's bracelet, but nonetheless, an unmistakable sign.

I brushed my finger over the treasure. "Is that what I think it is?"

His expression radiated excitement. "Yeah!"

"Cougar?"

"Cougar definitely has more swagger than wolf." He strutted in a circle throwing his fist in the air and pausing only to admire his bejeweled find. At that moment, a large white feather floated down and landed on my foot.

"Hey, what happened to you?" he asked, finally noticing the dirt streaks all over my white shirt.

"Fell down."

His shoulders shook with laughter. "Seriously? You should have worn better shoes."

"Humph. Thanks for the late advice. I got distracted."

"With what?"

"You'll think I'm crazy if I tell you, and it doesn't matter." From the corner of my eye, I spotted a black BMW racing out on the main park road where the bird was diving and chasing it.

"That looks like Emme Blackstone's car," he said. "Why would she be here?"

"Why wouldn't she be here?" How seventeenth century of them—witches gathering in the woods and leaving their marks to prove it. Well, they could conjure up and disfigure a thousand Voodoo ice sculptures of me. What did I care? After all, fire melts ice.

Caw, caw. The beautiful winged creature with its pure white feathers cawed from above, perched on a low-lying tree branch.

"There you are."

The bird seemed to stare right through me with piercing blue eyes. I'd never seen such a magnificent creature in my life, and my connection to it was immediate. I motioned to Mateo with a wave of my hand. "Psst. Mattyboy!"

"Huh?" The charm held him spellbound.

My voice dropped to a whisper, not wanting to scare the bird off. "Is that a white—raven?"

He looked up. "Ravens are almost always black except in mythology, but even with that color it does resemble a raven." The bird cawed again. "Sounds like a raven, too. Check out its eyes." He looked at me, and then back to the bird. "You know what this means, don't you?"

"What?"

He snapped his fingers in the air. "Girlfriend got herself a familiar."

I was thrilled at the idea. "I'm not saying I'm a witch, but I'd love to call him my familiar." Especially since he had chased Emme away. "What does a bird like that symbolize?" I didn't know much about their spiritual significance.

One side of his mouth curled up pensively. "Well, ravens in my tribe are known as divine messengers that represent magic and transformation. And this is a rare white raven. My mom, who's half Greek, would say he's worthy of Apollo's favor."

"The myth with Coronis, you mean?"

He nodded as he sized the majestic bird up. "Their appearance usually signals the fulfillment of a prophecy."

A sense of foreboding dampened my joy. "W-what prophecy?"

He shrugged. "It's your familiar. You tell me."

I sighed. "You already know too much." How could I explain a prophecy where, in the worst-case scenario, I die, Emme becomes the most powerful Chesapeake witch ever, and the coven gets destroyed? Plus Emme had a serious problem with boundaries. Who knew what she'd do to the ordinaries in town. Hmm. I couldn't explain any of that.

Another feather rocked back and forth descending like a snowflake toward the ground. I gently picked up the delicate plume. "Farewell, raven." With a wave of my hands, the majestic creature took flight and with every flap of his angel-like wings, he seemed to lift my spirit as high as he rose in the sky.

I inhaled a deep breath, the air stretching my lungs. I spun back to Mateo. "This really was an adventure." I stood on tiptoes and hugged him.

He wrapped his long arms around me, unintentionally lifting my shirt up a bit. His cool fingers pressed into the warm skin of my waist. Suddenly sensing he wanted more than friendship, I quickly shimmied out of his embrace.

I didn't feel that way about him. I stepped back. "I should go."

"Wait. What's wrong?" His voice sounded deeper as if discovering his cougar animal spirit had buoyed his confidence.

I hoped he would let the awkwardness fade away. "Uh. I have a lot to do."

"Wait, I can drive you home. I borrowed my dad's car."

"Walk. Walking is good." I flashed my hand in a wave and headed toward Flower Power, twirling my familiar's feather with my fingers.

Twenty minutes of cool autumn air blew away the weirdness, and before I knew it I was stepping into the shop. Aunt J busied herself by neatening shelves filled with distilled flower petals and herbal oils.

"Hi." She didn't seem to hear me. "Aunt J?" I asked in a louder voice.

"Huh?" She spun around, dropping a jar of Belladonna. The deep magenta powder spewed across the floor in a cloud of purple dust. She gasped and drew back, seeming frightened.

"I'll clean it up," I assured her, not understanding her fright.

"No. Don't move. You don't understand…"

"What's the big deal?"

"Belladonna is from the nightshade family. It's deadly in large doses."

"Jeez, I'm not going to lick it off the floor. Aunt J?"

She looked down at the contours of the powder as it settled on the wide floor planks. Her intense expression told me she was more than freaked out. She clasped her hand over her mouth.

"What is it?"

"Holy salt, sulfur, and mercury. This is worse than an oleander flower."

"Why is this bad?" I said, exasperated, watching her run to the back room. Within seconds, she raced out with the broom and dustpan. "Help me. Quickly."

I kneeled down next to her, holding the dustpan as she swept the powder into it.

"Now, dump it in a bag. Quickly, quickly," she urged.

I hurried as fast as I could into the back room and grabbed a trash bag. I dumped the powder in and knotted the handles. I rinsed my hands, now tinted pink. She came up behind me. "Is it done?"

"Yes. Will you please tell me what that was about?"

She exhaled a rush of air as if she had foreseen a tidal wave rise up from the Chesapeake Bay to swallow us whole.

"The dark cloud your parents feared is coming." Emotion rose up like hot bile in my throat. "I saw it in the Belladonna."

"Are you clairvoyant, too?"

"I talk to plants and sometimes, in their own way, they talk back."

"What did the Belladonna say?"

"Danger will befall everyone in town and our coven will be to blame."

My heart raced. "You saw this in the Belladonna?"

"Do you remember what I told you about the *Chesapeake Histories*?"

Dread weighed heavy on me. "How could I forget?"

She stared into my eyes. "There will be two, and then only one."

I was certain my magic was growing stronger, but what was worse was that I didn't know how to control it. The short hand on the wall clock approached eight. "Do you mind if I leave? I have somewhere I need to be." I hoped I did anyway.

She gestured to the door. I dashed out of the shop. When I turned the corner, I broke into a mad sprint with a sea of wavy hair trailing behind me.

As I approached the Calverts' property, I slowed and searched the street, making sure no one was stalking me. I shoved through the rusty gate and hightailed it to the back of the gardens. In the darkness, I approached the brick chapel.

The blackened windows offered no sign of him. I stepped closer. My heart pulsed faster as I grabbed the handle. Sure, we'd said some regrettable things, but he had said he wanted to help me, and if that were true, it was the only chance I had to change what my parents had feared the most.

I pushed in, my eyes drawn to the single lit candle set atop the altar.

"Hello?" My voice echoed off the walls. "W?" I spun around. "Are you here? Because—I need you. I mean, I need your help."

Silence dominated the chapel as I bathed in humility. I waited, inching closer to the altar, searching, but I found nothing beneath the candle. I dropped my face in my hands. I had screwed it all up. With one last glance toward the empty choir loft, I backed away and closed the doors behind me.

The next evening, Aunt J and I arrived early for the coven meeting. I excused myself to use the bathroom. However, I paused when I caught sight of Emme hugging her stiff mother. Not wanting them to see me, I stepped behind a column, but before I was out of sight I witnessed Mrs. Blackstone pluck Emme's hands from her rigid frame. Her mouth formed a scowl.

"Stop being so needy. I have a lot on my mind with your father's legal problems."

Emme slumped and receded from her mother like a melting glacier. "I thought you said he was handling that."

A slight scoff escaped her mother's plump lips. "I'm handling it now and there's nothing I won't do to fix it."

I felt sorry, not only for Emme, but also for whoever was dealing with Mrs. Blackstone. I skipped the bathroom and hurried back to the hall. Aunt J waved to me from our seats in the back as the other members filed in.

She'd filled me in on what most of the witches in the coven could do. Like her, many of the women owned small businesses in town, utilizing their innate gifts to make money like Missy Edwards's Charm City where Renner and Ava worked, Molly Dyer's Chesapeake Midwifery, and Liza Bennett's Witch's Brew, a beer and rum distillery. Then there were those who used their talents to secure high posts in the city government and businesses—like Mrs. Blackstone.

Mrs. Blackstone—wearing a black suit dress and showing an unnecessary amount of cleavage—took a pill and stuffed her familiar iridescent bottle in her pocket. "My dearest sisters, please be seated so we may begin." She shuffled her note cards next to *the* book on the podium.

Emme strolled to the back rows and descended into the empty seat next to me. Her black dress accented her thin frame and the midnight shade seemed to reflect her mood. I shifted closer to Aunt J as shrill mental alarms blared wildly in my head.

Mrs. Blackstone cleared her throat. "The first item on my agenda is the city's Two Hundred and Fiftieth Anniversary of the Annapolis Tea Party, which is approaching quickly. The city wants to coordinate with our civic club to help make the event—" she paused, her front teeth pressing into the tip of her tongue, "a *memorable* one."

The way she said *memorable* sent a chill across my skin.

"Through my channels at the historic foundation, I've learned that a painting, which was located in Philadelphia, featuring the *Peggy Stewart* ship in flames, will be shipped to the foundation in time to unveil it at the re-enactment. As a bonus, all members of our club are invited to attend the Governor's Ball at Carroll House afterward, and as a token of appreciation, we will organize a fireworks display that evening over Spa Creek." She started laughing and set her gaze on Emme. "I'm wondering if we should launch the special fireworks before or after the ball? Perhaps after. There's nothing quite like ending a festive occasion with a great...big...bang." Her eyes appeared blank as if she were playing out a fantasy in her mind.

Those in the back rows—minus Emme—looked around, seeming unsure what to think of Mrs. Blackstone's party plans.

"Don't forget who I married. I know you will want to look your best for this event. If anyone needs a little touch up, my husband is more than a wizard when it comes to Botox and fillers." She grabbed her oversized breasts and heaved them upward to create even more unnecessary cleavage. I stole a quick glance at Emme, thinking she must be so embarrassed, but she was busy simpering to her own image on her phone.

"Please stay seated. We have a fabulous guest speaker with us tonight. A very successful earth witch is here to give us tips on herbs and their cosmetic uses. Please welcome, Ms. Eliza Duncan."

While everyone else clapped, Emme examined her eyes. "Ugh. Are those crow's feet? I know those are crow's feet." She dropped her phone in her lap. "And my dad refuses to give me Botox. He's an ass," she said as if she were trying to connect with me on some plastic level.

I had heard about girls our age using Botox to prevent wrinkles, but I couldn't fathom the idea at sixteen, so I tried to ignore her. Not so easy breezy. She tapped her fake nails against her blue bedazzled phone case and jingled her gold bangles profusely throughout the rest of the meeting. Up front, the other two Queen Js periodically glanced back to check on their alpha. Their intermittent snickering triggered a headache.

When the meeting finished, Aunt J turned to chat with Missy Edwards, and when I tried to stand, Emme tugged hard on my sweater, yanking me back into the seat.

I slapped her hand off me. "What the hell was that for?"

Her smile thinned. "Listen to me."

Her condescending tone set my teeth on edge. "No. You listen to me. What were you doing at Quiet Waters Woods? I saw your car racing out of there and I know you and your Queen Js etched those symbols into the trees. Was that to mark your meeting territory?"

"Tree graffiti? That's what you're worried about?"

I knitted my eyebrows together.

"The Queen Js meet in the woods because it's private and we can practice our skills out there, especially with the talent exhibition coming up."

"So trapping sister witches in a dirt pit is one of your skills?"

She shrugged. "That was just for fun. By the way, did you like the party favor Arora and I left for you?"

"Yeah. The Voodoo sculpture was a real laugh riot."

She blinked her eyes over and over and bit her lip like she was trying to stifle a laugh. "You still up for joining our clique?"

Her invitation lingered like the putrid stink of a corpse flower. However, I still needed to know what that damn book was a clue to. "How could I join a clique when their leader is a thief?"

"Me, a thief? Everyone knows I'm rich." She swallowed hard as if she wasn't so sure about that. "Besides, what would I need to steal?"

"I saw you take that book from the library archives."

Her grin puckered. She strained forward in her seat to make sure Aunt J wasn't watching. "Are you seriously upset about that?"

I waited.

Her shoulders dropped, and she stared at her phone. "You don't understand. It was one book, and my mother made me steal it. I didn't want to."

I twisted my lips to the side. "You didn't have a choice?"

Her face filled with angst. "You don't know my mother. She's super intimidating when she wants to be."

That I believed. However, something was off. I eyed Arora sitting sideways keeping a subtle watch on us. "Emme, why are you sitting here? What do you want from me?"

She offered a coy grin. "I want to invite you to join us for some fun. No strings." She nodded to the other Queen Js.

"What are you talking about?"

"I'm talking about hanging with the Queen Js. We haven't exactly been fair to you. Consider this a peace offering after the ice sculpture. Is that so awful?"

"Why should I trust you?"

"You told me you were tough. Prove it. Take a chance tonight."

I ignored the after-school-special peer pressure. "So, knowing I'm a Fitzgerald, you really want to hang out with me?"

"Fitzgerald, Smitzgerald. Even with that Irish wizard blood in your veins, you're talented."

It sounded like she wanted me to thank her for forgiving me my ancestry. "Go on."

"I saw it with my own eyes. In fact, I can't wait to see what you do at the talent exhibition."

Lies, I thought. "Seriously?" I played along, wondering if she'd give me a chance to see that book. Even with the page missing, it might still help me understand what the key was. "I don't even know what I'm doing for the exhibition, but now that you mention it…"

"Tonight, we're gathering in the woods at Quiet Waters to practice. If you want, you can take a look at what we're going to do. It's too far to walk, so why don't you meet me somewhere and we'll drive together."

"Meet you where?"

"I have to drop my mom at home first, and then I can pick you up." She tilted her head as if she were considering her plan. "I've got it. I'll make you a deal. Let's meet at the library. I'll bring the book with me and leave it in the drop box, and then we'll drive to Quiet Waters together. Would you like that, Hannah?"

My gaze narrowed. "Only if I get to put the book in the drop box. Just to make sure it does get returned."

"Where's the trust?"

"Oh, I trust you," I lied, "I just want to verify."

She grinned. "See you in like twenty minutes." She flipped her hair over one shoulder and strutted away.

The library was too far a walk from St. John's campus, but not so far from the Rocas' house. I glanced at my watch.

"Aunt J." I tapped her shoulder. She turned with a gentle smile. "Can you drop me off at Summer's place? We need to work on a history project that's due on Monday," I lied to avoid the inevitable lecture. It felt like a betrayal, however, and I wasn't sure if it was against Aunt J or myself.

"Okay, but Mrs. Meier just asked about the talent exhibition and what you're preparing to do for it. We need to figure that out and soon."

"I know. Emme just reminded me. I'll come up with an idea tonight. I promise."

"Good. Let's go."

I followed Aunt J to the van. After a short drive, she dropped me off in front of the Rocas' house. I waited for her to round the corner before I took off in the opposite direction.

Above, clouds grumbled as they followed me to the library where I stood outside in the dark. Beyond the trees and the creek, I listened to the buzz of passing cars. I checked my phone. No messages. Whatever.

The gurgling of the creek drew my attention away from my thoughts. I paced back and forth along the bank near an old crooked tree with claw-like branches that stretched over the water. I trailed my fingers across the bark and the realization of the hallowed ground I stood upon shivered through me. I flashed my phone light on the plaque impaled near the darkened roots. The nearly four-hundred-year-old tree and its sturdy branches had served as gallows for three Chesapeake witches, including Lady Arundell—Witch's Grave.

I exhaled a gasp, fully aware of the tragic tale. How could I forget? Magic brought tragedy and death to those plagued with it. Waves of grief lapped at my heart as I hurried back to the library.

The wind picked up into howling gusts. I calmed myself by thinking of W. He said fate had not dealt him a fair hand. It obviously had something to do with the scar, but what? I recalled Mateo's mention of Chase's brother leaving school because of a weird illness. I grimaced, recalling the emptiness in the chapel.

Crash.

I stole to a window. A small flashlight glowed from inside. Did Emme break in to prove she was a badass? Because the nightmaring trick resolved any lingering doubts I may have had. I inched closer to the main door. A half-twist of the knob confirmed it was unlocked.

Caw, caw.

From a nearby tree, my white raven spied me. A shiver trembled down my spine. "Not now." My eyes flitted back to the light inside the library. I shouldn't have let Emme tempt me, but she had lured me into her web and there was no turning back now.

I sneaked into the empty library and tiptoed along the walls, inching toward the light. My heart pounded in my ears, silencing the sounds of the outside world. I stopped for a second to calm myself, but it didn't help. I pressed on. With a deep breath, I jumped out from the shadows and into the archives room, hoping to scare the witch a million times over for playing such a stupid trick on me.

On the desk, a pencil rolled to a stop. My eyes flashed around the bookcases.

"Emme? Is this some kind of stupid initiation?"

A picture crashed to the floor and the glass shattered behind me. I jumped back into the hall and swung around, my fists in front of me.

A husky figure appeared from behind a corner, jarring my heart to a standstill. "A Fitzgerald witch like you should be hanging from that tree out there, not breaking into a library," he said in a creepy stalker voice.

"You don't know me." He was tall and broad, but kept his face obscured with a black mask. Unfortunately, it didn't obscure the smell of his cheap cologne. He blocked my exit and peered around at the desolate library like he was delighting in the stillness.

"Since you're not hanging from a tree, there is something I need from you."

I swiveled my head toward the cry in the distance—police sirens. I gasped out loud. "No, she didn't!"

"I was told you have a special piece of family jewelry." Emme had obviously told him it about it.

"I'm—I'm not alone," I stuttered. "I came with my boyfriend."

He looked around. "I don't see a boyfriend."

"He's right outside and he's big," I bluffed as police sirens growing closer warned me to get the hell out of there. My eyes darted back and forth.

The only movement he made was a subtle shift of his body to prevent my escape. I was not going to jail because Emme wished it. I mashed my lips together.

With a fake shift to my left and a real one to my right, I ducked under his arm and raced down the hall. He lumbered after me. I spun on my heel and slipped into the reading pit.

"Where do you think you're going?" He stood at the top of the pit, blocking my escape. He lurched and gained a firm lock on my forearm, jerking me closer to him. Did he not hear the sirens growing louder?

I fought against his grip. "My date is waiting," I sputtered, staying focused on wriggling free. I tugged my arm in a downward motion, but he held tight. My heart raced. Adrenaline flowed to my legs causing my knees to shake like vibrating rubber bands.

He shoved me down on the floor with force. "You're going to give me that damn ring or I'm gonna take it." He held me firmly with one arm.

I searched for a way out. The windows were locked and there was nothing to grab but books. Then I spotted a possibility. His grip tightened. With everything in me, I fought, keeping my eyes on the red fire alarm switch, wanting the shrill screech to distract him long enough for me to run.

A chill brushed across my skin as the white willowy form appeared in front of me.

Lady Arundell.

She pressed a ghostly finger to her pale lips and with her other ethereal hand, touched the switch. The fire alarm screamed to life and the oaf startled.

"Who did that?" he bellowed.

"You're an idiot." I kicked and strained against him, imagining a parade of firefighters lined up behind the police that were nearly here.

He twisted me around, causing the soft fabric of my sweater to tear at the seams. He fumbled, trying to pin me down face-first. I struggled to get to my feet, but he was too big and relentless. He picked me up and slammed me against the wall.

"Ow!" My legs went numb. I collapsed, hitting the top of my head hard on the edge of a table. He dragged me toward him, my hands scraping against the rough floor.

Hot blood trickled down my face, but the pain was dull, a background throbbing to the pounding of my heart and the burning in my lungs. *He's going to kill me!* Then the magic whispered.

But before I could cast the spell and channel it, he jammed a foot against my back and wrestled with my arms. His hand found its way to my hand—and my ring.

No!

I tried to focus, but the room spun out of control and started to fade.

Through the blare of the alarm, a heavy thud crashed behind us, shaking the floor. Was Lady Arundell's ghost strong enough to knock over that dinosaur of a card catalog?

The pressure of his foot lifted. I didn't look up. I crawled to a table and pulled myself up, but my unsteady knees buckled, and I crashed to the floor again. Then man groans and growls, and flesh pounding against the floor, filled my ears.

He grabbed me again. This time I spun around and punched him. His body seemed firm beneath my fist, considering how paunchy he had looked in the hallway. The lunatic held me in front of him with both arms as I wrestled to free myself.

"Let me go!"

"Look at me." The familiar voice eased my desperation.

With eyes adjusted to the dark, I focused. W's brow bunched with stress. He wore black clothes and his familiar sunglasses. He panted, trying to calm himself and me too.

He gently gripped my arms. "We have to go. Now!"

With the thug down, my anger melted into a latent reaction. I trembled and tears rolled down my cheeks as I broke into heaving sobs.

He fell silent, slipping his arms under me. He cradled me against his warm, broad chest and hurried to his midnight blue Jeep. He slid me into the passenger seat and closed the door. I sank into darkness.

A nudge and his warm voice brought me to the surface. "Hannah." His voice lingered softly over my name. "I'm taking you with me. Okay?"

Flashing blue and red police car lights and screeching fire truck sirens broke through my fog. I nodded and moaned as the accelerating G-force pressed me into the seat. Shapes and lights blurred through the window. The pain from my head pounded violently in contrast to the quiet in the car. I dabbed my hand over the source. The wetness brought me out of the peaceful fog I'd slipped into. I hesitantly examined my hand. Bright red blood clung to my palm and fingers and flashbacks rotated through my memory, hitting me like cold, hard punches.

"What happened to the thief?" I barely got the words out as my breathing accelerated.

"Hopefully, the police got him."

I doubted that. If he found a way in, he'd find a way out. "Lady Arundell pulled the fire alarm. She wanted to help me. She wants me to return a stolen book."

"Please, Hannah, I need you to be quiet right now." His expression seemed strained, as if he were in pain.

I noticed a tremble in the other hand that gripped the steering wheel. "Did he hurt you?"

"That's not the problem."

"What is, then?"

He stared straight ahead. "I'm in pain, but it's not from the fight. You're safe. I promise."

His voice was soothing, yet with the way he spoke, part of me wondered exactly what I was safe from. I stared out the side window, the events painfully replaying in my head.

The car came to a stop on the street behind Calvert Manor. W stood in front of me with the door open. He carried me through a hidden opening in the brick wall that led to the chapel. With my nose pressed lightly against his chest, I inhaled his amber scent as he carried me to the loft and set me on his bed. A soft, warm blanket draped around me.

"Hannah, you're okay. Do you understand?"

His hands, strong and soothing, wrapped around mine as he tried to reach me. I nodded. He approached a side table with a crystal pitcher of water. The water gurgled into the glass.

120

I shook my head and ran my shaky hand across my face again.

"I want you to drink this." He pleaded as he offered the drink.

"My hands are too jittery," I whispered. He set the water down next to me on the table.

He looked down at my swollen and bloodied hands and then his fists clenched, the veins straining along the surface. "I know he wore a mask, but do you have any idea who he was?"

"No. Did you see Emme?" Was she outside laughing at me for believing they invited me to a witches' gathering in the woods?

"I didn't *see* Emme anywhere near the library."

I creased my eyes at the corners. "How long were you there?"

He didn't look at me. "Long enough." He inhaled a deep breath, the muscles in his face finally relaxing.

"I'm sorry for telling you to leave me alone."

He shushed me. "Stop. We both said how we felt at that moment, but feelings can change. I know mine have."

My eyes drifted to his face, hardly seeing the scar as I took in his other features—the square of his jaw and the perfect line of his nose. His rosy lips looked more inviting than last time. But he was more than that. Pained or not, he was good, down to his core, and his soul radiated a beauty that was easy to see once I looked deep enough. In fact, it was difficult to look away, so I didn't.

"How did you find me?"

A hint of a smile appeared. "I told you before. Like you, I'm good at finding trouble. I'm also good at slipping into places I shouldn't be."

A million questions raced through my mind. "Who are you? How did you end up in Annapolis or have you always been here?"

He held my hand. The touch of his skin sent tiny sparks flickering all over me. He touched a finger to the ring. "Is this a family heirloom?"

I remembered him noticing it at the car accident. I pressed my lips together, feeling nervous as we treaded near a dangerous boundary. "It's a family crest. I'm a Fitzgerald."

"You're more than a Fitzgerald," he said in a serious tone I couldn't understand.

"What are you talking about?" I squeezed my eyes shut, too exhausted to deal with his riddles. "Never mind. My head's in a fog."

He sat beside me, his closeness easing my nerves. "I doubt a fog could dull your curiosity."

I tried again to see beyond the sunglasses, but only caught my own reflection.

"I'll tell you this much. You're easy to read."

I sighed. "Tell me something I don't know."

He pressed his lips thin, looking deep in thought. "I will. I'm concerned. Whatever that man was after, he's going to try again." His serious expression caused my throat to dry up like cotton. "The determination in his eyes left me with no doubt."

I recalled the violent feel of the thug's rugged hands against my skin. My body trembled. I tugged the blanket up to my chest, squeezing it in my fists.

The protective part of him surfaced and he seemed desperate in his attempts to calm me. "Hannah, I won't let him near you. With everything I am, I promise you that."

Pain and anger penetrated his voice. I searched his face, wondering what he was feeling, but it was difficult without seeing his eyes. His jaw shifted back and forth and his hands quivered. His angry expression slipped into a troubled one. He pressed a hand to his forehead and passed me the glass.

"Are you okay?"

He nodded, but I didn't believe him. He leaned his head away, as if he were uncomfortable being near me, which couldn't be true since he'd gone to so much trouble to help me.

"Drink," he commanded, his voice soft and rough at the same time, like velvet.

I sipped slowly, unable to refuse his request. The water cooled my burning throat. I tried to control the memories that stabbed at my calm, tried to think about something else. I gulped the water in four swallows while my attention turned to the beautiful mahogany bed we sat upon.

I touched my hand to the side of his face and forced him to look at me. Sparks ignited every cell in my body. Desire took hold like a fiery addiction, consuming me in its glow. My gaze shifted to his mouth. My stomach tightened.

He waited, seeming patient.

"What's your name?" My lower lip trembled.

He sat silent for a long second before leaning closer. His breath tickled my neck, sending shivers through me.

I angled my head and let my cheek brush against his ever so slightly. Pleasure consumed me.

"William," he whispered beneath my earlobe.

"William," I repeated. The electricity between us built to an unbearable peak.

He glanced down at the closeness of our bodies and trailed his hand down my jaw to my neck. He let his fingers rest on my collarbone, and for a moment seemed lost in my breathing. Then he startled to his feet.

"You need to go home."

I jumped up and clutched my hands around his arm. My gaze locked on the tendons straining in his neck. Was he not feeling the same heart-sputtering electricity that I was? "I want to stay here." I searched his expression for a sign.

He uttered a scoff. "You must have hit your head harder than I realized."

"Don't do that. Don't push me away. I know what I'm saying. I want to stay here—with you."

He stared at the stained glass window barely breathing. "That's not possible."

I knew what I felt and had zero intention of taking no for an answer. I stepped into his line of vision. "Why not?"

He turned the force of his concealed gaze on me. His face distorted in pain.

I furrowed my brow. "What's wrong? I—I don't understand."

He disconnected. "How could you understand? You're this beautiful creature with so much potential, and I'm—I'm cursed." He seethed and grabbed my hand. There was frustration in his grip. "Look at me."

I mashed my lips together. "Curses are meant to be broken. Besides, the last person I'm worried about hurting me is you."

He gnashed his teeth. "Maybe you should be worried."

He spun away and groaned into his hands. I wanted to reach for him, tell him I trusted him, but instinct told me to wait. He lifted his head and raked a hand through his dark brown hair.

"Please, forgive me," he said, sounding more composed. "I don't mean to be so harsh, but you have to understand. You can never stay here with me. It would be too difficult if…"

I didn't want to understand. I wanted to be with him, secrets be damned. "If what?"

"Never mind."

"I won't never mind. You're hiding something."

"I'm—not like other people."

Everything about him exuded danger, but he would never hurt me.

"That's it?" My voice rose steadily in pitch. "You think I'm worried about you not being an ordinary? I already know you're not and that excuse isn't good enough."

He swallowed hard. "I've told you all I can for now. Let it be enough. I'll take you home in a few minutes." He started for the stairs.

A tidal wave of disappointment drenched my mood as I stared at the floor, feeling lightheaded. Suddenly, through the daze, I realized that him dropping me off was a bad idea. "Um…you can't. Not in the Jeep anyway."

He turned around with surprise in his expression.

My gaze drifted to the floor. "My aunt thinks I'm at my friend, Summer's house—because she dropped me off there. If she sees your car, she'll know I lied."

He sighed. "You did lie."

"I'm sorry I did, but her seeing us together will make my life more difficult than it already is, in ways you can't understand. I mean, you don't have a guardian overseeing your every move."

He winced. "I know you don't know much about me, but you shouldn't make assumptions."

"What are you saying?"

He ignored my question. "I'll walk you home so she doesn't see me." He paused. "And you won't have to worry about explaining the cuts and bruises." His lips thinned as he surveyed the damage from a distance.

"How's that?"

He disappeared down the stairs and reappeared a moment later with a warm wet cloth and a black bag filled with supplies. He inhaled a deep breath before he reached for me as if he were

124

shoring himself up for something challenging. Then his warm hands were on mine. "I've always been good at healing. In fact, I planned to go to medical school. Before…"

"Before what?"

He ignored the question as he inspected the cuts on my palms and forehead and wiped dried blood away with the cloth. He opened a small tube of ointment and dabbed the garnet-colored balm on the tender abrasions and scrapes.

I inhaled the fruity scent. "Smells like mulberry."

He cupped my face with his hands, gently tilting my head to the side to determine the severity of the cut above my forehead. "That animal doesn't deserve to live."

"He doesn't deserve to die. He's just a thug."

"He's a violent idiot."

I clasped his hand, causing him to hesitate. "Promise me you won't do anything."

He stiffened his jaw. "I won't if he doesn't."

Sparks flickered between our hands and my stomach flipped round and round as I studied his beautiful features.

Breathe, Hannah.

"I already feel better."

"They should be healed by the time we get you home."

I sniffled, coming back together. "Tell me why you were looking for me."

A soft smiled appeared. "Tell me why you went to the library."

"If it weren't so boring and predictable, I'd argue that I asked you first."

"Ha! You boring and predictable? Hardly." He started returning the supplies to the bag. His expression was so warm, it left me wondering if my heart was melting from the heat. "You're the most interesting and unpredictable girl I've ever known."

I stared at the gauze on my hand, impressed with his medical skills. "When I first arrived, all I dreamed about was being ordinary, or at least pretending to be."

I could feel his eyes burning into me. "That seems foolish when you're so the opposite of ordinary."

I blushed under his summation. "Emme told me to meet her there. She said she would return a stolen book if I did…"

"What?"

"I agreed mostly to get a better look at the book, but then she said she wanted to take me to a witches' gathering. I feel like an idiot because part of me believed her."

His lips paled. "So you wanted to believe there's good in someone like her. There's nothing wrong with that, but I doubt your instincts approved."

He was right about that. "Tell me, why were you there?"

He grinned. "I wanted to see you. I knew there was a coven meeting so I waited for it to end. I followed you in my Jeep out of concern. And then, at the library, I waited, not wanting to interfere. When I heard the ruckus, I raced in." He pressed his hand to his forehead."

"What?"

"The library was torn up. You must've put up quite a fight. I suspect if you had a few more minutes, you'd have had him running out the door."

I shook my head in disbelief. "Why do you have so much faith in me?"

"I've seen what you can do."

"Yes, you have. Hey, I have a question."

"Of course you do."

"This one's easy. What's your favorite food?"

He arched an eyebrow above the rim of his sunglasses. "Trying to figure me out?"

"Of course, I am."

"Chinese and picnic food."

"Huh," I said, surprised it wasn't something more exotic. "I like those, too. Tell me something else about you."

For a moment, he considered the request. "I used to go to London every summer. I'd attend concerts with my dad. It's where I fell in love with classic British rock like The Kinks and The Police. Do you know any of their songs?"

I was pleased he let me in on that much. "I wasn't born under a rock. Yeah, I like some of their music." I twirled a strand of hair tight around my finger as nervous butterflies took hold of my stomach. "So, um, do you think maybe you and I could get Chinese food one night?" *Like normal people*, I thought.

He subtly turned his scarred cheek away from me. "No."

My cheeks burned with rejection. "What? Why not?"

He sighed. "It's not because of you. It's just better if I don't go out." He paused. "But maybe one day."

His optimistic tone soothed the sting of rejection. "I'd like that."

"Since I've met you, I feel a change in me I never expected." He paused. "I only want an end to the pain she'll cause and that ending can only come through you."

He was frustratingly cryptic. I pressed my hand to his face, cupping it around the edge of his jaw. "I agree she'll probably keep causing trouble. I don't mean to disappoint you, but I think you're wrong about me being able to stop her." How could I stop her when I couldn't even stop my own magic from seeping out?

"If you let me, I can prove I'm not wrong."

I touched my hand to my chest, feeling his heartbeat as his words slipped inside my consciousness. "William, what am I going to do with you?"

He clasped my hand, sending a burst of shivers through me. "Keep me at arm's length while I help you, I hope." He grinned a frustratingly sexy grin.

"I think we both know after tonight that won't be possible."

ady Arundell's ghost had given me a brilliant idea for the talent exhibition, so the next evening I asked Aunt J for her help. For the next several hours, she watched me practice and gave pointers on how to present my talent.

By eleven o'clock, exhaustion got the better of us. She kissed my cheek and said goodnight. I crept up to the attic and curled into the red recliner, clinging to my dad's book as if part of him were still alive within the pages that contained his strange and mystical notes. He had turned his back on his magic in the hope that alchemy would change a dark outcome my mom foresaw, but his perceived failure to do so along with his fear drove him to his end. I winced with remorse, and then caught a glimpse of my tired reflection in my phone.

To what lengths would I go to alter fate? I thought as sleep pulled me under.

A brilliant light flashed. As the light dimmed, the familiar figure of the girl in fog appeared. She flung a finger at me and blew her glistening powder into the air, but this time the fog behind her cleared ever so slightly. In the dark distance, flashes of sparkling lights against a backdrop of midnight blue broke through the mist and the screams pierced my ears.

I jolted awake. Damp with sweat, I checked the time and raced to my bedroom to change.

According to Mrs. Blackstone's instructions, we were to gather at McDowell Hall at five o'clock for the talent exhibition. The secret recruiter would witness our skills as part of the decision process, and in a few weeks would choose the best witch or wizard to represent our coven for a summer at the international level. After everything I'd been through, the thought of the participating in a vapid talent display made me gag.

Aunt J and I arrived on time. Inside, chairs were assembled in a circle around a cluster of black-topped worktables brought in for the event. The blinds were drawn tight. A billowy, white silk banner hung above the double doors and blue blazing candles in the chandeliers added to the witchy ambiance of the event extraordinaire.

Brother and sister witches snatched up empty seats, including Mrs. Meier, Mr. Wardwell, the Queen Js and their proud parents, and three-dozen others. Liza, the beer and rum distillery owner, chatted up Aunt J—as if anyone could feel like socializing.

The buzz of hushed chatter reminded me of the crunching of dried flowers beneath my aunt's pestle until Mrs. Blackstone silenced us from the podium. She announced the order in which we would perform. The participants would follow Emme's lead. Naturally.

Still in shock and awe over her attempt to frame me for the library break-in, I cringed at the sight of the carefree head Queen J throwing up a beauty pageant wave. Where was her guilt? Her remorse?

Aunt J tapped my shoulder. "I still believe you need to embrace who you are, but for today I'm giving you a pass. Do your best, but not your best." We agreed it would be enough to please Mrs. Blackstone without drawing unnecessary attention. I pressed my hands to the sides of my head—irritated for having to perform. Emme may enjoy putting on a show, but it felt wrong to me because she didn't respect the magic for what it is—deadly power; the same power that had exacted its toll from my parents and was out of control inside me.

The older crowd took their seats while we waited, lining up along the sidewall. The girls were dressed in knee-length death-black dresses and the boys in black pants per the instructions. Mrs. Blackstone signaled with a nod for Emme to start.

"I will be creating Witch's Fireworks," she announced with confidence thrumming in her voice. Emme pointed to Arora who took her place beside her at the center worktable. "Hand me the first vial of white water."

Arora played with her white and black hairdo before following the instruction. Emme poured the milky water into a graduated cylinder.

"Charcoal liquid, please." Arora handed her the vial of inky black water. Emme curled her fingers around it.

"Sulfur."

Like a well-practiced witch, Emme pinched the glass stirring-rod between her fingers and stirred the gray mixture any chemistry student would recognize—liquid gunpowder. She uncorked a small flask of clear, liquid sulfuric acid and poured that into the mix.

The color and consistency of the individual ingredients reminded me of the powders and liquids my dad kept in the jars sitting in the attic.

"And a little bit of zinc for flair." She sprinkled the metallic powder onto her experiment; the substance glimmered on her fingertips like sparkly fairy dust. Then she poured the solution into a round beaker, swirled it, stuffed a cork in the neck, and faced the crowd, her eyes wide with excitement. But it was her smug grin that convinced us all she nailed the contest. "Now, watch."

Emme set the beaker above a flame and removed the cork. The swirling fluid ignited into a lapis blue spray of mini-fireworks. She corked the top of the beaker again and repeated. Each time, the solution exploded into a dazzling spray of blue sparks bouncing off the insides of the glass container.

Mrs. Blackstone smacked her hands together, leading everyone in a generous applause.

Mr. Wardwell stood up. "Witch's Fireworks requires precision in technique and measurement. How do you do that so well?"

"It's a natural talent." Her beautiful black velvet dress followed her movement as she folded over in a deep bow.

Mrs. Blackstone pointed to Arora. "You're next, dear."

Emme's assistant shifted to another worktable and set up her gimmick. "I will be creating—Black Widows." Arora acted like she was summoning a freaking miracle.

She set a stone chalice next to a bell jar that contained a black widow spider. In a glass bowl, she prepared a dilution with silver flakes. She poured it into the chalice. Next, she filled the cup with blue Rochelle salt crystals, a rare mineral that I recognized from my dad's notes and drawings.

She added a few pinches to the dilution. "Now, I will set the chalice above a flame." After a few minutes, she retrieved the cup from the heat and let the crowd watch her drop a dot of potion onto the spider. With a dramatic flash of her hands, she cast her spell. "*Araignée, araignée, noir et agile. Multipliez, puis vous mourrez.*"

Something, something, black and spry, multiply and then you die, was all I translated. My gaze flitted to the creature. One spider phased into two and multiplied again until there were dozens of replicas crawling about the table. However, as the last spider formed, the original withered and curled into a death ball.

"There's always a price to pay," she announced, although it wasn't costing her a bit of her life. With another swish of her hands, the replicas swirled into black dust. "Black Widows, ladies and gentlemen. Black Widows." The crowd applauded and she took her bow.

George Wardwell and Navan were next. She faced the spectators. "We will each choose one person from the audience and demonstrate our clairvoyant gifts from an object they present

to us. This will be a race to see which of us can see the past first."
She smiled curtly at her competitor and the two began.

She approached an unfamiliar woman in the crowd, probably
hoping it was the recruiter. The woman handed her a wristwatch.
Navan clasped it between her hands and closed her eyes. George
approached a man standing next to his dad who smiled with
delight. The man gave George a gold wedding band to read. He
wrapped a pudgy fist around the object and whispered to it.

Navan raised a hand in the air at the same time George did.
Everyone quieted. Navan stared at the woman. "Your watch tells
me you are married with a daughter and you have a black cat
named Felix. I see a green Subaru in your past, and you were
born in a northern state. I see water and whales, perhaps
Massachusetts?"

The woman nodded. "Yes. Nantucket to be precise." Everyone
clapped. Even I was surprised by the improvement in her
clairvoyance.

George cleared his throat and shook his fist in front of the
man's face. "Your ring tells me you are named Hartley, and you
work in the music industry."

"Oh. I'm sorry, George. That's wrong. My name is James, and
I teach history at the Naval Academy."

George's face crumpled in defeat. He handed the ring back to
the man while Navan curtsied to the entertained crowd.

The Queen Js completed their performances to perfection, and
then it was my turn. Aunt J handed me the large writing pad. Her
eyes filled with pride while my heart sank. The competition
wasn't what I wanted. Standing in the center of the room, staring
at the paper in my clammy hands, I wasn't certain I could pull off
the Lady Arundell trick.

I stared at all the waiting faces. Arora and Navan snickered
while Emme expelled a dramatic yawn, probably hoping to
influence the mysterious judge, but my attention locked on Mrs.
Blackstone. The vein in her head throbbed as if it were about to
burst if I didn't act and quick.

As my anxiety mounted, the whispering magic broke into an
ache-inducing screech inside my head. I grabbed the edge of a
black worktable and breathed through it trying my best to calm
down.

"Hannah Fitzgerald, you may begin. Hannah?" Mrs. Blackstone's voice cracked through my daze, and then her bony fingers snapped together.

My gaze traced over the paper in my hands and the thin satiny black fabric of my dress. I hated wearing black because the color whisked me back to their funerals. I hated showing off, and I really hated not having control of my destiny, but if I could take charge of it at this moment, what would happen?

I cleared my throat, thinking about Aunt J. "My dad once told me perception is reality. And everyone's perception in this room right now is that Emme Blackstone is the far superior witch among those of us presenting our talents." The paper trembled in my hot hands as if it was possessed by an angry poltergeist. "What I'm saying is, what is the point of presenting my talent to you when you have already judged who the winner should be?"

Mrs. Blackstone, looking on edge after George's total fail, stormed toward me, her faux violet eyes wide with rage.

With an unexpected flash, the paper exploded in flames in my hands just before she was about to grab it. It fell to the ground, trailing fiery embers in its wake. I stood there wide-eyed and breathless. No summoning spell and no control. I definitely had a problem of the genetic kind.

I doubted the recruiter would view my unrestrained display as worthy of an internship, but alarm filled Emme. She glared at me with dismay and pure hatred as if she didn't expected me to be a threat to her most prized possession.

Navan approached and leaned in toward my ear. "That little fiery outburst won't get you the internship."

"Oh, has your clairvoyance improved that much?"

Her cold fingers trailed the length of my arm. "I might surprise you one day," she hissed.

Opaque smoke and delicate ash scattered through the hall. My eyes flashed to my aunt, whose face had turned paper white. Mrs. Blackstone grasped hold of my arm and nearly lifted me off my feet. A hushed murmur rose from the crowd as she dragged me out the door and into the hall.

"Who do you think you are?"

My gaze narrowed. "I'm proud to say I'm a Fitzgerald." It was a step I was ready to take toward accepting my true self.

Aunt J raced up behind us and peeled Mrs. Blackstone's hand off me. "This is nothing but a show you set up to impress a recruiter who will report back to the International Witchcraft Club in favor of Emme. All Hannah did was ask the question we should all be asking." She turned her apologetic eyes on me. "I've got this. Now, get out of here."

I glanced at both of their heated expressions. "Bye, Aunt J."

"I *myrtle* you."

"I love you, too."

She nodded and I was off. I unbuttoned the black pearl buttons around the tight neck of my dress and tousled my blonde waves that had been brushed too neatly as I rushed to the boy who had offered to help me.

Four blocks later, I was standing in front of Calvert Manor, ever the dangerous magnet drawing me in. My heart raced and my head buzzed with thoughts of him. William was mysterious and different, and he was hiding something as mysterious and different as himself, which I had every intention of figuring out.

I skipped up the steps, pushing past the gate. I inspected the main house and noticed it seemed to be less saggy and broken down, as if the Calverts had begun renovations. Above the roofline, the half-disk of sun clinging to the horizon highlighted the September sky with a warm, pink glow that matched my changing mood.

I inhaled a deep breath, but it didn't settle the nervous rumbles inside. What was wrong with me? He was frustratingly what was wrong with me. What else could it be? My curiosity demanded to know everything about him, including the story he was hiding behind those damn dark sunglasses.

I broke into a run and hurried to the bottom of the vast garden where the chapel rose from the earth. I stood before the intimidating wood doors, which seemed ten times bigger than before.

With a shaky hand, I entered the abandoned sanctuary. The glacial gloom from his absence swept over me. I rubbed the chill from my prickled arms. Where could he be? I strode to the altar where an envelope waited.

You are like a Phoenix rising from the ashes of death, strong, but inexperienced. Summon the right amount of magic to bring

*new life to the Calvert gardens. Too much will scorch, too little—
you will not succeed.*

Beneath the note rested a packet of seeds in all shapes and
sizes. I inhaled a deep breath and snatched the seed packet. On
the one hand, I was still peeved about the vine trick, but on the
plus side, I hadn't gone crazy yet from the magic.

Outside, I brushed my hand along a rough hedge filled with
withered brown leaves. I needed to find balance in order to
control of the burgeoning power inside me, and with the
prophecy looming I had nothing and everything to lose. Emotions
were the perfect trigger so I closed my eyes and summoned a
memory.

It was the second to last argument I had with my mom. She
was out of her mind and giving up. I grabbed her by her
shoulders and shook her. Her wild blonde hair fell in her face,
sweeping away her tears. I had to do something, anything to keep
her going, so I screamed, mostly from the pain of feeling my own
heart break. I focused on that pain. Sadness and anger sprung up
along with the buzzing whisper of magic. I clenched my fists
tight.

"By the power of fire, I do summon and churn, and call thee
forth to blaze and burn." The whisper burst into a hot sphere of
energy. The heat rose like mercury on a hot day. The fire swelled
and surged with force to every muscle until I channeled it to my
hand in a slow, restrained way.

I kneeled down and sprinkled the packet's contents onto a
small pile of leaves. Still emotional from the memory, I aimed
my fingers at the straw-colored seeds and within a second, a
surge of long flames burst from my fingertips, scorching the
leaves and some of the seeds. I balled up my hands to stop it.
"Try again, Hannah."

I waited a moment and let my emotions cool before trying
again. I summoned the magic and aimed my fingers. I thought of
thin threads of fire, and that was exactly what sputtered out, in
pitiful little intermittent flashes. I urged the magic forward,
imagined the fire streaming out in a steady flow, and shook my
hands, but it fizzled.

I threw my head back, frustrated as the energy burned inside.
Think and feel. Needing to control it like never before, I let my

heart feel what it was feeling while I hyper-focused and thought of absolutely nothing but the task at hand. Then I tapped into the power and channeled it again. This time thin, fiery threads of magic blazed a brilliant, steady orange. I floated my hands over the seeds. A willowy trail of black smoke funneled toward the sky.

I exhaled a breath of relief. When I was done charring them, I drew the fire back inside. I stretched my tired muscles and yawned while the flames worked their transformation. A crisp autumn breeze swirled the smoke above me and cooled everything until it was touchable. With both hands, I scooped the warm seeds and leaf ash into my tender palms.

From what I had learned in my dad's notes, there was power in ash—spiritual, alchemical, and fertilizing power. I traipsed up and down the terraces unleashing the white powder and seeds. In my mind, I imagined the most beautiful plants and flowers in each plot. When I reached the top of the terraces, I spun back around.

Under the house spotlights, the gardens bloomed in all the colors of all the seasons. The sweet fragrance of spring perfumed the breeze that brushed over my face and arms, and for the first time since my parents passed, sad memories of their funerals melted away, replaced with the beauty of swaying flowers.

Behind me, a shadow rose up. I spun on my heels excited to show William the results. "It worked!" I glanced around, but he disappeared. "William?"

The murky purple sky faded to black as nighttime blanketed the town, meshing darkness with shadows. "Hello?" My voice echoed back to me without a response.

I dashed down to the chapel and swung open the doors. "William?" Maybe I was wrong. Maybe I had hallucinated the shadow because the sanctuary was definitely empty and he was nowhere to be found. Did that mean I was going crazy? I didn't feel crazy, but I needed to get home. I left the chapel and wandered through the stretch of woods at the back of their property, searching for the hidden entrance in the brick wall. Dead tree limbs and brittle brush slowed my pace. I ducked and leaped, getting smacked in the face with thin switches. Couldn't anything be easy? In the near distance, streetlights illuminated the top of the wall. I'd have to climb it. I threw my shoes over and crawled up, not giving a crap about ruining the ugly black dress.

A second later, the sound of breathing hit my ears. My heart thrilled until I smelled cheap cologne. In a panic, I scrambled to throw a leg over, but a strong hand grabbed my ankle and dragged me down. I dropped to the ground with a sickening thud. I clambered to a stand and whipped around.

My eyes settled on the paunchy masked thief. He reached for me with his gloved hands. With my energy totally drained, there were only two options and I wasn't running, which left me with option number two. I balled my right hand into a fist and threw a hard punch into his stomach.

His beady eyes widened with surprise for a second, and then he lunged.

I stumbled sideways, tripping over an ill-placed branch. Hyperventilating commenced until I drifted into a deep cloud of blackness. The last thing I saw was the stranger drawing closer.

The next morning I shot up in my bed, my head pounding like a jackhammer. My breathing came in panicked gasps as I checked for my ring. I sighed with relief at the sight of it glimmering on my hand.

"Good morning, sleepyhead," Summer said in her sweet, clear voice.

Sunlight streamed through a window. I blinked. "Huh?"

She swept her long, white hair behind one shoulder.

"What are you doing here?" The memory of running through the woods around the Calvert property flashed back to me. My pulse pounded. I grabbed her by the T-shirt.

"What's your deal?" She brushed my hands off her as if I was an annoying ladybug.

I scanned my arms for bruises and scratches, but there was nothing. Did I hallucinate the whole thing? How did I get home?

"Seriously? What are you doing?"

I blinked over and over, and then examined what I was wearing—my lavender-colored pajama top and bottoms. The horrid black dress sat in a heap on the floor along with the ballerina flats I had thrown over the brick wall. The clock on my night table flashed seven.

She blew a pink shimmery bubble with her gum and sucked it in with a snap. "Is today the day you lose your mind? I hope not because we have a history quiz." She chomped and chomped.

"Yeah, I hope not, too." I checked to make sure the pink rose bud wallpaper still lined the walls and my family picture was in its place. "I'm sorry. I just…I don't remember going to bed last night."

"That doesn't sound too crazy. Maybe you were really tired."

"You think I'm going crazy?" She had no idea how serious I was.

She shrugged. "No more than usual."

I groaned. "Thanks. What are you doing here?"

She smiled and patted my leg. "Your aunt let me in."

"Aunt J!" She'd planned to be out late last night after the exhibition. I doubted she had any clue about how I got home. I wasn't even sure, but I had to assume it was William. Who else was kind enough and strong enough? And then the obvious and most embarrassing question surfaced. Did he dress me in my pajamas? My cheeks flushed hot. I crossed my arms over my chest feeling way self-conscious.

"Yes. Your Aunt J. Very good."

"Shut up."

"I have news. Hannah? You sure you're okay? You look flushed."

"Huh?"

"News."

"About Calvert Manor?"

She drew back. "What are you talking about?"

The elusive and clever William was on my brain. "Nothing. Wait. You got up early to bring me news? You text." Her pursed lips betrayed her. Had to be big news.

"Did I tell you my mom is friends with Arora's mom?"

Who wouldn't want a Voodoo priestess for a BFF? "No, but go on."

"She told her mom who told my mom that Mrs. Blackstone is sending Emme away."

Emme had performed like a champion racehorse yesterday at the exhibition. Had she already been declared the winner? "Like forever?"

She busted out a laugh. "We wish. No, but for a week to some beauty boot camp."

"She already looks perfect, though."

"Right? I thought that was weird, too. I know the Blackstones are really into looking wrinkle-free and young. And her mom's boobs, jeez!" She cracked her gum.

"You're deviating. Where is she sending her?"

"Baltimore House. I think it's in Riverdale Park."

My curiosity tingled like the air before a lightning strike. "Isn't that a mansion used for weddings and stuff?"

"I don't know much about it, except one of my cousin's friends had a quinceañera there. She said the place has a garden, but it also has a graveyard. What kind of beauty boot camp is that?"

"Maybe she'll have to run laps around the headstones."

She snickered. "So that's why I'm here. Something's up with the head Queen J, and it smells rotten, so I thought it might be fun to figure it out. Now, snap out of it and get yourself dressed. I'm driving us to school."

10.

Summer's T-shirt said, 'Incans make sacrifices to do it.' At the end of the day, she slammed her locker and pursed her lips, looking like she was going to burst. "I have another fun idea."

I shot her a quizzical look. "Guys are going to get the wrong idea about you with those shirts. Or at least the wrong idea about Incans and baristas."

Her laugh exuded confidence. "I don't care what any of those weeny posers think."

"Seriously. Everyone should know you're more than a pretty face and a dirty T-shirt."

She considered it for a moment, then grinned. "How about one that says, 'Incans have big—brains'?"

A laugh snorted out of me. "It would be an improvement."

Her eyes widened with disbelief. "No, it wouldn't. We're passionate warriors who happen to be smart, too."

"Passionate and smart?" A thought of William flashed through my mind and I bit my lip.

She stopped short and held tight to my shoulders, staring me down. "All right, Missy. Who is he?"

This time I brushed her hands off me. I fanned my hot face. "What are you talking about?"

"The guy you're thinking of. It's written all over your fire-red cheeks. This is a good sign."

The blood continued to rush to the surface.

"Fine. Don't tell, but you can't keep secrets from me. I'm designating myself as your bestie so you have to share. Eventually."

"How did this conversation start?"

She stared blankly into the space above us and snapped her fingers. "Oh yeah. What I was trying to tell you is that there's a fortuneteller downtown. My mom went with a group of friends for a reading on their last ladies' night out and said the woman was spot on. Calls herself the Decrepit." She held a finger in the air. "No, that's not right. It's the Discerner. Thought we could pay her a visit. Maybe she can see what Emme's up to."

Unease gnawed at my bones. "Why do you care what Emme's up to?"

"I can tell she's got a problem with you, but if she thinks she's gonna mess with my bestie without me doing something about it, she's dead wrong. Now let's go."

I didn't want her getting involved, but she was too stubborn to stop and a fortuneteller sounded harmless. We raced to the parking lot and tossed our backpacks in the back of her white VW hatchback. A few minutes later, she was attempting to parallel park on a side street, but two SUVs sandwiching the spot forced her to leave the front end of the car jutting out. We both laughed at what had to be the worst parking job ever.

"Where is this Discerner?"

She pointed to a dark alley. "In there. See the sign?" Set inside the alley, a small wood sign with a carved crescent moon stuck out from the wall.

"She's not big on street presence, huh?"

"Who cares? You can ask about Emme, and while you're at it, your secret boyfriend, too."

Was she reading my face again? "Who said anything about a boyfriend?"

"We're not in second grade, Hannah. Boys don't have cooties. Well, except for the boy who rubs Elmer's glue on his ears and peels it off when it dries. There's also the manga boy in our history class, but other boys do not have cooties."

"I'm not worried about cooties." I was worried about what made William different. How he exuded equal amounts of danger and kindness. "Okay. There is someone."

She crossed her arms against her chest. "Who is he?"

"He doesn't go to our school."

"What's his name? Does he know you like him? Tell me he's swoon-worthy."

He was more than swoon-worthy. "Name's William. He's very mysterious and full of secrets."

"A man of mystery. Sounds perfect for you."

Could everyone read me as easily as my aunt? "Except I kind of have to know what he's hiding before I fall completely." Who was I kidding? My heart had already plummeted into the abyss.

She pointed a finger at me. "For a smart girl, you're an idiot, but while we're here, you should ask the fortuneteller about his big, hot, luscious—secret." She laughed as she dragged me behind her, racing up a narrow staircase like a kid dragging her doll into an American Girl store. The steps ended in front of an amber-beaded curtain where she stopped dead, as if the curtain were a magical boundary.

I ran my fingers across the strands of beads. "That's not hokey," I whispered, hoping she heard the sarcasm.

"Shh. You'll offend her."

I forgot my fierce Incan warrior bestie was superstitious. The clear golden and orange beads clacked together as we pushed them aside. The scent of mint and candle smoke swirled around us on a mystical current, and the sparkly orange walls reminded me of something from my childhood—I think my dad called the pigment antimony red. Hanging on the walls was a poster of the all-seeing eye and the Star of David within a double circle.

In the center, the Discerner had placed two black chairs and a table with a deck of oversized cards, a silver teapot with Hebrew symbols etched into the hammered surface, and two blue and white stoneware cups. A gray tabby wrapped its warm, furry body around my ankle and offered a purr as I stroked her.

"I see you've met Shepherd," the fortuneteller announced in a familiar voice as she entered the room through another beaded curtain opposite us. Her small, curvy frame was cloaked in a hooded black robe and her face was hidden by the billowy fabric.

"She's sweet," I said, shifting to see the face behind the hood.

"I'm afraid I'm closing to prepare a feast for Shemini Atzeret, so I only have time for one reading." She sat down without looking at our mystified expressions. The tabby raced toward her, circling her feet under the table.

Summer offered the spot to me with a shrug. "You're the one with all the secrets to uncover. Go." She nudged me forward.

I hated secrets, but I plopped in the rickety chair anyway. She glanced at Summer. "Privacy, please," she requested.

I looked back at my bestie and nodded. "I'll meet you outside after." As soon as Summer disappeared down the creaky stairs, the Discerner pointed to the strange-looking card deck marked with colorful images and Hebrew letters. "Shuffle."

She kept her face hidden beneath her hood. A wave of paranoia swirled around me. "Can you tell me who you are first?"

She sat back and lifted the hood with her softly aged hands, revealing her face and wavy auburn hair. "I'm glad to see you, Hannah."

My lips parted with surprise. "Mrs. Meier, I didn't realize you were a clairvoyant. Aunt J never said anything."

She offered a mischievous grin that tugged at her soft, round cheeks. "It's our secret. We don't want Mallory Blackstone to use my gift to her benefit." She exhaled a loud breath and placed her hands flat on the table.

Is everyone hiding a secret? I wondered. "I won't say anything. I promise."

"Would you like tea? It's jasmine."

"Yes, please." The floral-scented steam rose from the spout. She poured the hot golden liquid into the cups and pushed one toward me. The exotic fragrance filled my nose and warmed me from the inside. "How is Eve doing on Smith Island?" I cringed, regretting my mention of her daughter's banishment.

A mother's tender regret appeared in Mrs. Meier's kind eyes. She set her cup on the saucer. "Homesick. I forewarned her not to fall for the forbidden outcast, but love is stronger than a mother's rules. Or the coven's."

I thought of Aunt J. My stomach twisted into an anxious knot because of the potential trouble my choice might cause.

"I hope you respect your aunt's rules just as she respects the coven's rules."

"I try my best."

"I'm hopeful when it's your turn to fall in love, things will be different," she said as if she had foreseen a change in the coven, but I couldn't imagine any change with the pride Mrs. Blackstone took in the centuries-old histories and bloodlines. "You never know what the future holds."

I smiled. "Well, *you* might."

She chuckled. "I'm aware that your mom was a clairvoyant, as well." She played with the card deck.

My throat tightened. I didn't want to think about my loss. "I'm here because I have questions about something else."

"Of course. I apologize. You're here for a reading and a reading you shall get. I drank an organic spinach smoothie for breakfast today, and I'm still energized from the iron. Go on and shuffle the Kabbalah Tarot cards." She sipped her steaming tea and waited. I half-smiled as my fingers lingered over the deck, hesitating. "You're with a friend. You have nothing to fear."

What if she saw me with William in the cards? Would she keep that secret from Aunt J? I drew back and twirled my hair around a finger, considering what to do. Walk away or take a chance?

I wasn't a walk away kind of girl. "Fine. What do I do?"

"Shuffle and pull three cards."

I did as she requested, tugging three cards from the oversized deck and laying them face down on the table. She flipped the first card over and examined it. Her face crinkled with confusion. She flipped the next two cards over and held her expression. "Three more."

A hard lump caught in my throat. "Why? What's wrong with the ones I picked?"

"I'm perplexed. This has never happened before."

"What is it?"

"Rather than the first card relating to your past, they all do. The next three should relate to your present, if I'm reading correctly."

I chose the cards and set them face down again. She flipped them over and nodded. "Okay, the first set of three cards explains your past. *Di toyt*, the Death card, with the Nine of Swords and the Tower card—this combination represents someone or, in this case, two people you've lost." Her mouth softened. "You shouldn't be so harsh in your judgment of what they did, especially your mom. You don't know what she saw coming."

I tilted my head. "I didn't think of it that way."

"As a diviner and a mother, I feel obligated to say it." She continued reading. "*Zex fun shverdn*, the Six of Swords paired with the Wheel of Fortune and Strength cards, denotes your change in homes. Choose another card."

I laid it down.

"*Di mlkh fun pentakles*, the Queen of Pentacles. She represents a female ally in the home."

"That's Aunt J, right?"

She stared intently at the images. "Yes. Choose one more. I'm curious." I obeyed. "*Di riter fun shverdn*, the Knight of Swords. This is someone you met in the recent past who is upbeat and cheerful. A young man who is an ally in your world."

Upbeat? Had to be Mateo. "Huh? Interesting," I said, positively not revealing anything more.

She eyed me with suspicion. "The cards don't lie, but I won't ask." Her hands glided over the next three cards. "The present." She flipped over the cards. "Temperance, Justice, and *di keyserinye*, a goddess, a daughter of heaven and earth that represents the feminine principle. She is connected to the mystical realm and radiates her own inner energy."

She was beautiful. I edged closer, curious, and pointed. "What does the combination mean?"

She laid her hands flat on the table again and sat back in her chair, staring at me. "They tell of change and struggles you are going through, but more importantly the goddess represents what you are."

I grimaced from her implication and shook my hands in the air. "That's wrong. I'm so not a goddess."

Her lips pressed straight as if the news were serious. "She is symbolic of heaven, meaning a realm above the ordinaries."

I smirked. "Yeah, still not me."

She frowned. "I think you know that isn't true. You are special."

I stared at her, not up to lying. "I hardly know what I'm doing. I've been reading my dad's notes and using my inherited gift out of necessity, but after learning about the prophecy in the *Chesapeake Histories*, I'm scared."

She clasped her hands together. "Fear is a dangerous thing."

"So Aunt J said."

"She's a wise woman. You turned sixteen recently, correct?" I nodded. "Have you noticed your gifts growing stronger?"

Noticed? The Fitzgerald magic wasn't big on subtlety.

She reached across the table and took my hand in hers, snagging a closer look at my family ring. The dim lighting glinted off the gold surface. "Look at this. That's something."

"So my dad said."

She frowned again. "It seems you're very lost and your parents weren't able to prepare you properly. What I can tell you is that many of the witches and wizards from this area are descended from two royal witch bloodlines, including my late husband. His father was Jewish, but he was raised in his mother's pagan faith." She paused. "Oh, I can't tell you how my mother fought me on my choice to marry him." She smiled lost in her memory for a moment. "I'm sorry. I digress. Anyway, the prophecy foretells of two extraordinary witches that will come from the thirty-third generation. Thirty-three is a palindrome number. And your name—Hannah is a palindrome name. Tell me, what is your birth date?"

"July seventh." *Same as Emme Blackstone*, I thought.

"Seven-seven. A palindrome birthday."

"What do palindromes have to do with any of this?"

"Magical and healing properties are attributed to palindromes, which is why they are significant."

I swallowed hard and pushed away from the table. "I don't want to do this anymore."

She slapped her palms on the table. "Because you understand the seriousness of what I'm telling you."

Of course, I understood. Everyone was branding it on my brain.

"You must stay and listen. The time is nigh and your life could depend on it. Who do you know with a palindrome name and birthday besides my daughter, Eve?"

"She has a palindrome birthday?"

"May fifth."

I mentally ran through the coven names, in case there was the slightest chance it wasn't my frenemy. All three Queen Js had palindrome names. Then there was Renner and Ava, but they didn't stand out.

"I don't know who it is." My jaw ached from biting down so hard. "Aunt J said one of the two witches will die." And as ambitious as Emme had revealed herself to be, I didn't think she'd have a problem killing me off to get what she wanted.

"Let us continue the reading with the cards you've already chosen." She flipped over the cards. "*Der mkhshf*, the Magician, is a human bridge between the spirit world and Earth. See how he points to the heavens and Earth like he is saying, 'As above, so below, as below, so above.' He takes the magic of the Universe and channels it through his own body. He represents the duality of purity and experience, innocence and knowledge. *Di dus fun teplekh*, the Deuce of Cups, represents a union, but not without— *di sikrits*. Secrets." She lingered over the word.

I swallowed hard. "Do you know what his secrets are?" I compared William to all of the boys I'd ever met and realized how dim they were next to him even with his secrets. He was a mix of dark and brilliant like an eclipse.

She tapped a finger to her lips, seeming contemplative. "Pick one more."

I obeyed, quickly laying it face down. She turned it over and winced. "*Di lbnh*, the Moon. I don't know what the Magician's secrets are, but I see what your counterpart is working on— danger, darkness, and deception." Her eyes flashed to mine. "You have no idea who she is?"

She was working on something dark and deceptive, all right. And she was doing it at an old mansion in Riverdale Park. "Do you know specifically what she's working on? Can you see that?"

She stared hard at the card. "No. It's hidden in a dark fog. Do you know her?"

"That's not important."

"I fear it is."

"I don't know the girls that well."

She inhaled a deep breath while every muscle in my body tensed. "Let us read your future. Three more cards, please."

As I reached for the deck, the beaded curtain clacked from a gust tearing up the stairs and into the tiny room. With a whoosh, the heavy cards blew off the table and scattered. The teacups rattled in their saucers. Mrs. Meier's mouth dropped open. Her eyes filled with what could only be fear. She stood up signaling the end of the reading. "Time for you to leave."

My breathing accelerated. "Why?"

She wrung her hands. "Your future is undetermined and it is not for me to try to reveal it."

"My mom didn't believe it was undetermined."

"She was probably a better clairvoyant than me."

My jaw tensed. "All I want is a chance to fight the fate that's been outlined in the prophecy from the *Chesapeake Histories*. However, I'm not sure my talent will be enough to stop the other witch."

"You need to be sure." She glanced at the beaded curtain swinging to a stop. "Go now."

I jumped out of the chair, but turned back. "Wait. You won't say anything to anyone in the coven, will you?"

She glimpsed the cards scattered on the floor as if they were all whispering to her. Her deep-set eyes grew wide. "It's one of the three." Her gaze drifted to me. "Who is your counterpart?"

I cringed inwardly. "Aunt J and I suspect Emme is."

She wiped her nervous brow. "We will keep each others' secrets. You will keep your eyes open and prepare for the fight of your life, young witch."

I stood and backed away from the table, my eyes locked on the scattering of symbolic cards across her wood floor. I pressed my hands against the doorframe and in a flash, descended the stairs. I looked where Summer had parked, but didn't see her car. My pocket buzzed.

Had to go. Mom called. #Sorry.

Perfect. I was stone cold freaked out and without a ride, not that the house was far away, especially if I took a shortcut. I dashed through a parking garage and raced up West Street. After a few more dizzying blocks, I tried to orient myself, but the creepy feeling of eyes on me set off my internal alarm. I didn't glance back. Instead, I dashed up the street, desperate to get off the main drag. There were two places to hide—a cemetery or an open car wash.

I hated cemeteries. I hated the plastic flower arrangements. I hated the hard granite protrusions and the soft earthy indentations. I hated the memories, but there was no better option. I ducked into the tree-filled Catholic graveyard and hid behind an imposing stone angel.

Disappearing behind a cluster of black clouds, the sun cast one last long shadow that encroached on me quickly. My heart hammered as I prepared to face whomever it was. I stepped out from behind the angel. A slender, tough-looking girl in jeans and a skull shirt peeking out from her leather moto jacket stood five feet away. She offered a slick grin. I froze, confused. I surveyed her nefarious expression and stepped backward, desperate to generate a safe space between us until I could figure out my next move. However, she matched my pace. With a shaky twist, I spun and ran, leaping over short headstones as I dashed back toward the entrance.

Footsteps smacked hard against the ground behind me. Her ashtray-scented breath was on me before her strong hand. She seized my arm and tugged me backward. I hit the ground. The echo of pain vibrated through my head and body and I seriously regretted not having worked out more.

She pinned me down by my neck. Her big eyes traveled the length of my arms until they glimmered with intent. "I'm taking the ring, sweetheart. Don't make me hurt you." Her voice was deeper than I expected.

"How many idiots did Emme hire to get my ring?"

"You're the idiot who's about to be short one ring."

"I doubt that." The magic whispered from its dark void, louder and louder. I clenched my fists. Through gritted teeth, I whispered, "By the power of fire, I do summon and churn, and call thee forth to blaze and burn." The energy exploded. Every muscle tensed until the fire expanded and jolted through me. I turned my glare on her, feeling the anger and focusing on getting her off me.

"You like to smoke?" Concentrating hard on my target, I funneled the blazing fire from my core to my hands. Then I grasped the sleeves of her jacket.

"Yeah, I like my smokes. What's it to you?"

My eyes narrowed. "Then you should smoke." There was ice in my voice while fire raged within. I tightened my grip and thought of nothing but her sleeves.

She laughed. "Look at your f-face…" She stuttered, her cool-mean expression phasing to a baffled one. "Ow!"

She released her hold on my neck and flailed her arms like she was doing the Harlem Shake. I struggled to get to my feet while the smoke around her wrists gave way to the tiny smoldering flames I wanted to impart. She fell to the ground with a yelp. Her arms and legs swung wildly and panic filled her wide brown eyes, even though she had already extinguished the teeny fire.

I swiped the blowing hair from my eyes as a strange calm overcame me. It took a moment to figure out what it was and then it hit me. Confidence.

My attention shifted back to the thief who lay there on her back, panic-stricken. She examined her uninjured wrist over and over.

Tired and irritated, I tapped my ballet flat next to her head. "Did Emme hire you?"

"No, man. It was a random dude. I don't know his name, but he paid me fifty bucks and I really need the cash. Said you'd get the joke, and he'd return the ring to you later. I wasn't really gonna hurt you."

"Could've fooled me." I stuck my hands on my hips. "You seriously agreed to do this for someone without getting a name?"

She nodded furiously, keeping her eyes locked on her wrist. "Did you do that, man?"

"You mean the fire? You sound like an idiot, don't you?"

Her eyes grew wider. "Is this some kind of prank show? Am I being filmed?"

I rolled my eyes. "You are your own reality show gone bad. Tell me where you were going to meet this guy."

Her chapped lips trembled. "Corner of Prince George and Randall Streets. I swear."

She sprang to her feet and scurried off like a rat. I trailed slower behind her, scanning each man's face. At the corner, I spotted a guy wearing all black, checking his watch as he paced back and forth. I studied him and realized his height and paunchy build resembled the other thug. As I approached, I saw his pale clammy face, but I had no idea who he actually was.

He looked at me and froze for one telling second. His eyes, the same beady ones I'd seen behind the mask, flashed panic before he broke into a run. Without thinking, I pursued, dodging dog walkers and moms with strollers to catch him.

He took a left and dashed into the Historic Annapolis office at Brice House. Of course he went into a place connected to the Blackstones. I raced up and threw the front door open, my eyes searching the main level.

"Hannah Fitzgerald, exactly what do you think you're doing?" Mrs. Blackstone yelled from a hallway.

"Did you see that man…?" I panted, trying to catch my breath. "Doughy build? He ran through here a second ago." It took everything in me not to accuse her of helping her daughter scheme because she still had the power to whisk me away to Camp Sea Haven.

She sneered while her brow remained unnaturally smooth. "Why would you be chasing someone?"

I turned a cool gaze on her. "Because he's been after me for some time. Can you imagine?"

She pursed her lips in a pout of disbelief. "No. I certainly can't, and I saw nothing." Remnants of irritation from the volatile talent exhibition lingered in her voice, and there was something about the way she concealed her hands behind her back. She looked like a kid telling a lie.

The creak of a door hinge and a figure swathed in black drew my attention. The man dashed out the back toward Paca House. I flashed another glare at her. "Nothing, huh?" She shrugged without remorse. I raced after him, stopping when I reached the back of Brice House gardens. I cast my gaze far, but there was no one.

11.

aw, caw.

I jumped out of bed and greeted my familiar as he waited on the ledge outside my window. "What does my divine messenger want with me this morning?"

He leaned his head down and tapped his beak against a small black-lined envelope resting at his feet. My heart skipped a beat as I snatched it and tore the note out.

> *You're progressing well, but time is running out and your life means more to me than anything. In case you haven't noticed with us, storms happen when hot and cold collide. This time you need to pair your magic with nature. Meet me at Winchester Pond at eleven o'clock. I'll be watching with great expectation.*

~*William*

Saturday morning came early as Mateo requested my services as his personal good luck charm. "I told you I have to be at Winchester Pond at eleven, right?"

"Yeah, no worries. Where we're going is actually pretty close to it." He shot me a sideways glance. "What do you have planned? A hot fishing date?"

The pond was known for its abundant inhabitants. "Uh, no. Let's just say it has to do with my ancestry."

"Huh. Guess we have that in common this morning."

Classic rock thrummed from the Subaru wagon's speakers while Mateo tapped his thumbs against the steering wheel in time to the music. I peered out the open window as we drove over the Severn River Bridge. On the water below, several small sailboats drifted toward the harbor downtown, and the smell of brine and sea life wafted in. "Why is it Summer has her own car and you have to borrow your dad's?"

A small bellow rose up from his chest. "I lost a stupid bet to her."

"Which was?"

"I bet my car that I'd find my animal spirit before she did. Let's just say it's a sore subject I don't want to talk about." He bobbed his head to the music.

"Fine. Then tell me where we're going."

"The Severn River cliffs. I need to perform acts of endurance in a setting that replicates the mountains of Peru. So basically I have to scale a tall cliff," he said beating his chest with one fist.

"So it's just a typical Saturday morning for you then?"

He laughed. "I've climbed the four-story rock wall at the Y in Baltimore. I've got this."

He opened his window, thrusting his hand into the wind. "Wait until you see how tall this cliff is. It's wild."

"Sort of like the man climbing it."

His chest puffed up at the sound of the word *man*. "The Huarachicoy is also a celebration of our success from tests of endurance and strength. I'm just glad they've done away with the whole loincloth thing."

I threw my hands out in front of me. "Whoa. Loincloth?"

He snorted with humor. "Yeah. In ancient times during the ceremony, mothers presented their sons with their first item of man clothing, a loincloth. God. I'd just die a million times over."

"If I had to see that, I'd die too. I think the endurance tests are enough to prove you're a manly man."

"Definitely. So today, I will test my endurance, find three sacred objects, and cleanse my youthful past away in the water."

"No head-shaving or self-inflicted whippings?"

His Ray-Bans slid down his nose and he looked at me from above the black lenses. "This is serious."

"So you keep saying, but you're the one who brought up the loincloth."

He chuckled. "Merely providing background information."

We drove into a small sandy lot. He parked the car and pointed to our left. The cliffs were much more imposing up close. The uneven cliff edges revealed multicolored layers of Triassic rock. Tall, green grass layered the top level and wet sand surrounded the base. In the distance behind us, cars whizzed across the Severn Bridge.

"I just have to be careful not to get caught, right?"

"Yeah. The police would be my main concern," I said with sarcasm, "not falling down or faulty equipment." I glanced behind me at the entangled heap of climbing ropes and gear. "How long will this take?"

"That's the problem. I don't know how long I'll need."

"Not a problem at all. Would you mind if I wished you luck and got a jumpstart on what I need to do today?"

He eyed me up and down. "Since you're really not dressed for cliff climbing, I'll let you off the hook to go do your ancestry stuff."

"You're the best." I leaned over and plunked a light kiss on his warm cheek. "Keep your phone on," I said. "If I accidentally turn myself into a bird, I'll text you for help with my beak."

"You're funny."

We jumped out of the car. He broke into a sprint with all the ropes over one shoulder while I shook my head. There was no way he wasn't getting arrested. I waited until he was out of sight, then entered Winchester Pond into my maps app.

I didn't know much about fishing, except it was done early in the morning. After a twenty-minute walk, the pond came into view and just as I suspected, I was the only one there. Lush clusters of trees gathered around the pond's edge and wild strawberries grew in scattered tiny patches around the grassy areas. In the air, I smelled the sweet fragrance of overripe blackberries mixed with the freshwater scent of the nearby river. Close to the trees, I noticed a cluster of tall spear plants with spiky, sword-like leaves. The spears dipped low enough that I could grasp the seed casings on the tips. With a pop, one pod snapped off, then another. Remembering what Aunt J had taught me about the formidable plant, I stuffed a handful of pods in my skirt pocket for another day.

White, puffy clouds and carefree seagulls above, signaled fair, cool weather. I wasn't sure about a storm, but if wind speed was affected by temperature difference, I could work with that. At least I'd try.

I concentrated on William's warning about time running out. The stress caused my heart to accelerate. I imagined facing off with Emme and what she'd do to me and the coven if she had her way. The magic whispered, so I tightened my fists and whispered back.

"By the power of fire, I do summon and churn, and call thee forth to blaze and burn." The power exploded and fire surged. My body shuddered. Feeling the stress and focusing on the lesson, I threw my head back and funneled the fire out through my hands in a purposeful stream.

A small dust devil formed in front of me. Wildflowers and grass danced into its vortex. I laughed as I whirled my hands around, playing with the motion of the hot current. I continued, drawing out the energy and spinning the ribbons of fiery heat. As the devil grew taller, leaves and debris twisted around its center while tree branches swayed to and fro. After several minutes of practicing, I channeled the wind into a funnel that reached for the sky. Farther up, white cumulus clouds undulated against a backdrop of hydrangea blue sky, churning, swirling, and finally darkening to a deep, surly gray.

Winds whipped hard against my face. I leaned against a tree trunk for support and continued to draw fire out of me. A grumbling vibration shook my core; the inner force spun and ricocheted off my sides and then thunder rumbled through the sky. With a flash, a luminous white bolt of lightning zigzagged through the gray, striking the ground five feet in front of me. The ear-piercing crack of electricity tossed me backwards onto the ground. I steadied myself and stared at the white smoke rising from the charred earth.

"Whoa. Did I do that?" Feeling drained, I staggered to my feet and stared at the lightning mark. How did I not know I had this in me? I yawned and glanced at my watch. It was eleven exactly and I was already too wiped out to show William anything.

Oak leaves rustled above me. I glanced up and noticed my white raven sitting on a tall oak tree's limb. "What are you doing here?"

Caw, caw.

He must've followed me. "You need a name."

Caw, caw.

"My dad named his bird Gerry after our infamous ancestor, but that doesn't suit you. You are a courageous messenger." I tapped a finger against my temple. "What about…what about Siris?"

He bobbed his white feathery head up and down, nodding with approval.

"What does my messenger Siris want to tell me?"

He swooped down, his wings sweeping through the air with the grace of an angel. He landed on a low-lying branch. His intense blue eyes expressed a warning I didn't understand.

Snapping branches and a low, burly animal growl alerted me. I twisted around. A wolf stood poised with glistening, sharp fangs exposed by a vicious snarl. A white bandage was wrapped around his left foreleg.

My heart raced. Beads of sweat popped out along my brow. A wolf wouldn't scare as easily as a chain-smoking thief and most of my energy was already depleted. I cautiously stepped backwards without taking my eyes off the muscled predator. If the creature had been treated for an injury it might be in pain, which wasn't a good thing for me at the moment.

The gray wolf matched my pace, creeping closer. In a blinding moment of chaos, Siris swooped in, beating his powerful wings against the animal's face.

"No!" I screamed, fearing for Siris's life. I dipped to the ground searching for rocks, but instead found a large stick about an inch in diameter and four feet long. I gripped it tight. With wary eyes, I stared back at the animal while Siris continued to dive-bomb the wolf's head.

I had to stop this. Everything in me focused on the magic, but there was none left to summon. "Siris, go!"

He soared to a high branch and perched. I held the stick against my chest. "Please back off. I don't want to hurt you."

The wolf growled. Thick fur on its scruff stood on end while saliva dripped off its long, pointy canines.

I shored up my courage and stepped toward him. He held his ground, but his growl was deep and ferocious. I stepped again ready to swing with every bit of force I had left in me.

His hips slanted down and before I realized what was happening, he catapulted toward me. I fell backward with the snarling beast on top, his mouth lunging for my throat. I kept the stick between us pushing to keep his jaws from my neck. His nails dug into my skin. My muscles trembled. Then he clamped down on the stick, wrestling it away. As soon as I let go, he dropped the stick and snapped at my hand. I jerked back and clambered to my feet. I gulped enough air into my lungs to exhale a scream as I fought for my life.

Flapping his powerful wings, Siris latched onto the wolf and pecked at his head with his powerful beak. When I grabbed the stick, I felt a twinge of fiery magic, but not enough to channel outward. Then suddenly the ground rumbled beneath my feet and the trees shook. Patches of white and gray flashed before my eyes. Desperate, I swung at the gray. The wolf yelped. I'd hit my mark. I backed up fast, ready for his next lunge, but my foot caught on a tree root jutting out from the ground. The magic whispered faintly and the earth shook again, throwing me off balance. I tumbled backwards as I grasped at the tree to stop the fall. However, the friction against my hand forced the ring to slide off.

"No!" I yelled. I rolled down the embankment of a deep drainage ditch, my head landing hard against a rock. Everything went dark.

The fragrance of candle smoke pooled in the air and stirred me awake. I rocketed upright, fighting off a beast that wasn't there.

The chapel loft was comfortable and clean. A tall bookcase filled with books lined one wall. Another wall was taken up with an old wood desk replete with an Apple laptop, silver model sports cars, and a small speaker faintly humming classic British rock. Beside the mahogany bed, an empty chair rested, and on the night table was an old receipt for Chinese takeout from Joy Luck.

I tossed the covers off to search for him, but noticed a bandage around my arm and felt one on my forehead. Panic set in as I stared at my hand—the bare ring finger. I had to go back. I stumbled to my feet and bolted to the stairs, catching sight of William heading up. He wore a black T-shirt and dark jeans and his ever-present sunglasses. Against his side, he held tight to a handful of shredded fabric. "You're not going anywhere, yet. How are you feeling?"

I pointed to the torn up jeans in his hands. "Did the wolf do that?" My lips trembled as I surveyed his appearance, searching for injuries and bloodstains that weren't there.

"I was changing in a room behind the chancel and heard you get up," he said, not answering my question, which only led to a thousand more questions like, *Did you seriously wrestle a wolf?*

"What happened?"

His free hand gripped hard to the handrail. "Can I get you anything?" His voice seemed strained as if he were battling his inner demon again.

How could he act like nothing happened when his jeans resembled spaghetti? "You can tell me what happened."

He inhaled a breath through clenched teeth. "If you're feeling well enough, wait for me downstairs in the sanctuary. I'll only be a moment." He turned his face away from me, trying to hide the pained expression I'd already glimpsed.

I wished he'd tell me what was wrong with him. I descended the narrow staircase and sat in the first wood pew, staring at the tall silver candelabrum on the altar. My phone buzzed, nearly sending my heart into cardiac arrest. I snatched my cell and saw Mateo's missed calls. Ugh. How would I explain the inexplicable? I called him back.

"Where are you?" Irritation drenched his voice.

"What's up?"

"I called because there's a city wide alert about an escaped wolf from the Annapolis Wildlife Sanctuary. Tell me you didn't run into it." He spoke so quickly he didn't leave room for me to answer.

"Calm down, Mattyboy. I ran into a friend. I'm at their place."

"What was Summer doing at the pond? Is she okay?"

I exhaled a ragged breath not sure what to think of his opinion of my social circle. "I have more friends than Summer."

He hesitated. "Who then?"

I closed my eyes and inhaled deeply. "His name is William." I paused, realizing at that moment how strange it was that I didn't know his last name—not for certain anyway. "He's a friend I met outside of school." The words rushed out fast like the way I tore off a Band-Aid. I waited for the delayed pain. There was silence on his end. "He's going to drive me home."

"No. No. No." The Roca stubbornness surfaced. "I picked you up this morning, and with the escaped wolf, I feel responsible for getting you home. Besides, I don't know this guy. What if something happens?"

His pessimism rankled me. I stuck a hand on my hip, not that he could see me through his phone. "I know him and nothing bad is going to happen."

"Where does he live and when are you leaving?"

He always asked so many questions. "I'm leaving soon. Look, I'm sorry I didn't call sooner. I just came to." I groaned inwardly at the slip.

"You passed out?" He groaned outwardly. "I'm coming to get you. Tell me exactly where you are."

"Stop worrying."

"Your aunt will curse me if anything happens to you."

"She's not so much into curses." Unlike the Grey witches.

"Are you sure you're okay?"

"Positive. Hey, did you finish your endurance test?"

He paused, probably letting my explanation digest. "You changing the subject?"

"Yes, I am."

"Since you're tougher than you look, I'll let you this once." I could almost hear him shaking his head. "Yeah, I finished. Fast, too. And afterward, I found the coolest sacred objects around the beach. I'll show you when we catch up, which will be soon. And call me if he tries anything."

"I will, but nothing is going to happen."

"Your confidence underwhelms me." Disappointment shaded his tone.

"Bye." I slipped my phone in my skirt pocket and glanced at the dirt all over my arms, legs, and clothes. I was a federal disaster. I finger combed my mess of hair and tried to brush out the dirt embedded in my skirt. Then I touched a finger to the white gauze on my forehead.

"Ow." William was quite the medic, patching me up at every turn.

"How are you feeling?"

His daze-inducing voice reminded me of the ocean, inviting yet dangerous. I gently pressed a hand to my chest, reminding myself to breathe.

"Tell me what happened to you? I mean, how are those jeans all torn up and you're not?"

He rubbed his hands together seeming more at ease. "You don't remember anything?"

I shuddered as I thought back to my last memories of the wolf's snarl, the ground shaking, and me rolling down into a ditch. "I remember thinking I was about to become a chew toy."

He stole a glance at his hands and grimaced. He paced in front of me. "Nothing else?"

"Nothing. Did you chase the beast off? Because I don't see how you could've when it was thirsty for blood." My mouth dropped open. "Oh my gosh, did you see my white raven? Was he injured?"

He shook his head. "I didn't see him there." He dropped his head into his hands. "I lured the wolf away from you and chased him off."

My mind went blank, running out of imagined scenarios. "I was stupid and arrived at the pond early. I should've waited for you. Although I'm not sure that would have stopped the wolf."

He formed a straight line with his mouth. "I was there promptly at eleven."

"I didn't see you."

He exhaled a heavy sigh. "Today was about pushing you beyond your expectations. It was necessary for me to stay back and observe." His expression imparted deep honesty, but as he read my concerned face, he flashed his hands in front of me. "If you're going to survive Emme, you need to be tested. But I swear I didn't realize a wolf would be on the loose at Winchester Pond and that things would get so out of hand."

My pulse picked up as the realization settled uncomfortably in the pit of my stomach. "I don't understand. Are you saying you saw the wolf and allowed the situation to get out of hand?"

The straight line of his lips turned down at the corners. "When I saw the animal, I waited. I thought if it scared you, you would use your gift to stop it. If you could stop a wolf, you could stop Emme."

The blood drained from my face. I jumped up, the anger pulsing in my vocal cords. "That's your idea of testing me! I was already exhausted from stirring up a funnel cloud. I had nothing left to defend myself." I rushed toward him and smacked my palms against his chest. "I almost died!" Flashbacks of the wolf snapping at my throat hit me hard.

He glanced away. "I was careless. I'm sorry." Remorse saturated his apology.

"And the ground shaking?" I said. "Was there an earthquake or did I hallucinate it?"

"It wasn't a hallucination, but I can't help to wonder if…"

"If what?" I barked with impatience. I raised my hands to strike his chest again, but he wrapped his strong fingers around my wrists, halting my attack.

He tugged me closer and closed the gap between our bodies. Anger seared my senses, yet for one moment the fire blazed into something hotter. His breathing, quick and shallow, matched the rhythm of mine, and every inch of my skin became acutely aware of him. He leaned his head down, his lips poised. "You're strong, Hannah, stronger than you realize."

His expectations cracked through my daze. I pushed his hands off me. "What are you saying? It's my fault I didn't stop the wolf?"

His complexion heated to scarlet. He set his lower jaw in an angry thrust. "I think you caused the earthquake, and if so, then you had it in you to stop the wolf. You're capable, but you don't see your potential and your denial will be the death of you!" he raged.

My volume matched his. "I'm not in denial anymore, but Emme's gift is powerful." I tugged at my collar, releasing the heat rolling off my chest.

"If you believe Emme will always be better than you, I'm wasting my time."

His words stabbed into my heart causing a wound so painful I clutched my hand to my chest. I whirled away from him and raced to the front doors.

"Don't go," he commanded.

My hands froze on the handle. My muscles taut, ready to yank the door open.

"I didn't mean that."

My eyes narrowed as I spun around. "Yes, you did."

He closed the distance. "Nothing bad happened. Nothing bad will happen if you can forgive me and find a way to trust me again."

"The first time we met, you left me in a burning car."

"I know it doesn't make sense, but it was the only way I could save you that night."

"No. It doesn't make sense and it doesn't help your cause. Maybe it's not Emme. Maybe you're the one who's fated to kill me and you're just taking your time doing it."

He cringed from my harsh words, but how could I trust him when there was one thing I needed from him?

A church bell in the distance echoed its chime. We both turned our heads toward the ominous toll. "You decide. If you can't, this will never work. I'll leave you alone. You'll never hear from me again."

I winced from the thought of trying to take on my frenemy alone. I wanted his help, but I was pissed off. "I—I didn't say I couldn't forgive you, but I wasn't expecting you to test me like that."

"Tests are meant to prepare you for the unexpected or what's the point? This is a fight for your life and mine. Should we sit back and watch Emme's power grow darker and do nothing to stop her?"

I stared up at him, speechless. I felt like a child too stubborn to open her eyes and really see what was in front of her.

"I'll take you home now."

"Wait. How can I trust you when I can't even look you in the eyes?"

He turned the right side of his face away from me as if he was suddenly aware of the scar and he didn't want me to see it anymore. "It's better this way."

"You don't have to turn away from me. I saw your eyes the night of the car wreck and when Emme attacked me in front of Calvert Manor. Seeing them now won't bother me."

He faced me straight on. "My scar does. I saw you flinch before."

"I did, but I swear it wasn't from the scar itself. I'm sorry if you thought that, but I don't think it's the scar or your eyes you're trying to hide from me. It's the story behind the sunglasses you don't want me to know. *Quid pro quo.* Tell me what was so bad that it makes you want to hide from me and I'll give you my trust."

"Enough," he snapped.

I twitched my lips. "So you can ask for my trust without giving anything in return? Can't handle being pushed?" I stared, hopeful he would reveal something. At least tell me what he was hiding. However, his stormy silence revealed only his fear and vulnerability, which touched something tender inside me. I wanted to reach out and tell him it was going to be okay, but I couldn't.

He slid his hand in his pocket and retrieved an object. "Before we go, you'll want this." He grasped my hand with a tender touch and slid the gold ring onto my finger.

The crested bezel had popped open, revealing the mother-of-pearl cabochon, but under the dim chapel lighting the stone didn't look solid at all. The pearl looked like a liquid swirling around in its tiny container. A hallucination, I was sure. I pressed it closed.

My breath caught in my throat. "I thought I lost it at the pond." My eyes flitted to his face, wondering how someone as kind as he was could be so troubled. Overwhelmed by his sweet gesture, I leaned up. My heart sputtered. I shut my eyes and pressed a tender kiss to his left cheek. I broke away and studied his reaction, pleased with the warm flush that colored his face, even if it didn't change anything between us. "Thank you for this."

12.

Fallen leaves in shades of pumpkin pie spice blew about my feet in the school's quad as I thought about the raw and lingering silence between William and I. He was right about hot and cold colliding to create a storm, but neither of us had figured out what to do during the calm after, and the calm was slowly killing me. My heart, shattered because he didn't trust me with his secret, was only beating because of the survival instinct driving it to work—an instinct that didn't want Emme to be the death of me. Not yet, anyway.

"Hannah. How pleasant to see you." Her voice oozed liquid Splenda.

Frazzled, I jumped in her face and shoved a finger at her. "Cut the crap, Emme. I know you hired the doughboy to attack me at the library. You had the ovaries to call the cops, and let's not forget the leather-clad girl-thief who tried to steal my ring. And not that anyone missed you, but exactly what kind of trouble were you stirring up at Baltimore House?"

With a bored sigh, she perched on the concrete bench, pretending to pick lint from her black cashmere sweater and Burberry plaid skirt. She touched her fingers to her huge diamond stud earrings like a model and then swooped her freshly highlighted pony over one shoulder. "I'm flattered you're interested. Someone started a nasty rumor that I went to beauty boot camp," she said, patting her rosy cheeks. "But that couldn't possibly be true."

I sat next to her, leaving enough space to prevent catching her evil virus. "What I want to know is what were you looking for?"

She narrowed her eyes to slits and glided her tongue along her upper lip like a snake tasting the air. "A good witch, er, I mean a good bad witch does her research."

I crossed my arms over my chest wondering what she was hiding. "What you were looking for? Something to help you snag the international internship?"

She heaved her shoulders upward. "The internship? Ha. I'm not worried about winning that."

"Sure about that?" I asked recalling her enraged expression when I caused the paper to combust in front of everyone.

"Prada positive." She touched her nose and looked down when she spoke—a liar's tells. "I've got bigger ambitions than a little internship. I'm a queen without a kingdom, and I plan to change that."

Inwardly, I rolled my eyes at her inflated ego. "So, your demented highness, why spend time in an old mansion when you could be shopping or getting a manicure?"

She ignored my snappy insult. "When I discover a sister witch has been spending time with an ordinary from a very odd, oops, I mean old family, it requires looking into, and I did that on the grounds of Baltimore House. I even brought Navan with me." Her tone expressed her wry amusement with the idea of tampering with my life.

"And?"

Her eyes flirted with mischief. "Oh, we found the mother lode."

She had to be bluffing, right? Adrenaline lapped at the muscles in my fists. I bit down, staving off the rage. "No good will come from your dirty tricks."

"My dirty tricks?" she said. "You mean this." She lifted her hand to her mouth and blew a puff of air, imitating her nightmare-inducing technique. "Don't worry. I'm a novice compared to my mother and her bag of tricks."

The magic's whisper escalated into a scream. I focused my eyes on a tumbling leaf and counted to ten. Sparse threads of fire worked their way out through my fingers warming the air around my hands until the magic receded under my control.

"What's wrong with you?" Her harsh voice cracked my concentration.

The wind whistled into my wide-open mouth. "Shut up," I eked out, needing to catch my breath. I flashed a frustrated glare at Emme. "If you're looking for a fight, I'll fight you. If that's what you want, if that's what we have to do. I'll fight you because you refuse to see any other way, but leave everyone else out of it."

A depraved grin sprawled across her tight, chemically peeled face. "We both know that only one of us is going to survive the next few weeks, and in order to survive, everyone becomes a pawn."

Her voice was as cold and unyielding as steel. But even if she was more ambitious than me and I was the one fated to die, she didn't scare me. And she sure as hell didn't scare the fight out of me. "Haven't you ever played chess, Emme?"

She stared at her nails. "No, why?"

After I'd read Nabokov's *The Defense*, a story about a man's obsession with chess, I researched the game and learned to play a little. "You're thinking of pawns as worthless pieces to be sacrificed to keep the strong pieces safe, but pawns aren't weak. With a little strategy and luck, a little pawn can become the most powerful piece in the game."

Her gaze drifted to mine. "What are you talking about?"

She had no idea a pawn could become the queen. "I'm the only pawn you need to play with."

With a grunt, she dismissed me and checked her watch. "You're such a Fitzgerald."

"Thanks. That's the best compliment you've paid me."

She stood and spun on her heel, but turned back. "You want to know exactly what I was doing at Baltimore House? Meet me in the parking lot after school."

I rolled my eyes, unimpressed with her scare tactics. "Another sucky meeting?"

"Take it or leave it."

My curiosity tingled. "It will be you there this time and not the doughboy, right?"

Her gaze fell on my ring and her wicked grin straightened. "No doughboy."

After dismissal, I waited in the parking lot as all the cars left, except hers. From around the corner, she showed up with the other Queen Js in tow. I really needed to get a cool clique of my own together.

She spied my irritated expression and winked. "Don't cry. I didn't send the doughboy, and you never said I had to come alone."

I crossed my arms over my chest. "So what did you do there?"

"No. It's my meeting. I set the agenda. Girls, let's play a game first," she tossed over her shoulder to Arora and Navan.

Arora, wearing a khaki skort and a black argyle sweater that matched the stripes in her hair, stepped forward with her hands cupped together. She mumbled a spell in French and opened her hands.

A swarm of angry bats released, their high-pitched squeaks filled the air. They flitted and swatted at my face. I spun in a circle, freaked out. My hands and arms flailed in the air to shoo them away.

"Look at her. She looks like a crazy Fitzgerald. That's awesome." Arora laughed. "Hannah, the bats are witch holograms. They may look and sound real, but they're totally fake. Duh."

"Like your smile," I snapped. I finger combed my disheveled hair and reminded myself to stay in control.

She stuck her hands to her hips. "What a disappointment you are." She glanced back at Emme. "There's no way this one can possess a key to part of the Witch's Breath."

My gaze flitted to Emme, whose eyes suddenly bugged out. She whipped her arm into Arora's stomach, almost knocking her down. "Shut up about that."

Arora winced in pain.

I hesitated. "Wait? You think I have a key to the Witch's Breath?" The three stood blank-faced at the mention of the word. I glowered at Emme. "That's the dumbest thing I've ever heard."

Arora shot Emme a dirty look before speaking. "Of course it is. I didn't really think you could have anything to do with it."

All I knew was what Aunt J had told me about it, but now I questioned why Emme wanted to keep that info from me. Was it the page Navan had translated for her?

I locked eyes on Emme, but Navan stepped forward, getting in my face. "If you don't have it now, let's see if it's part of your future, orphan." Arora came from behind and grabbed my shoulders while Navan flipped my hand over and traced her icy finger along my palm.

Emme leaned in as I fought to get my hand back. "What do you see, Navan?" Navan shook her head. "I can't read her." Her green eyes went blank and she flashed a deceptive, smug grin. "Emme, it's—it's like trying to read your palm. I can't see anything."

"Arora?" Emme said as she weaved her fingers through the air. The fog she summoned between her hands condensed into a tall lump of ice. With a few swooshes of her fingers across the object she carved it into her desired shape. "I need a spell."

"I have the perfect one." Arora touched a finger to my icy doppelganger. "Pour les ennuis que vous m'avez infligé, la douleur en double vous sera retourné."

Emme flashed another wicked smile and held the sculpture over her head. "I'll translate. For the trouble you have inflicted on me, double shall I inflict on you." She tightened her grip around its center and the ice snapped in half.

The sensation of being punched in the gut tore through me. I wrapped my arms around my waist and doubled over. I stifled a groan in my throat. "Stop."

"Look at me."

I peered up at Emme while I struggled to stand upright.

"I'll never stop." She held her palm up to her lips and with a puff, she blew gold-colored mist up in the air.

My hands flew up to block the sparkly droplets, but they were already burning my eyes. I may have failed with the wolf, but I couldn't afford to fail with Emme. Her palpable hatred would only drive her to do terrible things to me.

Fury ignited my magic. With clenched fists, I dropped my volume to a whisper and recited the spell. Fire exploded in my core. I focused on the inferno, channeling it all outward without control or restraint. I thrust my hands skyward and released the energy.

When I flashed my tear-filled eyes open, a hot white bolt seared through the sky like a jagged glass crack. With a thunderous explosion, the strike split a distant elm right down the middle. The bewildered girls turned and stared, but didn't seem fazed.

I wiped moisture from my irritated eyes. Arora looked at me and laughed. "What the hell, Emme? Your new mist only made her cry. I can do that, too." I reminded myself to control the magic.

Arora leaned down and clasped her fingers around a small gray rock. "Solide à rampant est ma demande, un changement de forme je le commande."

This time I was able to translate a bit of her spell. Solid to slither? A moment later, she opened her fist and dropped a hissing black snake to the ground.

"It's my newest trick. Jealous?" The snake reared its head and hissed at me.

As much as I hated snakes and as real as its scaly skin looked, I refused to flinch. The witch hologram glided over my foot in a smooth motion and coiled around my leg. I closed my eyes and reminded myself the tightening sensation around my ankle wasn't real. I pried my eyes open, summoned a pinch of courage, and snatched the creeping snake by its neck. I tossed it at Navan. Before it hit, it disintegrated into thin air.

Navan tossed her ginger hair behind her. "Emme, she can't possibly have the key because if she did, wouldn't she let her decrepit aunt have a shot at the youth elixir?"

"I told you both to shut up! You're idiots," Emme yelled, her pale complexion burning a bright mercurial red.

She was totally off her broom. There's no way the rare elixir Aunt J had mentioned could be something as vapid as an anti-wrinkle potion. I wanted to laugh in their toxin-filled faces, but instead I glowered. "My aunt is not decrepit."

Navan took it as a challenge and narrowed her eyes at me. "Haggard. Ragged. And her forehead—get that woman to Dr. Blackstone, stat," she added. "I've foreseen that he could use the business." She laughed. "Am I right, Emme?"

Emme's eyes bulged. She stomped her feet in a tantrum. "Shut the hell up!"

My temper ignited again. I lunged for Navan, grabbing her by her hair and yanking her backward until she hit the ground. "What's inside is what makes someone beautiful, unlike all of you with your beastly personalities that can't be surgically altered."

"Get away from her," Emme yelled.

I squeezed my fists tighter.

"What are you doing?" Navan asked, confusion contorting her lopsided grin.

Again, I tapped into the waiting inferno and carefully channeled the energy where I wanted it to go. I threw my hands in the air, and with a rush, hot energy surged from my body. A second later, clouds rumbled and whirled. The wind rose and whipped around us.

Emme locked her claws on my arm, digging her manicured nails into my flesh. An unfamiliar ferocity took me over. I swung and knocked her down. I flashed a palm to the ground, directing the scorching heat from my core. Roots from beneath the pavement cracked through and wrapped around her flailing wrists. She glowered at me and then, with a whisper, she summoned her own gift. "Give to me, oh clouds on top, from the air, drops and drops." The clouds groaned before a torrent of rain burst down on us.

I pointed my fingers upward and several flashes of lightning illuminated the blackening space above us. A roaring crack in my head matched the boom echoing from the heavens. I pointed to an evergreen at the opposite end of the parking lot. An intense surge of electricity forked through the air and struck it. Smoke drifted toward us.

Navan and Arora coughed and screamed. "What is going on?" Navan whined. She waggled her wet hands above her, staring at the freakishly small amount of black sky that covered the parking lot only.

Fear and realization flashed in Emme Blackstone's eyes; she could summon rain, but now she knew—I brought the thunder and lightning.

Wheels screeched. We all froze as the VW van jolted to a stop in front of us. "Hannah, get in. Now!" Aunt J demanded.

I trudged to the van, my wet skirt plastered to my legs. I slammed the door shut.

She hit the gas pedal and the wheels squealed onto the main road. "Holy salt, sulfur, and mercury. Have you lost your mind?"

"Why did you interfere?" I snapped, watching the shops fly past us in a dizzying blur. A tremor ran through my fingers.

"You think you're prepared to take on that witch?"

I stared at my hands. "I've been practicing."

"Clearly, someone's been helping you, but I'm afraid to ask whom." She slammed on the brakes, flinging us both forward in our seats. She looked straight ahead.

"You're the one who wanted to see my fiery spirit again."

She flashed me a stunned look. "I don't know what's going on with you, but I can't lose you. I promised your parents I'd take care of you, if ever— And I *myrtle* you." Pain etched her tone.

Uh. She was hitting me with guilt. I hadn't thought about her losing me, and what it would be like for her, and suddenly I realized how selfish I'd been and it swallowed me whole.

A breeze through the cracked windows helped calm my heart rate.

She eyed the moody sky behind us and looked at me with suspicion. "The weather reports were not calling for an isolated storm today."

My face crinkled with disbelief. "How did you know where I was?"

She sighed with dark circles under her eyes. "Summer Roca called me. She couldn't find you after school and was *oleander*.

Concerned," she clarified. She wiped the stress from her forehead. "Hannah, this is serious."

I couldn't help to think of Mrs. Meier and the card reading, and William's tests. I grimaced. "I know, I'm fighting for my life."

"It's more than that. You're fighting for the survival of the coven, too. There was something else I saw in the Belladonna—the coven's demise. I warned you before that the ordinary locals will blame all of us for the danger that will befall them. What I didn't mention was that it will be devastating to us all. We will be revealed on social media as freaks and outcasts. Our businesses will close, our livelihoods will be destroyed, and our history will be scattered to the winds when they run us out of town."

I hadn't considered the value of the coven and what it meant to the hard working witches who were a part of it. I thought about Mrs. Meier, Ava, and Renner, and what would happen to all of us. And I hadn't appreciated the history that was coursing through my veins.

She shook her head. "What you did back there—that took great power. I spend a few hours preparing flower essences and balms and I'm exhausted. You summon lightning and thunder, and your muscles are only shaking."

"The magic is growing stronger, but it still takes its toll. I'm worn out and the magic is depleted." There was no denying how strong the magic was, and as dangerous as the lessons had been, the results were undeniable. I had William to thank. He knew exactly what I was and what I was capable of. However, it was time I knew his secrets.

"I want to assume you found the trunk key I left for you, and you've been studying your father's notes from the attic. If you've been up to anything more than that do not tell me."

"I have been reading his notes."

"Good. Keep doing that, but you should know something else. Your father's ring, the one on your hand—there is more to it than meets the eye. Your father was working on its secret before he died, but he never figured it out."

"He always told me it held a secret and secrets would reveal themselves to me once I proved worthy."

"That's true, and I have a feeling you're exactly the worthy kind of witch that ring deserves. You need to pick up where he left off. Uncover its secret. You might need it."

I stared at the Fitzgerald crest, the weight of my heritage falling heavy on my shoulders. "The way you say it scares me."

"You need to be scared." She stared straight ahead, but her knuckles on the steering wheel paled white as she gripped it harder.

"How much time do you think I have?"

"I don't know. Momentous events surrounding witches usually occur during planetary alignments or natural disasters."

I wasn't clairvoyant like Mrs. Meier, so predicting a volcanic eruption or tidal wave was out of the question unless the date came to me in a fog-free dream. However, I wasn't counting on that. I reached for my phone and Googled "upcoming astral events." I scrolled through the list. My eyes nearly popped out of my head—one impending big, amazing, blood moon-slash-total lunar eclipse. With anxious fingers, I checked my phone calendar. The eclipse was occurring on October nineteenth, the night of the tea party re-enactment. I swallowed the lump in my throat and slipped the phone back in my pocket. Aunt J would be there with other members of the coven for the painting unveiling and everyone else in town for the re-enactment. I sighed, frustrated. "Can you drop me off at Mateo's."

"Mateo? We're talking about your actual life, not your social life."

"I promised him."

She frowned. "If you *prunus domestica* to consider what I've told you."

"I promise that, too." We parked in front of Mateo's house. I waved goodbye to Aunt J and dashed to the front door.

Summer greeted me with a huge smile. "Come in. I'm glad you're okay." Her gaze drifted to the cloudless blue sky. "Why do you look so damp and disheveled?"

I sighed, filled with frustration and stress. "Long story."

"Mateo's in the backyard. He's been waiting to show you his stupid sacred treasures," she said, as if it wasn't a big deal to anyone except Mateo. She pointed to the sliding glass doors. "He's out there, but come back when you're done."

"Sure."

Mateo, sitting at the sunny picnic bench in the middle of the yard, eyed me up and down. He set his small brush down. "You look like you got in a fight with a fish and the fish won."

"Maybe I did."

"Seriously?"

I shrugged. "Emme."

"She doesn't know when to quit, does she?"

"That's for sure."

He puttered around with a shell thingy. "So you gonna tell me exactly what happened after you left the beach by the cliff?"

I slid onto the bench opposite him. "Stupid really. Went to the pond, got distracted, and fell into a drainage ditch."

He laughed. "I'm serious."

"Me, too. Fortunately, I didn't die there."

"What had you so distracted you didn't see the ditch?"

"Siris, my raven showed up."

He looked up from cleaning. "I thought familiars were supposed to be helpful."

"He was helpful. It was my fault. I wasn't paying attention."

"So what happened?"

I pressed my lips together, not sure how he would take the news. "That's where William found me."

He snapped his eyes shut and slapped his hands to the table. "He just happened to be at Winchester Pond?"

"Well, I didn't want to say too much before, but he was supposed to meet me there," I said.

"So he knows what you are?"

I narrowed my gaze. "Yes."

"And you wanted *him* to watch you practice your craft and not me?"

"This isn't all about you, Mateo."

He made a lemon face.

"There's a reason we're together."

"Which is?"

"Fate. Fate brought us together, and I think it's because we're kind of the same." What else could I say to make him understand?

"The same, huh? You like him?" he asked, dejection stinging his tone.

"Why do you care?"

"You're my friend. I care."

"I think we should change the subject. I seriously don't have the energy to fight anyone else today."

He picked up the brush again, tending to his treasures with great tenderness. "What happened with Emme?"

"She started trash talking."

"My uncle would say she was a hornet's nest, all wound up on the inside and ready to strike at the next person who pokes her."

I rested my elbows on the rough table surface. "So whatcha got there?"

His eyes lit up. He grasped a small triangular-shaped stone between his finger and thumb. "Fossilized shark tooth. See the black mineral replacement? So cool." He set it down gently and picked up the white shell-looking thing. "This is a giant tree oyster, which is as old as my Incan tribe. I found all this on the beach." He set it down with great care and picked up the next fossil that was smaller than the stone oyster. "This is a perfectly formed miniature conch shell. See the whorls? Dude, I can't wait for the ceremony." He examined his treasures with pride.

"When is it?"

"Next weekend." He looked at me. "Wanna come?"

"Duh. I'm your four-leaf clover. Um, you won't be drinking blood or sacrificing virgins, right?"

He laughed. "Nah. No loincloths, no blood, and no virgin sacrifices," he joked. "It'll be cool. You and Summer can hang out after she does her storytelling."

"They let girls participate?"

"Sure. I told you before, women and their connection to nature hold a place of honor among our people."

"Most patriarchal societies don't get that." I thought about my female ancestors and how they'd suffered over the centuries for their understanding of nature and science, some persecuted and hung at the gallows. "What story is she telling?"

"Our women, including my mom who is descended from a famous high priestess, are the history keepers because the Incans relied on oral tradition, and Summer will be telling one that has meaning to her."

"Wow. Sounds cool." Mateo explained more about what would happen at the big event and time got away from us. The sun dipped lower in the sky and the autumn air filled with a chill. "I need to get home and change out of these damp clothes, and Summer still wants to tell me something."

"Sure." We hugged and everything felt normal again, well as normal as it could be between an Incan warrior and a Chesapeake witch. Inside, I caught Summer staring at herself in the foyer mirror. "Whatcha doing?"

Her eyes smiled at me from her reflection. "Looking for wrinkles."

"Okay, Queen J wannabe." Was the whole town obsessed with maintaining their youth?

"I'm not, but I learned a tribal story about vanity and it freaked me out. And don't think those Queen Js and other girls in our class haven't had plastic surgery. You've seen Emme's tiny nose, right?"

"So bizarro."

She faced me. "She's been luring the other two Queen Js into her dad's practice. What's worse is that she does it because her parents need the money. Arora's mom told my mom they were in debt because of a few recent medical lawsuits. Apparently, one of the women, Mrs. Wardwell, sued him for a botched boob surgery."

"George's mom sued Dr. Blackstone?"

"Oh, yeah. For big bucks. Nearly bankrupted them. Can't imagine how much he had to pay out for the other lawsuits. Can you picture Emme and her mom driving around in anything less than a luxury German car or shopping at thrift stores?"

"No, I can't." Not at all. They were definitely used to the finer things that fashion and BMW had to offer, and I shuddered at the thought of the lengths they would go to maintain their posh lifestyle. "How does your mom know Arora's mom, exactly?"

"They both volunteer part-time at the Merkle Wildlife Sanctuary."

"So Emme's been bringing her friends to her dad for fillers and stuff?"

She shuddered. "Like girls with PMS to the chocolate factory."

I stuck my tongue out. "Bleh. Your analogies are horrible."

"I do that on purpose to gross you out. Want to hear my story?"

"Definitely." I tried to push the info out of my mind, but a feeling of dread stayed with me.

"It's about a woman who is growing old, and she worries about aging and dying. She wants to be young forever, and an evil spirit instructs her. He tells her in order to stay eternally young she has to travel the great desert to find the waters of youth, but every time she gets close, the waters disappear like an oasis. Her quest for youth becomes an obsession until she dies."

"She died from tasting the waters?"

Her eyes creased with disbelief. "The waters don't exist, silly." She angled her head. "How could they?"

"Right. They're mythical. Of course. So how did she die?"

"Vanity. Oh, and dehydration."

13.

eet me at Hard Bean Ice Cream & Booksellers. I've got news that only a sugar overload can help us make sense of, Summer texted.

In her world chocolate, sugar, and cream fixed everything. In my world, it was crab pretzels, but even that magical treat couldn't fix the trouble Emme blew out of her mouth. When I arrived at the quaint shop located inside the historic Market House, Summer was waiting at a round table in the window and bopping in her seat.

I tapped my hand on the table. She plucked her earbuds out while I read her T-shirt. *Warriors do it without fear.*

"What's up?" I asked.

She eyed me with a confident smile. "I'll trade you a scoop of information for two scoops of chocolate blended into a delicious milkshake then we can try to make sense of my news on Emme."

"Your shirt should say, *Warriors do it with carbs*."

She laughed. "I think we both acknowledge, with mutual respect, the carb addiction in each other."

"True that." I skimmed the menu hanging above the jars of mix-ins and the shake machine. "Chocolate Bomb or Death by Chocolate?"

"They have a new secret-menu flavor, Double Chocolate Afterlife. It's supposed to be more chocolaty than Death by Chocolate."

"Natch. I'll be right back." I placed our order, paid, and set the creamy dark cocoa-colored concoction in front of Summer.

She peeled the paper from the bendy straw and plunged it into the frozen creaminess.

I sat down, unbuttoning my sweater and tapping my anxious fingers against the tabletop. "Tell me what you know." I sipped my apple pie shake. The cold thickness dissolved on my warm tongue so only thinly shaved bits of tart apple and specks of tasty cinnamon lingered in my mouth. I sighed from the sweet carb overload.

"Wait, do I smell apple?"

I stared at her. "Never mind that. Spill!"

"It's apple with baking spices, isn't it?"

"Apple pie with cinnamon to be exact. Now, talk."

Her eyes lit up. "Ooh, can I try it?"

"Will it make you spill any faster?"

"Yes." She slurped. "Ooh. That's good. Bits of salty crust. Delish, but it won't be as good as my Double Chocolate Afterlife. So back to the scoop."

I leaned forward, eyes wide.

"Emme was hanging at that old house in Riverdale Park, right?"

"Yeah, and she took Navan with her."

She sniffed her milkshake. "Oh, this is definitely more chocolaty than Death by Chocolate."

"What's up with your sense of smell?"

She grinned. "It's sort of one of my super powers." She dipped her straw in and out, then plopped a frosty cocoa dollop on her tongue. "Mmm. I was right."

"Whatever. Back to what you were saying."

"Well, you're not going to believe what they did. It wasn't beauty boot camp. Remember I told you the place had a graveyard? They paid a man to open a sarcophagus."

Why was it not surprising Emme and Navan were messing with dead bodies. "And?"

She flung her hand out to the side. "You don't even look surprised."

"We're talking about Emme and Navan, so pairing their names with a word like sarcophagus isn't shocking."

She pointed a finger at me. "True that. Anyway, while I was in the girls' bathroom stall, I overheard Navan tell Arora that Emme was doing ancestry research in the cemetery there. The town was founded by a historic family, and we all know her family goes way back."

So did most of the families in the coven and even the Calvert family. They were one of the oldest bloodlines in the state. "That's so creepy, but it still doesn't make sense."

"The Blackstones have always been different." She slurped then stopped and pressed on the sides of her head with both hands. "Ow! Brain freeze."

"Why do you say that?"

"Take Emme's dad, for example. He's a plastic surgeon-slash-gun enthusiast. He hosts target-shooting parties in Quiet Waters Woods every few months."

"Yes, Emme and the other Queen Js like to hang out there, too."

"Doing what?"

"Sharpening their claws against tree bark."

She laughed. "Good one."

"Thanks."

"Anyway, my mom said the wildlife sanctuary where she works complains to the city every time because the parties disturb the endangered red-bellied woodpeckers' habitat, but Mrs. Blackstone is so well-connected with local officials the complaint gets ignored."

I pretended to sip my shake, but the icky, dreadful feeling returned as I thought about the Blackstones.

"Hannah?"

"Huh?"

"Do you want to hear my theory?"

"Sure." I dunked my straw over and over.

Her eyes widened. "I think they were making a Queen J Frankenstein out of the corpse parts."

I pictured it for moment and laughed. "I don't know what they were doing with a corpse, but they don't need to make a monster—they already are monsters."

As soon as I closed my eyes for bed, the bright light burst inside my head. The light dimmed and a different image than before came into focus. I saw a woman with long brown hair lying on a floor. I recognized the marble tile around her. Panic released me from the dream. I shot up, my heart racing.

It doesn't mean anything. It was just a bad dream. Breathe, Hannah.

During a break between classes, I saw Emme sling her plaid Burberry scarf around her neck. She stared at her face in the locker mirror, touching up her thick, black eyeliner with a pinky finger. "Hey Hannah, how are you?" She tossed a glance in my direction.

Her fake interest left me uneasy. "Fine, thanks."

She whipped around, her shampoo-commercial hair whirling behind her in bouncing waves. "Fine? Really? That's great."

"Are you feeling okay?"

She narrowed her gaze. "I'm feeling like P-F-M."

"Is that Queen J for pre-freaking-menstrual?" God, I sounded like Summer.

"Yuck, I take a pill for that."

Of course, she did. Probably got the prescription from good ol' dad.

186

"P-F-M means pure freaking magic, but I'm so busy I don't have time to chat." She checked the gold and diamond-encrusted watch on her wrist as she tapped her gray manicured nails resembling little headstones on the watch face. "I have a chess lesson to get to."

I rolled my eyes. "Whatever that means."

She slammed her locker shut and strutted away as Summer rushed up. "What's her problem?"

"She's playing nice."

"Snakes can't be vegetarians."

"I was joking. Let's get to class."

Ms. Russell, the strange guidance counselor, marched toward us with her blonde hair swooshing back and forth. She peered at me from above the rim of her reading glasses and winked as she passed.

I nudged Summer. "Did you see that?"

"See what?" Her attention was locked on her phone as she texted and bumped into classmates rushing into the classroom.

"Nothing."

After our last class, we headed to the parking lot. Emme's BMW was noticeably absent. "Wonder if Emme choked on her own venom and left early?"

Summer shifted her backpack onto her other shoulder. "Oh, she did. Leave early, that is."

"How do you know?"

"She wasn't in fourth period."

I shrugged, but a cold feeling snaked up my back as I recalled my eerie dream. "I need you to take me to Flower Power. Now!" I folded my trembling hands together.

Please be wrong, please be wrong.

"Sure. What's going on?"

My lips quivered. "I'm worried about Aunt J."

"You think Emme did something to your aunt?"

"No," I lied. "Of course not. Just need to get there."

We tossed our backpacks in her car and sped to Flower Power, running stop signs and almost crashing into the back of a seafood truck. After what seemed like an eternity of sudden jolts and quick jerks, we slowed. I leaped out of the car and ran into the shop.

"Aunt J?" I scanned the tiled floor and behind the counter, hoping my nightmare was simply that. My heart beat hard against my ribs. "Aunt J?" I dashed into the back.

She lay motionless, curled up on the floor. Her eyes were open and filled with the kind of terror only one person knew how to impart. With a glance at the glistening mist on her face, I knew exactly who was to blame. I draped my arm around her and sat her up, rocking us back and forth. "It's okay. I'm here. Nothing is going to hurt you now. Whatever you saw, it wasn't real." *Don't leave me. Please, don't leave me.* Tears streamed down my cheeks. It was my fault. I should have warned her. I should have kept her safe. "Aunt J, come back to me. Please." I sniffled. Summer came up behind me, kneeling beside us.

She softly pressed her hand to my shoulder. "What's going on?"

I choked back the tears as helplessness overwhelmed me. "I need to take her home."

"Sure. Let's get her to my car." We lifted her up, our arms supporting her around her waist and helped her outside. She didn't say anything. She just stared blankly into space. Her lips trembled. We shifted her limp frame into the front seat. Summer drove faster than ever before and parked in front of the house. We helped her upstairs to her bedroom.

A hot porcelain cup shook in my hands as I carried herbal tea to her along with a natural hops sedative I found in her night table drawer. After several minutes, she relaxed her face and finally closed her eyes. I clutched her hand and whispered the sentiment she said to me in her language of flowers. "I *myrtle* you, too."

Summer waited for me downstairs. "She's lucky you have such a strong intuition or was it something you saw?"

"It was a foretelling nightmare. I've had a few lately and I don't like them." I didn't care if she knew about that. However, Summer was a warrior and if she knew Emme was to blame, she would go after her without realizing how dangerous that witch was. "I foresaw her mix up her meds. I should have warned her."

When Summer left, I made sure Aunt J was resting soundly before I set off for the witch that wanted to teach me a chess lesson. I slammed my palms against the double mahogany doors of her house. A rustle in the bushes caught me off guard, followed by a sparkling mist that filled the air. A screaming pain penetrated like a thousand knives, stabbing into the skin on my face and delving into my gut. I dropped to my knees and stared up into her menacing eyes before the lethal fog rolled in. "Emme. Stop."

"You have ten seconds to tell me what you know about the Witch's Breath. If you don't tell me, I'm going to leave you hanging in this nightmare while I go after the next pawn you love. And I have a good idea he haunts the grounds at Calvert Manor."

My protective nature took hold and the magic blazed. I clenched one hand into a fist and lifted the other into the air. I cast the spell and streamed searing hot energy with focused precision into the sky.

The October wind howled sounding as enraged as I was. Gusts spun into a dark, thin funnel, sucking everything from the ground around it and nearly knocking my frenemy off her feet.

She flashed her eyes to mine. "Stop this!"

With a deadly serious glare, I imparted my refusal to relent. The hot, energized pressure in my core increased.

She counted down as the winds lashed our hair into our eyes, and leaf bits and dirt into our mouths. She sharpened her focus and cupped her hand to her mouth ready to blow the rest of her deadly mist at me. "Three-two-one. You asked for it." She puffed.

The fog in my head grew thicker and darker. The mist swirled around me in the nightmare. I wandered down a path and came upon a sign—Green Briar Center for Mental Health. I raced toward the cries drifting from my former psych facility. Behind a thick wall of glass, Aunt J rested in a drug-induced haze, her arms and legs bound to the bed frame and tears streaming down her expressionless face. The next moment whisked me to the cemetery.

"Not the cemetery," I pleaded. "Anywhere but there."

However, my feet stuck like sticks in mud. I plodded one foot at a time as if on a track, past the gravestones until I stumbled, landing in front of William's.

"No!" I writhed in the mud in pain. With one last burst of energy, I shifted my hand upward again.

Her cruel laugh burst through the nightmare at the same time as a bolt of lightning cracked like a whip in front of me.

The boom whisked me out of the darkness. I fought to open my eyes as another sliver of hot white light slipped in. Emme was struck. She flew onto her backside and wrapped her arms around her waist, shaking from the electric shock of the bolt.

"Don't come back here a-again," she stuttered, her teeth rattling.

The pain from my head traveled to the rest of my body like poison working its way out. Exhausted and dazed, I wavered like a zombie under her mist's influence, but as soon as I was far enough away from the Blackstone's house, I doubled over and wept. I wept for the loss of my parents, for what I had let happen to Aunt J, for the future of the coven, for what was coming to Annapolis, and for the impending battle I'd have to fight to my death.

14.

Windblown, exhausted, and sick from Emme's hate campaign, I hunched over on the edge of Aunt J's bed, holding her hand. She shivered, still living the nearly fatal nightmare Emme had introduced into her head.

I stroked her hand, desperate to reach her. "Don't worry. It's going to be okay. I'll take care of Flower Power and the house, and you rest." I wasn't sure how I was going to do it all, but I had to. Aunt J had been there for me when I needed a safe haven, and I planned to do the same for her.

However, something was going to break. Stress from Emme's attacks and worry from wondering whom she might inflict with her next lethal nightmare were crushing the air from my lungs.

I was emotionally and physically worn down when a terrible, rotten thought took root. I didn't ask where it came from, but it was there like a different whisper from another dark corner within me. How would Emme like it if I opened up a can of freaking nightmare on her mother figure?

They were obsessed with their looks and eternal youth, but obsession was a weakness—a weakness that gave me an advantage. I gently released Aunt J's hand, closed her door, and raced downstairs.

Her study was the daisy white room off the main hall. It was filled with ivory-colored furniture and bookshelves.

I scanned the ordinary-looking books when a plain, crackled brown leather spine caught my eye. Its musty scent and old-fashioned print betrayed its age. After an hour of searching through *Witches' Study of Plants*, I found the title of a recipe that sounded just right. The problem was, there was no list of ingredients or instructions beneath it. I flipped through the book and found no other recipes like it. Something was amiss.

I scanned the room. Vases filled with dried flowers and rows of books lined the shelves. On her desk rested an antique magnifying glass with a sterling handle engraved with swirls and flowers. Was it bewitched? I snatched it up and flashed it over the blank recipe page. Nothing. My neck muscles ached with frustration.

Perhaps the recipe needed coaxing with a Latin spell? I didn't know much Latin, but beginner French was close enough, right? I balanced the book with one hand and hovered my other hand over the page. "*Révèlez-vous.* Reveal yourself." I repeated the phrase. Still nothing, but as I held my hand there and felt my natural body heat radiate outward from my palms, and I swore I saw a shadow on the page.

Was it that simple?

I glanced around again and noticed an atomizer sitting next to a stack of antique books. I lifted it to my nose—her bee balm home fragrance. Bee balm flowers were acidic. Why would she leave that next to a stack of fragile paper books? Feeling love for my quirky aunt, I spritzed the fragrance onto the page and floated one hand above the blank space. With my other hand balled into a fist, I recited the spell.

"By the power of fire, I do summon and churn, and call thee forth to blaze and burn."

Magic surged and heat radiated from my fingers in a controlled stream onto the freshly acid-laced page. Within seconds, the reaction caused the invisible ink to appear.

Going old school, I snatched a pen from her desk and wrote everything down in case it all disappeared again. I reviewed the list and decided there was only one place in town to acquire the one rare ingredient.

I jotted down the nefarious plant's Latin name along with two benign flower varietals.

The next day after school, I checked on Aunt J. Having foreseen what happened, Mrs. Meier stopped by to help. We both made sure she sipped her tea and stayed in bed. Then I left them to dash across town to Mrs. Fairchild's Seed & Sow shop. Mrs. Fairchild sold seasonal stuff to the ordinaries, including heirloom seeds her own ancestors cultivated centuries ago, but for ladies like my aunt who were a part of the coven, she opened her special back room. It was full of the exotics a witch couldn't find anywhere else.

The two-story brick building with a green awning and huge pots of seasonal flowers beneath the main window consisted of the shop on the main floor and her residence on the second. Inside, the sweet fragrance of fertilizer and grass seed scented the air. Shelves and shelves of seed packets with the most colorful hand drawn art were lined up in long wood crates and twirling tree of life chimes beckoned to shoppers from where they dangled above their heads.

Mrs. Fairchild and Aunt J knew each other well since both of them were in the plant business. She waved to me with a green apron secured firmly around her robust waist. She was short with ginger-colored hair and a twinkle in her eyes. "Hannah Fitzgerald. Your aunt told me you were back. How are you, dear?"

"Fine, thanks. It's nice to see you again." Two ordinaries sized up the garden tools near us, so I lowered my voice. "I thought I would have seen you at *the* meetings."

She lowered her voice. "That's a younger witch's club, and I don't care to go to Dr. Blackstone's practice to look the part. By the way, how is your aunt?"

"She's fine," I lied, feeling horrible about it, but she would be fine. She had to be. She was all I had. "She sent me here on an errand."

"Certainly." Her eyes sparkled with delight. "Follow me."

We wound our way past several shelves and through the garden tool section. Once again, she looked around before sliding a row of tall wood trellises on concealed tracks to the side, revealing a narrow green door.

I had passed through the entrance only once before with Aunt J and my mother on a late night shopping trip for what I later found out were agrimony seeds, a powerful love potion ingredient. The concoction was crafted for a distant relative who had a crush on a special somebody.

The innocuous green door looked like it hid a dusty broom closet. She opened the door and led me inside.

Along the golden oak walls of the eclectic storeroom hung rustic iron mirrors and décor. Ivory statues rested on every surface and from the ceiling replicas of sparkling garden fairies dangled from fishing wire.

"Now, let me see what she needs." She lifted her green-framed reading glasses to her face and examined the list. Her glasses dropped. She eyed me, seeming puzzled. "This doesn't look like her writing."

My lips thinned. My pulse picked up a bit. "Um, no. It's not. It's my handwriting. She had a ton of distillations to do, so she, um, dictated the note to me." I swallowed hard and hoped she didn't hear the tremble in my voice.

Her eyes returned to the list. "Certainly."

I exhaled a quiet sigh, pleased the ruse was working.

"Follow me. One of these is a very unusual plant and I'm nearly out of the seeds. Do you know what she's using this for?"

From what I understood about witches, they liked to know what others were up to, but in this case she needed to remain oblivious.

"It's a pre-treatment for her flowers."

She stopped and faced me. Her brow creased. She pointed to the top name. "This one here won't have a good effect on fresh flowers. It will cause them to wither quickly. Are you sure you wrote these names down properly?"

"Positive. She checked them. Said it's for a special elixir that requires extremely dried flowers."

"Oh. Dried flowers. Certainly." She pointed a chubby finger in the air. "That makes sense. I've been shipping so many of the seeds to a local business, you're lucky I have any left."

I thought about why I needed them and wondered. "Who would want Senescent seeds in bulk?"

"Powder River Armory. The woman I dealt with said it keeps their explosive powders extra dry, so I guess that makes sense."

"Aren't there less expensive ways to keep powder dry, like sealed containers?"

"I don't know." She scanned her distressed sage green shelves. "Here we go." She plucked a tiny white envelope from her apron pocket and pinched it open. She scooped four seeds of Senescent Flower into it and did the same with the other seeds. She handed me the envelopes. "No charge. Your aunt is a good customer."

"Thanks." I snagged the envelopes and hurried home.

Into the dimly lit attic, I carried four pots of dirt and planted the Senescent seeds under the open hexagonal window where just the right amount of autumn sunlight filtered through. A breeze sent the chime into a melancholy song. My eyes lingered over my dad's jars resting on the desk, and then flitted to my phone where I caught my reflection. A reflection I didn't quite like. I looked away. My dad wouldn't approve of revenge, but I had to do something to get that nasty witch to back off. The angry memory of what Emme had done to Aunt J caused the magic to hum. I squeezed my fists tight and cast the spell.

"By the power of fire, I do summon and churn, and call thee forth to blaze and burn."

The energy exploded and raged within me. With a touch of my finger to the pots, I focused a thin stream of heat into the dirt. The tiny seeds sprouted into two starter leaves and then into full-sized plants with buds in a matter of milliseconds. The buds burst wide open into blooms the color of deep, dark amethyst.

I yawned, feeling drained. Tomorrow, I'd be rested and finish what she started.

15.

After filling orders at Flower Power, I rushed home to check on Aunt J. She drank a few sips of cool water and fell back asleep. I tucked the blankets around her before heading to the attic. I plucked the spray bottle filled with the withering potion and sniffed. The potent scent of rancid flower told me the liquid had intensified. For the rest of the day I busied myself with homework and chores while my nervousness reached a peak. Mrs. Meier returned at dinnertime with a special rejuvenating broth for my aunt and a container of stew for me.

At midnight, I jumped out of bed, wired. I dressed in black from head to toe. With the small bottle in my pocket, I snuck over to the Blackstones' house, sticking to side streets and alleyways. The waxing moon provided ample light once my eyes adjusted.

I threw a leg over their fence, but my pants caught on the sharp jagged tip of a picket. "Come on." The fabric ripped with a whoosh as I lost my balance and tumbled over. A groan stuck in my throat from the sharp pang radiating from my wrist. White sparkly stars flashed in my head and the pang radiated up my arm. I inhaled a few breaths and sucked up the throbbing before standing. When I stood straight, a burning sensation from my leg drew my attention. Beneath the torn fabric, a trickle of warm liquid ran down my calf. I pressed my hand hard against the cut, wanting to prevent a gory trail of DNA.

Within the boundaries of their yard, I limped my way to a tree by a back window left open. After a painful climb, I plucked out the screen, stifling another moan as my wrist bent in an awkward fashion. I fought back the anxiety of getting caught with the memory of Aunt J's terror-filled eyes.

I eased myself in, landing on a credenza. I slid to the floor and inched my way upstairs, tiptoeing. There was the only place Mrs. Blackstone would keep that iridescent bottle of pills—twelve inches from her mouth.

I creeped until I reached the second floor and there I eyed the long, wide hallway filled with closed doors—one, two, three, four, five, six, and seven. Six and seven were double doors, most likely leading to the master bedroom. Clinging to the wall like a moth, I shuffled closer.

A hissing beast pounced on the floor behind me. I startled and plunked my hand over my mouth. Sweat beads trickled down the side of my face as I discovered Mrs. Blackstone's emaciated family familiar. The feline arched its back, showing off its black glossy fur that shined under a ray of moonlight streaming in. It eyed me and hissed again.

I tilted my head as I considered how to scare it off. I extracted the spray bottle, aiming to the side of the agitated cat and spritzed. The burst along with its unpleasant scent caused the brittle creature to recoil and bolt into its mistress's bedroom.

Holy salt, sulfur, and mercury. Please don't meow the Blackstones awake.

My hand trembled. I nudged the door further open, breathing through the faint creaking of the hinges. The spacious bedroom, slightly illuminated by exterior spotlights, contained a huge gothic four-poster bed and a ginormous armoire, both adding to the haunted castle feel. I tiptoed closer to the bed and easily distinguished Mrs. Lump from the Mr. Lump hidden beneath the thick, gray comforter.

Their snoring vibrated at different intervals and shook me with each exhale, sending my pulse racing. With one scan of the room, I discovered what I'd come for on her night table. I snuck closer and picked the pill bottle up while keeping my eyes locked on both of them.

With a push and twist, the cap was off and between my teeth. It was now or never, and even though the spray was harmless, I cringed inside from the act. A boorish snort from Dr. Blackstone sent my heart into palpitations.

I spritzed the pills as much as I thought the capsules could tolerate without melting. I lightly jiggled the bottle to disperse the liquid and then I replaced the cap.

A rustling noise froze me still and then the fine, sharp pang of cat claws tearing into the skin of my ankle sent stars of agony bursting through my body. I bit my tongue and cried inside as the pain pulsed. Karma came in the form of a cat.

I gently set the bottle back on the night table and backed out of the room. I had one foot in the hallway when I heard the cat hiss and pounce on the Blackstones. They startled awake. My breathing stopped. I stood there frozen as Mrs. Blackstone struggled with the blankets and smacked her husband in the head.

"Stop, thief! Everyone wake up. Emme!" She screamed.

I inhaled a deep breath and ran. I stumbled down the staircase and scrambled to unlock the double front doors. I twisted the large metal deadbolt and yanked on the handles while a ruckus ensued upstairs. The cacophony of voices nearly drowned out the footsteps that were heading in my direction.

My pulse skyrocketed. "Come on," I pleaded with the door. With my fingers I searched for another lock. A second later I found it. With a quick turn, I was outside. Emme's voice echoed after me, but I didn't dare look back. Her feet smacked the ground as she raced after me, and then a whooshing sound came from behind. Suddenly the back of my head was smacked with a gooey awful substance that smelled like skunk.

I kept running while breathing through my mouth. Did they know it was me? I wasn't sure. I wasn't even sure the prank had been worth all the trouble. Guilt settled into my stomach like osmium, a metal my dad wrote about that was twice as heavy as lead. Perfect. I was sick to my stomach with a hair full of stinky goo.

The next day at school while I hid the bandage on my leg under a pair of leggings, Emme laughed out loud, strutting down the hall with the other Queen Js swarming around her like two desperate worker bees. She showed the girls something on her phone. They oohed and ahhed.

Was it a pic of my wet head from last night? *Stay cool*, I thought. I grabbed my books, trying to block out their vapidity. I slammed the locker shut and picked up my pace, but what I couldn't block out was the awful thought of Mrs. Blackstone popping her tainted pills.

"Oh, Hannah. Don't walk so fast," Navan shouted after me. "You have to read this."

I ignored her and kept walking.

She raced up and touched a long plastic nail to my shoulder.

I spun around, annoyed. "What?" I snapped.

"Someone didn't get her beauty sleep." She eyed my baby pink cardigan and gray leggings up and down. "Hannah, look. This is really funny."

I glared. "I doubt we have the same taste in jokes."

A snotty half-grin flashed. "You'll like this." She glanced back at the other Queen Js who watched from a distance. "We all think it's funny." A frenzied excitement filled her, reminding me of a shark smelling blood.

I stuck a hand on my hip. "What is it?"

"Read this text." She flashed the phone in my face. Her fake nails glistened from the bedazzling.

Hey, what's the deal with the weird girl trespassing on my family's property? Truth bomb, I think she's freaking ugly.

I searched for the sender and receiver names—Chase Calvert to Emme Blackstone. The blood drained from my face. I'd always liked that little rat. My head swam in embarrassment, but I didn't want Navan or the others to know the message cut deep. I leaned on a locker to steady myself and shoved the phone back at her, ignoring the lump in my throat. "This means nothing to me."

Emme approached. "I guess your stalker visits to Calvert Manor haven't gone unnoticed by the family," she said, knowing Chase had seen me there. She shot a look of satisfaction to the other Queen Js who bit their lips to keep from laughing.

"Your mother has ruined you," I said through a tensed jaw. I whirled away, my cheeks hot and my eyes moist with anger. I didn't care if he thought I was ugly. I cared that he'd said it to Emme. With my head down, I sniffed the tears back and raced to the cafeteria as the bell rang for lunch.

Summer caught up with me just when I spotted the texting Calvert doofus at a table with his pimply-faced classmates. She stayed back, probably sensing from my tense stance I was about to pounce. I grabbed him by his shoulder and shot daggers through him with my eyes. His face drained of color.

"Outside."

He followed without an argument.

I smashed my lips together, focusing my rage-gaze on him. "You sent a mean text about me to Emme? Of all the people in this school, you sent that vicious message to Emme Blackstone?"

He shrugged his shoulders, his eyes wide as he took in my crazed reaction. "I...I don't know what you're talking about. I never sent..."

My body shuddered. "Liar!"

He shook his hands in the air. "Whoa. I'm not lying."

"The text. The one you sent Emme Blackstone a little while ago."

Confusion swept over his face. "I didn't. How could I?" He hung his head back and his shoulders dropped. "My phone went missing this morning and Arora handed it to me before I walked into the cafeteria. Said she found it in the hallway. I thought I'd left it in my locker."

I shook my head. "You're telling me you didn't send any texts this morning?"

He retrieved his phone and scrolled through the messages. His eyes bugged out as he discovered the salacious message. He held his hands out. "Let's just say, Emme is the last person in the whole universe I would text. I swear. I didn't send this. I would never, even if I hated you, which I don't. I like you. And I know my brother likes you. He was so down last year and when he met you a few weeks ago, he became a different person; hopeful. I'm sorry. I couldn't say anything to you before about him being my brother." He glanced around and dropped his volume. "My family has secrets and it's not my job to share them."

"Don't worry. I already figured out your connection to him."

He shrugged his shoulders. "It's hard to keep secrets in a small town."

"There are so many other secrets he won't let me in on."

"He's good at keeping them, but it's only because he feels obligated to protect the people he loves."

"I know that, and I'm sorry for tearing into you about the text. Really."

"No worries. I'd be upset, too, if I read that and so you know, I'd never say, 'truth bomb'."

I lowered my voice. "I have to know. Are all the Calvert men wizards?"

He whispered. "We're considered crossbreeds because we have so much ordinary in our bloodline now, but technically, yes. If there's any magic in me, it hasn't come out yet. But William is special. Our uncle who used to be part of the Colonial Chesapeake Sons a long time ago is his tutor, and he thinks so too."

That explained how William knew so much about the coven and my family's history. We were connected that way. "Why haven't you officially informed the coven of what you are? You must know it's mandatory."

"You should ask William about it, but I'll tell you this much. We're not exactly the type they're looking for."

hile Mrs. Meier paid another visit to Aunt J, Summer offered to help me at Flower Power after school. However, Mr. Nickerson, one of our teachers, needed her at the history club meeting. I hoped business was slow, or my GPA was going to suffer. I kicked a pebble to the curb and watched it roll across the street toward the shop.

My gaze drifted upward, catching sight of an ethereal column of gray smoke funneling upward. Every muscle in my body froze, including my heart, as the realization settled in.

"Fire!" I bolted into a sprint, running around to the back of the building where a growing blaze devoured a stack of newspapers. Tiny embers leaped from the pile and clung to the back door like glowing orange magnets. The flames licked and sucked at the air, growing taller and stronger.

I scattered, searching for a hose or bucket, but there was nothing except crates, boxes, and a rat-filled dumpster. The fire crackled and hissed behind me. On the ground next to the newspapers, a charred matchbook flapped in the breeze next to a small wooden chess piece—a pawn. "That witch used my element against me!" I coughed and picked up the matchbook by its hot, chargrilled edges.

Carson's Gun Shop - catering to the unique needs and special orders of its customers since nineteen ninety-eight.

I dropped it and searched in desperation for something to douse the fire. I fiddled with the back door lock. I slammed inside the shop, filled two buckets with water, and dumped them on the newspapers.

The fire sizzled and smoked, but it had already taken hold of the wooden doorframe. My breathing raced out of control. I kneeled down low for air to breathe. Exasperation struck me while tears streamed down my face. Coughs and gasps shook my body as the thick smoke engulfed the back area of the shop.

What good was my fiery gift now? I hung my head low, but there was no time for the pity party I wanted to attend. The flames grew larger and hotter, stoking the fight in me. I raced back into the shop, exhausted and choking as I filled the buckets to overflowing again and again.

The blaze hissed like an undulating demon dunked in holy water. Through my futile tears, a laugh broke through as the attempt to destroy my aunt's livelihood was slowly extinguished. That's when it hit me. I didn't need to be like Emme to beat her. I only needed to be strong for the ones I loved.

With the fire reduced to a sopping, smoky mess, I inspected the blackened bricks and doorjamb. The damage was minimal, and I sighed with relief that the shop was safe. Aunt J would die without it, and I couldn't lose anyone else. I would die, too.

I glanced around, ready to clean up the mess before catching up with my studies. There was also a coven meeting to squeeze in.

At home, I changed into a daffodil-colored sweater set and paired that with charcoal-colored leggings. I checked on my aunt, tucking her in and keeping her as comfortable as possible. Her panic attacks had settled down and she was nibbling water lily flower crackers in between mutterings about the nightmare. I set a cup of hot Roman chamomile tea on her night table before leaving.

The blue-flamed candles flickered in the front windows, reminding me of my dad. Inside, I searched for Mrs. Blackstone, curious if the Senescent flower had worked. Near the front of the room, the coven leader, wearing a tight navy blue suit, whispered to Emme. Emme reached for her mother's hand, but the woman shooed her desperate fingers away. Instead, she retrieved a compact from her pocket and examined her sagging face, tugging at the corners around her eyes. Emme mirrored her actions as I snuck closer.

"I don't understand why your father's pills and potions work on everyone else in town, and suddenly they aren't working for me. I'd adore the person who could make these wrinkles go away forever," she whined to Emme. A glint of desperation shimmered in Mrs. Blackstone's eyes as she traded the compact for the iridescent bottle and popped a tainted pill. With a swig of expensive organic water, she swallowed.

Moments later, her brow creased with deeper lines than I'd ever seen and the same with her mouth. The temporary effects showed on her face, harsher than I expected.

I cast a glance back at the flickering blue flame and pressed a hand to my forehead.

Hannah, this is so wrong.

Nausea hit me and not from the sight of her. She looked age-appropriate for the first time, but the guilt for being the one responsible for her desperation gnawed at my soul.

I trudged to the back row of seats while Emme followed on my heels. I tried to lock eyes with Mrs. Meier or anyone else who would talk to me, but it was too late. Her shadow crawled past my feet. I spun and faced her. "I don't know how you live with yourself, Emme." I pointed a finger at her, but saw three pointing back at me. Ugh.

She checked her fresh, blood-red manicure. "Are you upset about the text message? I really don't understand how that happened. I guess we shouldn't have shown it to you."

"I don't care about the stupid text."

"What's the problem then?"

I seethed, thinking about Aunt J and her shop. I seethed, thinking about my mom and dad. Then I said it. The thing I shouldn't have said. And I said it through a terribly satisfied grin. "If you must know, I couldn't help to notice how old your mom looks. Did your dad come to his senses and leave with his crappy bag of tricks?"

Her eyes thinned to slits. "Speaking of mother figures, since your actual mother killed herself, how is your aunt doing? We all miss her so much." She tugged the corner of her lip upward with the satisfaction of a superior combatant withdrawing the dagger from her enemy.

My anger at her mention of my aunt triggered the magic, which screeched louder. The noise rattled in my head. I closed my fists and whispered the spell. Inside, everything burned and shuddered with ferocious energy. I focused on the target, pointed my fingers, and channeled the fiery magic. The double doors shook and rattled. The wind howled and gusted against the windows and the blue flames on the candles each shot a foot in the air. I drew the power back and relaxed my hands.

Hiding my exhaustion, I gnashed my teeth and leaned close so only she could hear me. "I found the chess piece you last played. I'm warning you, if you ever hurt anyone I love again, I'll bring a storm you'll never forget, Emme."

She grinned, unconcerned. "I've been wanting you to bring it, my little wannabe. In fact, I'll consider it your test. If you pass, you can be the alpha."

"Emme, what's going on?" her mother asked while her gaze drifted outside the window.

I backed away and closed my eyes, stunned at how far I let her push me. What was wrong with me? I hated the mean things I thought and felt when she was near me as if her toxic sludge contaminated me. And I hated what I was becoming—a shadow of her. "Go. Away. Emme."

She chuckled, seeming completely unconcerned. "Gladly." Her shoes clacked as she joined the other Queen Js in the front row. Mrs. Blackstone returned to the podium and snapped her nimbus mist-coated fingers, creating another stupid blue cloud above her thumb to garner the group's attention.

206

I remained in a weakened daze and sat on my trembling hands until Mrs. Blackstone adjourned the meeting.

"Please go forward and remember the great words of our ancestors. We are the daughters of the witches they couldn't burn."

I waited and followed behind them. Emme lowered her volume and leaned closer to her mom. "Have you arranged the fireworks yet?"

"It's all taken care of. It will be a spectacular surprise—for the whole town. Make sure you are inside Carroll House before they begin."

Was she afraid her plastic daughter would melt under the lights of the fireworks?

"And whatever you do, don't make it rain," she continued.

As the witches crowded the door to exit, I bumped into her mom. I slipped my hand into her pocket and retrieved the pill bottle. Regardless of her horrible daughter, and what she'd done to Aunt J, I needed to be better than Emme.

I slipped back into the crowd and waited my turn to leave. The Queen Js stood less than ten feet away and chatted among themselves, as usual.

"My idiot brother has been practicing a glow finger trick and I swear it looks like a lightning bug's ass when he gets it right." Arora chuckled.

"That's stupid. My little brother can spit actual fireballs. Now there's a trick for a Grey descendant," Navan chimed in.

Emme set her gaze on me while she spoke to her followers. "Listen up. My dad's throwing a little pre-shooting party at my house. Who's in?"

With a heavy sigh, I pushed through the crowd and broke out into the night air. I chucked Mrs. Blackstone's pill bottle in the trash, certain her husband could write a fresh prescription for her in the morning.

That night I drank some of Aunt J's lemon balm tea, desperate to avoid any weird dreams. I needed sleep. I closed my eyes and sank into my pillow. When I finally drifted into the dark, the burning white light flashed and faded and the strange image grew clearer. So clear, it scared me to death. Under the silver light of the waxing moon, William lay on the ground among a cluster of leaves. He was motionless. I jerked upright, my heart racing out of my chest. I was afraid, but thankful the lemon balm hadn't worked. I scribbled a warning to William and summoned Siris.

The fireplace at Inca Coffee Bean crackled with a glowing blaze that cast flickering shadows all around. Summer and I cozied up near the welcoming heat. "Mateo is prepping for his big day," she said.

I rested my elbows on the table, full of stress and uncertainty. Emme's killer instinct ruled her and my heart ruled me. I needed to use that to my advantage without betraying who I wanted to be, but how? I sighed into my hands and yawned.

"I'll be right back." Graceful and toned like a jungle cat, Summer slinked up to the counter and slinked back a minute later with drinks in hand. "Here you go." She tucked the tray under her arm and leaned down to my ear. "I asked our barista to add extra whipped cream for you." She slid a pumpkin Frappuccino under my chin.

I stared at the clear plastic cup filled to the rim with a nutmeg-colored coffee shake, thickened with ice granules and topped with a swirly mountain of whipped cream and caramel drizzles in two different shades of golden deliciousness. A big grin spread across my glum face, as the caffeinated and sugary drink was just what I needed. "Oh, I love that you get me."

She smiled. "And extra whipped cream, too. What are friends for?" She sucked on her double Incan frozen mochaccino with two shots of chocolate syrup. After a few satisfying sips, she leaned back and grabbed her suede, fringed jacket by the collar. Her T-shirt poked through. *Incans do it on mountaintops.* I shook my head.

"This beverage is delicious and super revitalizing, which I need after such a terrible history club meeting." She slumped in her seat. "I swear I thought Mr. Nickerson was going to hurl all over us when a fight broke out about what to call the Civil War-slash-War of Northern Aggression. That's the problem with Maryland—we're a border state."

I half-smiled. "That's Maryland's problem? Not the Bay pollution?" Or the impending coven prophecy that didn't bode well for the local ordinaries? I tugged my straw out of its paper sleeve.

"I know. I'm being dramatic, but there were only ten of us there so he could have hurled all over us."

"Was Chase there?"

"Maybe." She took a sip and bobbed her head up. "Speaking of cute guys, have you secured a date with the mysterious William for the Governor's Masked Ball, yet?"

With my index finger, I doodled squiggles in the condensation on my cup and took a sip. I thought about William. It had been too many days since we'd seen each other and I missed him. "Not yet."

"If you don't fix the sitch soon, I'm going to fix it for you."

The threat was real. I had no doubt she could blackmail a distant Incan cousin into taking me. "Don't do that. I'll make it happen. I swear."

"That's not convincing. Your aunt's civic club—" she paused, wrapping air quotes around civic club "—will be at the ball, too, right?"

The coffee caught in my throat. I coughed and pounded my chest. "Um, some of the members will be there to see a lost historic painting returned to the city, and they are overseeing a fireworks display for the evening."

"What do the Colonial Chesapeake Daughters do, exactly?"

"The *club* gives certain people like the Queen Js bragging rights. You've heard the claims. 'Oh, I'm descended from this duchess, I'm descended from this earl and, I'm descended from Queen what's-her-face.' I'm surprised the leader doesn't hand out her own royal titles and force the lower tier members to curtsy to the higher ones."

"You sound a little irritated. PMS?"

I stopped staring at the coffee and shot her a *Don't mess with me* look. "Are we really going to talk about hormones because, ew, gross. Not PMS." How could I tell her what was really going on? Emme was coming after me at every turn and Mrs.

Blackstone was keeping a close eye on the coven, ready to ship any one of us off to Camp Sea Haven if we broke a stupid coven rule. "I really don't want to go to the ball. You know Emme and the other Queen Js will be there."

She eyed my expression. "The keyword is 'masked' ball. You can wear a mask and you won't have to deal with her or any of them."

She was wrong. Fate wouldn't let me off the prophetic hook and with the lunar eclipse occurring that night, the blood moon would want a blood sacrifice in return.

"Hannah?"

"Never mind." I peeked at the time on my phone. "I have to open Flower Power. There's a ton of orders to fill. How could so many people order perfume and flower oils at the same time?"

She dipped her straw in and out of the drink. "Need help?"

I shook my head. "I like the work and it's the least I can do for my aunt. Besides, I have to grow up and take charge of me, now, and although that sounds super mature, it really sucks."

She bit her lip. "It'll be okay."

A breath of frustration expelled from my taut lips. I closed my eyes and sipped the coffee. The cool, creamy beverage swooshed over my tongue like liquid ice cream. "I hope you're right."

"Have you heard? Dr. Blackstone is arranging one of his crazy shooting parties."

She was trying to change the topic to relieve the tension, which I appreciated, but the new topic sucked crabapples. "So I heard. When is it?"

"Not sure, but my mom and the wildlife sanctuary are in a tizzy."

The ache phased to a severe pounding in my head as I recalled the most recent foreboding dream. The hammering grew louder. I closed my eyes and breathed. I gripped tight onto something.

"Hannah!" Summer screamed, drawing me out.

My eyes fluttered open. "Sorry!" I frantically grabbed napkins to sop up the mess that spilled from the cup I had crushed. Whipped cream, ice cubes, and coffee spewed all over her.

She dabbed herself with her own handful of napkins. "Hannah. I think you need to unfriend caffeine. Stick with carbs."

My heart ached worse than my head. "You're right. I'm sorry."

"You have been so on edge lately and you look really pale. You sure you're okay?"

Tears welled up in my eyes. "You have to tell me when. When is the shooting party planned for?"

"Probably in a few days, but my mom didn't say exactly when. Why?"

I dropped my head into my hands and my hair—held together in a messy knot with a pick—fell apart, draping around my face. My throat tightened and my nose leaked. I sniffled. "I don't think they're out to disturb woodpeckers this time."

"What are you talking about?"

"I had a bad dream, that's all."

"Who died?" She wasn't joking.

I was beyond stressed. "No one, yet." I was certain Siris had already delivered the warning to William, but would he heed it?

Summer reached over and touched my hand. "I need to say something to you and you're not going to like it, but I have to say it. Because you're my friend." She paused, tucking her white blonde hair behind her ears and looking very serious. She eyed me, making sure I could handle it. "I'm sure Emme is to blame for your stress. She's like nuclear waste and you are whatever mixes with nuclear waste and causes a huge radioactive explosion. The best thing you can do is stay away from her."

My shoulders tensed. "You still suck at analogies."

She chuckled. "I'm better with Incan myths, but you get my point?"

"Yes. However, we go to the same school. Our families are in the same—" I paused, glancing around "—*civic club*. That's just not a possibility."

She grimaced. "Then you need to do everything you can to avoid her because she brings out the worst in you. And she knows how to fire you up. I'd hate to see you do something stupid because she pushed you into it."

I shrugged it off. "I handled the text game well enough."

Her expression turned dark. "No, you didn't. I watched you nearly bite Chase's head off."

I wanted to roll my eyes, but she was right. Emme contaminated me, and I didn't like who I was when I was around her. "I'll try to stay away." Summer's silence frightened me. "What?"

"Promise me you won't do anything stupid at the Governor's Masked Ball, okay?"

That wasn't up to me. "I promise I won't do anything intentionally stupid."

She frowned still dabbing a napkin at the whipped cream stain on her tan suede jacket. "You control you and, hopefully, Emme will let up."

After lunch, I found myself standing in front of Ms. Russell's office door, my hand frozen in a fist hovering below her name plaque. I shook the nervousness out of my hands and knocked.

"Come in."

The fragrance of sweet bee balm pooled in the air and conjured images of Aunt J's house. "You like bee balm?"

She sniffed her wrist. "It's my perfume. I bought it awhile ago from a shop in town."

"Flower Power?"

"That's the one."

"That's my aunt's shop. She made it."

"Great place."

"But still not good enough for me to make a career of, right?"

She ignored my question and inhaled an impatient breath. "What can I help you with, Hannah?"

I stared at the rose painting. "I have questions." I plopped in the chair as a file dangling on the edge of her desk slipped off. She leaned over and picked it up, and when she did, a gold medallion slipped out from her collar. The engraving on it looked familiar. "May I see that?"

"See what?" She tucked the necklace back in and straightened her posture, paying too much attention to the manila files stacked before her.

I pointed to her neck. "The gold medallion on your chain. The engraving looks like a family crest. Is it?"

She glanced down, pressing her hand to her chest. "Oh, that? It's a holy medal."

My eyebrows furrowed together. "If you don't mind me saying, I don't think it is. I have questions. To start with, what are you hiding?"

Her lips pursed and she blinked rapidly as if trying to appear innocent. "I'm your guidance counselor and…" She paused to check her watch when the bell dinged in the hallway. "Oh, it's time for you to get to your next class, and I have a staff meeting to prepare for. Thank you for stopping by."

I stood and smacked my hands on her desk, tired of the secrets mounting all around me.

She lowered herself back down in her seat.

"Show me your medallion." I paused. "Please."

She exhaled a deep breath and pressed her lips together. She slowly reached for her necklace and extracted the pendant. She held it out for me. The backside contained writing in Latin. I flipped it over and gasped as I released it. I stepped back, my mouth still hanging open.

Her expression exuded distress. "I couldn't tell you before."

I sharpened my focus. "You're a Fitzgerald?" A flurry of thoughts swirled as I looked around her office. "Are you the secret recruiter sent by the International Witchcraft Club?"

"No."

"Then you're here without the local coven's knowledge."

She leaned closer. "Someone way higher than your leader gave me permission to be here."

"And why is that?"

She tapped her polished nails on the desk and stared hard at me. "I'm here for you, Hannah."

The unexpected response rattled like bad luck charms in my head, making me uneasy. I didn't need anyone else trying to change my life. Fate had already done a fantastic job with that. I eyed the door, part of me wanting to run away, but since I hadn't had any luck in outrunning fate up to that point, I stayed. "Why me?"

"Think of it as a family reunion of sorts. I'm a distant cousin, if you will." She stood and walked around her desk, peeking outside the door to be sure no one in the hall was listening, then she pressed it shut. "I traveled from Washington, D.C. That's what you wanted to know, right?"

Even with confusion swimming around my brain, her answer didn't completely satisfy me. "Why me, Cuz?" I'd never received a visit from any distant cousins from Washington, D.C. before.

She stole a glimpse of her wedding ring. "I owe someone a favor, and I'm repaying it."

"Who?"

"I'm not at liberty to say." More secrets. Perfect. She folded her long arms across her chest. "What else do you need from me?"

I played with my gold family ring with the crest that matched Ms. Russell's medallion. "Answers. Tell me what you know about my ring."

She seemed hesitant to reply. "It's a family heirloom."

"Obviously. What else?"

"Are you sure you're ready to hear it?"

The imaginary clock ticked in my head. "If not now, when? I'm sixteen. My parents are gone. I'm running my aunt's shop, extinguishing real fires, and dealing with frenemies from hell, all while maintaining a three point six GPA. I'd say I'm ready."

She lowered her voice. Her expression softened. "Your ring, according to information I have access to, is a key to finding..."

I clutched the chair arms. "The Witch's Breath?"

A curious crease in her brow formed. "I've never heard it called that."

I inched to the edge of the seat. Maybe it was a name only known among the coven, but she had to be referring to the elixirs. "Go on."

"What I know is that it's a key to finding a precious lion oil."

"What's a lion oil?"

"There may be more than one kind, but the lion oil I know about is a powerful potion, a lifesaving one. Even the name denotes its magical and healing properties."

"What do you mean?"

"The word 'lion oil' is a palindrome and there's ancient magic in palindromes."

I recalled Mrs. Meier saying something similar. How strange. "Tell me more."

"This particular lion oil can save a person, and only one person, from the brink of death."

One? Like one witch who was destined to die young? My hope shot up. "Where did you get this information?"

"I can't tell you. Not yet."

I wanted to rattle the details out of her, but I played cool, hoping for more info. "If the ring is a key to finding this lion oil, where is the lock?"

She leaned against her desk. "How old do you think your ring is?"

I smirked. "You're using the Socratic Method on me? Really?" Mr. Boyd had power drilled the Socratic Method into my head for a freshman writing assignment. I hated him for it, until now.

Her gaze exuded frustration. "You're a smart witch, Hannah, but you need to start thinking like one. You've spent too much time pretending to be an ordinary *ordinary*, and it has dulled your talent. What do your witch instincts tell you?"

I ignored the *ordinary* comment, mostly because it was true. "Hundreds of years old?"

"And where would you look for a lock that was hundreds of years old?"

"I don't know, somewhere equally old?"

"Your ring is older than the state of Maryland."

"Somewhere that has really old things, like a museum?"

She shook her head. "There aren't any museums like that in Annapolis. Try again."

"An antique shop?"

"Ahh. Now, you're thinking like a witch. Perhaps you should start browsing."

I furrowed my eyebrows. "How will I know what I'm looking for?"

"Consider this a quest where you must trust your witch instincts. I think you'll know when you find what you're looking for."

My lips parted with surprise.

"Shut the door on your way out, please. After all, I have a meeting to prepare for and transcripts to review." She winked and returned to her chair, delving into files.

"Aunt J?" I quietly entered her room. The sun radiated its golden light through the narrow slits in the blinds.

"Hannah? Is that you?" she asked, her voice raspy.

Relief settled over me. "Yes. I'm here. Are you feeling better?"

She pushed herself into a half-seated position. "I'm so achy. What happened to me?"

"You had—a nightmare."

"I'll say." She coughed and touched a hand to her head as if she were trying to remember. "Wait. I recall Emme at Flower Power. She asked me to look at her phone and then…and then." She covered her open mouth with a shaky hand.

"You're okay, now." I sat down next to her, the palms of my hands damp with sweat.

"It was horrifying—like the night of the car accident, but worse." She touched the quilt on her bed and pinched her cheek, probably checking to make sure she was awake. "I—I heard you crying outside, behind the shop. I tried to get to you. Smoke filtered in through the door. All I could think was you were trapped in a fire and I couldn't get to you. The smoke kept pouring in, burning my eyes and then…" A tear rolled down her cheek. "Tell me what happened."

My lips puckered, unsure if she could handle the answer. "Emme happened. She used her creepy mist and inflicted her nightmaring on you."

She wiped her eyes with her hands. "She tries hard to please her mother. She doesn't realize she can use her gift to inspire dreams like a sprig of holly tied to the bedpost."

Where I once felt pity for the cold-hearted girl with the heartless mother, I only felt numb now. "Emme has really perfected her talent. She'll make a great recruit."

She squeezed my hand hard. "That decision has not been made, yet."

"I'm sorry. I shouldn't have brought it up."

"Have you uncovered the ring's secret yet?" Her eyes flitted back and forth.

"I've started."

A cough rattled her delicate frame. "Finish. You must figure out its secret. Do it now before Emme gets any stronger."

"Aunt J, do you need a sedative? More tea?"

"I'm so thirsty. Tea would be lovely. And my robe, please." She nodded toward her poufy-sleeved pink bathrobe hanging on the back of her door.

"You shouldn't get up. Rest today. The shop is fine. You left plenty of inventory in the back that I've been using to restock the shelves. Business has been good."

She widened her eyes. "You haven't missed school to run Flower Power?"

"No." I assured her. "I've been running the shop after school and delivering phone orders when I can. You really need to go digital."

She relaxed into her pillow. "*Hydrangea*, my darling."

"You're welcome. I'll get your tea, now." I returned a few minutes later and made sure she was comfortable. Afterward I showered, dressed, and rushed downstairs, ready to keep my promise.

After my conversation with Ms. Russell, I racked my brain trying to think of other places with old stuff, but all I could think of were antique shops.

I whipped out my phone and after a quick Google search discovered three shops in the area, but only one that specialized in pre-colonial items—Crossland's Antiques on West Street. I locked the front door behind me and embraced the quest.

The small, dilapidated building with white paint peeling off the exterior welcomed me inside where a musty scent of old things wafted around me. I scanned the various rooms for something that stood out from the heaps of old chairs and stacks of pewter dishes.

Nothing sparked my instincts, but my determination pushed me onward.

Across the street, an old mansion converted into a shop caught my eye. I'd passed the building hundreds of times before, but this time I saw a small sign hanging above the front door, Ye Ole Book Shop of Otto. Above the sign was a crescent moon symbol. My witch instincts tingled. I strolled up to the door and entered.

Creaky hinges announced my arrival. In the grand entrance, neatly stacked books filled the ceiling-high shelves. A spiral wood staircase rose up from the center of the main floor to the second level where a casual layout of tables and chairs accommodated quiet readers. I sniffed the air, inhaling the delicious scent of mocha and sugar.

"Can I help you find something?" a gentleman behind the counter asked in an Irish accent. He was average in height with streaks of silver running through his chestnut brown hair. His ruddy cheeks sunk in around his mouth and his lean frame looked fragile. He looked at me over the rim of his reading glasses.

The wonderful fragrance filled the shop. "Is that chocolate I smell?"

"Yes. We sell hot chocolate and chocolate biscuits."

Biscuits? How cute was he? "They smell delicious."

"Would you like to try anything?"

"No, thank you. I'm searching for something with a lock. I know that doesn't make sense in a bookstore, but that's what I need."

He gripped his chin and rubbed it, pensively. "And you thought you might find it here?"

I glanced around at the enchanting bookstore and nodded. "Just a feeling." And the feeling was shaking my instincts like an earthquake.

"Will you show me the key?"

I paused, feeling slightly out of my mind and not sure how to respond, but the way he asked, he seemed to understand my request. I twirled a strand of hair around my finger.

"Miss?"

"Huh?"

"I assume you have *the key*?"

I slowly approached the counter and held my hand out, showing him my ring. "I believe this is the key."

He nudged the glasses up the bridge of his nose and lifted my hand, rocking it back and forth. The soft light glinted off the gold. He looked at me, examining my face. "You're younger than I expected."

I drew back, puzzled. "What do you mean?"

"I've been waiting for you. For a very long time."

I creased my brow. "That's not possible. I only decided to come here a minute ago."

He smiled. "Providence is a funny thing."

I gritted my teeth. "Not so funny to me," I said, feeling like a chess piece someone else was moving. Part of me wanted to leave. I eyed the shop door. What if I chose to do something unscripted? What would fate say? Then I recalled the upcoming shooting party and realized time was ticking.

"My name is Bob Reinier. I'm what someone like you might call an ordinary, albeit a knowledgeable one. Now, please follow me."

How did he know anything about my kind? At least, he seemed excited to see me in his bookshop. Would other ordinaries be so thrilled to know what we were? "How did you know I was…?"

"A witch, possibly something more than that?" He grinned. "Your ring. It's the Fitzgerald family crest. As an old book dealer, it's hard to not be a history buff. I'm also familiar with royal bloodlines, including yours. It's fascinating to have a family tree with a wizard earl and so much exciting history."

"Exciting? More like dangerous."

His eyebrows knitted together, telling me he didn't understand everything about my world. "Well, come with me." He locked the shop door, drew the blinds, and gestured for me to follow. He led me up the spiral staircase to the gallery that held more bookshelves filled with old, old books. The heavenly smells of chocolate and parchment followed us.

At the end of the gallery, we faced a narrow bookshelf. He searched the row with his index finger and tipped a copy of one of my favorite reads, *Beauty and the Beast* by Gabrielle-Suzanne Barbot de Villeneuve, toward us. The whole bookshelf slid to the right, exposing a dark entrance. "After you."

I gasped. This was way cool. I slipped into the darkness, placing one foot in front of the other.

"Stop," he instructed, flipping a switch to light up the room beyond the arched opening.

"Is that arch framed with—books?" I touched my fingers to the leather and cotton spines of all the classic novels.

"Naturally. Follow me." The room resembled a dark, but cozy great room in a castle. There was a table and high-backed, comfy chairs set in front of a huge fireplace with stone cherubs supporting the massive mantel. Above us, a swirly metal chandelier hung, adding candlelight to the space. "Take a seat." He scanned the shelves. "Aah. Here it is."

He set the small locked book in the center of the coffee table. "Go ahead," he encouraged, sitting across from me.

I ran my fingers over the rough edges of the book that resembled an ancient diary. Did this simple book hold something as precious as the secret to a lifesaving potion? Inset along the side was an intricate carved brass medallion the size of a dime. I ran my fingers over the tiny grooves of the mysterious engraving, which somehow looked familiar. As I traced the curving lines, I realized what it was—a mirror image of my family crest. I looked at Mr. Reinier, who seemed as curious as I was. His grin encouraged me. I glanced at my hand. With one tug, the ring slipped off. I pinched it between my index finger and thumb and pressed the gold face into the carving. With a tight twist, the lock released with a pop.

He clapped, excited like a five-year-old about to peek beneath shiny wrapping paper. I lifted the cover and peered into the hollowed out book. A thin wood disk about four inches in diameter was centered within. I picked it up with the greatest of care, and with my other hand I swept the interior, searching for a secret compartment. I felt my face go blank. I passed the book to Mr. Reinier so he could see it. "How long has this been here?"

"For as long as I've owned the shop. The previous owners explained the history of this room and what was in it. Said eventually various wizards and witches would show up to claim their family books."

"But I don't own this book."

"You have inherited it, like the key. It's yours."

"This must be a mistake. It's not what I was looking for."

"You must have more faith than that. Your ring opened the lock. It's not a mistake. Read the writing on the disk."

The etched words looked like calligraphy. "I can only read part of this."

"Let me see." He adjusted his glasses.

I leaned my elbows on the table, waiting intently for his thoughts.

"The etching is exquisite," he said, seeming to enjoy the mystery that left me with even more questions.

"What does the whole message mean?"

"It's definitely Latin, but unfortunately, I cannot translate," he said, handing it back to me. "I studied French."

"The parts of the message I can read are plant names. Why would plant names be used in this old message?"

"*Je ne sais pas.* I don't know."

I sighed with frustration. "Thank you for your help."

"It really was a pleasure." Mr. Reinier eyed the book like a treasure collector.

"Why don't you keep that? I don't need it, and it seems like the least I can do for you after keeping it safe all these years."

His withered face lit up. "I will, but if you ever need it, please return." He picked up his treasure and cradled it like a cooing baby. Down the spiral stairs and back to the counter, he set the hollowed out book down and placed the wood disk in a plastic bag for my safekeeping. "*Bon chance.* Good luck."

"Thanks." I tucked the bag in my pocket and left the bookshop for home, but every time I glanced over my shoulder, I noticed a shadow keeping pace with me. Irritated, I made a swift turn into a vacant, tree-filled park. Sure enough, the menacing shadow followed. I quickened my pace and slipped behind an immense oak tree.

As the shadow drew closer, irritation triggered the magic and the energy swirled inside. I clenched a fist and recited the summoning spell. With my free hand, I pointed my fingers to the ground and thought only of what I wanted to happen. Thin strands of fire surged out and penetrated the earth. A root peeked up from the dirt and curled around the shadow's ankle, gripping firmly.

Slightly drained, I peered around the trunk when I recognized the girl's scratchy yelp. "Emme, why are you following me?"

She reached in her pocket where she kept her vial and then placed that hand in front of her mouth. She exhaled and blew her harmful mist onto the root. The root writhed and twisted in agony.

I winced. "Stop it!"

"Do you really think a root can hold me?" She laughed. "Hannah, we never talk. Why don't you start by telling me what you were doing at the antique shop?"

I did a double take. She must not have questioned my visit to a bookstore as anything out of the ordinary. I considered it a small bonus for being a book nerd. "Your nightmaring mist works on trees?"

"It's very potent. I incorporate my essence into it with my breath. That's where the real magic comes from. Obviously." She stared at the root. "Actually, I never tried it before on plants, but apparently it does." The wood disk felt like an osmium weight in my pocket. "I'm going to make this easy for you to understand, Hannah. I know what you did. It was a dirty trick using plant magic to make my mother look old, although it was nice to see the darker side of you, and it was fun sliming your hair with my skunk goo."

"Yeah, lots of fun."

"You're more badass than I thought. Are you sure you're not a Grey?"

The question triggered my outrage. "Exactly what are you accusing me of, you who has taken up arson for amusement?" She really was a product of her bloodline, a very strong one.

She glared with ice in her eyes and stuck a hand on her hip for only a second before pouncing. She grabbed my arm and pinned my hand to the ground before ripping the ring from my finger. "This has to be the key."

With my free hand, I clutched onto her leg, trying to channel the fire to my fingers before she escaped with the precious heirloom. We landed on the grass, rolling in the leaves, but she held tight to my ring and jumped up, standing over me triumphant.

"I should have followed my mother's lead and taken care of my own business weeks ago instead of delegating it."

"Give it back. *Now!*" I pressed my fists to my head. Rage shuddered within me so hard, my entire body vibrated. I cast the spell, threw my hands out, and released the power with intention. It rushed into the ground below.

Beneath my legs, the ground shook and fractured as if it was being unzipped. Emme fell backwards from the quake that grew more violent.

The tearing was deafening, as if we were standing near a never-ending freight train, thundering past. Trees along the crack fell into the widening gap. Emme's eyes grew larger as the earth near her feet crumbled into the gaping fissure.

"Hannah, help me!" She grasped the ring firmly in one hand and shook it as an offering.

I inhaled a deep breath and calmed down. I glimpsed the outline of the old disk in my pocket, confident she'd never go after anything that wasn't made of precious metal. The quake settled to a subtle tremor and then silence. I set my clear gaze on her. "There is no eternal youth elixir, Emme. It's an oasis. It doesn't exist."

She seethed. "I've read about it. It does exist."

"You can read fake news, but it doesn't make it true."

She uttered a scoff. "The fact that this stupid ring bears the Fitzgerald crest does make it unlikely it could be related to anything so important, but there is a key, and if you have it, I'll stop at nothing to get it."

224

"Even if my ring was a key, you don't know where the lock is, do you?"

"Is that why you were out shopping today?"

I set my gaze on her and tried not to show a liar's tell. "Not that it's any of your business, but I was searching for an old time record player so my aunt could play her disco albums. Something to cheer her up, no thanks to you."

"Whatever," she snorted, seeming to believe me. "I'm going to make you a promise." She stepped around the fractured earth, smacking the ring in my palm and grabbing my shirt. A shadow fell over her and her eyes darkened to the point she didn't look like the girl I'd known these past few weeks.. A more wicked than usual smile crept across her face. "I'm never going to stop looking, watching, and going after the ones you love, until I get what I want."

I summoned my last bit of strength and ripped her hand from my shirt. I gripped it tight. "Are you willing to die trying?" As I looked into her soulless eyes, I saw her killer intentions. Disappointed, I released her. "You're pathetic, Emme."

A deep, low snarl rose up from behind her. A pair of large hands clasped onto her shoulders, and from the clenching of his jaw, it seemed like Mateo was restraining himself from doing something awful.

"Mateo, don't," I said.

Another deep animal growl vibrated from his chest, more intense than the last. He pressed closer to her ear as she writhed to escape. He reached around her collarbone, and with a subtle squeeze, he pressed the breath out of her. Her eyes watered as she struggled to clutch him with her demon-like claws.

"Everything okay, Hannah?" he asked keeping his eyes locked on Emme, whose face screamed with fury. She snorted for breath and scratched at his muscular forearm peeking out from the sleeve of his gray jacket.

"I was handling it just fine before you got here, but I'm not complaining about your company," I said. "Actually, I am in awe of your realistic growl."

"Ever since I found my animal spirit, I've really synced with it."

"Clearly. Now, can you knock it off before someone sees you?"

He glanced around. "There's no one here, but us, Hannahbell." He released Emme and stood next to me, shoving his hands into his cargo pants pockets. "Pretty cool, huh?" he said, totally ignoring her flustered state.

"To say the least."

"It's an Incan thing." He shrugged his shoulders as if it was nothing then flashed his gaze on Emme, who looked stunned. "My animal spirit, Apu, doesn't like evil. So you, especially, better watch your back."

She straightened her disheveled clothes, glaring at him as if she was adding him to her growing blacklist. "You both better watch your backs." She whipped around with a huff and marched away.

I looked up at Mateo who tried to contain a snort of laughter.

"You named him Apu?" I asked.

"Means god of the mountains, his natural territory, so yeah. Hey, don't forget. Tomorrow night. Nine o'clock. Need you there."

"Can you do that growl thing on command?"

He waggled his eyebrows suggestively. "You like that, huh?"

"Kind of." I pressed a knuckle to my lips as puzzle pieces swirled in my head. "How do you make the sound so realistic and terrifying?"

"Apu is a part of me. I can tap into his strength any time I need it."

I thought of Mateo embracing his animal spirit. He was between two worlds; human and mystical, like the Magician in the Tarot card, and he wasn't the only one. With a mental snap, the pieces fell into place. "I'll be there at nine, Mattyboy." I patted him on the shoulder. "Thanks for your help with Emme, but you didn't have to."

"I wanted to. See you tomorrow."

As fast as I could run on weak legs, I hurried to Calvert Manor to the family chapel and rattled the locked doors. I pounded wildly. "Dammit, where are you?"

A door swung open. William met my crazed expression. Even with his sunglasses on, his gaze welcomed me. "Hannah."

"I can dig around and find out what your secret is, but I don't want to do that. With everything that's happened between us, it would feel dishonest, so I want you to tell me."

He grimaced and dropped his head.

I kept my feet planted. "I'm not leaving without the truth."

"Fine." He snatched a key from a nearby table and locked the doors behind us, ushering me into his Jeep. The only sound was British classic rock on the radio, but it didn't alleviate the tension between us, which was thick and conflicted. Within minutes, we parked in an isolated cove.

"Why here?"

"It's private, which may or may not be a good thing, but here we are. Don't move." He clicked his seatbelt, ran around the car, and opened my door.

From the trunk, he removed a plaid wool blanket. His warm hand clasped around mine, sending a small shiver across my skin and causing my determination to falter.

He led me to a narrow strip of beach where the fragrance of sea life drifted off the small waves crashing against the shoreline. A blue heron, painted dark by the tree shadows, swooped low over the water, oblivious to us while it searched for dinner.

He spread the blanket on the sand in a spot where tall sea grasses and lush willows surrounded us, and where the sun shined through, casting a warm glow on our faces.

I lay back on the soft blanket, my stomach fluttering. He lay down next to me and leaned over, gently stroking the side of my face with one hand.

"You're making me nervous," I said.

"I'm the one who's nervous. I thought the splashing of waves on the sand would keep me calm, but my heart is racing a million miles per hour." He traced my lips with his finger.

An imaginary earthquake shook the ground beneath us as the wall of secrets crumbled away. "I'm nervous, but I'm not afraid. No matter what you tell me."

He tensed his jaw muscles. "You should be afraid."

"Tell me."

Sitting up again, he plucked an old oyster shell from the sand and tossed it into the water. With a *plunk*, it sent ripples racing outward. "I want you to know everything." He paused, staring into the distance.

I pushed myself up. "Whatever you're hiding, it won't change how I feel."

"I'm not worried about you liking me less. I'm worried about what could happen to you because you want to be near me."

My heart fluttered. "I told you I'm not afraid."

He grasped both my hands and stared solemnly into my eyes. "Hannah, what if I told you I was destined to kill you?" There was nothing ambiguous about the danger he imparted with his question. "Would you be afraid then?"

I stared at his tender lips and square jaw and the gentle way he tilted his head when he spoke to me. I considered his honesty, and how he had helped me see my magic as something important. "No."

His breathing picked up, he turned away, seeming distressed by my lack of fear. "My bloodline is cursed."

He paused, listening to my response the same way he had watched my reaction when he showed me the scar. Did he think I would freak from his confession when I'd always thought my own family was plagued with bad luck and misfortune? I maintained control, more curious than anything else. He reached for me, trailing his fingers along mine.

"The curse marks me inside and out as an outcast among the ordinaries and our kind." He pressed his palm to his forehead.

"Go on."

"The Arundell Curse, which I inherited through my family, became the Calvert's curse…"

I interrupted. My heart raced. "The night of the Annapolis Tea Party?"

"Yes, that fateful night, two hundred and fifty years ago. It not only disfigured my face, but it leaves the killer in me hungering for vengeance any time a Grey witch is near."

Aunt J hadn't been kidding about the story being more than an urban legend.

"This year you, Emme, Navan, Arora, and a few others, all Grey witches, came fully into your powers."

Denial rolled right off my tongue. "You must be mistaken, because I'm not a Grey."

He seemed certain in his conclusion. "I'm not mistaken. There is a drop of Grey blood in your family somewhere, because the curse doesn't lie."

I shook my head, but then I realized. The only family stories I ever heard were about my dad's side. I never questioned my mom about her side. Ugh. Was it possible I was related to someone like Emme? I thought of how I had sought revenge for what Emme had done to Aunt J, and how I had struggled with my anger around my frenemy. I dropped my face in my hands. "It can't be true."

"I'm afraid it is. That's why my father and I thought it best if I left Truxton High and lay low. No need to kill anyone."

His dark humor lightened the mood. I peeked up at him. "So you live in the chapel at Calvert Manor and that works for you?"

"It's safer if I'm isolated."

"You're not dangerous."

"I haven't lost control yet, but the pain it causes me, it's like my blood is on fire and the only way to cool it is, well, you know."

"What about the rest of your family? What do they think?"

A sad expression washed over him. "Chase and my father are supportive, and my uncle has helped me understand the burden, but my mother couldn't handle the stress. She left us."

"I'm sorry." My heart ached for him, mostly because I understood the pain of being abandoned. "I shouldn't have asked."

He stared into the distance. "Don't apologize, Hannah. I want you to know everything. Last year, sometime after I turned sixteen, that's when this wretched scar appeared." He touched his hand to his cheek. "And my eyes changed. The irony is that I've always been good at healing. However, this scar never heals. It's like the rot that happened to my soul is mirrored on my face."

"What happened after that?"

"You showed up in a burning car and turned my whole angry, self-loathing world upside down. Suddenly, it wasn't about me anymore." He turned his compelling gaze on me. "You're everything to me, Hannah. I know it's been stormy, but that's because we're both so stubborn and hotheaded."

"Yes, we are. I think that's why we get each other. You're the only person who has ever understood me, seen me for what I am, and I hope you know that I see you, too. You're this amazing boy who is fiercely loyal and protective. I've never met anyone like you. You're everything to me, too." A dizzy feeling encompassed my head. My cheeks heated. "I want to see you without the sunglasses."

He frowned, but his hand lifted. With a tremor, he slowly removed the sunglasses and set them down. I waited. My heart stalled.

His clear, arctic eyes gazed into mine. It seemed like forever since the first time I'd seen them.

"They're shocking, aren't they?" His glistening eyes, framed by curving black eyelashes and thick dark eyebrows beckoned my acceptance.

"Your eyes are lovely. Exquisite, really."

"They mark me as cursed. I'm cursed, Hannah. Even now, the pain of being near you is excruciating." His strained voice reminded me of the dream I had when he was still a shadow to me. "When I first saw you trapped in your car, I sensed you were a Grey just as I sensed Emme was, too. The pain and the raging fire in my veins that night alerted me."

I drew back. "Wait. What do you mean? Emme was there that night, too?"

"Yes. I'm certain."

"Of course, she was." I set my jaw, angry.

He looked away from me as if it hurt him so greatly to confess his terrible secret out loud. "That night—I feared the curse would take over so I forced myself to run away. If I hadn't? Honestly, it frightens me to think what I would've done. I couldn't hurt you. If you died in the car, it would've been an accident, and I wouldn't have been the cause. I can't tell you how much I hated myself afterward. But something else happened, too. When I look back, I realize it was that night that I fell under your spell."

I tilted my head slightly to the side. "My spell? If you're right about the Grey thing, then it was my ancestor, not me, who cast her spell on your family ages ago."

"It was you who bewitched me that night and in the best possible way. As soon as I saw you, I knew there was something about you and the strength you exuded. Even the ring on your finger declared you were special. Everything about you triggered a strong reaction in me. Something I'd never felt before." His fiery gaze drifted from my eyes to my mouth. "The two of us together, though..." His forlorn eyes seemed to plead for understanding. "Do you think we're pushing our luck?"

I shook my head, a lock of hair falling across my cheek. With his finger, he brushed it aside. "William, I trust you more than I've ever trusted anyone."

"Even after the wolf incident?"

I was immediately whisked back to our last fight. I recalled every detail of the attack. "Tell me what happened to you at the pond after I rolled into the ditch."

"When I heard you scream for help, I lured the wolf away. He attacked me, shredded my clothes, my skin, but I didn't care as long as you were safe." He smiled, seeming pleased with that terrifying thought. "My concern for you, for your safety seemed to diminish the pain that day."

"I didn't see a mark on you at the chapel."

"You wouldn't have. I'm a wizard with a few tricks of my own." He clasped my chin between his thumb and index finger, demanding my attention. He gazed deeply into my eyes. His lower lip trembled ever so slightly. "After we argued, I convinced myself that being apart was better for you. After all, you were well on your way to mastering your magic. You didn't need me any more, so why tempt fate? But I soon realized how foolish that decision was because keeping my distance from you is worse than the curse itself."

"What are you saying?"

"I can't live without you." He clasped his hand around mine.

I furrowed my eyebrows inward. "This curse is what you meant when you told me fate didn't deal you a fair hand."

He nodded and looked down, staring at nothing except the sand around us.

"It'll be okay." I touched my hand to the scar on his face, wanting the tenderness of his eyes back on me.

"Unfortunately, I don't think it will be."

"What do you mean?"

"Some people visited my family's cemetery at Baltimore House."

"That place is *your* family's ancestral home?"

"Yes, along with Calvert Manor."

My breathing grew shallow. What the hell was Emme up to?

"The problem is, they dug up an ancestor of mine and used witchcraft tools to extract something very telling from an ancestor of mine."

"How did you find out?"

"A custodian informed my father. He said two girls and an older man went into the cemetery and left an hour later, leaving the stone lid of a sarcophagus ajar along with their strange tools around the base."

I swallowed the lump in my throat. "The two girls were Emme and Navan." I stared at him, not wanting to ask, but knowing I had to. "Wh-what did they take?"

"They extracted a silver bullet."

I gasped as I thought about Emme's father's shooting party coming up. Desperation seized me. "Never mind them. Have you ever tried to break the curse? There must be a way."

"My father and uncle have been searching for decades without any success." His focus drifted for a moment. "On the bright side, if there is a bright side, one benefit of the curse is that I can't be killed except with time and," he paused, "one other way."

My heart raced. "A silver bullet." I hated what fate had handed us both. I wanted it to change or go away, but it was looming on the horizon like a big, fat, black hole ready to suck us in. I waited, my breathing silent.

"Through the heart."

"Like a werewolf?" There was a tremble in my voice.

"Yes, the Arundell Curse is similar to a were-curse in that way." He tightened his broad shoulder muscles and clenched his jaw.

My somber gaze met his. "You read the warning note I sent with Siris, didn't you?"

"You think Emme's going to take me down with a silver bullet?"

"I'm not saying it will be Emme herself, but I know what I saw in my dream and you told me she means us both harm. Promise me you won't take any chances."

"Of course I won't."

"She's d-desperate to hurt me," I stammered, "no matter the cost to anyone else."

He voiced a throaty growl. "It takes everything in me not to end that witch and she knows it." His body trembled. He grabbed his head with both hands and closed his eyes.

"Are you okay?"

"Wait," he eked out through clenched teeth and closed eyes. A moment later, his shoulders relaxed and he opened his eyes. Struggling with the pain of the curse seemed to be more than enough for him to bear.

"Don't worry about Emme. I plan to face her on my own, and you've helped me prepare for that."

He drew back. His temples bulged from the pressure of his bite. "You don't understand. Anything that threatens you or your happiness is my fight whether you like it or not." A snarl rumbled deep in his throat. "I can't let you fight her alone. She's too dangerous."

"You said you were dangerous, and I'm still here."

He creased his brow with concern. "Is that a joke?"

I needed him to chillax. "I have a plan."

"If I'm not involved, it's not happening."

"That's just it. You are involved. I can't handle what might be coming if you don't help me, and I'll be forever grateful."

"I don't need gratitude. I need you to be safe."

"Then let me show you how strong my power is now." Feeling exhilarated in his presence, I tapped into the buzzing magic with tightened fists and the spell on my lips. I channeled the fiery energy through my fingers in a thread-like stream over the water's surface to churn up my amusing idea. A small waterspout formed and danced in front of us.

The wind rolling off the misty twister tousled our hair and then the spout dropped onto the sand, leaving behind a clump of seaweed. I flitted my fingers in the breeze, releasing more energy. The wind blew the wet seaweed up the beach and coiled the grass around his wrists in a loose knot.

He grinned, tugging at the simple restraint. "Impressive, but I've seen you do more than that."

I blew a warm sweet nothing into the air and the seaweed dropped away. My muscles only felt a little bit shaky. "Do you really want me to summon a lightning strike? Because I'd like to save my energy for something else." Heat stirred the air between us.

A sexy grin tugged at his cheeks. "A bolt of lightning would be overkill, don't you think?" He took my hand and intertwined his fingers with mine. "Do you think you'd ever be able to consider...?" His fire-and-ice eyes invited me to come closer.

"Consider what?" I looked up at him from beneath my lashes. The tension between us reached a white-hot pitch. He slipped one hand around my waist and cradled my cheek with the other. The heat from his body radiated to mine. My breathing grew shallow and fast. He hesitated, holding my gaze before slowly leaning in.

There was no misinterpreting the love he felt for me. I wrapped my arms around his neck and closed my eyes.

He pressed his warm lips against mine. My stomach tightened. Our mouths parted and our tongues explored, tender at first, then hungrily. His pressed me closer to him. His racing heart pulsed against my chest. He inhaled a breath through his nose and pulled back, seeming light-headed.

"You okay?"

"More than okay. I don't feel cursed when I'm with you. In fact, I've never felt happier and the feeling scares me."

"Why?"

"Because I can't forget what I am and let my guard down."

Beneath my hand, his heart pounded. The rapid beat matched my own. "Shh. Calm down. Stop talking," I whispered and pulled him back to me.

He nuzzled his lips against the sensitive skin on my neck. "I want you to be mine," he moaned.

Flutters filled my body. "I am yours. All of me, heart and soul."

His lips brushed against my throat and beneath the hollow under my ear. "And your body?"

I sighed, wanting nothing more than him—all of him. "Yes, but not..."

"No. Not now. When this is over."

He trailed his lips from my jawline to my earlobe. Our passion heated to an unbearable longing. I slipped my hands under his shirt and explored the smooth skin of his strong shoulders and back.

Another moan tore from his throat. I ran my hands through his hair and pressed his face closer. I traced my tongue over his lips. Then I kissed him, my mouth on his, the fever building.

I pulled back and inhaled a breath. I blinked, taking in all the details of his face and thinking about being with him.

"You okay?" he said.

"Uh-huh." I paused. "I am curious about something."

"Go on." He sighed pleasantly. "I'll answer anything."

Me too, I thought. "After I brought the Calvert gardens back to life…"

"Yes, I remember. I chased your attacker away so I could take care of you, and then I brought you home."

"Um, but when you changed me into my pajamas—did you look?"

His cheeks flushed crimson. "No, I swear. I sort of fumbled it with my eyes closed." He stared at me. "Are you sure you're okay?"

"There's one other thing."

"Say it."

"There are rules I'm breaking."

His perfect lips pursed. "Coven rules?"

"Mm-hmm."

Reality settled into his brow. "I nearly forgot about that."

"I know it's ridiculous, but wizard or not, you would be perceived as an outcast by the coven. I would be sent away and Aunt J would be left behind to suffer the consequences of my choice."

He sat up. "Are you serious?"

I nodded. "Water witch serious."

He considered it for a moment. "So I'll remain isolated. It's probably better that way since I can't take the chance in losing control of myself around Emme and her followers."

"I'm tired of her winning, and I won't stop seeing you. I won't."

A half-grin lightened his expression. "Agreed. Let's keep meeting privately."

It was the only way because I couldn't live without him either, regardless of the short time fate was giving me.

here was nothing I could do with the wooden disk from the bookshop or my promise to Aunt J until I had more time. The last few days, perfume and potion orders rolled in at Flower Power. Summer was a lifesaver, offering to make all the deliveries in her little hatchback. She made three trips, returning at eight-fifteen.

I straightened up the receipts. "Thank you for helping me tonight. I owe you a lifetime of chocolate milkshakes."

"No probs." She glanced at my face. "You look really pretty tonight and you're not even wearing makeup, not that you ever wear much."

"Just lip-gloss, but thanks. I decided I'm not a big fan of pretending to be something I'm not."

She kept staring. "There's something else, too."

"What?"

"What's put the smile back on your face?"

I neatened a stack of invoices. "Huh?"

She arched an eyebrow. "Or should I say who?"

My smile widened. "I've been spending more time with William."

"Awesome. So that means you've secured him for the ball, right?"

I threw my head backwards. "Ugh. I've been so busy I haven't even thought about that."

She stomped her foot. "Hannah! Seriously."

"Stop worrying."

"Fine. Hey, I gotta get going. Big night."

"Yeah. I'll be a few minutes behind you." I counted the cash in the register.

"You can ride with me."

"I've got to close up. You go ahead."

"How are you going to get there?"

I waved her off. "Stop worrying. See you in a few."

I wiped the counter down, locked the register, and yanked the floral pick from my messy knot. I shook my hair loose so it cascaded over my shoulders. I rolled Rusty from the back room out to the area behind the shop and shoved the oversized black helmet on my head. With a twist on the handlebars the engine revved and I was on my way to Summer and Mateo's uncle's farm near the Severn River. Fifteen loud minutes later on several bumpy back roads, I parked the bike next to a tree in a grassy makeshift parking lot.

South American music played and a bonfire cast its glow around the fields. The summer smells of burning charcoal, fragrant chili peppers, and roasting tomatoes filled the air. A dozen male Roca family members stood around the fire, wearing grass skirts and umber and carmine headpieces with long dark feathers jutting straight into the air. Summer strolled past me, mumbling in a zombie-like state.

"Summer! Wait up."

She twisted around. "I'm so afraid I'm going to mess up. An annoying twin brother I can handle, public speaking, not so much." She held a piece of paper in a death grip.

"Is this the story of the vain woman searching for the waters of youth?"

Her gaze drifted back to the paper. "No. It's a story about Mama Ocllo, the Incan goddess of spinning, and I have to recite it from memory. My mother told me this story when I was little. She mixed Incan mythology with Greek to explain the power of fate. It's not pure, sort of like my mom who is Incan mixed with Greek, but I like it. It's representative of my and Mateo's family history."

"It's nice you have an Incan tribe to belong to. We should form our own group. A clique with you, me, and who else?"

"I thought we already were a clique, unofficially."

I laughed. "I guess we are."

"We need a name. Every official clique needs a name. What do we call ourselves?"

"Hmm. You and I are pretty fierce. How about the Warriors?"

She laughed. "You know I like it. We're officially the Warriors. Now, let me practice my story on you."

"Go."

She held the paper at her side and recited the tale. "For each human life, Mama Ocllo spins a thread, determines the length, and cuts it. The thread is known as fate and it is unique to every individual. One day, the high priest heard his child was ill. He sent for medicine men to heal him and high priestesses to pray over the child. Sacrifices were offered to appease Supay, the god of death, but to no avail. As the boy weakened and Supay summoned him, the high priest turned to Mama Ocllo, pleading with her to extend the boy's thread of life. She, merciless and without pity or remorse, ignored his pleas. As the boy grew sicker still, the priest decided to take matters into his own hands and change his son's destiny no matter the cost. He sailed out to the center of the great lake and dumped into the water an offering of emeralds and gold for the goddess Copacati who dwelled at the bottom. He prayed for her to intercede. When Mama Ocllo learned of the priest's transgression, she punished him. After the boy died, she spun strands of sickness and disease into the threads of every child born in the village from that day forward. For generations, the tribe suffered great losses and learned to never interfere with fate again."

I stood there like a hungry bird with my mouth open. "That's an amazing story. They're going to love it!" But as I pondered the meaning, my stomach twisted into a loose knot. "So the moral is, don't interfere with fate or everyone has to pay?"

She nodded. "Exactly."

"That's not fair, though."

"No, it's not, but we were taught as children to accept what fate has laid out for us."

"What's wrong with wanting to alter it?"

"Trying to alter fate is like trying to turn a snake into a vegetarian. And we both know that's not possible."

It was the last thing I wanted to hear as my own fate played out like a tragedy. "Sounds like a warning."

She shrugged her shoulders, not understanding my meaning. How could she? We were officially part of a clique, but she didn't need to know I was allocated a fifty percent chance of living beyond sixteen. Not now. My eyes drifted to the waxing moon hanging in the sky.

"Are you okay? You look suddenly preoccupied."

"Um, I'm fine, really, and tonight isn't about me. It's about Mateo."

"And don't think he isn't loving the attention. He's such a butt-face."

A small laugh escaped my throat. "Speaking of Mateo, he told me you know a lot about Annapolis history, and I wanted to know if you could help me with something."

"Tonight?"

"Of course not. But soon. I made a promise to Aunt J and I'll need help with it."

"Absolutely. Anything." She paused. The tribal music in the background played louder, inciting the crowd to dance. Her gaze drifted over my shoulder. "My mom is signaling to me. Ceremony's about to start." She flapped her hands, shaking off the excitement. "Come on."

We raced toward the crowd. The adults were passing around cups of corn beer Summer called *chichi* while the bare-chested boys, including Mateo and Blaze, followed behind his uncle, the leader, who signaled for silence. The wind instruments withered to quiet before he spoke.

"Tonight, we gather to induct these boys into our tribe as young men. They have performed acts of valor, endurance, and bravery. They have discovered their animal spirit guides and tonight we celebrate."

Family and friends broke into raucous shouts and cheers. The uncle tossed a handful of pellets into the blaze and the flames exploded to new heights, hissing and crackling. Louder cheers ensued. The boys circled around the fire and the uncle blessed them in their exotic tribal language.

Summer approached the circle and stood next to Mateo. She recited her myth with unbridled enthusiasm.

After the final blessing, the uncle introduced each boy with his new tribe name and then the women opened the lines to the tables layered with decadent displays of ancient Peruvian foods and sweets. I pushed through the crowd until I stood face to face with Mateo. He yanked me into a bear hug, smearing red war paint all over my yellow sweater, which looked like ketchup on a mustard background. We looked down and laughed. "You feel like a man, now?" I said, trying to talk over the boisterous crowd.

"Look at me. War paint, gauchos, animal spirit guide…that's gotta make me a man." He took his finger, dabbed it across a line of red paint on his chest then smeared the red pigment across my cheeks. "Now, you look like you fit in around here."

I smiled, touching my fingers to the oily red streak on my face. *Caw, caw.*

I whipped around. "Siris?"

Mateo followed my gaze. "What's your familiar doing here?"

"Ever since we discovered him at Quiet Waters Woods, he's been showing up at—unusual times."

"Looks like he wants your attention. I'm gonna feast on my aunt's roasted salsa and tortillas."

"I'll hurry back." I padded to the water's edge. Siris glided in, landing on the rail of the dock. I slowly approached him, noticing he rested on one foot. Clasped in his elevated talon was a small roll of paper. His ice blue eyes beckoned me closer.

His feathers tickled my hand as I reached under and plucked it from his grip. When I unfurled the paper, another floated out. I snatched it up before a breeze swept it out to the river. Under the radiant torchlights, I skimmed over the information. The first was the torn page from the stolen gold book with Navan's handwritten translation beneath the Latin. I read part of it.

The twin potions of the Witch's Breath have mirror effects— one brings immortal youth and the other causes rapid aging.

I gasped. It was an ancient version of fake news, just as I suspected. The gold book was a ruse that had fooled Emme and Navan. I glanced at the second slip of paper, a receipt for a custom order placed at Carson's Powder River Armory. These two pieces of paper could only have come from the Blackstones' house and there was only one person who had told me he was good at slipping into places he shouldn't be. William. I paused, recalling Mrs. Fairchild mentioning the Powder River Armory, and then I saw it—one case of sterling silver twelve-gauge shotgun shells and one box of sterling silver bullets. My mouth dropped open.

"No!"

Caw, caw. My raven's angelic wings beat the air like a drum. He nodded his head and took flight, soaring toward the grassy parking lot.

My heart pounded. The whole world blurred around me as I raced to the moped and jumped on, leaving the helmet behind.

The raven flew ahead of me while I maneuvered with one eye on the road and one on the sky. I didn't know where he was going, but I trusted him. I zipped into Quiet Waters Woods behind him, the area as black and grim as my fears. When Siris perched in a tall oak, I leaped off the moped. My feet hit the ground in a panicked run and I raced into the deepening dark. My legs moved like heavy rubber. I had to focus on putting one foot down and then the other to be sure I kept going. "William!" I screamed. My pulse hammered in my ear. "William!"

The crack of a rifle shot shattered the silence of the woods. I should have known better.

Another crack.

It wasn't a party. It was a single shooter. I ran toward the shots, tripping over stumps and uneven ground. Thorns on wiry stems scratched at the tender skin of my ankles. "William!"

With a snap followed by a discernible groan of agony in the near distance, I realized he was down.

I ran in that direction, my shaky legs extending as far as they could go, and my lungs working double time. A figure writhing on the ground brought me to a standstill. "W-William?"

"Hannah. Get out of here. Now!" he commanded. His velvet voice was gravelly and pained.

I slammed into the ground next to him, my hands searching for the sticky dampness of a gunshot wound. "I'm not going anywhere." I couldn't. Fate had brought us together, and a common enemy had melded us into something extraordinary, the way hot white lightning fused sand into a glass sculpture. "What happened? What's wrong?"

Crack.

I jumped to my feet, my senses on high alert. My heart stopped. The terror-filled shot echoed all around, but it was louder than before, closer.

"Get out of here. Please. I'm begging you. I can't live if anything happens to you. I can't."

I kneeled down beside him, shielding him with my smaller frame. "Why are you even here? You read my warning note." My hands trembled as I continued to search for the cause of his injury.

"Yes, but then Chase received a text. Thought it was from you. Message said for me to meet you here and that you were in danger."

Emme, I thought. "I didn't send him a text."

"I know, now." His breathing grew labored.

"Where's the pain coming from?"

"Ankle."

Cold metal met my touch with an unwelcome harshness. "What is this?" I strained to see in the dark.

"Trap. Can't pry it off." He growled. "Hannah, I'm struggling to control myself. You need to get out of here before I do something I'll regret."

"Don't talk like that. Just breathe and find a focal point," I said, recalling the Green Briar mantra. "I'll work on the trap."

He dug his hands into the earth, grabbing hold of whatever he could. "If I don't kill you, the shooter will. He's still out there. Leave me!"

I clenched my jaw as the magic fired up. "I trust you and I'm not leaving." I was resolute in my promise.

Another shot cracked through the silence, this time within a hundred yards. William's groans grew louder. The shooter would find us for sure, but how could I quiet him?

My thoughts raced as fast as my pulse. I could barely see, but I could smell and feel. "I'll be right back." I darted to my feet and searched. My hands patted down every tree trunk until I found what I needed—the hop vine. I plucked three mushy cones and dashed back to his side. "I trust you. Now trust me and eat these."

He moaned and took my cupped hands in his, pressing his lips to the hops and eating them. "Stay down and let the hops do their thing. Don't fight the drowsiness. Everything will be fine."

William obeyed. As soon as he closed his eyes, I darted away from him. I grabbed whatever I could find—pinecones and rocks—tossing them hard to lure the shooter toward me. "Come on, give me what I need," I eked out under my breath.

Crack. Whizz.

I dove on the ground. Another bullet sped past. "Perfect." Wrapped in darkness, I looped around a tree and raced toward the shooter with fists tensed. Whoever he was, he deserved the ass kicking of his life, and I was just the witch in just the mood to serve it up.

The man's paunchy silhouette stood poised. With a click, he reloaded another shell and cocked the rifle.

I leaped, my momentum knocking him to the ground. His head hit with a hollow thud and he whimpered.

With a furious rage igniting the magic, I cast my spell. The energy exploded. I channeled the fire to my fist and thrust it skyward, concentrating. Thunder rumbled. Winds groaned and began to gust at a speed that matched the pace of the adrenaline coursing through my veins. I commanded the wind to pick up two vines and entwine them around his flailing arms. I kneeled beside him and knotted the vine ends around his wrists.

"Let me go!"

"Who are you?" I asked, catching my breath. A brilliant, jagged ribbon of white gold crackled through the night sky, illuminating the coward's chubby face.

"Name's Kalvin. Let me go."

Suddenly drained, but undeterred, I beamed my phone light on his face. He was the same man I'd chased into the Historic Annapolis office. He looked older, like he was in his forties. "Well, Kalvin, if you ever go near me or my loved ones again, or if you ever do anything to hurt us, it will be the biggest mistake of your life." I snatched the rifle from the ground and demanded the rest of the shells. He nodded to his right. I scooped the ammunition up, leaving him bound.

"Get me out of here. You can't leave me like this."

I tossed a glance over my shoulder. "You left my beloved stuck in a painful trap. Consider this more humane."

With little energy, I managed to carry the gun and shells to the beach and toss them into the murky water. As soon as I heard the splash, I returned to William who lay asleep from the hops. I searched the trap for its hinges. With a hard push, the retreating inferno surged. I channeled the fire through my arms, to my hands, and directed the molten-hot strands of fire into the metal springs. The trap heated and glowed orange. Within seconds, the bolts softened and drooped. Once they melted, I pried the heavy metal pieces apart.

I slumped with relief before flashing the light from my phone on his swollen and bloodied ankle that was already healing. I leaned down and pressed a kiss to his cheek. He stirred. "William. We're safe. For now."

he next evening, I checked on William, and for the second time I was thankful for the foreboding dreams. What if Siris hadn't shown up? If he hadn't led me to the woods? Would Kalvin what's-his-face have succeeded with Emme's silver bullet plan to capture and kill my king in the twisted chess game we were playing?

The countdown clock ticked in my head. I hated it. I hated not having control of my own fate. This was my life and it was slipping away. With Emme blinded by ambition, fate would easily exact its toll.

I texted Summer to meet me at my house and bring her history expertise with her. An hour later, she arrived, wearing a black zip-up jacket with her black jeans, which made her white blonde hair stand out even more than it usually did. "How's your aunt doing?"

"She's sleeping, but feeling much better. Come in. I need your opinion on something."

"What happened to you after the ceremony?"

"Long story." She followed me to my aunt's study. "Here." I handed her the eighteenth century wooden disk I had retrieved from the old bookshop.

"Do you have a desk with a lamp?"

With a flip of the switch, light flooded the small room. Her green eyes grew wide as she absorbed the titles. "Wow, look at all these witchcraft books. Fascinating."

"Any chance you know Latin?"

"Of course."

"Of course?"

"Yeah, picked it up from the internet."

"Right." I shook my head, not sure whether to be impressed or ridiculously concerned with how she spent her free time. "Then read this."

She gripped the small disk and skimmed the etched words in Latin, concentrating on the clues in each line. Within seconds, her expression told me she understood what I didn't.

"Well?"

"*Maio florentem fructum* and *sub quercum et stilla ad glandes*? What's with all the plant references?"

"That's the Latin I could translate, but what about the rest?"

"It's weird. It's like a riddle. It says, 'In the yard of the flowering branch of the Jesse tree, a vine bearing foliage and grapes, within the shadow caster of Garrett's stone, the secret shall be concealed'." She glanced at me. "I also think it's a religious reference."

I creased my forehead with confusion. "What do you mean?"

"Well, the flowering branch of the Jesse tree refers directly to the Jesse Tree."

"I'm sorry. I don't know what that is."

"It's the lineage of Christ, but it is also symbolic of members of his family. The flowering branch of Jesse probably means a woman who was flowering, which is so cliché for being fertile. Ew, right? So either Mary or her mother Anne."

"So the secret is in the yard of Mary or Anne. Within the shadow caster of Garrett's stone..." My mind combed through the words. "Stone like a headstone?"

"And the yard would be a graveyard, right?"

"Yes, but which graveyard?"

Her eyebrows knitted together. "Um, St. Anne's or St. Mary's. Annapolis has one of each. However, this round, flat disk thing looks old. If it's from the seventeen hundreds or earlier then it's probably St. Anne's Church in the circle. Most of those graves start from the seventeen hundreds and..."

"What?"

"Garrett might be Amos Garrett, the first mayor of Annapolis. It would make sense if he was buried there, but what's a shadow caster?"

I smiled. "A shadow caster, of course, would be a tree."

"How do we know if a tree that was there in the seventeen hundreds is still there?"

I shrugged. "I guess it will be really big or unusual. We'll have to look around."

"If the secret is concealed within the shadow caster, or tree, how do we get it out?"

I smiled wryly. "Leave that to me."

"Wait. For what we're about to do, you should change into black, like me. Also, we'll need a flashlight and maybe a small shovel, just in case."

"There's a pocket flashlight in the kitchen, in the cabinet under the sink, and we won't need a shovel." I padded upstairs and changed into a black jacket and pants.

Summer waited by the front door for me, clutching her hands together. "This is going to be so much fun. Warriors rule!" She clapped her hands and was the first one out the door and in her car. I was less excited about hanging out in a cemetery.

Within minutes we arrived at the church only to spot a group of ladies wearing neon glow bracelets and pins on their jackets that said, *Kingsport Book Club*. They circled around a tour guide with a bright flashlight—a ghost tour.

After ten long minutes of spooky tales, the ladies moved on, leaving us alone with the deceased VIPs of colonial Annapolis.

We followed narrow brick paths between the stones, stepping on crusty leaves as we searched.

Summer flashed the light onto the face of each stone, searching. After twenty or more epitaphs, we finally found Amos Garrett's tomb. "Now what?"

"Look around for the oldest or most unusual shadow caster, I guess." My instincts were on high alert.

She snickered as we arched our necks. "They all look the same."

However, one seemed to call to me. Its leaves rustled in the night breeze, sounding like the whispers of children. "Over here. I think it's this oak." I touched my hands to the gnarled trunk and felt a weathered carving beneath my fingertips. Was it possible? I traced the swirling lines—the tree of life, an ancient goddess symbol that Aunt J liked. "Flashlight," I requested. She pressed it into my hand and I confirmed my suspicion. Perfect. "This is definitely the tree and now I know where to apply the woodwater."

"The what?" she whispered.

"It's a recipe my aunt taught me that will soften bark."

"Okay. What are we looking for exactly?"

I recalled the necessary ingredients. "I need you to find a small rock while I search for something gross."

"Works for me."

I checked all the tree trunks for the one thing that wasn't guaranteed to be in the churchyard, although Maryland had an invasion of the creepy crawlers earlier in the year. With a sweep of light around each tree I found nothing.

"Hannah, will this work?" She offered her find for inspection. The gray stone was the size of a small fist.

"Perfect. Now, if I can find what I need."

"What disgusting thing are you looking for? Eye of newt, toe of frog?"

Witch humor—awesome. "Hardly. I need one cicada exoskeleton. You know the amber shell they leave behind as they morph?"

She stuck her tongue out. "Yuck. That's almost as bad as eye of newt." With a few clicks on her phone's Google app, she seemed ready to help with the task. "Okay, I've got this." She lifted her head, sniffed the air, and began prowling.

I smelled the air, too, but sensed nothing out of the ordinary. "There's no way you can smell something that small."

"I told you it's one of my super powers, and in the dark it's heightened even more."

I flashed her a look of disbelief.

"Trust me. I'll work on the bug shell. You take the rock."

"Fine." I tiptoed to the sidewalk outside the churchyard and scraped the rock against the cement of the street curb, cupping my hand underneath to catch the sodium-filled powder. Outside of the cicada shell, the other ingredients would be easy to find. I plucked an evergreen leaf from a nearby rhododendron bush, ignoring the fact that rhododendron in Aunt J's flower lingo meant 'beware'. Then I gathered a pinch of brown pine needles from the ground beneath an obliging loblolly and scooped up a handful of damp peat moss from a flowerbed.

Summer approached me dangling the fragile amber shell in front of my face. "Here you go."

"I'm afraid to ask."

"Apparently, cicadas have a faint Limburger cheese scent when they decay, so the shells do, too."

"Wow. You're kind of weird in a good way, but at least you dare to be yourself."

"Aw, thanks."

I kind of loved that I was daring to be, too. I smashed everything together with my hands and mixed in a few drops of rainwater from a nearby puddle.

"Is this a witch's mud pie?" The snark was obvious.

I laughed. "You'll see." I smeared the concoction over the symbol in the trunk. Excitement stirred my magic. I clenched my dirty hands into balls and subtly whispered the spell. The power exploded. Concentrating hard on the spot, I emitted just enough fire to spark the chemical reaction. Within seconds, the crusty bark softened and thinned from the warm witchy solution. Then, to my surprise, a small hole appeared like a slot about four inches long.

I stretched my tired arm muscles before reaching in my pocket. I retrieved the disk. It fit perfectly and with a little push, it disappeared into the trunk. The bark around the slot fizzed and peeled away, revealing a larger hole. I reached in, hoping I wasn't disturbing a family of feisty chipmunks. Instead, my fingers brushed across a hard rectangular box. I reached both hands in and extracted the curious item. As soon as I set it on the ground, the hole in the trunk closed up. Summer rushed over.

"That was cool."

"Like an otherworldly vending machine, huh?"

"What's inside?"

"Let's find out." The box resembled the hollowed out book from Otto's so I felt along the side for the dime-sized lock. I removed my ring, inserting it as I did before. With a pop of the hinges, the cover lifted.

Summer shined the flashlight on the interior. "Is that a tiny scroll?"

I gently unrolled it while she held the light. "This one is written in English."

"Show me."

> *Virtue escaped ole Bladen's noose,*
> *and when he turnt to dust and bone,*
> *a secret she hid beneath his stone.*
> *A shield and knight watcheth over him in death,*
> *while Bladen watcheth over her clew to Witch's*
> *Breath.*

Summer seemed pensive. "I know who Virtue and Bladen are. Virtue Violl was the last woman to stand trial for witchcraft in Maryland thanks to Bladen, who was an eager attorney general from like the early seventeen hundreds."

I nodded. "Virtue was acquitted, but she was revealed as a witch to the town, which you can imagine didn't do much for her reputation back in those days. What about the rest of the poem?"

She turned her eyes back to the lines. "Not sure what the secret is, but according to this, I have a good idea where it is."

I grabbed her by her shoulders. "Nearby?"

"Yup. Follow me."

We tiptoed through the graveyard until she stopped in front of a large sarcophagus. She beamed the light across the surface where William Bladen's name was etched, and carved above that was an engraving of a knight and shield.

"Bam!" She giggled, seeming thrilled with the evening's adventure. "My mom would kill me right now if she knew what we were doing."

"Now what?"

"The rhyme said she hid the secret beneath the stone, so I guess it's inside the sarcophagus. Did you know sarcophagus means 'flesh-eating'?"

Bloody zombie images flashed in my head. "Is that factoid really important right now?"

"I know Mateo complains I'm a fountain of useless knowledge, but not so useless now, huh?"

I flashed my eyes to the ominous sarcophagus. "This is actually where Bladen's corpse is resting." Angst filled my voice as I thought about what lay inside the box.

"Does that freak you out?" She probably noticed my horror-filled expression.

Why couldn't the secret just be in the tree? "Well, unlike Emme, I've never seen a real corpse that's been rotting for hundreds of years, and I really don't want to."

"After all this time, there probably won't be much to it."

I cringed again. Dry and dusty like the crypt keeper. Perfect.

We both instinctively looked around and listened, hoping for no more visitors. The silence assured us we were alone with the former Governor Bladen and his guests. Summer moved to my side and we both pushed against the solid lid, grunting. She turned around pressing her shoulder blades into the lid while pushing with her slender legs.

The lid didn't budge. Not an inch. "Do you think they sealed it with some kind of mortar?"

I shrugged, having no idea how they buried people in the seventeen hundreds. "You're the keeper of useless knowledge, you tell me." I inhaled a deep breath, not wanting to dwell on the creepy factor of what we were doing. "Let's go again. Really dig your shoulders into it."

We grumbled and pushed. The stone refused to budge. I eyed our not-so-muscular frames and realized why Emme had brought a guy with her to the Calvert family cemetery. "We need something more than brawn."

A grin curled across her pretty face. "Something like Incan magic?"

I creased my brow. "Huh?"

"I thought Mateo might have told you."

"Told me what?"

Her green eyes filled with mystery as she held the flashlight out for me to take. "I have a secret, witch. Stand back and watch."

I walked a few steps back, curious and unsure what was about to happen. As soon as she started taking her clothes off, I threw my hands up. "Whatever you're doing, please stop."

"Give it a chance."

I turned away. "I can't watch."

"Suit yourself."

Seconds later, the throaty chuffing of a big cat forced me to spin around. Summer Roca, with her exotic coloring, had morphed into the most beautiful white jaguar. Her wide emerald eyes glistened and her white blonde hair was now plush fur.

I slapped my hand over my mouth to contain the shock. She slinked right up to the stone coffin, ignoring me completely. She rose up on her hind legs and pushed her big cat shoulder against the stone. The lid slid far enough to one side.

"What an amazing little secret you've kept. I guess that explains why you have such a great sense of smell."

She chuffed again.

What I really thought was that our clique was way cooler than Emme's. We could crush them. No probs unless Navan's foresight improved even more. I stepped closer. I shored up my courage with a deep breath and beamed the flashlight in. Thick webs filled every crevice around the old man's bones. "I'm a little freaked out right now, Summer." What if I accidentally disturbed them? What if a skeletal hand broke off and grabbed me?

Chillax, Hannah.

The light reflected off the spider silk like high beams in fog. I swept my fingers around the empty space between him and the stone encasement.

"Bladen watches over her clue to Witch's Breath," I recited, moving my hand closer toward his skull. I touched something small and leathery. My breathing stalled and I prayed to every star in the sky that it was not his brain.

Snap.

A twig cracked in the distance. Every muscle in my face tensed with urgency. I pinched the object between my thumb and index finger and snatched it out.

I flashed a panic look at Summer, the jaguar. "Shut the lid fast and change back. I hear someone coming."

I stuffed the flashlight in my pocket while she jolted to the other side of the tomb and shoved the five hundred pound stone back in place. Then, with a shake, she morphed back to herself and slipped into her jacket and jeans.

With my hand covered in cobwebs, I passed what felt like a small journal to my friend. Reading my serious expression, she tucked it in her waistband while I wiped the ick off my fingers.

The jingle of metal drew our attention to the cloaked figure in the graveyard. "Well, well, well. What are you two doing?" Navan said, flipping her copper-colored hair over one shoulder, the bangles jingling again. "Wait. Let me guess." From beneath her black wool cloak, she produced a glass ball that filled her palm. She raised it up, seeming mesmerized by what she saw within its center. "Oh my."

A swell of nausea rocked my stomach. "Enough with the drama. It's none of your business what we're doing. Now, leave us alone."

"Huh. That would be convenient—for you. However, my new crystal ball has shown me you were going to find something here tonight."

"Just a red-haired rat," Summer interjected while I stifled a snort.

"Something I want. I mean, something Emme and I want." She stuck her free hand out. "I'll take it now. Thanks."

I waved my empty hands. "That's weird because I don't have anything."

She glanced in the ball and her eyes popped. "Lies!" Her reddened cheeks tightened and she jumped in my face.

Startled, I shoved her backwards. She crashed to the ground with a hard thud. The crystal ball rolled free and landed next to Bladen's sarcophagus.

Navan lay there frozen with a stunned expression. I couldn't afford to waste the opportunity. I grabbed the precious globe as she shot upright.

"Summer, run!"

"Give it back, Hannah Fitzgerald! Taking my crystal ball won't change anything, including our date with destiny," she shouted after us, "and your time is running out."

We were already on the move, but her ominous warning resounded in my head. *Our date with destiny?* Did she mean with all the Queen Js or just her? We headed toward Main Street. One block down, we cut through a parking lot and came back up Franklin Street. Near the corner, we dashed into the unlit patio area behind Reynolds Tavern and ducked behind brick pillars, panting.

Summer wiped her sweaty brow. "What the hell was Navan doing there without her gaggle of witches?" She eyed me. "No offense."

"None taken, kitty cat." I held the fortune-telling ball in the air. "But I thought it was Emme's gaggle of witches. At least Navan didn't foresee my reaction."

She snickered. "Hard to foresee something spontaneous and badass like that. So what are you going to do with that thing?"

The cold crystal weighed heavy in my hand while the dread of her improved foresight remained fresh in my mind. "I'll give it back, but not until we're done tonight." I set the ball down carefully by my feet. "Give me the book and hold the flashlight over it."

With a click, the light beamed over the small treasure. I examined the one-word title, *Veritas*, then I read a few passages, written in English. It looked rare and was interesting, but there was nothing about the Witch's Breath and the text wasn't written in Latin like I expected. I dropped my hands.

"What's wrong?" she asked in a whisper.

"I think this is a mistake."

"How could it be? We followed the instructions."

"I know. I don't think we messed up, but this book isn't what I thought it would be." I peered through the wrought iron fence to make sure Navan was not closing in on us.

"Let me see." She fanned through the pages then flipped back to the front cover. "Do you realize what the title means?" She held the book out with the flashlight over the words.

"What?"

"Truth. Does that mean anything to you?"

I gasped as Lady Arundell's words flashed back to me. "Actually, it does. Summer, this is going to sound crazy."

"Are you kidding? You just watched me morph into a jaguar and you transformed the trunk of a tree. I don't think it's getting any crazier tonight."

We'll see.

"Do you remember going to the library a few weeks ago?" She nodded. "What I didn't tell you was that Emme stole a book that day, one of the ghost's books."

"From the archives?"

"Yes. That book mentions two potions, but the information is wrong. I think a different book in the archives has the true answers we need."

"What if Emme went back for it?"

"She's too lazy to figure out that what she has may not be the pot of gold she thinks it is. And she might also be afraid of the ghost."

Her forehead crinkled. "You're not?"

"Ghosts I'm cool with, especially since she was a witch like Virtue Violl. I'm guessing Virtue left this to be found, knowing it would lead back to the protector of the true book."

"Appease the spirits, my uncle always says."

"What do you mean?"

"The ghost tour lady said Lady Arundell was a rare book collector, so I'm betting she's willing to reward a sister witch for finding a rare book like this."

She had no idea how right she was. She shook *Veritas.* "You think it's safe to go back to my car now?"

"Navan was so mad, she's probably halfway to Eastport looking for us."

We circled back to the other side of the church and jumped in Summer's car. Within minutes we were parked outside the library.

"You really think the ghost will show herself?"

My heart thumped hard with excitement. "I'm counting on it." I stepped into the shrubbery beneath a library window and studied the lock on the other side of the glass. Exhilaration brought the magic to life. I tightened my fists, cast the spell, and aimed an energized breath of hot air between the window separation. The lock jiggled, popped, and unlatched. We climbed in.

"Summer, give me the book," I whispered.

"Gladly." We tiptoed down the hall and into the archives room. She clicked on the flashlight and swiped the beam around the bookshelves. "Look at the dust in there."

I yawned, feeling slightly tired. "I don't think she likes visitors, including cleaning people."

"Can you summon her or something? This room gives me the creeps."

As soon as I brushed my fingers over a row of books, the temperature dropped several degrees in the already cool room and the white radiant glow appeared. Summer saw it first, silently nudging me in the ribs. I whipped around as Lady Arundell phased into her willowy white form.

She moaned and knocked an unopened box of archival gloves off the desk beside us. Summer jumped and yanked on my arm. "Give her the book, give her the book. Please, give her the freaking book."

"Be a brave warrior."

"I have no problem with flesh and blood enemies, but what am I supposed to do against a ghost?" Her teeth chattered.

"We've gone to too much trouble tonight to leave empty-handed. Close your eyes," I told her. Her shivering seemed to subside right away. I faced Lady Arundell's ghost and held the book in front of her.

Her figure undulated. On the wall she wrote, *Are you a worthy witch?*

"I found *Veritas* with Bladen. I think it's the truth you asked me to bring you."

Her ghostly head nodded. *You have earned your reward, then.*

She floated toward the shelves and pointed to a book on the bottom row.

"That one?"

She reached for the wall behind her. *You must return it.*

I dipped low and retrieved the book. The simple lead-gray cover revealed nothing, not even a title. "Thank you. I will."

What of the Book of Lies?

Book of Lies? She had to mean the golden one Emme stole. After reading Navan's translation, I knew something was wrong. "I'll do my best to return the other one." I waited, trying to interpret her ethereal movements. Her glowing form surged brighter for a brief moment and disappeared into the wall.

I elbowed Summer. "She's gone."

"Really?"

"Yes. Open your eyes."

Her eyes fluttered open. "Can we please go? I'm freezing!"

"Lady Arundell is too cool for school." I smiled. "Come on. Let's drop the crystal ball in Navan's mailbox then go back to my house and figure out why this book is so important."

In Aunt J's study, I gently flipped through the pages. Summer stood over my shoulder. "Some kind of history?"

"Yes, but that's not what matters." I opened the book to the first page and showed it to Summer.

"Latin again." She grinned and winked at me. "Fortunately, I can translate this, too."

"Read on, Miss Internet."

"*Te sunt coniuncta ad naturam. Habes vitae. Coelibatum salva. Elige sapienter misit mittique,*"

"And?"

Summer translated the message to English on a separate piece of paper, revealing the truth about the Witch's Breath. "The translation indicates there are two elixirs. The white one is a lifesaving elixir, known as the Breath of Life. The black one, the

Sigh of Death, will bring death to the uncursed or death to a curse."

"To a curse or a cursed person?"

Her gaze fixed on her writing. "I'm pretty sure it means death to a curse or else it would just say it brings death."

"I need you to be really sure."

She glanced at it again. "I'm really sure."

Her confidence was unwavering. "No mention of immortal youth, right?"

"Not that I see, but this part is interesting." She pointed to two lines, *Signa te, signa, temere me tangis et angis* and *In girum imus nocte et consumimur igni.* "You tell me, witch. Are these…spells?"

I glanced at the Latin phrases both in palindrome form. They were spells. "Even your guesses are right. It's so annoying."

"Thanks. So it seems you were on a quest," she said. "Those clues you uncovered were meant not only to prove you were worthy of the elixir, but also to teach you what it is and how to use it."

"It's hard to imagine I could be worthy of something so precious."

"Not so hard for me." Her gaze drifted back to the book. "You should also know your ring is more than a key."

Surprise settled over me. "What do you mean?"

"Your ring is the actual vessel, the key and the lock for one of the elixirs."

"Which one?" I pushed the clasp. The engraved bezel popped open, exposing the rounded mother-of-pearl cabochon. "I guess it's not a stone after all."

"And I guess from the color it's the Breath of Life."

At that moment, my hand felt like it weighed a hundred pounds, carrying around such precious oil.

Her eyes filled with concern. "What are you going to do now?"

"Someone unworthy is after this and the only chance I have to change my fate or cause some kind of change is to give them a choice."

"You can't change fate," she warned.

"I have to try, Summer." For so many, I had to try.

As the world outside went dark, the brilliant radiance hit me. The blinding light flashed brighter than ever before. It burned with ferocity. Then it dimmed. I watched the fog roll out to the water and the back of the familiar girl appear. She seemed different this time. What had changed? She didn't blow the powder into the air. Instead, she pointed a finger toward the fireworks exploding over town. A trail of sparkles rained down on the crowd. As the debris settled, people burst into screams. The elderly collapsed on the creek banks, but others raced toward the girl, wanting her to save them. Their faces aged and wrinkles deepened, even in the young.

Another spray of colorful light illuminated the mysterious girl's face as she turned in my direction. I bolted awake and gasped with recognition.

The girl was me.

"No. That can't be right. I'm not sure I can even save myself." The dream was more disturbing than all the others combined. I wiped the sweat from my brow and glanced at the reflection in my phone. In the eyes looking back at me I saw the inevitable— no matter what moves I made, a queen, whether she began as a pawn or not, would be taken before the game was over.

William said he was worried about me because of how pale and worn out I appeared, but how could I explain that searching through graveyards and haunted libraries for coven secrets drained a witch, even one with the power of fire at her fingertips?

With a little coordination, Chase arranged for William and I to spend time alone together, and since their father was still out of town, it made the most sense to meet at the Calvert chapel.

I waited until dark. Clouds obscured the moon, aiding me in my covert effort. I hurried past the front of the manor house, pausing only for a second to take in its changed appearance. The ivy was long gone, the landscaping refreshed and lush, and the brick walls had been recently power washed. I was pleased to see it as I dashed around the corner, slipping through the narrow opening in the brick wall where William waited.

I bit my lip, filled with excitement at the sight of him. I reached for his hand, but paused. "Why are you wearing your sunglasses?"

"I wanted you to have time to…"

"To what? Your eyes are beautiful and mysterious, like you." I reached up and removed the black spectacles.

His gaze sent butterflies fluttering about my stomach and his grin invited me into his arms. I swept into them with enthusiasm, the two of us nearly tumbling backwards into the grass.

He laughed. "My ankle is not completely steady, yet."

I shifted my feet so I wasn't leaning into him as much. "Sorry. How does it feel now?"

"Better since you got here." He rested his hands on my hips and a warm current took me under. "I don't remember what happened."

My head felt light from being near him. "I—I gave you something to sleep then I, um, took care of the shooter."

He laughed again. "I can only imagine what happened to him. But it's my job to protect you. Not the other way around."

"I'll make a deal with you. If a Calvert enemy ever comes after me, he's all yours. But my sister witches and their hired hands are my territory." I touched his cheek. "Do you mind if we don't talk about our families and breaking rules? Not tonight."

Concern filled his eyes. "I'll agree to that if you show me something you've worked on."

"Right now?"

"Yes. I can't relax unless I'm sure you can properly defend yourself."

"It'll wear me out," I whined.

"Save enough energy to be with me."

Unable to resist his request, I conceded. I focused on the intensity I felt being near him. The magic's hum started low and deep, then grew louder. With clenched fists and the spell floating off my tongue, the magic exploded like a bursting star. I threw my head back and flashed my eyes open, thinking of the only thing I needed to make the evening perfect. I wove my hands together, spinning the thinnest ribbons of fire skyward. Half-drained of energy, I stopped.

Clouds separated and sailed toward the east, revealing thousands of diamond-like stars that blinked above us.

He grinned a crooked grin. "Impressive. You've been practicing."

It was hard not to. The potential consequences of the coven prophecy provided enough incentive. "Are we good?"

He nodded. "We're going to be." I stared at the inviting chapel doors behind us. "Hannah?" He joggled my arm and brought me out of my daze.

"Y-yes?"

"Where are you?"

My head throbbed. "Oh. I was just thinking of…it's nothing. Tell me about this place. I've always wondered about its history."

He shook his head, not believing me. "You want a history lesson? No. Something's wrong. You look like you saw something terrible."

I shoved the latest revelation from my mind. I sighed and looked up at him. The jagged scar I'd come to hardly notice did not hinder the concern he exuded from every muscle in his face. "I want tonight to be about tonight and nothing more." I wanted to smooth out the worry lines on his brow with my lips and explore every inch of his hands with my fingertips. "Can you give me that?"

"When you look at me with those bewitching gray eyes, there's nothing I can deny you."

"Good. Let's go inside." He clasped my hand, his touch forcing me to catch my breath.

The interior of the sanctuary had been altered. The wood pews were gone, leaving an open area. Several lit candles on the altar dimly lit the space where a picnic dinner of parchment-wrapped sandwiches, grapes, and oatmeal cookies was laid out on a red gingham blanket.

He squeezed my hand a little tighter and led me to the blanket. "Where did the food come from? And what happened to the pews?" I asked. He smiled, as melodies from the outdoor concert playing from the park floated through the double doors. "Oh, the music is beautiful."

"I'm glad you like it." He extended his hand.

"What are you doing?" I laughed, hesitant as nerves gripped my tongue.

"Dance with me."

"I'm—I'm not sure that's a good idea."

"It's easy. I'll lead, and as much as you like to fight it, you follow." He slipped a decisive hand along my waist. My breathing came in shallow gasps.

"That's not what I'm afraid of."

The creases returned to his forehead. "Then what?"

I stared at his shoulder, ignoring the nerves that were taking me under. "I'm afraid of how much I want you." I peeked up.

The crooked grin lifted his cheeks. "Is that all?"

"That's kind of everything."

He pressed his strong hand into the small of my back, forcing me closer. With his other hand, he caressed my cheek. "No. That's the *beginning* of everything."

Nothing else mattered; no one else existed except us at that moment. It felt like we were floating around the chapel.

"I want you, too," he whispered, "but I won't rush this."

I wanted to rush. Rush right into the fever I was feeling deep inside.

He leaned down, his breath catching on my neck. I tipped my head back, my eyes closed as he lowered his lips to mine. He tasted sweet, like a ripe summer plum. I raked my hands through his hair, tangling my fingers as I tugged him closer. He was mine. He had always been mine. Whatever time fate granted us, I wanted to spend it with him.

When the music stopped, he trailed his lips along my throat, breathing in my fragrance. "Your perfume is driving me crazy."

I bit my lip. "It's called enchantress rose, named after the rose in *Beauty and the Beast*. Do you know the story?"

"I do, but refresh my memory." His voice was low and seductive.

I inhaled a shaky breath. "Because the beautiful girl desires a rose, she ends up living in a cursed beast's castle, and in the end, it's her sacrifice and her love that breaks his curse."

"So that's the effect of a beauty on a cursed beast?"

I stared at his shoulder and his neck, before forcing my eyes slowly upward. The bottomless pools of ice blue held me in a daze. He leaned down and pressed his face into my hair as he cupped his hands gently around my face.

"Hannah, I never thought I could ever be myself with anyone. Then you appear like a brilliant star casting light into my eternal darkness."

"It's wrong to make me sound so selfless." He held my face firmly while his eyes explored mine. My cheeks flushed hot. Then honesty welled up. "My motives are completely selfish when it comes to you."

"Do you think I mind?" He paused, looking serious.

So serious it worried me. "What's wrong?"

"I almost forgot something very important I wanted to ask you." He inhaled a ragged breath as if it was something awful. "Chase told me about the Governor's Masked Ball and I wanted to know if I could go…with you?"

My stomach flipped as if I was upside down on a roller coaster. "No." I hesitated for a second, playing out the scenario. "I mean, there's nothing I want more, but…"

"You don't want to go."

"No. That's not it. It's just…what if someone from the coven sees us together?"

He raised an eyebrow, making me think he'd already considered that obstacle. "It's a masked ball, Hannah."

Summer had already reminded me of that detail, but a mask would offer little protection from Emme's killer plans. "You're right. I'm just being ridiculously cautious, but nevermind that. I want to go with you, so I'm all in."

he next evening, I hurried to Flower Power, spinning around every few minutes, pretending the book I was holding in front of me was William and we were still dancing in the chapel.

The bell jingled as I entered the shop. I locked the door behind me, leaving the closed sign in the window. On the counter, I set my aunt's book down and examined the flowers in the refrigerator case, figuring a floral essence shop was the perfect place to assemble what I needed.

Summer tapped on the glass.

I dashed to the door. "Come in, quick." I looked behind her, making sure no one followed.

"Hey, Hannah." Her eyebrows bounced up while her voice dropped to a whisper. "I wore black again in case we were doing more grave robbing and breaking and entering."

I inserted a finger in the air. "We did not grave rob. That book did not belong to William Bladen, and as for the breaking and entering, we didn't break anything. Anyway, we are staying in tonight. Thought you could help me."

Her lips formed an O shape. She peered around the counter at the flowers I assembled. "What are we doing?"

"Taking this to the back room." She followed me through the door. I set the flowers and greenery on the worktable, along with the witchcraft plant book. I skimmed the flower meanings. "There is meaning and magic in flower combinations. See this one here. We need to put this combination together."

She spun the book around. "Is this revenge for something Emme did?"

I shook my head. "I'm done with revenge. It's not my bag, but I've come to the conclusion that Emme and I need to have it out, and hopefully, before she hurts anyone else."

"So what's this?"

"We're making a little distraction for Mrs. Blackstone."

She looked at the plants. "English Philpot and moon daisy?"

I glanced at her in surprise. "How do you know what they are?"

"I'm Incan."

"What does being Incan have to do with flowers?"

"Nothing. I just like to say it." She laughed. "Actually, we had a dog that got dizzy for three days from eating moon daisies, so I know they're not good."

"They're not bad, either. Taken in the right amount, this combo will make it difficult to differentiate reality from fantasy and that is the effect we're after."

She crossed her arms over her chest. "How are you going to get Emme's mom to eat it? Toss it into a fat-free salad?"

"She won't be eating it."

"Huh?"

"Adding a little bit of flower essence to her wineglass isn't going to kill Mrs. Blackstone." I didn't want to judge, but it was kinder than what she planned to give the whole town. She eyed me with disbelief. I held my hand up. "I swear."

With that promise, she agreed to help. We chopped and minced the flower parts to tiny bits according to the recipe. I carefully measured out a quarter teaspoon of each and set them in a bowl to dry.

"What are you hoping she'll hallucinate?"

"I imagine her hallucinations will reveal her greatest desire or her worst nightmare." I shrugged my shoulders. "Depends on what's in her heart."

"Sacred Incan priestesses!" she declared, her eyes wide. "What's in her heart? From what you've told me, you know exactly what's in her black heart." She shook her head. "Why are you going to this much trouble?"

"I need her distracted."

"Why? What's going on?"

"There are some bad things going down at the Annapolis Tea Party Re-enactment. The Blackstones plan to cause trouble."

"Then you need to stay away from them."

"I'm afraid my chess piece can't leave the board until the game is over."

"Huh?"

"I mean, fate won't allow that. There's a good chance that between Emme and me, only one of us will be leaving the masked ball alive."

She widened her eyes, this time the horror apparent.

"Relax. I don't plan to be the one who dies."

Her mouth dropped open. "What about Emme?"

"I don't want her to die, either. I'm trying to figure out a way for both of us to live through this and the only way is if one of us can make a different choice. Like you said, I can't change fate, but I'm still going to try. Emme's not going to give me a choice, but I can give her one, and I need her mother to stay out of it."

Summer looked down at her hands, still covered with bits of plant. She wiped them on her black pants and looked at me. "Are you as strong as she is?"

I smiled. "I don't want you to worry, but you'll have to wait and see. I might have a secret you don't know about."

She waggled her eyebrows and looked at me like I was crazy. "Can you shift into a jaguar, too?"

I laughed. "I wish."

"You do wish."

She smiled, seeming assured. Me—not so much. Emme was powerful and determined and I could only hope my plan worked.

"I'll add the moon daisy to her mom's drink, but what about the Queen Js? Navan and Arora won't let you take out their leader. You'll need more than just me." She pursed her lips, deep in thought. "I'll recruit Mateo and Blaze."

"Good. I'll get Chase Calvert."

"After that cell phone prank she pulled, he's definitely in."

"Oh, and I have something for you. I think it could come in handy." I retrieved the African spear plant seeds and poured them into her cupped hands. "I've enhanced them so all you have to do is throw them hard at the ground and they'll spring up around anyone you're trying to contain."

She eyed the dried seeds in her palm. "You really are preparing for a battle."

"That's exactly what I'm preparing for."

I didn't want to scare her, but the reality was Emme, with help from her mother, was capable of unleashing hell on all of us, including the town. A tap on the door interrupted our scheming.

"Who's that?" she asked, her eyes wide as if she were guilty of something.

I peered out the back room door and squinted, not believing my eyes. I stepped lightly and with a click of the lock, I threw the door open.

She stood there looking like a rebellious witch in black, her hair wild and her eyes glinting with mischief. "Eve! How did you get out of Camp Sea Haven?"

She winked at me with a half-smirk, somehow also managing to look very ticked off. "You'd be surprised what I can do." She let herself in. "My mother foresaw that you're going to need a Jewitch like me. So here I am, at your service."

I thanked the stars for Mrs. Meier. "Summer, I want you to meet the newest member of our clique."

Wearing a white apron over her avocado green mini-dress with bell sleeves, Aunt J stirred a pot of vegetable broth with turnips and greens, looking like her old self again.

I leaned against the counter, contorting my lips as I thought about Emme. "You okay?"

She smiled; her pale skin seemed pinker and her eyes clearer. "Better." Her voice vibrated with strength.

I glanced around for something to chop or dice. "Can I help with anything?"

"No. It's a simple recipe and in a bit I'm heading to Flower Power. I'm ready to get back to work." She smiled until her eyes settled on my face. She seemed to be reading my mind. "However, you look like you need something from me."

I grinned. "I might, actually."

She set the spoon down and wiped her hands on her apron. "Let me leave this here to cool, and we can take a look around my study for what it is I think you need."

She dialed the flame to low and gestured for me to follow. We stood side by side, scanning the bookshelves. A curious-looking book spine seemed to catch her attention. The leather appeared as old and cracked as her plant witchcraft book. She tugged it from its snug spot. "Perhaps what you seek will be found in here."

"Is this a copy of the *Chesapeake Histories*?"

"Something better. Take a look." She handed me the book and perched in her chair. I leafed through it, wondering what she wanted me to find in an old book of poetry. Then the pages fell open to where a thin stack of letters rested. I held them up. "Did you know these were in here?"

"Oh. I suppose I did," she said. "I believe they are addressed to a witch named Elizabeth Fitzgerald."

I glanced at the writing. "Who?"

"Your paternal seventh great aunt from the story of the Arundell Curse." She turned her attention to the letters. "They were written in the seventeen hundreds. Read them."

I carefully opened them one at a time unable to squelch my interest. The old-fashioned handwriting was legible enough. Once I got the hang of it, the sentiments were beautiful and intimate. Then I read the last one.

I have loved you as no man has ever loved a woman. Meet me at the harbor tomorrow evening. There is a question I desire to ask you.

Her admirer signed the letter, *Your Eternal Love, Benedict.* The man could write from the heart. "So what happened to them?"

"Do you see the date of the last letter?"

"October eighteenth, seventeen seventy-four."

"That's the day before the Annapolis Tea Party. The next night that's where they were discovered and the Arundell Curse was cast. Benedict Arundell was the forbidden ordinary she married."

Of course. I hadn't put the pieces together. Elizabeth Fitzgerald became Lady Arundell, the ghost in the library, and one of the witches who hung at Witch's Grave. She was part of my family history. I pressed the letters to my chest.

"Don't you want to know about their children?" She grinned when I nodded. "Their descendants married into the Calvert family, of course."

"The Calvert family?" My cheeks heated. Did Aunt J know about William? I twisted my mouth into a knot as I looked at her.

"I may have been out of it for a while, but I'm never blind," she said sounding cryptic, then she shrugged. "Plus, Mrs. Meier stopped by."

"She told you what she saw in her cards?"

"Yes. A union and a love interest."

I stared at the floor, feeling busted. "I don't know what to say." I grimaced and tucked the love letters back in the book. The letters were a part of my history and William's, too. They were a reminder that being a witch and the choices I made were a dangerous business.

She crossed her arms against her chest. "He's a forbidden outcast and a dangerous choice."

"I'm sorry."

She sighed out loud. "We can't choose what our heart wants, but you must be prepared for the consequences," she said, probably referring to Camp Sea Haven.

I wasn't worried about me, only the punishment Mrs. Blackstone would make her suffer.

She adjusted herself in the chair as I returned the book to the shelf, wondering if she was completely disappointed in me. "Hannah, there's something else."

I spun back around. "Go on."

"Do you know much about your mom's ancestry?"

"I only heard dad's family stories, but I've recently wondered why that was."

Her wary expression sent waves of trepidation through me. "Her mother's maiden name was Grey."

"So it's true. I'm a Grey?" William had sensed it all along.

"Yes. Your mom hated what they stood for, and she didn't want you to be a part of it, but like I told you before, you can't suppress what you are. Only in accepting your true self can you live a happy life."

When I went after Mrs. Blackstone to hurt Emme, I was certain it was the Grey in me surfacing. A knock on the door jolted us out of our family secrets, and a sigh of relief escaped my lips. I dashed to the foyer as Mateo walked in.

I wiped the stress from my brow. "What's up?"

"Hey, Summer said you needed to talk to me."

"I do. Let's walk."

We headed to the harbor where the *Peggy Stewart* ship and its British cargo had burned centuries ago. The smell of broiling crab cakes spiced with Old Bay seasoning wafted out of a restaurant and filled the air. In the distance, the State House with its glimmering, eight-hundred-pound, gold acorn topper dominated the skyline, and around us, tourists and midshipmen filled the Main Street shops. We chose a bench near the water and stared out at the sailboats gliding lazily along the glass-like harbor.

"You bringing anyone to the masked ball?" I asked.

"Nah. I have to help my mom serve coffee drinks, but I can't wait to see the fiery re-enactment. You still going to the dance?"

"Yeah."

"With that William guy?"

I didn't have a problem talking with Mateo, but the strange conversation left me unsure what to say. Maybe I didn't want to hurt the feelings I sensed he had for me or maybe I didn't want to damage the friendship I was growing to love.

"Yes."

His pursed lips shifted into a pout. He lifted his head, but didn't meet my gaze. "Hannah, can I say something?"

"Sure." Anxiety gripped my stomach.

He leaned closer, his body heat radiating off him and cutting through the chill of the October breeze sweeping off the bay. He touched a finger to my jaw and tilted my face toward his. The firm and unexpected press of his lips to mine sent a ripple of discomfort through me. He pulled back.

I studied his bewildered expression for a moment. "Why did you do that?"

"I had to know."

"And?"

He frowned. "Weird. It wasn't what I expected."

"Hmm. Not sure I like my kissing described as weird, but in this case it's okay, Mattyboy." I stared at my hands. "It's okay because I think we were fated to be friends, but sometimes things get confusing." I glanced up at him, hoping he understood.

He stared hard at the horizon. "I am confused. We like to hang out together. You smile big when you see me. I know I smile too. I don't get it."

I closed my eyes and puffed my cheeks with a frustrated exhale. "You don't have to understand it with your head. Your heart is telling you how it is."

"But you and I are good together in every other way. Maybe if this William guy hadn't gotten in the way, it would just be…"

It was time to spill. "William is William Calvert."

He leaned back looking overcome with shock. "William Calvert? As in the Calvert boy who left school with a weird disease? Are you kidding me?"

"It's not a weird disease. It's something else, Mateo."

He shook his head. "He's sickly and everyone knows it."

I shook my head, disappointed. "You're better than that."

"When I heard you were hanging around their property, I thought you were playing matchmaker for Summer and Chase. I should've guessed."

"He's a good guy."

"How do you know he's good?"

"How do we know anything? How do you know I'm going to be alive next week?"

He dropped his mouth open, stunned by my words. "What the hell does that mean?"

"Nothing. Look, I know things are weird between us right now, but I need to ask for your help."

He waved his hands in the air. "They're not weird, and I'm not a baby. Remember my man ceremony?" And just like that, the awkwardness melted away. He was my friend again.

"Yes."

"So lay the favor on me."

"I need your help at the tea party re-enactment. Emme has horrific things planned, and not just for me. I need help from my friends to keep her friends away from me so I can stop her."

"Wouldn't it be easier to not go?" His anger was talking.

"That's like trying to avoid throwing up when you have the flu. Sure, but not going will only delay the inevitable, so might as well get the yacking over with."

He tossed his head back and roared out a laugh. "You just compared Emme to throwing up. Classic." He grabbed my hand. "I've got your back. You can always count on me. Always."

"Thanks."

"Hey, I learned something during my initiation stuff. Let me try it on you."

"Okay."

He took my arm, wrapping his strong fingers around my wrist and pushing my sweater up my forearm.

"Is this going to take long?"

He chuckled. "Give me a minute, Miss Impatient." He took an artsy-looking black gel pen out of his back pocket and began sketching a paw print on my skin. He hovered his hand over the art and closed his eyes. Then he summoned the cougar growl from deep in his chest. "There."

"What did you do?"

"I imparted my animal spirit. Offers temporary protection if anyone messes with you."

I shrugged. "Can't hurt." We stood up and hugged, friends forever.

"What are you two...?" William's deep voice sounded from behind me.

I stepped out of Mateo's embrace and read the angry expression beneath the sunglasses. He seemed focused on Mateo's hand touching my waist.

"Mateo was helping me with something."

A sneer twitched on his cheek. "So I see."

I creased my brow. "It's not like that, William. Mateo's my friend. If you can't handle that, then you need to leave."

They glared at each other like enemy gang members fighting over turf, and I was the turf. I grabbed both their forearms and shook them. "Enough."

21.

That night, I let William cool off at the chapel while I worked in Aunt J's attic, continuing my search for clues in my dad's notes. Page after page of symbols and experiments were interesting, but had nothing to do with the answer I needed. Frustrated and tired, I sat back in the red recliner and blew a wisp of hair from my eyes. My eyelids grew heavy as if tiny osmium weights were attached to them. I nestled into the fragrant leather and drifted asleep, holding tight to his book.

With a lurch, I sat up, nearly flinging myself out of the chair. In the dream, my father had asked me if I remembered the cloud experiment we worked on together when I was younger.

My heart raced as I tore the book open to the page about the jars. Along the bottom of the page there were odd sayings he had jotted down, which at first glance seemed like a strange spell, but actually contained a hidden meaning and the answer I needed; the answer they must have hoped would give me, along with the coven and the local ordinaries, a fighting chance.

> Hannah,
> Tracy, no panic in a pony-cart.
> On tub, Edward imitated a cadet; a timid raw debut, no?
> Sir, I demand, I am a maid named Iris.
> Egad, a base life defiles a bad age.
> Eel-fodder, stack-cats red do flee.
> Delia, here we nine were hailed.
> Too hot to hoot.
> He lived as a devil, eh?
> Eve saw diamond, erred, no maid was Eve.
> Cain, a maniac.
> Live not on evil.
> O gnats, tango!
> UFO, tofu.
> Dog, as a devil deified, lived as a god.
> Seven eves.

As I read the palindrome phrases, I wiped tears of relief from my face and got to work. I gathered items from the kitchen and raced back to the attic, locking the door behind me. I set a plastic sandwich bag on the desk and stared at the four jars of compounds.

My parents' love for me urged me on. I removed the lids from the four jars. The strange foggy vision with the girl was a clairvoyant warning of what was to come if I didn't figure out how to stop the catastrophe Mrs. Blackstone and Emme had planned.

I stared at the designs on the jars that contained the three powders and the liquid. I mixed the gray powder, which was silver dust, into the yellow powdered iodide and set the combo aside. I poured the white salt into the jar of clear liquid Aqua Fortis and swished the two ingredients together. After a minute, I sprinkled the silver iodide powder into the liquid and held a fiery finger beneath the jar for two more minutes. As the Aqua Fortis burned off, the mix quickly dried, producing a new powder. I shook it loose, dumped the warm compound into the baggie, and went to my room to dress.

Outside the window, smoky red rust rolled across the silver of the full moon that glowed like an ominous warning to all of Annapolis.

A colonial white and gold gown hung from my closet door. The dress was a gift from Aunt J along with a pair of gold heels she had left next to my bed. I stood up and slipped my bare foot into one of them. My foot slid right in and I was surprised that what I thought was leather was actually pliable metal and as comfortable as my worn ballet flats. How was that even possible? Then I remembered her fragrance accident that had changed the flexibility of metal, including the gold-plated shoes she owned. I lifted my foot and pointed my toes to see the glimmering slipper better. Oh, how it shined. I shimmied into the gown with the built-in corset and hooped petticoat, and fastened a few hooks. The exquisite silk fabric embraced my torso and floated over my legs. At last, I slid the other shoe on.

I inspected myself in her full-length mirror. The top of the gown exposed a subtle amount of cleavage and the very short sleeves wrapped around my upper arms, leaving my shoulders exposed. I felt like a real colonial girl going to a ball. Well, a colonial witch girl.

I brushed my blonde hair back into a pony and draped the curled ends over one shoulder. Thinking of William, I spun around, and when I did, the voluminous skirt floated up around my ankles and for one sublime moment I was living a dream. I just hoped the dream had a chance to continue beyond the night. I stuffed the bag of powder into what décolletage I had.

I tried to relax, but a knock on the front door sent my heart fluttering. I carefully maneuvered down the stairs, not used to wearing high heels and swung the door open.

I took William in with my eyes. He was more than handsome in his colonial suit, tricorn hat, and black mask that dipped low on both of his cheeks. The suit jacket was tailored to fit his strong shoulders. "You look amazing."

His cheeks radiated a jubilant glow, sending a flurry of flutters through my chest. He grasped my hand and looked into my eyes.

From behind his back, he revealed his other hand, which was holding a colorful corsage.

"Where did you get an Enchantress rose?"

He grinned, looking pleased with himself. "Where do you think?"

"And purple and orange roses together?"

"Your aunt was very helpful in picking out just the right combination of roses for me when I told her what I wanted."

I swallowed. "You saw my aunt?" Then the selection of flowers held the meaning I interpreted. She would not have steered him toward those colors without knowing his feelings— deepening love.

"I love you, Hannah. I always will." He slipped the corsage onto my wrist.

My head spun as my heart skipped a beat. "Here." I picked up the boutonniere made of Sweet William, naturally, and pinned it to his lapel. "Now, we're ready."

A horse's whinny sounded from behind him. I glanced out the door and spotted two white horses attached to an elegant carriage. It was like something from a fairytale. "The corsage is beautiful and the carriage is amazing!"

"I'm sorry about Mateo earlier. I don't know what got into me."

"There's nothing to be jealous of. We're friends and he's a bit protective."

"Not more than me." His fingers gently pressed against my hand and wrist. He lifted my arm and inspected the cougar paw print. "Why did he draw that?"

"For good luck," I replied as I touched the gel ink marks with my fingertips.

He sighed. He had seen something in the way Mateo looked at me and he obviously didn't like it.

"William…"

He pressed a finger to my lips. "Enough about him. You look more beautiful than usual and it's not because of the dress." His pale blue eyes drank me in as if he were a thirsty man and I was a distant oasis, pleasantly visible, wholly desirable, but fleeting, as if I might disappear if he stopped watching over me. I wanted to lose myself in those concerned eyes forever. "If you're ready, our carriage awaits."

I grabbed my white, sparkly mask and slipped it on. He opened the carriage door and helped me with my dress, before taking his place beside me on the cushioned leather bench. "You've surprised me."

"I'm glad you like it."

"So do you prefer a horse drawn carriage to your Jeep?"

He grinned and shook his head. "Hardly, but this seemed more appropriate for the evening."

The coachman tapped the reins and we were off. The clip clop of the horses' iron shoes against the street echoed a pleasant rhythm. William clutched my hand. His warmth penetrated deeply and assured me of his strength, but physical strength didn't matter when dealing with witches. With the moon eclipsing above us, the surprises Mrs. Blackstone planned to unleash on the town, and Emme's deadly ambitions, the rising tension was as thick as crab dip.

"Are you okay?"

I bit my lip. "Butterflies."

His brooding eyes lifted to meet mine. "Hannah, you have something on your mind that you're not telling me, and I think it has everything to do with the ball tonight."

I stared at the corsage, not wanting to lie, but knowing I had to keep him unaware to keep him safe. "You're wrong. Everything is fine. Everything will be fine."

He clasped onto my hand again, staring at our entwined fingers. He had pushed and inspired me to strengthen my magic, but old doubts creeped in like the blood swirls consuming the moon. Was I ready? My stomach ached. I inhaled a deep breath and tried to relax, falling into the clip clop of the horses' steps. "You think you need to protect me, don't you?"

He laughed softly. "I don't think I need to, but I can't help myself, especially if I think you're in trouble. My gift may not be as powerful as yours, but I am more dangerous, and I don't care what that means."

It was exactly why I made Chase promise to keep William busy and as far away from Emme as possible. "Stop. You don't need to worry about me tonight. You don't need to do anything stupid, either."

"I will always worry about you and, so you know, I don't plan to let you out of my sight. Not for one minute." He tried to sound lighthearted, but the serious edge in his voice was as formidable as a steel blade.

"You know the coven will be there. And Summer will want to hang out with me, too. And Mrs. Blackstone has requested that Aunt J and I are present under the VIP tent for the painting unveiling, so while I'm doing that,it's probably best if you hang out with Chase. Besides, you don't want to be around Emme and me at the same time."

He narrowed his gaze. "Are you worried about me losing control?"

"I want tonight to be amazing, and I don't want to take any chances."

"I have every reason to be in control." He gently touched my cheek, drawing my face closer to his. He dotted a delicate kiss on my trembling lower lip, lingering for the slightest wisp of a moment before pulling away. A nervous smile appeared. "I love that we're spending the evening together in the real world. And I love—I love you."

I caught my breath. I wanted nothing to come between us, ever, but especially not tonight. The carriage slowed to a stop in front of the entrance.

"Why do you do that?" he asked, making me aware of the tendril of hair I had wrapped around my finger in a strangling motion.

I grimaced. "Nervous habit."

He clasped his hand over mine, pulling it free. "Come on. Let's join the party."

I touched my hands to his shoulders, feeling the firm muscles flex beneath the jacket as he slipped his hands around my waist. My feet barely hit the ground as William lifted me out. "There's nothing to be nervous about," he said.

I glanced up, seeing a few white clouds gather in front of the reddening moon. I pressed my hand to my stomach and tried to breathe. He escorted me around the outdoor event where we both enjoyed the sight of bustling food vendors and the rousing marching music from a fife and drum corps. Waiters hurried to load trays of appetizers onto high-top tables, and Mateo and Blaze helped Mrs. Roca refill industrial-sized urns with fresh coffee.

Inside the VIP tent, a huge crowd of beautifully dressed people in masks socialized and several couples waltzed near the easel that held the canvas-draped painting. I glanced around for Mrs. Blackstone, since she had the job of removing the canvas once the speakers were finished. She wasn't in sight, but Summer was.

She sat under the edge of tent near the water, her unique white-blonde hair giving her identity away. She wore a pink gown with a black and white mask. She gave me a wink and a thumbs-up to assure me she had delivered the moon daisy package, but I didn't recognize the date holding her hand. "Is that Chase?" I said, mostly to myself, but William overheard me.

"He's had a crush on her since his first day at Truxton High."

Summer and Chase rushed up, still holding hands. She held her full skirt out with one hand. "What do you think?"

"Beautiful," I said.

She turned to the guys. "Why don't both of you grab some tapas from the Jalapeños table. I'm starving." She held tight to my arm, holding me back.

William's eyes locked on mine. "Chase can do that." Desperation edged his tone.

"Go with him," I said. With the greatest reluctance, he left. I clutched my chest, feeling a crippling pain that threatened to rob me of breath. I grabbed onto her arm and lowered my voice. "Is Emme here, yet?"

"The witch just arrived with her subpar clique. You okay?"

"I'll be fine." I caught my breath as she followed me under the big tent and guessed the identities of several masked partygoers, including Aunt J and Ms. Russell, who was no doubt a fan of our town's colonial history.

I spotted our newest member, Eve, wearing a decorative mask and pewter-colored gown, standing next to her mom. I had given her a task to perform, one I thought she might enjoy. After all, Summer may have dropped the moon daisy into Mrs.

Blackstone's drink, but I needed to make sure she drank it. That's where Eve's secret talent came in handy.

In the center, Arora and Navan mocked passing ordinaries while Emme blew glow mist on them. A security guard scolded a small boy for spreading the luminescent liquid. The Queen Js erupted in laughter.

Chase continued to keep William's attention diverted while Mateo and Blaze, taking a break from serving coffee, resembled Secret Service agents keeping watch over Summer and I.

It wasn't long before Emme, in an expensive black and gold gown and black mask, snatched a microphone and informed everyone to gather closer. The group pressed forward and Mrs. Blackstone, wearing a purple corset gown that forced her cleavage to bubble over, took her place up front for the unveiling. The moon daisy seemed to be kicking in as she held the podium with both hands to steady herself.

William rushed to my side, leaving Chase to carry two plates of cheese quesadillas. He wrapped a strong hand around mine. "Everything okay?"

I forced a smile, but inwardly I groaned. "Great." I hoped it was convincing. His life depended on it.

Summer and Chase noshed on the appetizers while everyone crowded together. Eve continued using her power to keep Mrs. Blackstone animated and out of trouble. Behind us, the fife and drum corps continued to play.

Arora, wearing a designer gown and mask in silver, and Navan in a shimmery orange dress and matching mask, stood near the podium, probably wanting to be seen by the who's who of Annapolis, including the mayor and his wife. Mrs. Blackstone tightly gripped the gold rope attached to the canvas cloth. A bell rang to quiet the talkers.

"We have a wonderful reason to celebrate this evening at the Two Hundred and Fiftieth Anniversary of the Annapolis Tea Party. We are thrilled to share a piece of history with those who should appreciate the value of Maryland's past, including its dark days."

The mayor tore his mask off, his eyes wide.

"Historic Annapolis, under my leadership, has acquired an oil painting from a private estate in Philadelphia. After diligent negotiations, 'The Night the Peggy Stewart Burned' has returned home to Annapolis."

I glimpsed Aunt J who wore a concerned expression as she watched Mrs. Blackstone.

"Tonight, it is my honor to introduce Ms. Kelly, a historian who is here to tell us the painting's story. Ms. Kelly, please do us the honor."

Ms. Kelly approached the microphone. She was a slender woman in her fifties with mousy brown hair wound into a tight bun on the back of her head and thick black-framed glasses.

She adjusted them and cleared her throat. "On this day in seventeen seventy-four, revolution was in the air and patriot fever was spreading. The loyalist-owned ship, the *Peggy Stewart*, arrived in Annapolis laden with contraband, two thousand pounds of British tea. When the patriots discovered the ship's owner paid the much hated tea tax on the cargo, tempers exploded. Mr. Stewart and his family were considered enemies to the liberties of America and threats were made against them. Although the merchant and his family survived, the *Peggy Stewart* burned and sank in this harbor with all her sails, rigging, and cargo. In the painting, you can see several notable colonials from the time, including Anthony Stewart. I present to you 'The Night the Peggy Stewart Burned'."

Mrs. Blackstone tugged gently on the rope, revealing the painting. My eyes drifted to the artwork. A massive gold frame surrounded the oil painting. Curious, I stepped closer and removed my mask. I couldn't deny the resemblance of the scene to one of my strange dreams and it reminded me of the story my mom had told me.

Mrs. Blackstone pressed a hand to her forehead and waggled her hands for balance. I glanced at Eve who was distracted by her chatty mom instead of working her telepathic magic on Mrs. Blackstone.

She pressed the microphone back to her mouth. "A valuable lesson was taught that night to a witch…a Fitzgerald witch who was later hung by ordinaries like you, Mr. Mayor," she yelled and nearly fell over.

Ms. Kelly drew back, her face filled with horror. Aunt J's mouth dropped open. Everyone looked around at everyone else with dismay.

The mayor, with an appalled expression on his face, marched to a waiting limousine outside the tent. Eve worked her hands like a puppet master trying to get Mrs. Blackstone to cover her mouth, but it was too late.

Mrs. Blackstone couldn't miss a chance to impart one last reminder about breaking coven rules like the hypocrite she was, but I couldn't worry about that. I had to focus on my task—get the silver powder into the clouds before the fireworks show.

"Nobody leave. The Colonial Chesapeake Daughters has a surprise for everyone!" She yelled to no one in particular, sounding drunk.

Summer grabbed my arm. "Looks like the moon daisy has gotten hold of her tongue."

William wrapped his arm around my waist and tore me away from the crowd. "What's wrong?"

The fireworks, I thought. "Nothing. No. Something. It's just the sense of fate—the *Chesapeake Histories*, the fireworks—it means…" My ribs tightened. Even giving Emme a choice, it didn't mean she would take it. Fate was owed a death tonight and it might be mine. "I need air. Now."

He escorted me outside the tent. Emme's mother stumbled toward us, oblivious to who William was with his mask on. She latched onto his other arm.

"You look very helpful, young man. Would you mind helping a lady, I mean, helping me march to the ball at Carroll House?" she slurred. The sweet odor of Chardonnay and moon daisy rolled off her breath and added to my haziness.

He kept his pale blue eyes averted and tried to ignore her, but she wouldn't relax her grip. "If you give me a minute, I'll help you."

She eyed me up and down before retrieving a compact from her dress pocket. When she glanced at her reflection, her smile withered into a terrified gap. "Aaahhh," she screamed, freaking out at the hallucination she was seeing. "My face, my face, I'm a mummy. Some of the aging powder must have gotten on me. Help me. Grab my wizard, I mean my husband. I'm dying." She wobbled back and forth, slurring her words and her hand went up to steady her big updo topped with a fake tiara. She wobbled and plopped on a bench.

"Let me get her some help," William said. Chase eyed me through his mask. Then he grabbed William by the arm and imparted an urgent message. He had played his part well. William looked at me with concern. "Will you be okay for the next five minutes? Chase needs me."

"Go. I'll get someone to help Mrs. Blackstone, and I'll meet you at Carroll House in a few minutes."

"Save the first dance for me."

"I will," I assured him, somehow keeping my voice from wavering.

On the water, male actors dressed in colonial costumes rowed a small boat out to the wooden ship that was dressed up with canvas sails to replicate the eighteenth century brig. Throngs of costumed onlookers along the docks cheered and tossed dissolvable tea bags into the water before the crew set the ship ablaze. Cheers exploded while the fife and drum corps played louder than before.

Eve looked panicked as she searched in every direction for her puppet. Aunt J followed. I threw a hand in the air to flag them down. "Eve, she's here. You have to stay with her."

"Got it," she said, lifting her hand in the air to elevate Mrs. Blackstone to her feet. She made a walking motion with her fingers and Mrs. Blackstone's legs followed suit. Aunt J shook her head while grabbing Mrs. Blackstone by her elbow to make her look more graceful. She gave me a worried glance. All I could do was shrug.

A loud whistle blew from the leader of the fife and drum corps, signaling the start of the short march to the ball. With shouts and cheers, the boisterous crowd followed the corps' lead down St. Mary's Street to the historic Charles Carroll House where the Governor's Masked Ball was being held.

As we neared the house, I stared at the grand white steps, trying to squelch the painting surprise that had left me lightheaded. I pressed my hands to my head, feeling the blood drain from my face, and then I checked to make sure the small bag was still in its secure hiding spot.

Crowds of costumed Annapolitans headed toward the house, ready to shake hands with the governor and dance the night away.

Antique furnishings, ornate silver candelabrum, and massive portraits decorated the grand colonial home. Servers in colonial wait staff uniforms moved through the wide main hall with silver trays held high above their heads and the smell of fruit-filled pies and chocolate cakes saturated the air.

I rushed past the receiving line and toward the grand staircase. A cool breeze wafted down to me from an open window on the second floor. I followed it up the steps, feeling weighed down by the layers of my dress. Once I reached the top, I leaned myself against a wall and peered out the window.

The moon bled its rust colored light on the garden where Summer stood face-to-face with Arora, who was tossing hologram spiders at her. That witch was so out of her league if she thought fake spiders would scare my bestie. Above, Siris circled, and there was no sign of Chase or William, which meant the plan was in motion.

I yanked the bag from my cleavage and unsealed it. I thought of everyone I loved standing under the eclipse, waiting for fireworks. The magic shuddered to life.

"Like a fly in my web." Navan's voice came from behind and seeped into my ears like toxic sludge.

I dropped the bag on the windowsill and spun around. I wrung my hands together while the foreboding clock in my head clanged with chimes of doom. "Navan? Where's Emme?"

She tore off her mask and snorted with contempt, sending the hairs on my neck straight up. "You fool. Emme was never your counterpart. I knew that the first time I read her palm, not that I told her. Are you surprised?"

More than I should've been. "Where's Emme?"

"I told her I foresaw you hiding in the garden and that she should give me her ring for safekeeping." She flashed her bejeweled hand at me.

Her stone-cold green eyes locked on me. She pulled something from behind her back and tossed it at my feet—the stolen book.

I looked at her. "What's this?"

"Something Emme was dumb enough to share with me." She laughed at her betrayal to her leader.

A mix of rumbling and starburst explosions sounded at once and shook the house. Dread filled me as I realized what it was. Fireworks.

"I know about your ring being the key to part of the Witch's Breath," she said, dragging her shimmery orange dress train to the side.

I didn't have time for whatever crazy future she'd dreamed up in her crystal ball.

Caw, caw.

I swung around. Siris picked up the bag in his beak. Was there still time to counteract the aging powder? I lowered my voice to a commanding hush. "Hurry, Siris! Empty the powder above the clouds." I made sure he took flight before I turned back to Navan.

"It's a family thing, right? I heard the wizard earl talked to birds, too, or are you just losing your mind like your mother did?"

"I used to think I had family issues, but not anymore." My throat went dry, worried about the hundreds of ordinary spectators celebrating the re-enactment, not to mention the rest of the town that would be drinking the water tonight. The magic screeched loud inside me. "Navan, you need to shut up and listen to me. There's no fountain of youth in my ring."

Her eyes sparkled with evil delight. "I never thought the elixir was *in* your ring." She hesitated and stared at Emme's ring on her finger. "Wait—are you telling me these suckers actually contain the two elixirs of the Witch's Breath?" She gasped then chuckled. "No, there's no way this could be so easy."

"You don't understand. The information you translated was wrong. It was a lie from the *Book of Lies*."

She scoffed at me. "That's inconvenient, I think, for you."

From downstairs, Mrs. Blackstone's voice echoed up to us. She was shouting. "Fireworks are starting! Everyone go outside except Emme and me. We'll stay back and guard the wine," she yelled, still sounding drunk.

My breathing accelerated. I recalled the acronym formed by the first letter of each palindrome phrase in my dad's notes, *To Seed the Clouds*. If Siris didn't seed them with my dad's compounds, the Senescent flower powder hidden in the fireworks would fall into the water supply, aging everyone in town and driving droves of them to Dr. Blackstone's office.

"I won't give you my ring without a fight. It's your choice, Navan."

Her eyes glinted with confidence. "Consider this your Queen J test. If you win, you can take my role as the new leader, but if you lose, you die."

I couldn't shake the twist of fate. There had been moments when I saw a glint of ambition in Navan's eyes, but I'd never suspected she was the other one. "This isn't a test. It's a choice. What happens tonight all comes down to what you decide to do."

"There's always a test. So if it all comes down to what I decide, then you lose."

"Why don't you take your test and stick it up your plastic nose." I inched closer to the window, wanting to put as much distance between her and me as possible. Outside, a girl's scream followed the battle roar of two wild cats.

Navan cupped a hand to her ear, listening to the fight outside. "Did I mention that my gift has vastly improved? I forewarned Arora about Summer's talent and had her baby brother drop off a surprise a little while ago. That's right, a very big cat trap."

I felt nothing but pity for her. "Summer's the smartest girl in school. You think she's going to fall for a cat trap?"

A gunshot cracked through the air. I froze, petrified with fear for the target of the bullet. My fingers brushed across the velvet petals of my rose corsage. All of my loved ones were out there, each carrying a piece of my heart.

A groan, followed by Chase's scream lifted to the window on a gust—then a cry for help. I pressed my face to the glass and made out a lone figure lying in the grass. I smacked my hands against the panes. William.

A scream fizzled and died in my throat. Hadn't he suffered enough? The magic yearned for release. I squeezed my fists tight. "By the power of fire, I do summon and churn, and call thee forth to blaze and burn." The inferno radiated throughout my chest like an expanding sun. My back arched and my skin tingled. Threads of fire surged from my hands. Thinking a show of power might end our battle, I pointed to the clouds, which were turning stormy gray from my dad's powder. Instantly, a searing surge of white electricity zigzagged to the ground. Screams came from the crowd below as they ran for cover from the impending deluge. I whipped around and glared at my true enemy.

Navan combed her fingers through her red hair. "You'll never impress me, Hannah Fitzgerald." Her mouth puckered, her green orbs narrowed to slits. She lunged. She gripped tight to my arm, then sucked in a breath and released me. Her pale face tightened in pain. Smoke rolled off her hand. "Ow!" She screamed like a banshee. The veins in her slender neck bulged as deeply etched animal scratches sprung up on her palm.

I looked to where she'd touched the Incan cougar print on my arm. I flashed my eyes at her. For William, I had to do something. "Navan. Think. We can both live."

She turned her hate-filled glare on me and shook her hand in the air. "No, we can't. It's dictated in the coven prophecy, and since I'm the one who's descended from Queen Jane Grey and the famous alchemist, Henry de Grey, minus any dirty Irish wizard blood in my veins. I deserve to be the one who reigns. And by the way, Emme may have thought you were good enough to be part of the Queen Js, but I never did."

I listened in disbelief as my confidence swelled. "You're right. I was too good for it." My voice vibrated with conviction.

She lunged again, this time grabbing my other arm.

My pulse pounded in my ears as I controlled the inner tempest. Every part of me wanted to run to William. I forced my mind to stay put and shoved Navan off. "What did you do to William? Tell me!" I raged and cast a finger out the window again. Wind, roaring like a freight train, shook the old house down to its foundation. Thunder rumbled.

Her eyes grew wild and frenzied. "As a bonus tonight, Emme's helper brought his special ammunition to fire into your forbidden boyfriend. You know, the Calverts have been cursed for some time thanks to Emme's and my mutual ancestor, and when he left school last year, I suspected what the reason was. What I didn't know was that silver bullets were the only way to kill cursed crossbreeds like him. Emme and I figured that out at the Calvert family cemetery. It was the answer needed to solve the problem of the potential witch killer you were so interested in that you couldn't stay away from his family's property." She bit her lip and grinned. "Silver bullets. Who knew?"

"He has done nothing to you!"

"He's fated to be a witch killer."

"So are you if you go through with your plan."

"This isn't going to be murder. This is your punishment for breaking coven rules. You fell for a forbidden crossbreed."

"You are not my judge and jury!" I struggled as the magic felt like an internal nuclear reactor exploding. My ribs ached.

The evil grin spread wider across her face. "Your death will bring a big change for me. It will prove I was the one fated to be the most powerful witch in our coven's history. I'll change everything. The forbidden ones and outcasts will be eliminated. As for the ordinaries...Mrs. Blackstone is right about them. However, I'm not afraid to show them what real power is, that's if her plan doesn't kill them tonight."

The continued booms of Mrs. Blackstone's fireworks display resonated through the sky. "No!" My eyes darted to the window, catching sight of the green and pink sprays of light bursting beneath the billowy rain clouds. *Where is the rain?*

"The Blackstones have always had a flare for the dramatic, haven't they?"

Light raindrops pelted the roof. Desperation to save the ordinaries, the coven, and William gripped hard. I gnashed my teeth at her. "You don't have to do this."

She drew back with dismay. "You think either of us can change what's fated to be? No one can."

Tears streamed down my cheek as an imaginary alarm screamed in my head.

"What about our sisters? What will become of them when you take over?" I asked, desperate to make her think. "You can't see everything that's coming."

"I can see more than I could before."

"So were you able to see that Mrs. Blackstone has already put us all in a perilous situation? Once the ordinaries realize Emme and her mom are the witches who poisoned them with the Senescent powder, they'll come after all of us. They'll hunt us down and drive us away, including you."

"That's weakling talk. We're better than the ordinaries, even you. We're powerful and they respect power. Now, give me the ring, Hannah."

I stared hard at her face. "I can't do that."

There was no containing the magic now. It seeped out. I looked away from Navan, instead focusing on the trees outside the window. I whispered to my parents, sensing they were with me in spirit and I summoned the magic again. The fire spun from my fingers. A violent shaking commenced. The tree roots funneled underneath and cracked into the center of the house, vibrating the structure like an earthquake. Guests below us screamed and ran. Lights flickered. Panic abounded downstairs.

Rain now poured down in a deluge thanks to Siris. A roar of thunder rattled the windows. Navan grabbed hold of the banister, unfazed by nature going haywire around her. Her eyes laughed with a mix of delight and insanity.

I maintained my footing as she inched toward me. With a swirl of my hands, the breeze around me heated and every upstairs window whooshed open. Luxurious curtains tore off the rods, and winds rushed in, funneling around us and slowing her pace. I stared at the ring on my finger, William's only chance if I could get to him in time. Then an idea hit me in a flash. I tugged off the ring and held it tight. Her eyes gleamed as she locked onto the golden target. She patted the pocket in her dress skirt and seemed to be calculating her timing.

I threw my head back and stretched my arms out, releasing the inferno within me.

Waves of the hottest heat rushed out from my fingers. The storm raged as the energy drained from my body. Rain pummeled the windowsills. Gale force winds lifted us from the floor and sent furniture flying. Tree branches grabbed hold of the house, breaking through glass windows and shaking the structure up and down. Amid the chaos, I shifted my hand in front of me and dangled the desired object.

Her fiery red hair whipped about her face, but her eyes remained locked, as if she were hypnotized by it. She struggled to gain her footing, and then slyly extracted a metal object from her pocket. A curved witch's chisel glimmered in the light.

When the house shook again, I bolted past her. She grabbed hold of my skirt and ripped it as she dragged me back, maneuvering the sharp tool. I kicked and yelled, but when I inhaled a breath, the wind carried William's agonizing groan to my ears. I swiveled my head away from Navan and wriggled to reach the stairs, but she held tight, refusing to release me. My plan was definitely not working. I channeled one more surge of fire to my free hand to get her off me. She spun me around. With a fierce jab from her, a burning sensation penetrated where the chisel plunged into my abdomen.

"Uhh," I screamed. A warm bloom of crimson spread across the front of my dress. I pressed my fingers to the wet seeping through the white silk. I peered up at her. "The ring will not bring you what you want. I swear."

She kept a grip on me with her other hand, scraping to get at the heirloom.

The hammering of my heart filled my head. Still holding tight to the ring, I pushed and shoved her, but it was no use. She was too determined and my life was trickling out of me in a scarlet ribbon. The struggle brought us to the edge of the staircase. A dizzy and cold feeling began to take me under. I didn't want to die. Everything in me wanted to live.

At that moment, a church clock tolled its ominous chimes. Navan thrust her weight against me. I grabbed onto the railing as she pushed forward with violence in her eyes. I held as tight as I could with my remaining strength and whispered, "This is for my mom and dad, for William, and for the witches who didn't survive their wicked sister witches' ambitions." Before the eleventh chime clanged, I tossed the ring into the air, hoping she'd make the right choice.

I barely remained anchored in place when she lunged. With her entire body stretched and poised, she reached for the ring, seeming to move in slow motion. The gold brushed her fingertips as she extended every muscle and tendon to pluck it from the air.

However, the ring plummeted beyond her grasp. Her momentum carried her down the hardwood steps, one hard, vicious tumble after another to the first floor where she lay motionless. Her head and neck tilted at an unnatural angle from her shoulders.

I averted my eyes from the horror. It didn't need to end like this. Or if it did, I wished it didn't. I sucked in a breath, holding back the agony. I staggered as I descended the stairs. I had to get to William before it was too late.

In the abandoned foyer, Mateo, his clothes ripped and his hair and skin soaked with rain, dropped his phone. He grabbed me and spun me around, staring at the growing stain on the front of my dress.

"Where do you think you're going?" His face paled as his eyes fixed on the scarlet pooling around my feet.

"To the garden. William…needs me."

"Hannah, you're wounded. You need to sit down and let me take care of you since all the freaking EMTs took off in the ambulances with the governor and his security detail."

"I'm the only one who can help him." As I wrestled against Mateo, I noticed the sparkle of Emme's gold ring on Navan's lifeless hand.

"There's an ambulance coming for him." He shook his head in a foreboding way. "He's not in good shape."

My heart stopped. The breath rushed out of me like wind deflating from a boat's sail. "Where's Kalvin?"

Confusion creased in his brow. "Who's Kalvin?"

"The shooter."

"You mean Emme's dad, Dr. Blackstone?"

"Emme's dad is the shooter? Paunchy guy?" He nodded. I gasped. Emme had been using her dad all along to help her. The thought had never occurred to me. Maybe it should've. "What happened?"

His eyes relayed the terror before the words came. "It was crazy. Dr. Blackstone had a rifle. My adrenaline kicked in and I

Leigh Goff

morphed into a cougar. Summer and I scared the hell out of him. He's unconscious, lying inside a circle of spear plants Summer laid down around him and Arora. There's no way they're getting out without a chainsaw, but William. He...he..."

"Stop!" My lips trembled. "Don't. Say. That."

His eyes, warm and tender, held me in place. "Hannah...it's too late."

"No!"

"Let me take care of you." He held tight to my arm.

With my last bit of strength, I wrenched myself from his grip. "You don't understand. He'll be fine. He has to be."

I broke away and leaned down next to Navan. "I'm truly sorry it ended this way." I picked up my ring from the floor and tugged Emme's ring from her hand before shoving through the back door. I stumbled past the terraced gardens as groans of sheer pain tumbled off my lips. I passed a small gardener's shed and staggered to a landscaped area where I spotted them. Chase held his hand, tears streaming down his cheeks.

"I tried to keep him safe. I tried," he cried as the clouds splattered on us.

I didn't feel the rain. I pressed my hands against my abdomen, trying to stop the bleeding, but the wound was too deep. "You were up against forces greater than...than we imagined. It's not your fault." I bit my lip, staving off intense pangs. "Go wait out front for the ambulance. Tell them where we are." He kept his tear-stained face turned away and ran.

I dropped beside William and tore the mask from his face. My shaky hands loosened his collar and pressed against his neck, searching for a pulse. His heartbeat was weak, his breathing shallow. I searched his chest, my bloodied hands sprawling across the snow white of his shirt. His colonial jacket was soaked with rain and blood. "William, don't leave me. Please."

Navan was dead and I would die, too, regardless of what the *Chesapeake Histories* foretold. With one last moment together, I wanted to change the hand fate had dealt William.

With a pop, Emme's family ring opened. I pried off the glass cover, exposing the black liquid. Even if it started to kill him, the Breath of Life elixir would counter the deadly effect. I recalled the first Latin palindrome spell from Lady Arundell's gray book.

If there really were magical and healing properties attributed to palindromes, I needed that to be true, now more than ever.

"*Signa te, signa, temere me tangis et angis, Signa te, signa, temere me tangis et angis.*"

I dripped the liquid into his mouth, desperate to break the curse.

The Sigh of Death elixir seeped in between his lips. Then I searched for the latch on my ring and pressed. The clasp stuck. Sobs welled up in my throat. "No. No!" I wrestled with the ring, but to no avail.

Beneath my knee, a small rock dug into the skin. I reached down and pinched it between my thumb and a knuckle. It was large enough. I knocked it hard against the clasp, trying to undo the damage. I pressed the clasp again. It wouldn't budge. "Dammit! Open!" I pried it with my fingers and suddenly, the bezel popped, revealing the rounded pearlescent face. My heart thumped and stuttered. I whispered the other Latin spell into his ear.

"*In girum imus nocte et consumimur igni. In girum imus nocte et consumimur igni.*"

With bloodied fingers, I dripped the iridescent oil onto his lips, making sure it trickled into his mouth.

"I love you, too." I squeezed his hand.

"Hannah!" Mateo shouted in the distance. Ms. Russell followed behind him, unable to keep pace with his longer stride.

I lay next to William while the cold and blackness enveloped me. The increasing heat from his body and a now steady pulse from his wrist was the last thing I felt.

Sunlight filtered into my eyes and a girl's voice grew more distinct. The angel plopped on the bed, shaking me out of my lucid sleep. "Wake up, Hannah. I can't wait a minute longer to fill you in on everything that's happened the last few days," she said in a bubbly voice.

My eyes fluttered open. "Days?"

"You must've hit your head. Don't you remember being in the hospital? The ride home in your aunt's van?"

Memories of doctors in white jackets and tubes attached to my hand came back to me. "I thought it was a bad dream."

"No doubt. You lost a lot of blood and needed a transfusion and you're not going to believe who donated his blood."

My eyes focused on Summer's.

"Are you going to guess?" She said it as if she was talking about someone casually giving me his phone number instead of his blood.

"Who?"

"William Calvert. He insisted, and since the hospital confirmed he was a safe match, they went ahead. As soon as they hooked you up, your vitals improved immediately. The doc said William must have super blood. He also thinks you hit your head during the storm-slash-earthquake-slash-ecological disturbance that totally damaged Carroll House and that's why you've been out of it for a few days. My mom thinks it was caused by fracking. Have they been fracking in Annapolis? Anyway, you should've seen the governor being hauled out of there on a stretcher. And also, after the chaos ended, I found the gold book Emme stole. So I took your gray book and returned them both to the library. Appease the spirits, right?"

"Did anyone else get hurt?"

"The governor sprained his wrist. I went easy on Arora although she didn't deserve it after her brother brought that stupid cat trap that Emme got caught up in. Seriously? Anyway, the only ones who really got hurt were you, William, and poor Navan. Yikes. I can't believe I said poor, but not even the red-haired witch deserved to die. She broke her neck falling down the stairs. The police arrested Dr. Blackstone. He's in jail and he's going to lose his medical license, which probably isn't a bad thing."

"Oh my God. You're talking so fast."

"Before I got here, I downed like two of the new South American coffee drinks we started serving at the Bean."

I sat up, letting the super blood work its way back to my head. "What about everyone in town? Is everyone okay?"

"Yeah. Why?"

I sighed with relief. "It's not important. Hey, I'm über-tired. Do you think you could send Aunt J up? I need to talk to her. Alone."

"Sure." Summer smiled and squeezed my hand. "Mateo wanted me to tell you that he makes a badass cougar. He can't wait for you to see, but poor Blaze still can't morph into a wolf."

I waved goodbye to her. A few minutes later, Aunt J entered with a plate of buttery sunflower crisps and set them on the night table. "You always liked these as a little girl."

"I remember."

She sat down next to me. Her brunette hair was styled with a flower headband and she looked like she was wearing blush.

"How are you doing?"

"Well enough. What happened with Mrs. Blackstone?"

"Mallory was arrested when the police discovered what was in the fireworks and how she planned to disperse it into the air and the city water to bring patients to her husband's plastic surgery practice. Fortunately, the fireworks tainted with the aging powder hadn't been set off yet. She lost her job at Historic Annapolis to an ordinary historian named Mr. Clark. Then the coven demoted her for breaking the rule about using witchcraft to benefit and not harm the chapter. Her behavior certainly reflected poorly on all of us."

Would any of that change Emme for the better? "Who's in charge now?"

"Funny thing. Liza Bennett, the distillery owner, turned out to be the secret recruiter. After Eve demonstrated her telepathic magic, she was the obvious choice for the internship." I was happy for Eve. "Then Liza designated Mrs. Meier as the new interim coven leader. She's the first Jewitch to lead the coven, and I think she'll do a fine job until you are old enough to take over."

"Me?"

"Yes. You will lead us one day."

It was way too much to consider at the moment, especially when I had other things on my mind. I'd deal with it later. "So the coven is safe for now?"

"Yes. I think it's going to thrive, too. Mrs. Meier told me she was already planning on reworking some of the rules she felt were holding us back." A slight grin appeared.

"I like that. I saw Ms. Russell under the VIP tent."

"Yes. She said she needed to talk to you when you were feeling up to it. Said you knew how to get in touch with her."

I nodded. "I do, but I really want to see William first. I need to know he's okay." Was the curse broken?

"Of course he's okay, and I understand."

I touched my hand to the chisel wound that was still tender to the touch.

She smiled and cupped her hand to my cheek. "However, Ms. Russell seemed pressed about hearing from you first."

"She didn't say why?"

"No. Only that it was urgent."

She checked my temperature with the back of her hand and tucked me in, even though I was well beyond the age of needing tucking. Still feeling sore and drained, I didn't fight her.

"I'm sorry I didn't tell you everything that was going on sooner."

"Shh." She paused, setting her gaze on the wilted corsage resting on my night table. "I understand."

"I'm glad you do. So why are you all dressed up?" I glanced at her pretty dress.

"Now, that you are feeling better, I'm going on a date."

"Who with?"

She picked up a nutty cookie and chomped into it as if she wanted to delay answering. She swallowed and smiled. "Liza."

"Well, you look really nice."

"Thanks. We're going to meet for a glass of wine. I'm kind of excited."

I bit my lip, my heart bursting with happiness for her. "I'm glad. You deserve it."

She stood up, handed me my phone, and left looking happier than I'd ever seen her. I dialed Ms. Russell, curious.

"Hannah, I'm glad you called."

A nagging feeling told me I wouldn't like what she was going to say. "What's so urgent?" I remembered her warning me about Chase and his family situation. She must've known the Calverts were cursed to kill Grey witches, but why did she want to protect me? We were distant cousins, but that didn't really explain it.

"I was a witness to your power the other night, and I must say, I am very impressed. You are the first witch in centuries to demonstrate such a strong and powerful connection to your magic and that makes you worthy of great honor."

I'd tried to suppress it, fought against being a witch and a Fitzgerald, and now she was telling me I was worthy? "Are you sure?"

"A superior witch changes the world starting with herself, and it will be amazing to see you lead your coven with those talents one day," she said. "But it is my job to inform you that as a witch, you are invited to join the Rosicrucian Order of the Golden Dawn."

"Wait. Rosicrucian as in the secret society of alchemists?" I'd done some research since learning of my dad's experiments.

"Alchemists, witches, wizards—it's for those who desire to study the Laws of Nature in their highest form like your thirteenth great grandfather, the Wizard Earl of Kildare, once did. It is a great honor and only for a handful of rare witches like yourself."

That explained why she hung the rose painting in her office. "Will it take long?"

"Take long?" She hesitated. "Do you remember when I told you I was here because I owed someone a favor?"

"Uh huh."

"That someone was your mother."

"Oh."

"She knew of my connection to the Order."

"What was the favor she did for you?"

She paused. "She gave me hope when I was desperate for love and then she asked your aunt to craft a love potion for me. That's how I attracted my husband."

Sounded like my mom with a little help from Aunt J. "One made with agrimony?"

"How did you know?"

"I have a good memory."

"Of course. So, that's why I'm in Annapolis."

"Now what?"

"Now you will understand that your mother wanted this for you and I'm hoping that will be enough to convince you to join. If you do, you will be inducted into the Order, where you will be able to replenish the lion oil for your ring."

I grazed my fingers over the heirloom. How had I ever not wanted to be a part of the Fitzgerald legacy? "I thought the elixir was a one-time only deal?"

"I've recently learned that there is more than one type and that the plant materials required are very rare, but apparently, we are able to do that."

"The offer sounds tempting." I thought about how Emme's lion oil broke his curse and mine saved William and I from death's grip. It would certainly come in handy if I had to battle another witch like Navan. "And I appreciate that my mother wanted this prestigious position for me, but she never asked me if it was what I wanted. I'm sorry, but I don't feel ready to take that on."

"You have a wonderful future ahead of you and I do hope you will keep us in mind when you are ready."

"I will, and thank you for the invitation."

I ended the call as the rumble of his Jeep's engine alerted me. I needed to see him, to be assured he was alive. I hurried as fast as I could to the door and he rushed to meet me. He wore a baby blue button down and black sunglasses, which fell away as he swept me into his arms.

I wrapped my arms around his neck. His sigh told me he was as relieved as I was.

He gently pressed me to his chest "You shouldn't be out of bed," he scolded and pulled back. He laced his fingers through mine.

"Back at you. You lost so much blood. I thought, I thought…"

"Shh." A slight smirk lifted the corners of his mouth. "I know," he said, sounding relieved.

I glanced up and noticed his right cheek. The angry scar had been replaced with a perfect layer of ivory skin. His eyes—the otherworldly paleness had darkened to a deep sapphire blue. The sunlight sparkled in them casting a brilliant glint that caused my heart to race. He loved me and the curse was broken.

"Hannah."

He clutched me in his arms and tucked me under his shoulder. Dizziness and laughter filled my head at the same time. I held tight, pressing my hand to his chest. His heart thrummed against my fingertips. He was alive and my heart thrilled.

He held me out. "They said you needed blood. I thought you were going to…you were so cold and the pink in your cheeks that I love was fading."

A twinge of tingling around the injury remained, but I wasn't about to be coddled. "I'm fine now."

"Are you sure? Because if the wound hasn't healed, I can help," he urged.

"I'm fine."

"Chase said it was Navan who stabbed you."

"All along I thought Emme was fated to be my counterpart. She convinced me she was, and I let her ego blind me even when Navan hinted she was the one." I stepped on tippy toes and leaned into him. My heart raced as if we were about to share a first kiss, but in a way it kind of was a first. We were different now. Changed. I stared into the pools of blue. He pressed his warm lips to mine, his touch warm and sweet like summertime.

He drew back and smiled, unable to help himself. He cupped a hand to my cheek. "I'm so sorry I wasn't there to help you. I said I would be and I wasn't."

"I told you to leave the witches to me. However, you ended up saving my life anyway."

He arched an eyebrow. "You sound like you have a problem with that."

A chuckle escaped my lips sending a pinch of discomfort. "Definitely not a problem."

"Do you need rest?"

I needed an escape. From the *Chesapeake Histories*, the Blackstones, and fate. "I only need you," I whispered.

"You've got me," he promised, grinning his seductive grin.

"I want to run away. Just the two of us. Together. I want to get in your Jeep and drive."

"Where do you want to go?" His lighthearted tone meant he didn't understand I was serious.

My unchanging expression relayed my intention.

He frowned. "I don't want to run and hide anymore."

Tears welled up. I sniffled them back.

He touched a hand to my cheek. "I understand. You've been through a shock. Watching Navan die and…and…"

"Say it. Unleashing myself on her and Carroll House." I knitted my brow. "I won't ever get over it, William. It's changed me. Everything I went through the last few weeks has changed me."

"Running away won't change you back. Trust me." His eyes were solemn as he spoke from his experience. "Besides, why would you want to change back?"

"I used to curse my gift and what I thought it took from me. Because of my grief, I was desperate to be an ordinary girl, but I'm not grieving anymore and I don't want that."

"Thank God. What makes you different is what I love most about you, and ordinary has nothing to do with it."

I gazed upward. "What about you? You've changed, too."

"Yes. Your fiery heart broke through my eternal winter." He grinned. "Which means I don't want to kill you anymore." He was letting his dark sense of humor show. He lifted my chin with one finger, urging a smile from me, then wrapped his arms around my waist, pressing the small of my back closer to him.

I brushed my fingers through his hair as I traced kisses from his mouth to his neck, tasting the sweetness of his skin.

He broke away and looked at me. "I've changed my mind."

My eyes popped wide open. "About what?"

"I like the hand fate has dealt me. In fact, I wouldn't change anything. If I didn't inherit the curse, I wouldn't have met you, and that just wouldn't do."

I thought about the *Chesapeake Histories* and how, even though fate had demanded a young witch's life, I had escaped and without blood on my hands. "I like it, too."

"Good. Now, come with me. There's someone I want you to meet."

"Who?"

"My dad. He's been in Europe until now looking for a cure to the curse. When Chase called him and told him what happened to me, he flew home. He's waiting and Chase is ordering Chinese food for all of us."

"Eating Chinese food together. That'll be a first for us."

"One of many to come."

"So your dad—did you tell him about me?" I asked, wondering exactly what he would say.

"Don't worry. I told him how amazing you are and he said, and I'm roughly quoting him, 'I want to meet the young witch who brought your smile back and found a cure to the curse I've spent a lifetime searching for'."

"Oh. I like that." He was no longer a cursed creature and I was no longer a grieving girl afraid of embracing her own power. I'd never know whether or not I'd altered fate, but I did know that fate had changed us into so much more than we ever thought possible. Even if we wanted to be ordinary, we no longer could be; however, it wasn't the magic that made us more than ordinary. Ultimately, it was our courage to embrace what made us different and the grace to accept those differences as gifts, not curses.

My loving alchemist, slash wizard, dad might have said the transmutation of lead into gold was a metaphor for the transmutation of a soul from dull to radiant and that such great change can only be fueled by an abundant source of power—a magnificent power that was in every one of us, lying just beneath an ordinary surface.

The End

We appreciate every like, tweet, facebook post and review and we love to hear from you. Please consider leaving us a review online or sending your thoughts and comments to info@mirrorworldpublishing.com

Thank you.

Acknowledgements

A published book is a work from many, not just one so I'd like to acknowledge a few of the wonderful people who helped bring Bewitching Hannah to life.

My husband Brian has provided constant love, support, wisdom, and a perfectly timed sense of humor.

My sons, Carson & Chase, have given me their teen input, suggestions, and love. Thanks, guys!

Bernadette has supported my writing efforts from the beginning. I thank her from the bottom of my heart.

The Kingsport Book Club has provided their continued enthusiasm and generous support, and I am so grateful—seriously!

My book angel, Angela Kelly, has offered wise writing suggestions that I couldn't have done without.

Historic Annapolis, the foundation that maintains many beautiful historic homes in Annapolis, offered their historians to provide an accuracy check of Bewitching Hannah. Thank you for your expertise!

The Mirror World Team, which includes Justine Dowsett, Murandy Damodred, Robert Dowsett, and Lauren Ridgewell, has continued to strive for excellence in editing and publishing, and they put together great cover art! I am eternally grateful for the opportunity to work with all of you.

Authors Moving Forward has included me in their super cool author group and I couldn't do without their optimism and social media expertise, especially Sloane Taylor and my Mirror World authormate, Sharon Ledwith.

The Deviant Art artists, especially Jan Doseděl, have generously donated the rights to use their artwork for my cover, which I love, love, love!

My mystery beta readers (you know who you are) have provided insightful and constructive feedback, and I thank you.

And to the many others who have helped me along the publishing path in your small and wonderful ways—your support is forever appreciated.

About the Author

Leigh Goff lives and writes in Annapolis, Maryland. She is a University of Maryland University College graduate, a member of the Society of Children's Book Writers and Illustrators (SCBWI), and a volunteer with the Juvenile Diabetes Research Foundation. Fun fact – her eighth great-grandmother was Elizabeth Duncan, an accused seventeenth century witch from the Chesapeake area.

Also by Leigh Goff:

A forbidden love. A dark curse. An impossible choice...

Descended from a powerful Wethersfield witch, sixteen-year-old Sophie is struggling to hide her awkwardly emerging magic, but that's the least of her worries. When a dangerous thief tries to steal her mysterious heirloom necklace, she is rescued by the one person she's forbidden to fall for, a descendant of the man who condemned her ancestor to hang. He carries a dark secret that could destroy them both unless Sophie learns how to tap into the mysterious power of her diamond bloodcharm. She will have to uncover dark secrets from both of their families' wicked pasts and risk everything, including her soul to save them from a witch's true love curse, but it will take much more than that.

YA, Fantasy, Romance, 266 pages

Available from Mirror World Publishing, wherever books are sold!

Why 'Mirror World'?

We publish escapism fiction for all ages. Our novels are imaginative and character-driven and our goal is to give our readers a glimpse into other worlds, times, and versions of reality that parallel our own, giving them an experience they can't get anywhere else!

We offer free delivery within Windsor-Essex,Ontario, an all-you-can-read membership program, blind-dates with books, and you can find our novels in our online store, or from your favorite major book retailer.

To learn more about our authors and our current projects visit: www.mirrorworldpublishing.com, follow @MirrorWorldPub or like us at www.facebook.com/mirrorworldpublishing

Or keep reading for a sneak peek of:

By Sharon Ledwith

1. Leader of the Pack

"Silly, stupid humans!" Whiskey hissed.

Creeping through the ductwork was becoming harder on her old bones. Layers of dust tickled her pink nose and made her facial whiskers twitch incessantly. Her stomach retched at the stale odors. However, Whiskey, a fifteen-year-old calico cat, ignored these annoyances and persevered. She had to, knowing that she was the only link, the only form of communication, between the cat floor and the dog floor at the Fairy Falls Animal Shelter. This was what made her special, gave her life purpose. This quiet night was no exception.

What the humans called a *crisis* had happened at the shelter today and Whiskey had to relay this information to the canine pack leader. Nearing the entrance above the dog floor, the thick fur on the back of her neck rose. Some of the dogs she tolerated, some she abhorred. Her ears flattened. Whiskey knew she would have to scale across the top of Mary Jane's gate in order to get to Nobel's cage and deliver her report. She also knew to be extra careful not to shake the little bells attached to her red collar that would jingle out her presence. Reaching the opening, Whiskey extracted her long claws and pushed the dusty register aside. Looking down, she sighed, thankful that Mary Jane, a black and white pit bull terrier, and a long time resident of the shelter, was asleep. Carefully, Whiskey jumped down, balanced on the top of the fenced gate that faced the hallway, and started to slink across it. Then she sneezed and her bells jingled.

A growl and a snort sounded from below. "Who dares to wake me?"

Whiskey peered down. Mary Jane's eyes were rolled back, her tongue hanging limply out one side of her mouth. A quilted blanket on the cement floor was half-shredded and inches away lay a rubber toy, which would normally be stuffed into Mary Jane's powerful jaws to exercise the constant frustration of being incarcerated for so long. Whiskey watched Mary Jane lunge for the toy, shaking her thick head and neck in anger.

Whiskey leaned over into the cage and purred, "Someday, I hope you choke on that thing."

Mary Jane dropped the toy and lunged at the smug cat. Whiskey had just enough time to recoil and land feet first on the hallway's cement floor. She groaned, feeling her arthritic back legs cave slightly. She was not a kitten anymore, that was for sure. Mary Jane rattled the kennel door, snapping, growling, and barking. Slobber ran down the white patch on her neck and dribbled onto the floor, making it too slippery for her to balance on her hind legs. She slipped and fell with a loud thump and knocked the water bowl, spilling water all over. Whiskey flattened her ears and shook her head. This dog could easily have been the pick of the litter when it came time to receive the sleep needle, but since this shelter had a 'no kill' policy in place, all of its residents, including Mary Jane, remained safe and alive.

Suddenly the kennel next to Mary Jane's came alive and the one after that. Whiskey heard a whimper from the cage down the hall where the new dogs were kept. These were the dogs whose owners would either still rescue them or would condemn them to live here in the shelter until they were adopted by a new human.

"You sure know how to make an entrance, Whiskey."

Whiskey's ears pricked up. The right ear had been badly frostbitten once upon a time, but her left ear was still intact. Half her face was masked in black; the other half a mixture of white and orange. The rest of her small body was a patchwork of black and orange fur, with the exception of a white belly. She preened her whiskers, licking the pad of her front right paw until she realized all she tasted was watered down bleach. Cringing, Whiskey slowly sauntered over to Nobel's kennel—the biggest—at the very end of the hallway. She plopped her bottom on the cool concrete floor and stretched.

"You're certainly a deep sleeper, Nobel. Are you sure you used to be a watchdog?" Whiskey asked, preening the area above her yellow eyes.

There was a low growl, and then a high pitched bark. It was Nobel's way of laughing. "I'm part Husky, part Doberman, and part mystery mutt, so sometimes I get all messed up about my job. Do I run as fast as I can or do I stand and fight? It's darned confounding, I say."

Although it was dark, Whiskey could see the amusement in Nobel's light blue eyes. His fur was a mixture of black, tan, and grey, and standing on all fours he would be at least three cats tall. Nobel's kennel was well-kept, with a thick, comfy blanket set up in front and a pan full of water at the back. He'd been at the shelter for as long as she had, so Whiskey felt a sense of oneness with Nobel, even though he was canine.

"I smell feline! Feline! Feline! Feline!" a dog from the middle cage barked.

Nobel rolled his eyes. "You're dreaming again, Louis. Go back to sleep!"

Whiskey heard a snort from the big Rottweiler mix, followed by a whine. "Dreaming? Hmm, yup, silly me. Must be dreaming. No felines on the dog floor. Silly me."

She heard Louis yawn, fart, and then settle back down on his papered floor. Louis tended to pee in his kennel, so he wasn't afforded the luxury of a cushy blanket like Nobel's.

"Dumb as wood, that one," Nobel muttered.

"Yet he trusts you completely," Whiskey mewed, scratching her chin.

"That's because I'm the pack leader. It's not a choice, you know."

Whiskey nodded. She understood all too well. Dominant and submissive. There were leaders and there were followers. It was the same for cats as it was for dogs. The problem was that there were far too many cats in this shelter, so most tended to break off into separate colonies. Poppy, the fat, white Persian was one leader. Boscoe, a slick black domestic short-hair was another. Then there was Shadow, a grey tabby mix, and the meanest leader Whiskey had ever encountered in all her years.

"You have some news?" Nobel asked, cutting into Whiskey's thoughts.

She jumped. "Yes," she answered, and then decided to lick her leg. "This morning, while I was curled up on the chair in the office, I heard the Bossy One talking into one of those small, shiny things humans call a phone."

Nobel lay on his blanket and crossed his big paws. "Did you understand any of her words?"

Whiskey stopped grooming. "Some, but you won't like it."

Nobel's ears rose. "I don't like the Bossy One to begin with. What comes out of her mouth is mostly garble and she stinks like a dead skunk."

"I think you've just insulted skunks everywhere, my friend," Whisky mewed.

Nobel growled impatiently. Whiskey sighed and said, "From what human words I know, I heard 'no money' repeated many times."

"Money?" Nobel asked, inclining his furry head. "What is money?"

"Something humans need to survive on."

"Survive on? Explain."

Whiskey frowned. Sometimes dogs were thick-headed. "Money, my friend, allows the humans to eat well, sleep in a safe place, and cover their bodies with the strange hairless outerwear they call clothes. Clearly, 'no money' means the humans cannot function very well."

"So how does 'no money' affect us?" Nobel asked.

"I also heard the word 'shelter' after 'no money', meaning that the humans who care for us can no longer provide us with the food we eat, the blankets we sleep on, and all the comforts we've come to expect of this place." Whiskey's ears lowered. "No money, my friend, means this shelter will not be around much longer."

"What?!" Nobel howled. "But this is our place, our sanctuary! She can't make it go away!"

"The Bossy One will if she doesn't come up with enough money soon. I sensed her fear, her desperation. She sounded broken."

Nobel snarled. "The Bossy One has become weak! Her weakness endangers the pack! Do you think the other Ones who take care of us will do something about this?"

Whiskey sat silent for a few moments. *Who might challenge the Bossy One?* She thought about it. *The Kind One? The Loud One? The Quiet One? The Quick One? Which human might be dominant enough to do this?* The whimpering had dulled down and snoring replaced the barking. Her body twitched as if electricity surged through it.

Louis stirred in his sleep. "Get her. Bite her. Chew. Chew. Chew." He snapped his jaws and flailed his long legs.

"Shut up, you fool!" Mary Jane growled. She picked up her rubber toy and shook it viciously.

Whiskey's ears pricked up as she realized something. "Fool, no. Genius, yes."

Nobel leaned closer to his kennel door. "I don't quite follow."

"That's because you're the pack leader. You never follow. Don't you see?"

Nobel gave her a vacant look. His whiskered brown brows bobbed up and down in thought.

Whiskey fluffed her jowls. "It's simple. The shelter needs a new pack leader to survive. In order to do that all the animals must join forces to help find a stronger human who can stand up to the Bossy One."

"And how do we do that, seeing as most of us are in cages?"

"By using what nature gave us," Whiskey meowed, locking eyes with Nobel. "We send our thoughts to any human who will listen."

Nobel's brows rose. "But...what if it doesn't work?"

Whiskey stretched again, allowing her paws to knead the air before her. "Then, my friend, we will need what humans call a *miracle*."

CPSIA information can be obtained
at www.ICGtesting.com
Printed in the USA
BVHW030207091120
592836BV00023B/101